PRAIS

"Khan Wong ~~~~~ ~~~~ ~~~~ ~~~~~ ~~~~ ~~~~~~~
conversation with this thought-provoking and ultimately
hopeful novel, weaving together three very different
lives across time. *Down in the Sea of Angels* is a poignant
exploration of the resilience of compassion, humanity's
(re)connection with the earth, and the bright beacon of
community in dark times."

Ren Hutchings, author of Under Fortunate Stars

"These vivid worlds will make your mind expand and
maybe burst; these flawed wonderful characters will make
your heart ache and maybe break."

*Sam J. Miller, Nebula-Award-winning
author of* Blackfish City

"A dazzling, time-bending thriller about three people living
in San Francisco, separated by centuries but united by
disaster. I was sucked in immediately, and delighted by the
incredible worldbuilding and finely drawn characters. Every
time I thought I had figured what was going to happen, it
would get weirder and more fascinating."

Annalee Newitz, author of
Autonomous *and* The Terraformers

"In this beautifully intricate story, Wong shows how our
past, present, and future are all connected, and how we can
build towards a brighter world."

Sunyi Dean, bestselling author of The Book Eaters

'With its visceral imagery and seamless blending of past and future, *Down in the Sea of Angels* is a treat to read."
      Ciel Pierlot, Compton Crook award-nominated author of
                    Bluebird *and* The Hunter's Gambit

"*Down in the Sea of Angels* is a beautiful, generations-spanning story about resilience, permanence, and hope. A story about the lies we tell ourselves and the lies that reshape societies, and the weight of truth that can act as a counterbalance. A tale about the horrors of oppression and the strength of connection. An absolute must read that strikes a multitude of chords in these turbulent times and leaves you feeling like you can still make a difference."
      Dan Hanks, author of Captain Moxley and the Embers of the
                    Empire *and* The Way Up is Death

"Khan Wong has made the book for which so many of us have been yearning! *The Circus Infinite* is not only a gripping science-fiction tale set in a lushly imagined universe teeming with fabulous aliens, extraordinary powers, and political drama, but also a story that celebrates our real, lived spectrum of gender and sexuality. To top it all off, it revolves around a circus, the perfect manifestation of outsider community, artistic expression, and a sense of wonder. *The Circus Infinite* renews faith in the power of science fiction to represent our world even as it lifts our imagination beyond it."
                    Justin Hall, editor of No Straight Lines

"*The Circus Infinite* is both elegiac and majestic, with vibrant characters and a real sense of art at its heart. It soars like a trapeze artist."
                    Ferrett Steinmetz, author of Flex

Khan Wong

DOWN IN THE
SEA OF ANGELS

ANGRY
ROBOT

ANGRY ROBOT
An imprint of Watkins Media Ltd

Unit 11, Shepperton House
89-93 Shepperton Road
London N1 3DF
UK

angryrobotbooks.com
twitter.com/angryrobotbooks
The future is now.

An Angry Robot paperback original, 2025

Edited by Desola Coker and Travis Tynan
Cover by Sarah O'Flaherty
Set in Meridien

ISBN 978 1 91599 836 1
Ebook ISBN 978 1 91599 837 8

Printed and bound in the United Kingdom by CPI Group (UK) Ltd, Croydon CR0 4YY.

The manufacturer's authorised representative in the EU for product safety is eucomply OÜ - Pärnu mnt 139b-14, 11317 Tallinn, Estonia, hello@eucompliancepartner.com; www.eucompliancepartner.com

9 8 7 6 5 4 3 2 1

MIX
Paper | Supporting
responsible forestry
FSC
www.fsc.org   FSC® C171272

For the future

CONTENT WARNING

Down in the Sea of Angels contains racist language and attitudes, sexual assault, sexual harassment, the historical sex trafficking of minors, acknowledgment of the forced labor of minors, physical and verbal abuse, violence, drug use and drug-related death.

1.

MAIDA

March 4, 2106
Marshall Cove, San Francisco

A dozen drones buzzed right in my face when I got there. Beside the bonfire, a scruffy guy in coveralls fidgeted with a tablet, tongue stuck out of the corner of his mouth in concentration, presumably controlling these things. A tinkerer of some kind? Amber and green telemetry twinkled in the glass of his goggles. The drones turned away from me and back towards him in a sort of swooping torus configuration, the trails of their little lights making loops in the air. It was quite lovely, actually.

"Hi!" someone called, waving. The fire roared behind them, masking their face in silhouette and haloing the cloud of their hair. "Are you Maida?"

"That's me." Something whirred by my head – a mosquito? Big one, it sounded like. But then the blinking light caught my eye – another drone, larger than the others, flying obnoxiously close. How many could this guy fly at once?

"I'm Aviva," said the stout, brown-skinned woman who greeted me. "Lead Archivist." My new boss. She bowed her head and shoulders. Was this a thing with cultural workers, or this city in general, or was it her own personal thing?

"Happy to meet you." My return bow was more awkward than I wanted, and the growler I had hooked on one finger hit my sternum a couple of times. "I brought some Old San Francisco amber."

"Oh, you're fancy." Her laugh rang bright as crystal. "I hope you didn't expend luxury credits for this."

"What are they for if not to expend? Anyway, I was raised better than to show up at a party emptyhanded."

"That's kind of you. Just put it with the rest of the drinks over there." She pointed to a spot on the other side of the fire.

"Hey –" a jovial voice wavered toward us. The drone flyer, obviously tipsy, set one of his devices whirring around us in low, overhead circles as he ambled up to me and Aviva. It looked like he'd put the others away, and his goggles were now atop his forehead. "Are you the new psychic?"

"That I am." It was a struggle to keep my annoyance at the term "psychic" out of my voice. Nul-psis – that is, people who do not have psionic abilities, which was most of the population – tended to default to the term "psychic," an old-school term that evoked associations with turban appropriating charlatans waving their hands over crystal balls. I wasn't going to say anything, since I was going to be working with these people for a while, plus the tide of common vernacular was sometimes just too big a thing to hold back. At least he wasn't being hateful about it. Still, I decided to push myself and establish boundaries, given the opportunity. "The proper term is 'psion'."

I managed to keep my voice steady, but my palms were damp and my face flushed hot and felt warmer than the bonfire-toasted breeze. I hated confrontation, no matter how minor. Luckily, my pulse sounded only in my ears. I hoped there wasn't a telepath around.

"Right," he said, nodding. Was he really taking it in? "The last one was clairvoyant. What kind are you?"

"Roan, you could at least introduce yourself before you start demanding typology." Aviva met my eyes with a sympathetic look and seemed to be apologizing for her colleague – now my colleague, too.

"I'm Roan Flynn, Technology Specialist for the Cultural Recovery Project." He performed an exaggerated bow. "I get old devices to talk to us again and help maintain the Precursor Cultural Database, as well as our division's archive of field recordings. And now that I have shared my specialty, won't you share yours?"

"Psychometry. Do you know –"

"Is that the one where you talk with animals?"

"No. That's a telepathy variant."

Roan whispered "psychometry" to himself over and over. "You know the distance of things?"

"Maybe you could let Maida tell us," Aviva chided. She gave me a little nod with a hint of a smile.

"It's the ability to know the history of an object by touching it. Where it's been, who's owned it. All the way back to where, when and by whom it was made."

"Maida is a recent graduate of the Circle of the Eye Academy," Aviva explained. "One of the quickest to pass the trials. She was recruited for the Islais Cove haul. But I'm sure her talents will prove useful in other areas as well."

Roan's eyes narrowed as he examined me with refreshed interest, his drone buzzing over his shoulder. "I don't know much about psych – psion training. What does it mean you passed the trials quickly?"

"We spend eight years at the Academy, both for standard

curriculum and training our abilities," I explained. "In the final year, we concentrate on mastery of our own psionic discipline and control of our brainwave states. There are written and practical tests. Some folks attempt the trials multiple times over a year or two before they pass. I passed my first try." I didn't really expect a nul-psi to get it. Really, only other psions that have graduated the Academy understood the rarity of what I'd done. Talk about limited clout.

Roan didn't follow up on the topic, and instead asked, "Is this your first work assignment?"

"I've worked on remediation projects, like everyone. But this is my first specialized vocation assignment."

"Well congratulations and welcome to the team. This haul is from a lost neighborhood of San Francisco, one that seemed to have a lot of character pre-Collapse. I bet you'll have fun with it."

The process of using my ability was intense and draining and beautiful at times, but I wouldn't have called it fun. But that was a me thing. "I'm looking forward to it."

"Let's get you a drink and I'll introduce you around." Aviva walked me over to the refreshments area where I poured myself a cup of ale, mostly just so I'd have something to do with my hands. A stream of faces and names flowed into and out of my consciousness as Aviva led me around.

The birthday girl had donned a sparkly tiara and a bow of what must have been fake feathers – throwbacks to fashion elements of the precursor world. Fake feathers were a thing for some reason, but where did that tiara come from? The sparkle of the gems mesmerized in the flickering light of the bonfire – were they real or fake?

"It's an artifact," she said when she noticed me looking. "Cubic zirconia, not actual diamonds. Aviva would never have let me wear it out otherwise. I'm Lorel, by the way."

"Maida."

Recognition lit up her eyes. "You're the new psion. Psychometry, right?"

Well, someone had paid attention to the personnel memo. That was a check in the positive column for Lorel.

A bright eagerness swept over her face when I nodded. "I don't want to impose, since we just met and you just got here and all, but do you think you could…?" She touched the tiara.

Using psychometry as a party trick really chafed, but she had been considerate enough to pay attention to who the new team member was. And anyway, it was her birthday. So even though I normally wouldn't have, I held out my hand to receive the tiara. Besides, I wanted to make friends – I knew no one in San Francisco, having spent most of my life moving around for my father's assignments and then up north on the Mendocino coast for my time at the Academy.

A few folks standing close by noticed the interaction and a hush descended. The tiara was heavier than I'd expected. I closed my fingers around it and breathed deeply. Tendrils of stories reached out through the psifield, reached through time and tickled the edges of my awareness. At first, it was all a rush – darkness broken by sudden light, then a face. A face of someone I had met earlier in the flurry of introductions. What was his name? Bertrand. Then a box inside a larger box, in a closet, in a house underwater where it had lain for years. A young woman put it away – she was unsure what to do with it and had set it aside, thinking she'd deal with it later, but she never did. It had been her mother's, who had just died, who had received it from her grandmother. Now, a younger woman: the grandmother, when she was young, wearing the tiara and a slip of a dress, sheer, barely there, dancing in a desert. A huge bonfire. And fireworks and pounding electronic music. Maybe she was high on something? A man, also barely dressed, took her in his arms. An argument – crying, tears, recriminations. A broken engagement. The final polish of the maker before delivery to the bride–

"It was made in 1998 by a maker named Theo Lovelight. He was a friend of the woman who commissioned it, Lola Chen, who had ordered it for her wedding. She discovered her fiancé had been cheating on her with her sister and called off the wedding, but she kept the tiara. She was a party girl, and a devotee of the music festival scene of the early two thousands. She wore this to go dancing, quite a lot. She met the man she'd eventually marry at one of these festivals – on the dancefloor, while wearing this tiara, in 2004. Her daughter wore it to something called "prom" in 2023, then again to a gala in 2033. A fundraiser for the Symphony. After that, it remained boxed in the closet of the house on Beach Street, where it sat on a shelf, forgotten and abandoned. There it remained from the start of the Collapse in 2052 until two months ago, when it was discovered by Bertrand Lowell, marine archaeology, at the site recovery of January 4, 2106. Currently, the item is claimed by the Golden Gate Cultural Recovery Project, in the possession of the San Francisco unit, and currently in the temporary possession of you –" I handed the tiara back to the birthday girl, "Lorel Santiago."

"It's true," someone said. "I did find it." A man with round glasses and tufts of auburn hair poking out from beneath a beanie took a bow. Bertrand Lowell, presumably. People seemed to bow a lot around here.

Everyone clapped, and my face flushed – just a quick bit of hot. The last bit of the tiara's story faded, and I got that feeling of being left alone at a party by the person I had just had a great conversation with who went to go say hi to someone who just arrived.

"I wish we'd recorded that," Aviva said. "Will you remember what you just spoke? Can you repeat all that to a scribe?"

"Sure." I really didn't mind; this sort of thing was what I was brought on for, after all.

"I got it." Roan tapped a slender recording device and slipped it into his pocket. "I'll attach it to the item's record."

"Thank you, Roan," Aviva said. "Always prepared."

I looked at him with new appreciation – he definitely rubbed me the wrong way at first, but competence almost always balanced out pushiness. Almost.

"Thanks," Lorel said as she placed the tiara back on her head. "So how does it work, exactly? Your ability, and psionic abilities in general?"

I groaned a little bit on the inside. It got old, explaining it over and over. But still, these were my new colleagues, and they were only trying to understand my experience. "Are you familiar with the psifield?"

Party chatter had resumed, but Lorel, Roan, and Aviva still paid me keen attention.

"Okay. So you know how we're surrounded by microwaves, and broadcast transmissions, and wireless communication frequencies all the time, but unless we have the proper device and tune into those frequencies, we don't perceive them at all?"

I waited for my new colleagues to communicate their understanding before I continued. "Well, there is a range of sensory perception that is constantly around us that psions are able to perceive when we bring our attention to it. This field emerges from the overlapping waves of the fields of consciousness and matter – that's a whole big infodump I won't get into now. But that's what we call the psifield, that gradient of wavelengths. Telepathy, telekinesis, clairvoyance, clairaudience, claircognition, clairsentience, and my ability, psychometry, are all different ways of perceiving different types of information and energy within that gradient. In the case of telepathy and telekinesis, it could be argued practitioners are manipulating the energy too, not just receiving information. Think of it like: telepathy is a two-way radio, but clairvoyance is television, and psychometry is… I don't know, television through a time warp. Nul-psis, people without psionic abilities, like yourselves, are unable to tune in, but the signals are still there."

"Okay, I get it," Roan said. "I think."

"That was a good explanation." Aviva looked at me with a sly smile. I got the sense that she was giving me her approval or that I had passed some sort of test.

"So this tiara hasn't been worn since 2033?" Lorel asked.

"That's right."

"Have you encountered many items that have gone unused for as long as that?"

"Not many. But I'm just starting out doing cultural recovery work, so we'll see what the future brings."

"So am I part of the record now?" Her eyes were wide with hope and curiosity.

"Not unless you take possession of it. You'd have to purchase it, or be gifted it, or steal it."

She laughed. "I don't think any of that is happening."

After some getting-to-know-you party chat with Lorel and a few others, I took a seat on a log at the edge of the fire and gazed into its flickering tongues. The mesmerizing crackle, light, and shadow couldn't quite distract from the looks that everyone was trying really hard not to throw at me and that I was trying really hard not to notice. It had been thirty-four years since the Bloom, when the abilities of those who came to be called psions were switched on all at once. The how and the why of it remained a mystery. And although most folks knew at least one psion, even if only distantly, we were still a novelty to a lot of nul-psis.

"That was cool to witness."

Pulling my attention from the fire, I turned to see Roan standing close by. He gestured at the empty spot beside me and I nodded. "You put the drone away," I noted.

"Yeah. Lorel asked me to record some of the party, but I've imbibed too many intoxicants to fly responsibly." He paused, the fire igniting his eyes for a second before he turned to face me. "It was like you went into a trance." He picked up a stick and began tracing lines in the sand.

"It does kind of feel like that at first." I hadn't meant to leave an opening for follow-up questions, but I reminded myself that making friends required making an effort to talk to people.

"What do you mean 'at first'?" His expression was earnest, and his curiosity seemed to be the kind that sought understanding rather than titillation.

"When I begin a scan of an object, I get a rush of images and feelings – emotions – first. That part feels like a trance, like the 'me' part of myself is pushed aside to make room for all this stuff coming off the object. It doesn't always make sense and it isn't always chronological. But I'm still aware of myself and my own thoughts. Then that settles down, and the story of the object clicks into place – the provenance and bits of the life of the object become clear. It's like I suddenly just know everything about it. That phenomena is called claircognizance. Are you familiar?"

He shook his head.

"It's when the knowledge of something you're focused on just comes to you."

"That's fascinating."

Sometimes, when I took a step back and considered my situation objectively, I understood the fascination nul-psis had for us. But I didn't like talking about it all that much. Mostly, I preferred not to reveal my psion status at all, though social occasions with people who didn't know had been rare since I started at the Academy. But this was a specialized vocation posting, and everyone knew I was the new psion on board, so of course I'd get questions.

When my ability first manifested, other kids stayed away from me. They didn't tease or make fun, but they were clearly scared, and I couldn't even move things around with my mind or hear their secret thoughts. Not that I had to hear their thoughts to know what they thought of me.

"I'm sorry if I came on too strong when you first got here," he said. "I let my enthusiasm get the better of me sometimes. I'm fascinated by psych –" He caught himself. "By psions. I guess everyone is though, huh?"

"The ones who aren't freaked out." Most people were curious about us and found our talents useful, but every so often, I would encounter somebody who got flustered once they knew what I was. They often couldn't get away fast enough. I had it explained to me once that they were afraid we'd all read their minds, as if every psion was telepathic. Ironically, it was a telepath who told me that. Maybe that's why I tended to keep it to myself unless whoever I was talking to had reason to know – like co-workers.

A burst of laughter rippled over to us from the distant side of the fire, the birthday girl at the center of it, firelight glinting off her tiara.

"My parents always said in the years after the Bloom, it was like everyone snapped awake. They were kids when it happened, but they always told me about how the sky was lit up with auroras for a whole year and people were crying in the streets. My mom said people were filled with joy and wonder for a while, and that's when the confrontation of history began, and the Reconciliation. It seemed like humanity took a big step forward, but then slowly the effects of it wore off. But some people still get powers."

I couldn't quite parse his look; was he resentful that I got something he didn't? I'd run into that type before. Maybe I was just being paranoid. A telepath would know.

"Is it like you're there? When you do your thing? Like you're in whatever time period the object is from?"

"Not exactly. Sometimes it's like watching a movie sped up. Or cut up into random scenes that are all out of order. Once in a while, I get a burst of emotion if an owner had some charged feeling around the object. Grief. Anger. I scanned a trophy once that had been used as a murder weapon. That was fun in the sense that it was horrible." An echo of rage, a flash of blood splashed against green tile. I shoved that memory aside – not my memory, not really. A memory locked in an object that I perceived. Someone else's memory. Yet it popped into my head during a casual conversation, so did that make it mine? Did every story I received with my talent become part of my own? I didn't want that to be the case, but I'd come to terms with the fact that my want was futile in matters related to being a psion.

"Oh, wow. You never know what you're going to get, huh?"

"Nope."

"Well this assignment will be an adventure for you, won't it?"

I chuckled. "I guess we'll see."

Aviva called my name and waved me over. "Come meet some folks!"

I stood up and brushed off my pants. Roan stayed seated, kept tracing little circles in the sand. Now I was the one leaving someone alone at a party. "Welcome aboard," he said.

Aviva welcomed me warmly into the circle she stood in and made another round of introductions. I made a mental note to review the personnel manifest over the next couple of days; there was no way I would remember everyone's names in that moment. What was that old saying? "Strangers are just friends you haven't met yet"? I wondered which of these folks might become friends, and which would just be faces in the crowd, colleagues I knew by name. I supposed that time would tell. My ability gave me windows into the past, but I walked into the future just like everyone else.

2.

LI NUAN

January 17, 1906
Chinatown, San Francisco

Laughter and chatter and the occasional curse from the gambling house next door clatters in through the window as Li Nuan brings the Boss his tea. He likes to take it in the back parlor with the shades drawn; they're a good shield against the midday glare, but they do nothing to dull the noise. Why does he not settle in a quieter spot like the front room? She would have.

She serves with the jade tea set, his favorite according to Madam Bai, who had told her once that Boss Fong's family had received it as a gift from the emperor himself. Li Nuan doesn't really believe that, but it is a nice set. It felt familiar the first time she saw it. And the cups, in particular, vibrate with light and color and almost seem alive, or enchanted.

Now is when she admonishes herself for allowing her mind to take such flights of fancy and her attention snaps back to cold, hard, reality. On paper, she is Boss Fong's orphaned niece, but actually, her father had sold her to cover his gambling debt. When she was told she'd been sold to this stranger and was being sent to Gam Saan, a name which in English is Gold Mountain, she had sobbed and pleaded. Her mother told her to submit and do her duty to the family. Was that a girl's place in this world? To be passed along from man to man to cover a debt, to serve? Was she mad to hope that one day she could choose her own path?

Today, Boss is meeting with one of the Chinatown merchants. She doesn't know who this one is, but sweat beads on his brow and he can't stop shaking his right leg. He flinches when she steps up from behind him to place his cup. He is in trouble, isn't he? When she pours the first cup for Boss, he just stares at the other man, face utterly still. Though his face is blank nothing, fury burns behind his eyes. She breathes a prayer of compassion over the guest's tea as she pours it. Nobody gets called before the Boss for no reason. It isn't her place to know these things, but she is glad she does. Knowing is better than not knowing. After setting steamed buns and pastries on the table, she takes her leave, avoiding eye contact with the pair of the Boss's men who stand silently by the door.

The son that everybody calls siu wong dai or "little emperor," accosts her in the corridor. He is supposed to be learning the family business, but the only thing he seems to be interested in is reminding everybody who his father is. He doesn't know anything of running anything and does not seem to want to. He wants the glory of the role but not the duty. He would probably take his role seriously if the Boss disciplined his son the way he disciplines the girls at the Lotus Pearl. She had hoped he wouldn't be around, but she should have known. Little Emperor is always waiting to pounce.

"My favorite flower," he says like he does all the time, "You are too lovely to be a housemaid." And as she does all the time, she presses herself up against the wall and sucks her breath in tight and fast to avoid contact. His breath smells of rice wine, though it isn't yet noon. "You should be the prize blossom at the Lotus Pearl."

She hugs the empty tray across her chest and forces her face to stay calm even as disgust roils inside her. She knows what the Lotus Pearl is. She knows what the flowers there do.

"I know my father promised yours to keep you from all that. What a shame." He leans with both hands on the wall at her back, his fingers drumming on either side of her face.

"I have more work to do." Her voice is quiet and soft, yet her tone does not waver. "Housekeeping, and then the evening meal." They both know who she works for. And Little Emperor wants the evening meal too.

"I could take you if I wanted to. You would enjoy."

"Please." She releases the tension of her held breath, the tray a shield pressing Little Emperor away. "Your father will get angry if I do not complete my duties."

He scoffs, taking neither her nor his father seriously. "You will service me one day." His gaze is intense, but she avoids it, avoids his eyes, casting hers instead to the stained cuffs of his sleeves. To the dust on the table across the hall that she still must get to.

Finally he relents, lifts his grubby hands from the wall, stands back. "Get back to work, dutiful girl."

She makes her way back to the pantry and chokes down her useless rage. What is the point of being angry? She cannot do anything about it.

"Anger is a luxury our sex is not allowed," Madam Bai likes to say. She manages the Lotus Pearl. She has a special relationship with the Boss and visits frequently. After her first beating at the Madam's hands, even though she wasn't one of those girls, Li Nuan understood their relationship.

She hangs her apron and grabs her coat. It's time to go into town to fetch the laundry, and a chicken for the night's supper, and the teahouse should have a new shipment of the Boss's favorite tea in by now. Wu Jun, her assigned escort, waits by the servant's entrance when she gets there. He knows the day's agenda and is always right on time. She isn't allowed out without him.

The pair step out of Sullivan's Alley and onto the bustle of Jackson Street. She'll pick up the chicken and the tea first, then make the laundry the last stop before returning to Boss Fong's. She refuses to call that place home. Cantonese chatter fills the street, and for a moment, she can almost believe she's someplace in Guangdong Province, where she'd spent her girlhood, maybe even Hong Kong. There are docks and ships there too. She hasn't been anywhere near the ones here since her arrival, but she remembers the shadows of the ships in the night, the salty sea air, the sound of lapping waves. As a child, she thought that ships setting out to sea meant adventure, seeing the world, but now all she can think of is being brought to a strange land against her will. All she can think of is those ships taking people away from their lives, making their lives and their bodies the property of others.

Most men on the street – and it is nearly all men – cast pitying or lustful gazes at her before taking note of Wu Jun and looking away. They know she belongs to someone – she is maybe even a whore sent out to run errands. Her escort's presence is a deterrence from even lewd comments, and a moment here and there, she is grudgingly thankful for his company. But of course, he isn't there to protect her. He is there to make sure she doesn't run.

Moon Goddess Teahouse is her first stop, and Bao, the proprietor's son, is sweeping the sidewalk out front as Li

Nuan approaches with her guard. He smiles warmly as he does every time she comes by, a rare gesture of kindness that she appreciates.

She meets his eyes with a slight nod as she scuttles into the shop. "Old Man Chan," she says in greeting.

The shopkeeper behind the counter grins in welcome – father and son have similar smiles. "How can I help you, little sister?"

"Pu-erh." She hands over an empty tea tin. "For the Boss."

The shopkeep nods, taking the tin and knowing just how much to measure. "You know, my son thinks you are lovely," he says as he brings a jar of loose tea over to the scale. "I could arrange for him to be behind the counter next time you come." His eyes twinkle as he measures out the leaves, then scoops them into the tin Li Nuan had handed over.

She can't believe the old man would speak of such things. As if she could speak to the son if she wanted. As if she could be courted like a normal girl. But maybe her life is normal, and what she always thought of as normal was a fantasy. Whatever the case, she likes being talked to like a person.

Old Man Chan hands back the tin; there is no price on the tea since it is part of the shop's tribute. She takes it back and drops it into her satchel. "I never know when that will be."

"Hmm. Maybe customers will like seeing his handsome young face back here? Or will they wonder what the little monkey knows about tea?" He laughs at his pet name for his son. "Bao cannot even say a proper hello with the guard at your heels." He meets her eyes. "Not your fault, I know."

Her cheeks flush.

"Oh, I know! Next time you come, I'll offer the guard some dumplings and tea and make you stay. Then you and Bao can talk."

Does the old man really believe any of what he says is possible? This idea of a future with his son that he offers is meant as kindness – she knows this – but in light of the reality of her life, it feels cruel to offer hope and a dream of courtship. "The Boss won't be happy you said that."

"Don't tell him."

Despite herself, she laughs. Every little bit of lightness is a boon.

As she exits, she nods again at Bao, with a bare hint of a smile this time. He is sweeping the same area of sidewalk as when they arrived. At what must be a stern expression from Wu Jun looming behind her, he quickly looks away.

The Garden Corner, what the Americans call Portsmouth Square, bubbles with gossip, and the clack of mahjong tiles, and old men practicing tai chi or else smoking cigarettes. No women. What would it be like to have leisure time to sit in a park all day, doing this and that, doing as she pleased? The thought brings a rush of guilt, like she's stealing a comfort she has no right to, and she pushes it aside.

As they draw close to the market, the calls of the fishmonger grow louder, along with the clucks and squawks of chickens. She walks down a narrow aisle in between stalls of vegetables that line the front of the market, making her way to the butcher in the back.

"For Boss Fong," she says to the gruff man behind the counter with blood smears on his apron.

The merchant wraps the largest of the birds that are already dressed and hands the parcel over. No other words pass between them, as usual. She knows what kind of girl he assumes her to be and she sees no point in correcting him. What difference will it make? Still, she bristles at the notion that even speaking to her will taint him somehow.

Without even a word of polite thanks, she places the chicken in her satchel with the tea and heads back out towards the street. Wu Jun stays right with her, and for a moment she imagines that he is at her command, protecting her because of her importance to the community. It is not a fantasy she indulges for very long.

Steam billows from the laundry's vents as if it is blowing out its own weather. The pick-up includes linens and towels for Boss Fong's home, as well as some linens for the Lotus Pearl. She is amazed that the blood and the sweat and the other excretions that soiled these sheets can be washed away so effectively. Do the fibers retain any memory of how they had been defiled? As usual, the laundryman bundles the linens with heavy twine, creating straps Li Nuan can sling over her shoulders to carry the load on her back. Wu Jun stands outside smoking a cigarette as she struggles to get everything set just so. She has to walk hunched over to carry the laundry, and the sack that holds the chicken and the tea bumps on her backside uncomfortably. Wu Jun doesn't help at all, of course.

The guard disappears as soon as they arrive back at the apartment. She sets aside the chicken and the tea and attends to putting away the linens first.

"Mui tsai!" Boss Fong calls from the back room. Little sister. Household servants are all little sister. The girls in the brothels are all little sister. Every girl in Chinatown is little sister until they get married off. They are rarely married off. Mostly, they are just sold and resold until they die.

With a sigh, she obeys the call. The merchant from earlier is gone, along with the two guards that had been stationed at the door. But on the table, in the place where he had been sitting, lies a finger. A pool of blood surrounds it, dripping onto the floor. The first time she had seen evidence of Boss Fong's anger, she had fainted. Now she can at least pretend to not be bothered.

"Clean that up," the Boss says without looking at her. "And bring me more tea." He is settled into his armchair now, smoking as he gazes out the window at the goings-on of the gambling house. Can he spot cheaters from up here?

The blood around the finger is just beginning to coagulate as it continues dripping, splattering the floor. What had the merchant done to earn that? He probably held back on tribute. He probably did not give the Boss what the Boss is due. Stupid.

After bringing the tea, she cleans up the finger and its mess, and then burns it up along with the bloody rags in a burn bucket in the back alley. Her next task is to deliver the Lotus Pearl its linens. She hopes this will be quick – the unexpected clean-up of the finger set her back in her schedule a fair amount, and she still has dinner to prepare, and she doesn't like it at the brothel at all. Madam Bai is waiting for her when she arrives.

"One of the girls hung herself," the Madam says as casually as if she were announcing the time. She doesn't say who – they are all the same to her.

At the shocked look Li Nuan can't hold back, Madam Bai clarifies, "Chun Hua." She clearly hates saying their actual names.

The news saddens her, but a little bit of relief mixes in too. The girl whose name means "happy spring" is free.

The Madam isn't finished. "You will work her place tonight. After Boss Fong's dinner. He has ordered it."

"What? But I–"

"Yes, yes, the promise Boss made to your father, that you would be set to domestic work only. This is an emergency – you don't want to lose the Boss money, do you? The punishment for that is worse than what I ask."

The bloody finger on the table flashes through Li Nuan's mind. "What... acts must I...?" Her question barely a whisper.

"Whatever the men ask."

"I've never –"

Madam clucks her tongue. "You have to grow up sometime. You are already a little old."

She is sixteen.

"I will have one of the others show you the basics before your first customer. Are you going to cry? Don't cry. You'd rather work in a sweatshop? This is better. You give some pleasure and don't ruin your eyes sewing all day. Now you better get going; you still have dinner to cook."

Li Nuan's heart pounds and her stomach grows leaden, heavier with each step, as she makes her way back to Boss Fong's. No no no no no! Tears sting her eyes as she chops the ginger and scallions the chicken will be steamed with. Terror and dismay and disgust grip her as she prepares a vegetable side dish, as she starts the rice. Is this her forever place now, or is it just for tonight? Shame swells as she wishes for another girl to come and take her place, to relieve her of this vulgar duty.

She brings dinner for the Boss to the same table where he takes meetings. "Have you spoken to Madam Bai?" He still sits in his big chair, cigarette smoke curling around his face. He keeps his eyes on the gamblers next door.

She manages to choke out, "Yes. I –" She wants to beg him to relieve her of the duty. She wants to remind him of his promise to her father. But her father is nothing but a debtor, so why would the Boss care? Their gazes lock for a brief second, and the plea in her eyes is met with a face of stone.

"You promised." She can barely squeak out the words.

"You are lucky I kept you from it this long. It is just until the next shipment. Just until next week."

The next shipment. He means the next batch of girls, who will be for sale at the next auction. Boss Fong will certainly bid on a few of them. Or maybe he will send Madam Bai. Thankfully, she didn't go through an auction herself. She was purchased directly from her father before she ever got on that boat. She wishes that boat had sunk. Why couldn't she have drowned in the sea?

The Boss says nothing else. He just sits down at the table and helps himself to steamed chicken. He seems to have sensed her fear and dismay in the look they shared, because he doesn't look at her again or say "thank you" when she serves the food, which he normally does, even though he doesn't have to. He waves a hand to dismiss her, and she goes back to the pantry to wait for him to finish eating so she can then clean up and go do her other job. Her new job.

She should have some rice and vegetables, but she is too distressed to eat. In the privacy of the pantry, she lets her tears flow. She doesn't belong to herself – not since her father sold her has she been her own person. Maybe not even before that; she just didn't know back then. What must it be like to be your own person, to have control over your body and your mind and your life? She will never know, will she? Her whole life will go by, and she will never know.

"Mui tsai!" comes the call she has been waiting for. Wiping her eyes, she pulls herself together. When she gets back to the kitchen after cleaning up the remnants of dinner, Wu Jun is there. She understands – he is tasked with escorting her to the Lotus Pearl. To make sure she doesn't try to run. She knows she can't run – where does she have to go, anyway? She has to do what she is told. What else is there?

3.

NATHAN

June 1, 2006
SOMA District, San Francisco

"Form and function in perfect harmony," Accounts VP Kendal Jakes says as she wraps up her pitch. "Link. By Portal Technologies."

The last slide appears, and the design Nathan had busted his ass over for the past year is up there on the screen for the client to see and to judge. His colleagues had seen multiple iterations, and this one was agreed upon by the team, so he at least knows that somebody in the room likes it. The wait for the client's response is still anxiety provoking though. Nathan is proud of the sleek form factor, the feel of the buttons, the typeface. He loves the matte finish, and the colors chosen for the line: black, space grey, a brilliant red. It all goes together so nicely. He looks around the table and tries to gauge the response of the client team from their expressions. A couple of them nod, so that's good. But it's really only one person's opinion that matters: Zack Oja, CEO of the client company.

Proud as he is of his work, Nathan can't shake a tickling sense of futility. His job is to imagine the future – of consumer electronics, anyway – and it is a privilege to have it, he is well aware. Yet, the thought of his mark on the world being a snazzy new design that will dominate for a season, then be overrun with imitators, then be replaced by the next snazzy new design, makes him queasy. As cool and comfortable as it is, is this all his life is going to be until the end? Applause bursts through his pondering – a warm reception for his work, for him, from the assembled teams: the campaign and design leads of Phase Designworks, his employer, and Portal Technologies, the client. Despite his existential worry, he appreciates the validation.

Kendal joins the applause, then calls out, "Design Lead Nathan Zhao." She gestures his way with her clapping hands.

Nathan blushes at the attention, though he does like it. He bows his head – gracefully, he hopes.

"I think I speak for the full team when I say fantastic work," Zack Oja CEO says. "The concept works for me. The design, the campaign, all of it. Home run."

From across the table, Kendal sends an approving nod Nathan's way. That's as much as he can usually expect from her in a public setting – that shout out was a surprise. She typically doesn't offer public accolades, to prevent anyone from getting a big head, although Nathan thinks, as he has for a while, that the biggest ego in the room is usually hers.

"Let's get this thing into production," Zack continues. "And we won't let those stupid protestors get in the way of launch."

Portal Technologies has, in recent weeks, been the target of protests against unsafe working conditions in the manufacture of some of its products. But that negative attention doesn't seem to bother the company's CEO.

"Glad to hear it," Kendal says. The negative attention doesn't seem to bother Nathan's boss either. But of course, she could just be taking her cues from the client. She sticks to the business at hand. "We'll get proofs and a detailed timeline to you by end of week. And have your team contact Nathan directly to arrange looks at the models."

Nathan exchanges cards with someone on Portal's team, and after Kendal escorts the Portal delegation out, it's time for a round of celebratory drinks. They hit the wine bar-art gallery Kendal likes for some sparkly and to bask in the glow of satisfying another happy, well-paying client.

"You seem kinda down for someone who just designed the flagship product for a major tech firm." Lili Nakamura is Nathan's work-wife and the product-namer who bestowed the moniker "Link" on the company's latest success. He marvels at Lili's work – hours of market research and focus groups to arrive at a four letter, single-syllable word. The name for the thing he designed. It's her triumph as much as his. Nathan can sense Lili scrutinizing his face for the barest hint of his true feelings. Everyone's always masking, she likes to say.

"No, I'm great." He takes a fizzy sip. "Proud." He looks up at one of the gigantic paintings that comprise the current exhibit: elaborate portraits of Hindu deities done in a comic book, superhero style. Kali stares down at him, the vanquished villain's head in one of her hands, bloody sword in another, her eyes wild, the promise of destruction unfurling from her long tongue.

"Are you caught up in your impermanence trip again?" Lili sips her customary rosé; champagne always gives her a headache.

"I just want to…" He trails off as he looks over the crowd. There are his colleagues mingling and basking in self-congratulatory bliss, there are some finance bros in their vests, and people in sharp suits that he guesses are attorneys.

God, what is it all for? His work? All that effort and all those resources devoted to creating gadgets ruled by some ever-shifting notion of 'cool' and planned obsolescence? Gadgets the people in this room will no doubt salivate over and flaunt for a season until the next new thing comes out? He chides himself for being such a downer. This is supposed to be a celebration.

"You going to finish that thought?" Lili casually swirls the wine in her glass as she awaits his, no doubt, profound pronouncement. She knows how he gets.

"I just want to make something that's as meaningful as it is 'elegant and groundbreaking in its fashion-forward lines.'" They exchange a look and bust out laughing over their favorite quote from a review of their last major product launch, the Groov mp3 player. There's a lot of pompous language in the world of design review.

"I get that, but you should enjoy the now moment too."

"How very zen of you. I'll keep that in mind."

Nathan stays for just the one round, since he has a meeting of Camp Tomorrow's Yesterday to get to. That would be the group he camps with at Burning Man, the annual arts festival in the Nevada desert where tens of thousands gather to form a temporary city full of large-scale art, music, and radical self-expression. A lot of people like to say the event is over, that it's jumped the shark, ruined by newbies who were drawn in by the press it's gotten from MTV and WIRED Magazine but don't get it at all. But he maintains that a person gets out of it what they put into it, and for him, it's the biggest, most beautiful and profound party in the world. It's only as shallow or as deep as you make it.

No doubt, the inherent character of the event has evolved since its origins – a couple hundred hippies in the desert is far different than over forty thousand of all sorts of people. The hippies in the crowd are now joined by ravers and clubkids, and crusty punks and goths, and artists and musicians of all stripes, and libertarian techy types, and professionals like doctors and lawyers and accountants wanting to let their freak flag fly. Black Rock City, the temporary city that emerges during the event, is apparently one of the largest cities in Nevada for the week that it exists, and then it's all broken down and the desert cleaned up and reset by a crew of mostly volunteers. There is no other city like it, as far as he's concerned.

The meeting is at Mason's loft in the Mission District, a rustic yet artfully decorated space of raw brick and large windows. Nathan greets everyone as he makes his way to the kitchen to grab a beverage and a couple of cookies – oh, and pigs-in-a-blanket. With this snack that will likely end up being dinner tonight, he settles in on the sofa next to his boyfriend Remy, known for spinning house tunes as DJ Aspect. This camp is a joint endeavor of Remy's crew, Awaken Beat Collective, and Nathan's friends, the crew of an art car, the Fish, which was a big silver fish. This will be their third burn together as two crews in one.

As usual, Mason takes on facilitation. "Let's start with the Fish," he says, with a glance at his clipboard. "Tell us about it, Danny."

The Fish had begun its existence as a 1965 Dodge RV that Danny got for really cheap. "Let's do something with this thing," he had said on that fateful Sunday four years ago, when he had the gang over for a barbeque. Nathan's design talents were called upon, and when he learned that the theme of that year's burn was going to be The Floating

World, an ocean theme, he worked out a design to transform the RV into a sea creature. Something simple but with a distinctive silhouette. They took apart the whole structure, leaving only the engine block and chassis and the base, and rebuilt it in the shape it is now, a sort of flounder-like thing.

"She's looking good," Danny reports. He remains the owner and captain of the vehicle. "We got a new alternator in –"

"So you finally got that tent-stake out?" Nathan asks with a smile. One of the bolts securing the Fish's alternator had broken on the way back last year, just outside Reno. Nathan had had the brilliant idea to jam a tent-stake into the connector in lieu of the replacement bolt they didn't have. Trouble was, they couldn't get it out for a while after that.

"It took some of Sid's magic pixie dust to remove it," Danny says.

"What'd you do?" asks Remy, turning to Sid, who is perhaps the handiest member of the bunch. He's an electrician, after all.

"My ways are mysterious," Sid says as he strokes his beard, which is dyed a vivid purple. Sid's wacky that way.

"We need to re-upholster some cushions, and replace the lights, and lay the wiring for the new sound-system," Danny continues. "All doable. We've got twelve weeks before we roll out."

"I'll work on cushions," Nathan volunteers.

"And I'll work on the sound," Remy says. It makes sense that he'd take that on; it was his sound-system that was going to be thumping out in the desert night after all.

"Lights," Sid calls out, raising his hand.

"Great." Mason scribbles on his clipboard. "Let's talk shade. Annika?"

Annika has been part of the camp for as long as Nathan and is a fantastic artist – a couple of her paintings are up on Mason's walls now. While she and Nathan are friendly, and once had a long, rambling, childhood-and-universe-encompassing conversation on mushrooms, they don't know each other all that well – even though they knew each other deeply, for a moment. She takes on organizing the shade structure every year, a key element for comfort and survival out on the playa.

"Bigger camp means bigger shade," she says. "We have the green one from last time and it's still holding up. We could use another the same size this year, I think. In addition to the Quonset hut. I propose paying for it out of the camp fund."

"Everyone okay with that?" Mason looks around at the gathered, nodding faces. "Great."

"I'll get it ordered," Annika says. "And we should do a practice set-up at some point. I'll let everyone know."

Mason, an attorney when he isn't herding this bunch of weirdoes, runs down the rest of the checklist with assured efficiency: power, water, kitchen, fuel, bike parking. Nathan tunes out a bit, having done this enough to know how it goes. He settles back into the couch, finishes the last bites of food on his plate. This part of his life – the community, the collaborative creativity, the fun adventures with this crew – is the part he loves the most. This part feels meaningful to him and is what his work and his salary supports. But it's not enough. He wants his work to fulfill just as much as his personal life. Is that greedy? Is that expecting too much?

"Finally, we have the Time Machine," Mason says, bringing up the last bit of camp business. "Delilah, want to take us away?"

The Time Machine is the proposed art project offering for this year. For the past couple of years, the camp has applied for, and received, theme camp placement, which means a reserved footprint. As a condition of such placement, camps are required to make some kind of public programmatic offering, or gift, at the event. In the past, the Fish and the dance parties were considered to be the camp's offerings. The crew has always been dedicated to not being dicks and letting anyone board the Fish as long as there was room – as opposed to certain other crews of larger, flashier art cars – or mutant vehicles, as they are also called – who only let people board if they're deemed hot enough. Or if it's somebody famous. The parties thrown by Awaken Beat Collective are popular affairs; they take the Fish out to the deep playa, crank the speakers, and colorful, saucer-eyed dancers would stomp in the dust 'til dawn.

But this year, Delilah Wick, Pilates studio owner and Nathan's best friend, got a bug up her butt to do an art project. She calls it the Time Machine. "I got us a salon chair," she informs the group, "for the traveler. It spins around a full three-sixty, so it's perfect."

"I'm mostly done building the frame," Sid says. His handiness is called upon for multiple projects for the camp. "It's pretty simple, really."

"And I'll be sewing the covering with Delilah," Nathan adds.

"And we've got some strobes and a fog machine that can go into it," Remy says, speaking for the Awaken crew. "You wanted that, right?"

Delilah nods enthusiastically. "Yes, that sounds perfect." She claps her hands and wiggles in her seat. "This is so exciting!"

"What's the deal with this thing, again?" Danny asks. "I missed the meeting when we decided to do this."

All eyes turn to the mastermind behind the project.

"I got inspired by our camp name, Tomorrow's Yesterday, right?" she begins. "The structure will be a small yurt, just big enough to house the chair. The chair will be in the center of the space. Maybe on a platform if we can swing it. We'll get it set up with an LED underlight, and maybe some blinky things too, right? Maybe have some calm music – like that Japanese flute music they play in spas all the time. We welcome the time traveler into it from the back side that faces camp, and get them seated –"

"I think we should hot box them," Remy interjects.

Chuckles all around. Delilah replies, "Maybe as a special deluxe experience. With the participant's consent, of course."

"Of course," Remy agrees.

"Anyway, we get the flashing lights going, and turn on the fog machine, and spin the chair and we'll have *woo-woo* sound effects, and whoever's around can come shake the yurt to make it like it's really hurtling through time and space, right? Then the chair stops spinning, and we open the tent on the front-facing side, and the attendant says, 'Experience the yesterday of tomorrow, today.' And we usher the time traveler out into the rest of their day. It's using the trope of time travel and longing for adventure to comment on being present in the Now, yeah? Make today your adventure. Maybe a cup of tea after."

Danny sticks out his lower lip in an exaggerated pout, bobs his head in a way that's somehow both nodding it and shaking it. "Okay. I dig it."

"It'll be fun," Nathan says. "Can I be a shaker? I want to be a shaker."

"Whoever's around," Delilah says. "I think it might be best to make this offering during scheduled times. Maybe we can have folks commit to manning it during those times, but as long as we all agree to shake the yurt when we're around, that'll probably be fine. It won't take much."

"I'll be at the workshop this weekend," Danny says. "Work party for the Fish on Sunday? The usual pizza and beer?"

Everyone agrees and the meeting adjourns. Delilah catches up with Nathan before she goes flying out the door. "Let's sew this week. I'll call you!" She flips open her phone and pulls out its little antenna and hits one of her speed-dials. "I'm on my way…" she says as she hurries down the sidewalk. She probably has a date.

Danny hugs Nathan and Remy goodnight before they part ways. "Let's grab drinks sometime," he says to Nathan.

"Sure thing."

Remy takes Nathan's hand in his and gives it a squeeze as they walk into the brisk night. They're heading down Valencia Street, which is crawling with hipsters making the most of a Thursday night – the unofficial start of the weekend.

"How'd the presentation go?" Remy asks.

"Client loved it. It's going into production. I'm getting a fat bonus."

Remy shakes their joined hands up and down excitedly. "Congrats, babe. You worked so hard on that thing! And hooray for a fat bonus. Ibiza, here we come!"

The two share a laugh before Nathan rains on the Ibiza parade. "I'm using all my PTO for the burn and after. Black Rock City is my only vacation anymore. Maybe one day we'll have a vacation that isn't so much work."

"That's crazy talk. You want to get a drink to celebrate?"

They're strolling by Blondie's now, and one of that establishment's famously lethal martinis does sound tempting. "I've got a lot going on tomorrow. Don't wanna be hungover."

Remy nods in understanding. They walk for a while in silence before he asks, "Are you happy about it? You seem kind of... ambivalent."

"No – I mean, yeah." Nathan sighs. "I'm proud of the work, and the money's good –"

"But you want to channel your creativity into something more meaningful." Remy is well versed in this little loop of Nathan's. "You'll figure it out. You just need that catalytic spark. Keep yourself open to possibilities. I believe in you."

As flighty and inattentive as Remy can be sometimes, he's as supportive a boyfriend as anyone could want. He found his passion – spinning house music for frenzied crowds reveling in the ecstasy of the dancefloor – at age thirty after having found success in his day job as a sound engineer for Dolby. He'd considered leaving that job as invitations to play at festivals began rolling in, but he decided he liked having health insurance. Remy had found his thing, and Nathan wishes he would find his, already. He already has his dream job, but boy oh boy is it time to find another dream. Is this ennui a standard feature of his age? Of the times? Is he just another lost soul seeking purpose? He hates the thought that he could be so typical, and yet...

They get home and immediately go to the bedroom to change into loungewear. Nathan kicks off his shoes – a new pair that he loves, but they're not quite broken in yet. He sits on the edge of the bed in his underwear and rubs his feet. He hadn't realized how sore they were until the shoes came off.

Remy stands in front of him, mesh basketball shorts in hand, but he hasn't put them on yet. "We don't have to get dressed, you know." God, he's beautiful.

"What did you have in mind?" Nathan asks with a sly smile. Remy tosses the shorts aside, walks over, naked, and bends down for a kiss. Oh, this felt good. Any misgivings he has about the direction of his life evaporate in the kiss. Remy drops to his knees, and Nathan lays back on the bed with a sigh.

4.

MAIDA

March 5, 2106
Golden Gate Cultural Recovery Project, Presidio Campus

My first order of business was to review the artifact manifest, arranged in batches according to where the items were found. The Islais Cove haul was a top priority, but I wasn't really sure why. These were from a restored area in the southeast quadrant of the city, a neighborhood once called Glen Park. The cove, as I understood it, was named for the creek that it once was. The watershed reasserted itself in a big way once sea levels hit their highs in the 2070s and 80s. The items I'd be working with had already been recorded in the database, and holographic scans taken. My task was to scan and record their histories. The more interesting or beautiful items were to be included in an exhibit at the Precursor Historical Galleries here on campus.

The lot I grabbed contained several items that had been found in a time capsule. What was particularly interesting about this batch was that it wasn't a historical society or museum project, but appeared to be an individual person's collection of private memorabilia. That was where the rich stuff lay – the bits of regular people's lives that comprised the warp and weft of the Record of Civilization. It was in such items that the story of how people really lived could be found. It was those stories that drew me to this work; it was those stories that had fascinated me about my ability once I stopped being freaked out about it. The Precursor era was such a different reality – social mores, the economic and political structures – all of it was so different, and built around a mindset of extraction, exploitation, and domination that we just didn't operate by anymore. Not here in the Region, anyway. Thank whatever deity that may or may not exist. That world of the Precursors, up through the mid-twenty-first century, was as different to us in 2106 as the early colonial days of America must have been to them.

A lot of my peers from the Academy went into law enforcement – mostly in other Administrative Regions. The Sierra Northshore Regional Alliance was a famously low-crime, high-enlightenment area, but not all the zones of the former United States were like that. Some seemed intent on repeating the tragedies of the old world, and some of my classmates left for those regions to lend their talents to criminal investigations. I knew from the moment I started at the Academy that wasn't how I'd want to use my ability. That one time scanning a murder weapon was enough for me. No, I was more interested in how people lived than how they died.

The items in my cart winked at me from their trays as I wheeled them to my workstation. They beckoned me to unlock their stories. All together like this, a larger theme emerged – those artifacts and gizmos and trinkets told the story of a people who believed their days would continue on in glory, who had no idea of the storm they'd wrought. What lessons might we learn from such a people? We lived with the consequences of their choices, the aftermath of the civil wars and political turmoil and economic collapse and natural disasters and deterioration of the social order – collectively referred to as the Collapse. It spanned from roughly 2052, when several states seceded from the U.S., through 2072, the year of the Bloom. Although some folks believed the Collapse was truly starting as early as the 2030s. Could we gain insight into why? Why they made the choices they made, why they lived the way they did? I supposed that if nobody thought that we could, we wouldn't have been doing this work. This entire project would not even exist. And if I didn't believe that we could, or that such insight would be valuable, I certainly wouldn't have wanted this assignment.

The batch of items included a telecom device – a flip-phone, they were called. There were some postcards with images of old San Francisco, including a couple of the bridges, one of a row of brightly colored houses that were old even at the time these postcards were printed, some reproductions of artwork from various ethnicities: a Chinese watercolor, Japanese anime, Mexican sugar skulls and flowers for Day of the Dead. Also included were pieces of original artwork signed by the artist, somebody named Annika Blake. Alongside these was a packet of photographs of what looked like a party taking place in a desert setting – people dressed in colorful, outlandish clothing or barely dressed at all, smiling under a hot sun or else at night, huge fires burning behind them. A laughing group standing in front of a vehicle that looked like a fish. There was a ring connected to a medallion with an emblem engraved on it: a representation of a man with a sort of diamond shape for a head and what looked like stylized parentheses opening outward.

There was some currency – the strange green paper that had been used across the former United States, along with some coins. The paper had a particular scent to it: the ink plus a faint hint of incense. I looked over the money and marveled that this paper had had so much impact on people's lives. As I understood it, people needed it to pay for housing, food, healthcare, clothing, and everything needed for daily life. From some of the research I'd done during my studies, I knew people worked jobs they hated in order to get this paper in order to pay for things to just simply live.

In the Sierra Northshore Regional Alliance, housing, food, and healthcare were provided to everybody. Housing stock was managed by Specialized Vocation Administrata – the Department of Infrastructure, for example, or Utilities Maintenance. In my case, my basic needs were met by the Department of Culture, under whose purview the Golden Gate Cultural Recovery Project operated. The GGCRP was assigned an inventory of housing stock to maintain, and the housing was provided to its workers. Everybody put in shifts in community gardens or the food forests, which provided plenty of fresh vegetables, leafy greens and fruits, and the Department of Sustenance grew other crops like grains and rice and legumes.

The only wages we received were luxury credits, and those were generally used for things like alcohol, or prepared meals, or fancy-dress clothing – niceties not required for survival. Given that the population of the world was just a bit over half what it was in 2035, there had been a lot of built space and clothing and so many other things salvaged. We used as much salvaged material as we could – everything from fabric to furniture to tools were salvaged from the old world. There were no more resources to waste – the Precursors had seen to that. What new materials we needed, like paper or textiles, were now produced with fast-growing, sustainable materials like hemp and bamboo. New technologies had been developed, of course – augmented reality devices, superfast tablets and computers – but those were usually kept as work tools by the relevant Divisions and weren't sold as consumer products the way they used to be, although everybody got a node.

I set the currency down and went through the other items. A datastick with a label stuck to it: *music*. At the party, Roan had said his specialty was technology – how did he put it? He got old devices to talk to us again. Maybe he could do something with this. I set it aside along with the telecom device to pass on to him later. The source of the earthy, musky scent that permeated all these objects appeared to be a packet of incense. A herbaceous top note – patchouli, maybe? There was a clay tablet with a spiral carved into it, a pair of sunglasses, a hairclip with an ornate feather. Lastly, a small bundle wrapped in yellow silk. I untied the ribbon holding it together, pulled back the fine fabric to reveal a teacup. It looked like jade.

I folded the silk back over it when I set it back down, but left the ribbon undone. It was the most interesting item there, and I wanted to save it for later. Given that this group of items was found in the same capsule, I had expected a single owner, but that didn't appear to be the case.

The time capsule itself gave me nothing in the psifield; it was totally inert, a dead channel. Whenever I used my ability, the things I touched either lit up in my inner sight, giving me visions, or sometimes I heard voices or even music, or sometimes I just knew whatever there was to know about the thing. But this canister gave off nothing at all. The pieces of technology, the incense, and the currency were like the capsule: blank. To be honest, I knew this would likely be the case. We practiced on different items during my training at the Academy, and one of the lessons we learned was that most utilitarian items, particularly those whose very nature was "transient," like bits of technology and especially currency, held very little psychic charge. Currency, whether from the Precursor era or modern currency from other Administrative Regions – we don't use physical currency here in Sierra Northshore – is by its nature a tool of exchange. Thus, it never really belonged to anyone, no matter who happened to be in possession of any piece of it at any time. If there were any universal truths to my ability, to the cosmic laws governing the lives of objects, this would seem to be one of them.

The other items that had been inside the time capsule, however, were a different matter entirely. The original art pieces were a triptych of tiny paintings of landscapes with geometric patterns etched over them. Annika Blake's work. When I cupped one of these miniature canvases in my palms, the psifield tingled, and when I closed my eyes, I got flashes of her studio and glimpses of her loving attention as she painted this piece. It depicted a purple-tinted sky with wisps of silver clouds and an emblem that looked like a heart made from a key and chain links combined – had it been created for a lover? Maggie? I sensed that it had been in Maggie's possession for a brief time before ownership reverted to Annika. Guess it didn't end well.

The photographs told a story too, but there was no echo of ownership in them. They were probably printed for the express purpose of being included in this time capsule and never actually belonged to anyone. So instead of using my psychometry to scan them, I laid them out on my workstation and examined the images printed on them, like a nul-psi would. In the envelope that contained the photos was a ticket to an event called Burning Man. The year on the ticket was 2006 – a hundred years ago. It looked like some kind of festival or gathering. They seemed to be camping in a desert.

The people in the photographs looked to be in their thirties or forties – it was hard to tell with the dust that seemed to cover everybody. They looked like they were having the time of their lives. I spotted a woman with long, brightly colored ribbons braided into her hair and I knew right away it was Annika, the artist. There was a group shot of twelve or so standing in front of a vehicle built to look like a fish. Then a shot of a man holding up a medallion in front the fish vehicle, giving a thumbs up and beaming happily. The medallion... I just saw that.

I turned my attention to the other items and found it, the disc with the stylized and embossed diamond-headed man-symbol attached to a ring. I compared it to what the man in the photograph held and saw that I held the same object. I folded my fingers closed around it and concentrated, brought my focus to the psifield, and opened the channel to it. The man's name was Danny, and he was well-loved. This item, a key ring, had been a gift, something given to drivers of what were called mutant vehicles at this Burning Man event. It had only been in his possession for a short time – days – before being placed in the capsule.

There was a rush as I held it: flashes of a blindingly hot desert day when Danny was given this token of appreciation. He stood in front of the Fish – the fish vehicle, it was just called "the Fish" – and a line of other outlandish vehicles stretched behind it, most notably an enormous flower that towered over everything else. Suddenly, it was night, and music pounded – electronic, artificial, and yet a feeling of transcendence pulsed in it also. People danced together to the music booming from the Fish. Dust blew through in thin curtains and ribbons and swirls – the remnants of a passing storm or strong wind. A huge fire in the distance, swarmed by colorful lights. Danny making out with somebody.

The signal faded.

I tapped some notes on what I scanned into the database, then put the keyring back in the tray with the other items and looked through more of the photographs. Annika the artist was in a couple of them, most notably one in which she was laughing, her face covered in colored powder. There was a shot of someone behind some sort of console, headphones askew on his head, that same man in the arms of another and they were laughing and smooching. Another group shot – everyone standing in front of a sign that read CAMP TOMORROW'S YESTERDAY. What a fun bunch of friends. A pang of envy surprised me then, stirred up by the friendship, the camaraderie, the love so evident in these photographs, among these long-dead strangers. I never had a lot of friends. That wasn't on purpose; life just worked out that way.

Okay, that packet of photographs was a rabbit hole! I gathered up the photos and put them back into their envelope and turned my attention to the item I was most curious about: the teacup wrapped in silk. It seemed a bit out of place among the rest of this stuff, and that might have been what had me so curious. But there was also the odd sense of familiarity it gave me. One of the things we trained for at the Academy was trusting our intuition, discerning true intuition from merely being reminded of something, or fearing something, or wishing something was true. This familiarity I felt in that moment was the true intuitive kind. But why would that be? The green jade the cup was carved from sang against the golden yellow silk that wrapped it.

Little white and pink flowers were embroidered into the fabric. The cup itself was cool to the touch –

– sudden years burned through my sight and my knowing, embers and ash and hot rushing air as the life of the cup took over my mind in a blazing flash. Blood and weeping. Pride. Comfort. An old woman showing the cup to a little girl – a granddaughter? A voyage on a stormy sea. A housekeeper filled with terror. A party boy filled with all the wonder of the cosmos. Violent destruction – a falling building. Fire. Displayed on shelves for years and years that flicker by in a second, then years and years of darkness. More fire – the same fire? The joy of finding a calling. The confusion of being lost. Lostness. Grief. Belonging.

A sob burst out of me before I could fully grasp what I was feeling, which was all of it. Everything, all at once.

I dropped the cup and stumbled back a couple of steps. Tears flowed as the knowledge settled in – this cup had been engulfed in flame and didn't burn. This cup had been through more than one end of the world.

"Hey, are you all right?" Roan stood in the doorway of my office, concern etched across his brow.

"Yeah…" The sobbing had subsided, but my voice still quavered. "I got a really intense wave of stuff…" I pointed to the teacup, then wiped my eyes with my sleeve.

He walked over to the table where the cup sat swaddled in its silk finery. I almost called out a warning when he picked it up, but of course he was nul-psi and wasn't going to collapse in psychic overwhelm at the barest touch.

"What do you know about it?" He was completely unperturbed by the entirety of the cup's existence that it was transmitting through the psifield, that still wavered inside me even though the signal was fading.

"It's all a jumble right now." Closing my eyes, I brought calm to my mind and let all other thoughts not related to the subject – in this case, the cup – drop away. This was a skill all students at the Academy had to master before we were allowed to graduate. In this mental and psychic calm, details clicked into place. "It dates back to the 1800s in China, and has been in this area for a long time – since the 1900s, I think? A couple of people really stood out to me…" I trailed off as I flashed on the maid, on the old woman. Were they the same person? And the party boy, the hedonist – he had come through loudly as well. Yet there were others in the mix – shadows, echoes. Why did those two in particular arise so vivid and clear?

"You with me?" Roan asked. The concern in his voice prompted me to open my eyes. He peered at me with furrowed brows.

"Yeah. That was just a lot." My temples throbbed as I looked at the cup again. What came off it just now was way more intense than usual. "I'm a little scared of it now."

"Well I find food helpful in moments of stress. I was heading to the commissary for lunch. Come with me." His expression had shifted from concerned to inviting, and actually, I was hungry. He probably didn't know it, but after using my ability for an extended period, eating did ground me and help settle my internal state.

"Lead the way."

"How's your first day been?" Lorel asked as Roan and I joined her at one of the outside tables. It was a warm day – it was always warm, a state of affairs that wasn't true in the time periods I perceived through the cup. The breeze that blew through was hot and dry, the kind of brittle air that often preceded wildfire. I was thankful for the umbrella providing shade. "Scan anything good?"

I appreciated how welcoming these two were being. Because of dad's work studying recovering estuary systems, we traveled a lot – as much as local politics and border concessions allowed. Travel was limited, compared to how it had been in the Precursor days, but we still did a lot more than most people. Consequently, I never had consistent peers in my life until I went to the Circle of the Eye Academy, but there, people kept their distance, lest some stray psionic emission trigger a response in another person unawares. Or maybe that was just me.

After chomping down a big bite of salad, I launched into an account of what I gleaned from the photos. I told them about the group of friends who'd put this time capsule together a century ago, and of the big festival in the desert they all attended together. I told Lorel about the cup.

Roan chimed in on that part. "She was sobbing. That's what made me go check on her."

"Wow," Lorel said, eyes wide. "What do you think that's all about?"

"I'm not really sure."

"Do you think maybe you have some kind of connection to those two?" Roan calmly took a sip of tea after asking this question.

"What makes you ask that?" There was a prickle of familiarity – intuition letting me know he was onto something.

"Well, telepaths have a stronger psychic connection to people they're connected to in some other way, like blood relatives. Also, don't their powers work over distances only with people they've already connected with? You had this intense connection with people in the past, and time is a sort of distance, isn't it?"

Lorel and I both looked at Roan quizzically.

"That's so poetic," Lorel said. "How unlike you."

Roan scrunched up his face at her and stuck out his tongue.

"How do you know that?" I asked. "About telepaths?" That telepathy functioned in the way Roan described was common knowledge among those trained at the Academy – the standard curriculum included the basic mechanics of every psionic talent – but in my experience, most nul-psis had no idea how any of it worked.

"Oh." He seemed to fumble for an answer. "It's just what I've heard, I guess. Are you going to scan the cup again after what happened earlier?"

This question felt like a transparent attempt to change the subject, but I didn't press the matter. I pushed my salad around on my plate, took a bite of avocado. "Of course I am." Honestly, I was a bit offended that he thought I'd scare off that easily, but I tried to keep my annoyance contained. "I'm not done with it. I still have work to do, more data to log. I have a job. I can't just push it aside because I'm uncomfortable."

He smiled and nodded. I got the feeling that I'd passed some sort of test I didn't know I was taking.

"Did you get the memo about the site visit?" Lorel asked.

"I saw something about that." I pulled out my node, now reminded that there had been a memo from Aviva in my inbox that I hadn't read in the moment because I was so anxious to get started in the lab. It was a notice that Assessor Prime Julian Linstrom and some of his senior staff would be conducting a site visit next week. The artifact labs were on the itinerary.

"The top leader of Regional Administration coming here," Lorel said. "I don't think the other ones ever did."

"I can tell Aviva is stressed out even though she hasn't said so," Lorel said. "Like she needs more to deal with on top of Rebecca."

Roan nodded in agreement, which prompted me to ask, "Who's Rebecca?"

Lorel pulled out a tablet and tapped up a picture. "She was the Project's Liaison Officer to Regional Administration before she went missing. She was who Aviva reported to, and she approved new personnel and equipment and housing stock and all that stuff. They were friends, I guess. Anyway, Rebecca went missing a few months ago."

The bulletin displayed on Lorel's tablet was a Missing Persons notice for one Rebecca Morgan, thirty-eight years old, last seen on December 21, 2105. Seeing the notice made me go cold. Such notices were common in the Precursor days – not everyone knew somebody who went missing, but most people came across notices for missing strangers with some regularity. But since the Bloom, such cases had been exceedingly rare.

"I'm surprised I haven't heard about this," I said. "Clairvoyants can't find her?"

Roan shook his head. "They've tried, and there's nothing. That's why Aviva is so freaked out. They're even keeping it quiet on the newsfeeds. They don't want people to know someone can go missing and not even be found by a clairvoyant."

Lorel put the tablet away. "Nothing we can do about it."

An uncomfortable silence came over us. We didn't want to talk about the missing woman anymore, but how does one carry on a conversation after such a downer of a topic? Work. Bringing it back to work and something we can actually do; that was always a good tactic. "You said the previous Assessors Prime never visited. Why do you suppose Linstrom is?"

"Maybe he has a particular interest in Precursor history," Roan offered. "You better get your workstation in shape." He gave me a playful wink when I looked over at him.

"Are you going to give a demo of your little toys?" Lorel asked Roan teasingly.

"Don't call them that." His annoyance was clearly pretend because he was smirking as he replied. "My drones," he explained.

I remembered him flying them around at Lorel's birthday party. "I figured."

"He has a whole bunch of them," Lorel went on, "They're all coordinated. It's cool seeing them in formation, actually."

"Those are for fun, not part of my official work," Roan said. "I want to recreate drone shows like the ones I've seen footage of from the Precursor days. They were set to music and choreographed."

At the mention of music, I remembered an item from the time capsule. "Oh, hey, before I forget. I've got something for you back at the lab. A datastick. With music."

Roan raised his eyebrows with interest. "How do you know it's music? Did your powers tell you?"

"Yes, my powers of reading that allowed me to discern the label stuck to it."

Roan laughed. "Psions are so amazing."

We finished up lunch with me promising Lorel that we'd grab drinks sometime, then Roan and I headed back to the lab.

"I'm looking forward to this," he said when I handed him the datastick. He held it between thumb and forefinger and gave it a wiggle. "There was a remarkable range of music styles back then." He glanced at the items on the table. "May I?" He gestured at the photographs.

At my nod, he picked up a stack and started flipping through them. "This datastick was in with these items?"

"Yes. All bundled together in a time capsule. Why?"

"I'm wondering if the music on here was made by somebody in this group. Like this person, for example." He held up the picture of the man with headphones.

"Why him?"

"He looks like what was called a 'DJ'. They played music at parties and festivals and such. That's what the gear is for." He pointed to the console full of knobs and levers in the photo. "This could be a recording of a set played by this person. Maybe even what he was playing in this moment. Have you picked up who he is yet?"

I shook my head.

"Good-looking man," Roan comments wistfully. He flicked through a couple more, then set the photos down. "We should have a listening party when I extract the contents."

Once Roan had gone on his way, I was alone with my work once more. I avoided the cup for an hour or two, diverting my attention with the other curios in the batch: the clay tablet with a spiral carved into it and the words "a dreamer" on the back – it had been placed into the capsule by somebody named Remy. The feather hair clip had been the possession of somebody who had the improbable name of Sugar Bunny. Throughout all of that, the teacup called. It still sat where Roan had left it, and more than the other objects in this batch, it had a presence. It possessed a gravity that pulled at my attention – and at something deeper than attention: a knowing. A knowing deep inside me.

"Oh my god, lighten up," I muttered to myself. "It's just a cup." But the rush of images and emotion that came upon me the first time I touched it came back to me, and I braced myself.

The whole life, the whole history of this thing pressed at me through the psifield, and I struggled to keep myself partially closed, to open my Sight and my Knowing slowly, slowly, so as not to be overwhelmed like I was before. The stone itself was sourced from the Uru River Valley in Southeast Asia. This cup was a piece of a set carved by an artisan named Jing Yu, in Beijing, in the year 1860 during the Qing Dynasty. The set was given as a gift to a merchant named Fong Yu Chun, who then passed it onto his son, Fong Lin Chun, who brought it with him to the United States in 1890. During a storm at sea, as he made that journey, the cup jostled inside a trunk nestled in a berth that Lin Chun shared with others. A feeling of awe at the storm-swept ocean, a fear of dying, a calm sort of acceptance. Fong Lin Chun settled in San Francisco and later went by the English name Lincoln Fong, but he came to be known in his community as Boss Fong.

Then a sudden wave of bliss, blurry lights in vivid, saturated colors. Another fire, a bonfire, huge. Warm wind against my skin, but it wasn't terrifying like before; this time, it felt good. Sensual, even. People cheering in the distance – a celebration of some kind? A woman took my hand. *"You're a good friend,"* she said. Not my hand, the party boy's hand. *Nathan.*

Then, rage and a conflagration burned right through my inner sight. Emotional fire, but also actual fire and thickening smoke. The cup taken by someone full of bitterness and wrath. *Li Nuan.* Li Nuan was her name, and the cup was hers now. Voices calling for help. Screams.

I dropped the cup, coughing – it actually felt hot to the touch for a second. And why was I coughing? Why did I smell smoke? From the fire. The doorway of a burning building filled my mind, but beyond the burning building there was a burning city.

The cup sat on my workstation, and it was a weird thing, reconciling the inferno that had just engulfed me with this piece of carved stone. My breath was rapid, my brow was damp, and I was afraid for my life but also angry. There was an adrenaline rush as I ran for the door – no, not me, I wasn't running for the door. Her. Li Nuan, the third owner in the lineage of the cup. I was very clear that the emotions quickening my heart were not mine, but hers. While I did sometimes pick up emotional resonances from objects I scanned, they had never been as intense as what I got from this Li Nuan person. Who was she?

"Everything okay?"

I started at the voice – the second time today somebody has caught me unawares after I scanned the cup. It was Aviva.

"Fine," I said. "Just getting my bearings after a scan." I wasn't sure why, but while I was comfortable sharing my experience with Roan and Lorel, I didn't want to with Aviva. Maybe because she was my boss, and I was just starting this work and I didn't want to show weakness.

She cast a glance at the cup, then back at me. Her gaze was penetrating, but kind. "All right," she said. "Please know you can come to me if you ever face any difficulties in your work."

"All right. I will. Thank you."

She flashed a smile, then was on her way. That was random.

The cup stared at me as I entered preliminary notes about it into the database. The smell of smoke still lingered in my nose, which was unusual. It clearly held more story, but I wasn't up for gleaning more in that moment. Just then, my node pinged. Lorel. *Drinks!*

Normally, I would have begged off with the excuse that alcohol didn't agree with me, said that I had to settle in. But that was how I had always been: holding myself back. When I accepted this assignment, I told myself that things would be different. I told myself I wanted friends. Might as well get started.

5.

MAIDA

March 5, 2106
North Beach, San Francisco

"This is the oldest bar in San Francisco," Bertrand Lowell informed me as he brought a round of drinks to our table."Specs' Twelve Adler Museum Café, established in 1968. At the time of the Collapse, as late as the 2040s, there were older bars, some dating even to the nineteenth century. But those are gone now, mostly due to earthquakes or sea level rise. This place survived all of that, plus the many eras of the United States. It served as a community gathering place, even during the Collapse. One hundred thirty-eight years in continuous operation, which isn't that long compared to some other places in the world. But for this region, and the culture that built it, it's a long time. A blip in the grand arc of history, but an artifact of a gone world nonetheless." His love for this place was clear in his voice and eyes – I didn't even need to be a telepath to sense it.

The place smelled like booze and old wood. Photographs from many chapters of history covered the walls, along with odd knickknacks and clippings from old newspapers bearing dates that seemed fictional: 1968, 1975, 1989, 2001, 2025,

2036. That last year being the year that most historians considered the start of the Pre-Collapse period, when the socio-economic and political fractures threatening the Precursor world became glaringly, unavoidably evident even to deniers, when the environmental stressors were asserting themselves with even more ferocity. But it wouldn't be until 2052 that the United States ceased being a nation-state, and that year was generally considered the official start of the Collapse period.

The wonder that came over me as I perused these dates was less about the amount of time that had passed, and more about the fact that these years were before the Collapse and, more importantly, before the Bloom. The Collapse was the end of a social, political, and economic order that could no longer stand, but the Bloom was the transition of humanity into a new way of being in relation to the planet and all life. The Collapse represented the change of outer circumstances, the Bloom the change of inner life. Those years on the wall were coordinates on the other side of a barrier, markers of an alien world. This place was a remnant of a world that fell all around it, yet here it still stood, serving tumblers of whiskey to groups of friends after work.

This establishment was full of objects I was curious to touch – it looked to be as chock full of stories as a historical society gallery. Hell, it could have *been* a historical society. And "Museum" was in the name, after all. But after the day I had, I needed to give the psychometry a rest. I made a concerted effort to raise my psionic defenses.

"Here's to your first day, and new friends," Lorel said as she raised her glass.

"This is my first San Francisco bar," I said. My first sip was sharp, a little sweet, delightfully warm going down.

"Have you been to the city before?" Roan asked.

"Once, when I was a kid. I came with my parents. My father was here for work. I remember they were still daylighting some of the creeks." The city of San Francisco was situated on a watershed, a fact most inhabitants over the course of its history had no idea of, which both surprised me and didn't. Waters flowed over this land that had been poured over with concrete, and most of the people in the Precursor era had no idea they stepped over it every day, that there were living streams under their feet, beneath the asphalt. In the years since the Bloom, many of these streams were freed from those concrete prisons, and a public transit system that followed the flow of water was developed.

But back to the conversation. "This is my first time as an adult."

"Well I'm happy to show you around," Bertrand said.

Roan nodded approvingly. "He does know all the best places to go."

We were sitting in an alcove in the back, and there were a few tables arranged along a side wall to the front; the bar dominated that part of the room. On the wall beside our table hung an old black and white photograph. The label identified the group as "Beat poets." I wasn't really sure what that meant, but it seemed meaningful.

Bertrand saw me looking and took the opportunity to explain. "They were a groundbreaking literary movement. Despised by the establishment of the time, but their stature and reputation grew. Collectively, they pushed the boundaries of subject matter and form, addressing such topics as disillusionment with the American way of life, and sexuality, and drug use, and altered states of consciousness. In my view, their greatest contribution was a sort of wanton outlaw posturing in the stuffy world of letters. They were influential for a time, and their influence waned. Like with everything. But they certainly broke new ground and paved the way for other literary movements down the line. One of them" – he leaned toward the picture, his eyes scanning the faces – "him, Ferlinghetti –"

"Like the Ferlinghetti Center!" I exclaimed. When we first arrived, Bertrand had pointed out the Ferlinghetti Center for Precursor Literature that stood on the other side of the parkway.

"That's right. The Center is named for him. He was affiliated with the Beats."

"Bertrand will take any opportunity to display his erudition," Roan quipped with obvious affection.

"And you will take any opportunity to use a word like 'erudition,'" Lorel teased.

Music started up, cutting through the white noise of chatter. Roan and Lorel bopped up and down in their seats excitedly and began crooning, off-key, to the song coming on.

Bertrand sipped his drink and rolled his eyes, shook his head. "These two love this stuff. I don't quite understand it."

The song was percussive, a bit repetitive, and the singer's breathy voice had clearly been processed by whatever means music producers did such things back then. Still, there was an undeniable charisma to it all.

"Don't let him naysay," Roan said. "This is a classic of turn-of-the-millennium pop."

"It's from 1998," Lorel added. "Britney Spears. 'Iconic' was the word they used to describe her back then."

For a moment, my head swam deliriously as we sat in this bar that had already been around a while when this Britney person recorded this song in a world that no longer existed.

And there we were, over a century later, and what would have been an old bar to her was even older in a world she would not have recognized.

"Her biography has gaps in it," Roan said. "But based on what I could find in the internet records of the Precursor world, it seems like she had a tumultuous life, though she reportedly died a rich old lady. Another round?" He got up and headed to the bar without waiting for anybody's response.

Lorel continued singing along to the song and kind-of-sort-of dancing in her chair while Bertrand looked on in amusement. I decided in that moment that I really liked these people, and I hoped we could go on to be friends. It was a cautious hope, though. There was this girl, April, that I knew at the Academy, and I had thought we were friends, and she called me "bestie." But one day, I picked up a sweater of hers that she left in my dorm room and it told me that the last time she had worn the sweater, she had been making fun of me to other people in the dorm. She said I was a weirdo. I kept to myself after that. I didn't want to be like that here.

Roan returned with the drinks, and I polished off my first one that I had been nursing and started on the second. Another song came on, one sung in a mixture of English and Korean, and the conversation rambled on about celebrities and fame and what it all meant and was it all a big distraction from the real problems facing the world, like what we now know was happening at the time with the biosphere, and sea levels, and the forests, and and and...

But the world was how it was, wasn't it? We could learn lessons from the past, but what use was there wallowing in if-only's? We could lay the blame for the Collapse and its aftermath that our grandparents and our parents and now we have to deal with, but what good would that do, really, ultimately? We still have to do the work in front of us. Whoever was to blame for the mess of the world didn't change the fact that the mess had to be cleaned up. I wondered if they'd be sorry, the Precursors, if they understood the world they imposed on us? I still wonder.

The evening was crisp when we stepped outside, but that same hot breeze I noticed at lunch was blowing, and it carried the ever-so-slight tinge of far-away smoke. I could have been imagining it – a lingering trace of my cup-induced vision – but something was always burning somewhere. It was easy enough to disregard; we were all used to it by this point in history.

"Let's walk to Chinatown," suggested Lorel. Her cheeks were flush with the drinks, and she was slightly giddy. "I could use some dumplings."

"Food does sound like a good idea," Roan said.

Bertrand took the lead and guided us through the trees and gardens of the parkway that was once known as Columbus Avenue, as a plaque informed us. It had been a road for the cars that used to be so prevalent in Precursor culture, but now was one of the city's many food forests, and as such it was full of fruit trees – plums in particular, and apples – as well as edible plants and decorative plants and flowers. Running its length was the algae-powered pathway for the lightrail, which glowed softly green in the evening dark. A stand of chefs lined the edges of a small dining plaza, their booths piled with baskets of greens and apples, herbs and edible flowers – all of it harvested from this garden. They prepared salads for anyone wanting a light meal. Anyone who put in shifts at this garden could eat gratis, and from others, a donation of luxury credits was requested, but nobody was ever turned away.

As we crossed the parkway, we encountered a clutch of young people handing out leaflets in front of a table laden with literature and bearing a banner that read *Freedom Faction*.

"Help us contain the psion menace," an earnest young man said as he tried to hand me a flyer. I refused it and recoiled from him. I could only blink in response and willed my words to return to me, to no avail. I hoped my revulsion wasn't too obvious, but so what if it was?

My initial shock passed quickly, and I recovered my ability to speak. "What psion menace?"

"Don't buy into their usefulness to society," a woman behind the table said. Her demeanor and affect were friendly, even though her words were not. She wanted me to think she was helping me. She wanted me to think she was revealing some hidden truth. "It's unnatural. They're unnatural."

"The Bloom was a natural phenomenon," Lorel said.

"It happened over thirty years ago," the woman countered. "Were you there? How do you know what it was? We only know what the pro-psion agenda tells us."

There was a part of me that wanted to tell them I was a psion, but my hands went cold at the thought of it. From the way my heart was beating, it would seem I was sprinting away from these people, fast as I could. But I stood still. I said nothing.

"Come on," Lorel said, tugging on my sleeve. "Dumplings."

I gave in, but really, I was just using her as an excuse to avoid unpleasantness. I knew it, and I pretended not to. We walked away from that group, none of us saying anything until Lorel asked, "Are you okay?"

I was flustered, and my cheeks were hot with the shame of not standing up to those proselytizers. But I nodded. "Yeah. Just annoyed, is all. Do you know anything about Freedom Faction?" I avoided an altercation by not revealing what I was, but truth be told, the safety achieved by that felt fake.

My companions all shook their heads.

"Never heard of them before," Roan said. "Just a bunch of bigots, seems like."

If history was any indication, bigots could do quite a lot of harm – there was no "just." I was more annoyed than shaken, or so I told myself, but I was a little freaked out by that open display of hostility to psions. I didn't say anything more about it and my companions didn't press the issue.

We walked a few blocks and the streets narrowed, and Chinese signage adorned the buildings with more frequency. A night market was in full swing, and strings of lights zigzagged overhead, casting a warm glow on the milling crowd, the bustling fruit and flower stands, the band playing at an outdoor café. The clack of mahjong tiles clattered from a teahouse, evidence of a recent revival of the game. A dumpling shop that my companions seemed familiar with beckoned with white light through steamy windows. As we headed toward it, a wave of vertigo hit me, and my nose was full of the familiar scent of smoke. I stumbled, reached out, and Roan caught me.

I heard him ask if I was okay, but his voice was barely discernible over the sound of roaring flames. Voices called for help, then the pleas devolved into screams. The blaze whipped tentacles of hot air in all directions. I reached the bottom of a staircase just before it began to collapse behind me. I pressed my way to a door, to outside, clutching something tightly in my hand. When I stumbled at last into the street, fire blazed all around. Then, just as suddenly as they sprang up, the flames were gone and my friends were standing all around me, staring at me with grave concern.

"What happened?" Roan asked as he supported me with a gentle hand on my back.

"It was a scene I got off the teacup," I explained shakily. "From the time capsule."

"But you're not touching it now," Lorel said.

"No. I'm not."

"What does that mean?" Roan asked. "Is it like a flashback? An echo?"

I leaned against the front wall of the dumpling place as my friends hovered around me. Bertrand stepped into the shop, leaving me with the other two. "After lunch today, I scanned the cup again…" I told them about the two lives I witnessed with unusual vibrancy, the one in the burning building, the other brief flash with the bonfire and the colorful lights.

Bertrand came back out, handed me some water and a steamed bun, which I accepted gratefully. I took a bite of the bun before continuing. "It was like I *was* those people. In their bodies, in their heads. That's not how it usually goes. And also, there were other people in the fire. With Li Nuan. That's her name, the one in the burning building." Nobody had said her name; I just knew that's what it was. That's who she was. "They were speaking Cantonese, but I could understand them even though I don't know that language."

"That's so cool," Lorel said.

"Sure, when it's not causing bouts of vertigo and panic attacks," Roan quipped. "I mean that's what looked like was happening from my perspective. What do you call what just happened to you?"

"A mind-splitting vision of the past?"

"Okay, let's think through this." Roan paced as he spoke, gesticulating with his hands as if he was stirring his thoughts with them. "The one with the colors – that was just a quick flash, right? So let's set that aside for now. The big fire is what you just experienced again?"

I confirmed this with a nod.

"And what time period do you think Li Nuan lived in?"

"I think it's 1906." My reply was met with brimming excitement from all three of my companions.

"You don't suppose… the big fire that you saw…" Lorel didn't finish her question, but I knew exactly what she was getting at.

"I think so. I think it was the 1906 earthquake and fire." The event was a significant piece of the history of this city – the major earthquake and subsequent fire that levelled the entire city on the morning of April 18, 1906. Two hundred years in the past for us, but the lived present of the girl whose life I was catching glimpses of through the psifield. The perch between unfolding disaster and settled history was dizzying, and I had to close my eyes to my companions, to the streetlights, to the world. After a moment of darkness, I felt okay.

Lorel, Roan, and Bertrand were all staring at me when I opened my eyes again. Were their expressions confused or amused?

"This sort of thing is going to happen a lot with you, isn't it?" Lorel asked.

"I think we all know the answer to that," Roan quipped.

"No judgment," Lorel was quick to add, holding her hands up. "I just need to know. For future friendship reasons."

Well, that was sweet.

"And you're not touching the cup," Roan went on. "Has this ever happened before? You getting a bout of psychometric spasming when not in contact with the object?"

Psychometric spasming. Never heard that one before. I liked it. It was accurate. I shook my head. "Never."

Lorel chimed in. "Okay, well I'm no psion, but it seems to me there must be some connection between you and these two people."

"You could try searching for them in historical records," Bertrand suggested. "Records from before the Collapse are spotty, but you might come up with something. I could help. Did your family ever have a family tree done?"

I shook my head. "Our knowledge of family history was broken. I never knew my grandparents, and my parents didn't know theirs. And we don't have any family stuff from before the Collapse anyway."

They all nodded. It was a common story.

"Why would she need to search records anyhow?" Lorel asked. "She's witnessing history through her psychometric connection."

"But that connection doesn't tell her why. And that's what you're wondering now, isn't it? Why you're getting this vision or whatever when you're not even holding the object?"

"Yes. But I don't want to get hung up on this." I appreciated their concern, but it was starting to feel a little bit intrusive. Or maybe I could just let people care about me. "I'm sure it was just a fluke. And anyway, I've got work to do, and I don't want to get distracted. I mean, it is an interesting question, but it's not crucial to my work. For now, I'm content to just let it lie and chalk it up to psionic weirdness." I winced at the pounding of my rattled brain workings. The comedown from this one was going to hurt.

"You should take something for that headache," Roan said.

"Are you a telepath now?"

"Not sure I could handle telepathy, to be honest. But I don't need it; it's all over your face."

"I'm fine."

My new friends didn't look convinced, but none of them said anything more.

6.

LI NUAN

January 24, 1906
Chinatown, San Francisco

Fear marks her first night at the brothel. Her first customer is a young man newly arrived from Guangdong Province who is on his way to work on the railroad. So many are coming for that, and for gold.

"You will be the last girl I touch for a long time," he says. He isn't handsome, but he is young and fit. Is he Madam Bai's way of easing her into the business, a customer who is not old and reeking of cigarettes? He takes her maidenhood in a single thrust and seems almost apologetic after she cries out from the pain of it. After he notices the tears and the blood.

Apparently, he tells Madam Bai about it because she who rules the Lotus Pearl pulls her out of the room and admonishes her in the gaslit corridor before her next customer. "Never cry in front of them," she hisses. "What is the matter with you?"

On her second night, a sort of horrified resignation sets in. On her third night, Li Nuan finally makes herself go numb and cold. Her emotions shrivel and still, and everything, the entire world, is muted and far away, as if glimpsed through the fog that rolled in over the hills. For the rest of the week, she goes away completely as the men do their business upon her. She can't be there, in her body, in her mind, while it is happening. Madam Bai says to think of home, but that makes everything worse. What a stupid idea. Home sold her into this life. So she goes away, becomes an empty vessel.

They don't even have proper rooms to perform their duties in; all the girls in one large room, with sheets hung between thin mats on the floor. Cribs, they are called. Though she doesn't see the other girls at work, cries, whimpers, and grunts disturb the shadows. At sixteen, Li Nuan is one of the older ones. Most, she guesses, are between twelve and fourteen, though a couple are younger. Word is, they die of one disease or another and are tossed away well before they reach Li Nuan's age. Some of them – the ones who can most easily put on a pleasant face and manner – are stationed behind barred windows that face onto the alley. Their job is to grab the attention of passing men with their charms and promises of illicit pleasures.

Some of them, like Li Nuan, had been sold into servitude. Some had been kidnapped and others had been promised more fortunate fates that turned out to be lies – they were to serve as domestics for wealthy white families, or be brides to waiting husbands. Instead, at the end of a month-long ocean crossing, they were taken off the boat only to be stripped and bound and sold at auction. She had heard Boss Fong speak of something called "the Queen's Room" which she had imagined as a special place where the more successful merchants gather to share gossip, food, and tea. But then some new girls are delivered, and Madam Bai says to one of the guards, "Fresh from the Queen's Room. Looks like good quality. Good price." And Li Nuan understands.

There are a couple of prettier girls that entertain in the private rooms upstairs – the parlor rooms, they're called. They "host" the wealthier white men who come around. Madam Bai takes it as a point of pride that these men frequent her establishment. Some of them are even city officials or from the police department, so says Madam Bai. Important men in the community. These girls, the prize flowers, get better clothes, have their hair done nicely, put powder on their faces and rouge on their cheeks and lips. They look more glamorous, better kept, but they are owned like the rest of them. Madam Bai, too, is owned, even though she is in charge of them, even though she pretends she isn't.

While fetching soiled linens from the room where the girls sleep, Li Nuan finds one of the new arrivals curled up and crying, and when she goes to take the sheets from the bed, she sees the welts – raised red lashes raging across the girl's back. What had she done to earn this punishment? It could have been something major like trying to run away. It could have been something minor like an insolent look in her eye. It could have been for nothing the girl had actually done, just a beating to put her in her place, to remind her who is in charge. Li Nuan doesn't ask her what she did. The girl looks younger than her, perhaps twelve years old.

"It isn't fair!" the girl manages to huff out between sobs. "That we must do these things. They told me when I was still in my father's house that I would be a housekeeper. Not this."

Li Nuan doesn't know how to comfort the girl. She was told the same lie, after all. She retrieves a clean cloth and a clean basin and some soap and washes the girl's wounds. She wishes she had salve. All she can offer is a minimum of care. It's the best she can do, and it has to be enough.

Even after the new girls arrive, Madam Bai requests that Li Nuan be brought in on "busy nights." Boss Fong allows it. But he also allows her to continue to sleep in the servant's room in his apartment since she is still expected to carry out domestic duties during the day. She understands that for the Boss, this amounts to a special concession, a sort of twisted reward for her service. She counts it as a blessing that she doesn't have to sleep in a room with eight or twelve others on straw mats on the floor. She doesn't have to relieve herself in a shared bucket in a corner. A blessing.

The son accosts her in the hallway as she brings tea to the Boss. "Father says I can take my pleasure with any whore at the Lotus, but I must leave you alone." He smiles, baring his teeth as he leans in close. "Lucky for you, I am a disobedient son. Everyone says so."

She wants to spit venom in his face and watch him claw at his blinded eyes. She wants to hear him scream. Pushing his imagined cry of agony from her mind, she says calmly as she can manage, "Please. Your father will be angry if his tea is cold." She hates pleading with the boy to allow her to serve his father, as if it's a big favor.

He scoffs, as if to let her know he isn't afraid of his father. But she knows he's terrified of him. Everybody is. He steps back. "One of these days, pretty thing."

She gathers her composure as she makes her way into the parlor. Boss Fong is sat with Madam Bai at the table where the merchant had lost a finger. The bloody flesh flashes through her mind and she hopes the horror of it doesn't show on her face.

"The new girls will take some time to adjust," Madam Bai says. "A couple of them still think other work is waiting for them. Can you imagine being so stupid? I had to beat one of them until she understood her true situation."

Boss Fong grunts as he sits back, awaiting his tea. Li Nuan places a cup in front of him and pours. Most service would consist of serving the guests and women first, then the host last, but things don't work like that in Boss Fong's home. Madam Bai holds herself stiff and upright in her seat. She's stopped speaking as she watches Li Nuan as if looking for a reason to reprimand her. Li Nuan picks up the other cup –

–and immediately her eyes burn and her nose stings with heat and smoke. She is in a burning room, panic rising up in her. Then other visions swarm her mind: bridges twist as the earth shakes, buildings crumble and fire sweeps the streets. Then other places show themselves – places she doesn't recognize: forests ablaze, houses washing away in flood waters and mud, enormous waves driven by terrible storms, piles of trash as far as the eye could see, air choked with smoke that isn't quite smoke. People walking hazy cities wearing strange masks, bodies thrown into mass graves. Bombs fall in a war carried out by so many machines she doesn't understand. Then someone dances nearly naked in a desert, and there is more fire. Then the sky fills with swirling lights of pink and purple and green and gold.

She drops the cup, and it rolls off the table into Madam Bai's lap while tea sloshes from the teapot in her other hand. What was all that? Her brow and armpits grow damp and her heart pounds as she hastily sets the cup aright in front of the Madam. Is she cursed now?

"Clumsy girl!" Madam Bai snaps. "I hope you are not so careless with our customers!"

She wants to scream *our customers don't have me pour tea you wicked shrew*, but instead she offers a meek "I'm sorry."

She hates that her voice shakes, but that quiver is from the waking dream that just came over her, not shame for her ineptitude. The Madam will take it as the latter, and it's probably better for Li Nuan if she does.

"No candied ginger?" the Madam asks. "No preserved plums?"

"We ran out." Li Nuan glances nervously at the Boss. No other guest would dare question the refreshment being served, but he allows Madam Bai to speak to him in a way nobody else would dare to. Familiar. Demanding.

"Go fetch some from the shop," Boss Fong says.

"Get back before the tea is cold." Madam smiles her demon smile, which, like Little Emperor's, offers no reassurance, only cruelty in displeasure.

Li Nuan's blood curdles at receiving orders from the Madam, but there is no denying it: she works for both of them now.

Bao is behind the counter when she arrives at the teashop, his father asleep in a chair in the back corner. "I didn't want to wake him," the younger man explains with a smile. There is love in his voice and kindness in his face, and Li Nuan's eyes well up with the ache of what she does not have. Her voice cracks as she places her order. Bao furrows his eyebrows at that. As he wraps her items in paper he says, "You're sadder than usual."

A sob bursts from her, then she swallows the rest. She doesn't want to cry in front of the shop boy, in public, with Wu Jun standing just outside. She regains control of herself quickly – she is getting good at clamping her feelings down.

"I've seen you being escorted to the Lotus Pearl the past few evenings," Bao says, dropping his voice to barely above a whisper. He meets her eyes, and in his expression she sees understanding and pity. But not judgment.

"I go where they tell me."

"I have heard of some girls who have gotten out," he says, handing the parcels of sweets over. "With the help of the white woman up the hill."

Her heart races at these words. There is a rumor that the brick house at the top of the big Sacramento Street hill is a haven for girls like her who ran or were saved from the brothels – well, saved according to some. Boss Fong and the other Tong leaders consider those girls kidnapped. Stolen. Some of the brothel owners say they have been taken by the white devils to be kept as their own. It has to be true – the white Americans would never let such girls live among them as equals. And how could they possibly survive if not as servants? Some of those runaway girls have been reclaimed by the Tongs that owned them and must be beaten back into submission. According to Madam Bai.

But why is Bao bringing them up? Is he suggesting – no, she doesn't want to even think about what he is suggesting. "I don't have money," she says, so flustered by the hint of running that she forgets for a moment that the shop is one of the Boss's. Bao shakes his head and waves the suggestion of payment away. "For the Boss," he says loudly as Wu Jun sticks his head in the door.

"Time to get back," the guard says. He hadn't heard what Bao said, had he? About the runaways? She shudders at the sort of punishment the Boss would inflict on someone even hinting to one of his brothel flowers that she could do such a thing as escape and seek asylum amongst the Americans or Irish or whatever they were up the hill.

Without another word to the shop-boy, Li Nuan takes her leave. Once they are a few steps away from the shop, Wu Jun says, "Put it out of your mind."

She is about to ask what he is talking about, but she doesn't have to. With a glance, she knows he heard the talk of running. Her brow breaks into a sweat as she thinks of what to say to beg his secrecy – should she offer him the things she does at the brothel? But before she can say anything at all, he adds, "I say nothing. But you be good and don't think you can run."

A swell of gratitude fills her, and then resentment, and then hatred. Yes, she is grateful Wu Jun will keep his silence, but why should it matter? Why shouldn't she be able to leave if she wanted? She shakes her head – stupid girl. *That is not our place.* Wu Jun sets a brisk pace for the walk back, which is thankfully only a couple of blocks. It's as if he knows the guest will be impatient for the sweets she had been sent to fetch. How much does he hear of what goes on in the apartment? Probably everything.

Once back, Wu Jun locks the door behind them, then heads to his room where she imagines he sits in silence, waiting for the Boss to summon him. She is certain he has no other life outside of working for the boss. Could *he* leave if he wanted to? Does he even want to? Does he miss Guangdong? Does he miss his family? And does he cry when he is alone, sitting on his bed? Maybe the gruff face and manner are things he puts on to do his job, like part of a uniform. She has never before thought about his situation, how he came to be in Boss Fong's employ, what the terms are. He may be owned as much as she is. But he doesn't have to pleasure dozens of strangers a night in that dank hole of a basement. She pushes these unhelpful thoughts aside and sets her mind back on her task, unwrapping the sweets and placing them onto small plates before bringing them to the parlor.

"Took long enough," Madam Bai says as Li Nuan sets down the plates along with an empty dish for the pits of the plums. The Madam really likes to remind her and all the girls that she is above them in station, that they answer to her. Boss Fong, on the other hand, says nothing as he reaches for a preserved plum. He doesn't have to say anything at all.

7.

NATHAN

June 30, 2006
Chinatown, San Francisco

The space is more crowded than Nathan expected. Though he isn't sure why, exactly, he thought attendance would be lighter. Usually, the opening night of these sorts of things are the most packed, at least in his experience, and this show opened weeks ago. DIASPORA: PAST & FUTURE is the name of this exhibit at the Chinese Culture Center, a facility dedicated to the cultural life and history of Chinese Americans, which occupies the third floor of the newly rebranded Hilton Hotel San Francisco Financial District – it had been the Holiday Inn Chinatown until earlier this year.

The facility consists of an auditorium, classrooms, a shop, and offices, but it's the gallery Nathan strolls about now, clutching a little plastic tumbler of white wine. He eyes a large watercolor done in the traditional Chinese style, though the subject is San Francisco, famous bridge and all. The skyline, rendered in impressionistic blue-black ink, is clearly recognizable, and the fog is suitably ethereal and fluffy. The golden orange of the bridge is the largest splash of color, the only other color being the pale-yellow specks of light in the windows of the Transamerica Pyramid. Nathan doesn't know much about the techniques of this style, but he appreciates the delicate brushstrokes that hint at the fog juxtaposed against the heavier lines of the buildings. It's lovely work.

The program coordinator catches his eye and signals that it's time for him to do his thing. In addition to the watercolors and paintings hung on the gallery's walls, the space is dotted with pedestals, each of which holds an object of some kind – artfully piled silk, calligraphy sets, a few daggers and knives, a sculpture of a horse. A tall plexiglass case holds a set of faded blue linen trousers and a matching shirt – the standard garb of the Chinese laborers on the Central Pacific Railroad. Nathan takes the few steps from the watercolor he's been admiring to a close-by display – his family heirloom, a jade teacup. It glows atop its assigned pedestal, set in the center of a square of brilliant yellow silk decorated with pink and white blossoms.

The program coordinator, a young woman named Abby, pings her champagne flute. "It's time for our next Insight," she says. For tonight's program, individuals with a connection to any of the objects on display are speaking about the history of their respective item, or the intent of the work in the case of the original art created for the show. Abby continues, "Next, we have Nathan Zhao. Nathan is an industrial designer with Phase Designworks, where he has led the development of products for an impressive list of tech companies. A fourth generation San Franciscan, he is going to tell us about a family heirloom on loan for this exhibit."

Nathan gives a nervous wave to the faces gathering around him; they look inquisitive, or else bored. He gestures to the cup. "This has been in my family for as long as we've been in San Francisco. It's made out of jade, and the story is, it was carved by the Emperor's personal jade carver – but I don't know if that's actually true. Makes for a nice story, though, so let's say it is."

A few chuckles throughout the crowd.

"The story passed down to me is that my great-grandmother received it as a gift when she left China to come here. My grandmother told me that my great-grandparents ran a teahouse – my great grandfather inherited it. It was lucky she married into a business because there weren't many opportunities for Chinese women in those days. She would have worked in a laundry or been a servant for a wealthy white family, if she was lucky. And that work paid better than the living she would have eked out back in China. Anyway, this cup was one of her very few possessions, and probably the most valuable – that's a nice piece of jade."

More laughs from the audience while Nathan smiles back the way he's supposed to. But he's just repeating the story he was told as a child. The cup had always been explained to him as being a family heirloom, something passed down daughter to daughter on his mother's side until his generation of sons. But he doesn't know more than what he's been told, and now he wishes he had asked some more questions. Though it was more than twenty years ago when he was just a child, he remembers his grandmother being on the verge of tears as she showed him the cup and explained how long it had been in the family. He wishes to this day he had thought to ask why she was so sad about it, but he was too young, and now his grandmother is gone. His mother might know, but they don't really talk.

He continues, "It's been handed down from daughter to daughter on my mom's side of the family, but my mom only had me and my brother, and I got it, I think because I loved it more. I used to play with it as a kid. I pretended it was a hovercraft and I flew my action figures around in it."

Someone in the crowd says "cute," and Nathan flashes a smile in the direction of the voice. "There was a time when my dad's cousin had possession of it for a while because Dad bet it in a poker game and lost. But then, years later, my mom won it back in a mahjong game. And then she gave it to me." He grows pensive. "I don't plan on having kids, so I'm not sure who I'll pass it to. Maybe I'll bequeath it to this place; who knows? Anyway, that's it, that's the Insight."

A polite round of applause as folks start milling around the gallery again. A few step closer to the pedestal and look at the cup with interest.

"Is it very heavy?" an older woman asks. Her blue eyes twinkle behind cat-eye glasses.

"Not really." Nathan reaches for the cup and the woman lets out a gasp.

"Are we allowed to touch it?"

"Well, it is mine." Nathan picks it up and the heat and roar of flames erupt in his mind. It isn't just the building he's in now that's burning though, but the whole world. And more: infernos engulfing forests, patches of flame in the ocean – the ocean, burning! Then massive winds as hurricanes slam into coastal cities, and floods and tsunamis, and people by the millions seeking refuge from the storms. He sees parts of San Francisco flooding and panicked people evacuating Glen Park, the Marina, the Embarcadero. The Bay Bridge shudders and twists and cracks down the middle, cables on the Golden Gate snap. Then piles of bodies in the streets of many places, mass graves, mass pyres, more fire, and the putrid smoke of the burning dead.

He drops the cup. It bounces on the top of the pedestal, and the woman Nathan's speaking to catches it before it flies off onto the floor. Sweat beads on his brow as his face flushes with the heat of fire that isn't there.

The woman eyes him with curiosity. "If I didn't know better, I'd say you just had an acid flashback." When he meets her eyes with a befuddled gaze, she adds, "I was a flower child. I know from flashbacks. Are you all right?"

Nathan nods. "Yes... I –" He steadies himself on the edge of the pedestal, thinks about how nice it would be to use the silk to dab his sweaty forehead. Luckily, he has his wits about him enough to know not to do that. But what the hell?

The woman weighs the cup in her hand. "It is lighter than it looks," she says before placing it back in the center of the yellow silk. "What fine craftsmanship."

"They knew what they were doing back then, I guess." Nathan has regained his composure, but he looks at the cup like it might leap out and sting him with more visions. Because that's what it felt like just now – visions. But that's crazy, right?

"How wonderful to have such an object connecting branches of your family tree."

"Yes, it really is." He's put his charming party demeanor back on, but the scent of smoke still stings his nose, and the air around him still feels hot, like the burning ghosts haven't quite finished passing through just yet.

When Nathan arrives at the Stud for the camp fundraiser event, Danny is outside giving a tour of the Fish to a group of young women in party dress and one dude who looks annoyed to be there. Nathan recognizes the type: the "that's not so great I could do better" type who actually has never done any such thing as turn an RV into a fish. Danny always brings the Fish to camp events, and it often serves as a chill space away from the main party. Luckily, the thing is street legal.

"Nathan!" Danny calls. He strides his burly self over and enfolds Nathan in a big bear hug. He's a really good hugger. "This here is Nathan," Danny says to his audience, and for a second, Nathan feels like he's Danny's item on display at an exhibit. "But his playa name is Juicy Fruit. For all the salacious reasons you can imagine."

Nathan blushes at this, but honestly, he doesn't mind Danny calling him Juicy Fruit with his arm around him.

"Did you work on this?" one of the women asks, gesturing up and down the height of the Fish as if she were a model on a game show presenting a prize.

"I did all the upholstery on the inside," Nathan answers. "And my boyfriend installed the sound system."

"His boyfriend is DJ Aspect," Danny explains.

"Oh wow, he's great!" one of the other women chimes in.

"Yeah, he is pretty great."

"Well, come on board and do some shots," Danny says to the group, indicating that they should board the Fish via the back steps. "Join us, Nathan?"

"Maybe later. Gonna check it out in there." He jerks a thumb towards the purple exterior walls of the venue.

The scent and sound of burning air still haunts him as he steps into the Stud. He stops at the bar and grabs a vodka tonic before heading into the party proper. Not even the acrid smell of the fog machine's vapors can dislodge the phantom smoke as Nathan winds his way across the dancefloor. It's a good turnout, and despite the distraction of his experience with his cup-induced visions, he's happy for the crew. The additional shade, the Time Machine, and the Fish upgrades were all going to run up the costs, and this event would help defray some of that.

The performer onstage now is a burlesque dancer named Pussy Boom-Boom, who slinks across the stage, giant pink feather fans fluttering coyly about her bare shoulders and spangled, pasty-tipped breasts. Shoved to the side of the room, a juggler tosses softly strobing orbs that leave multi-colored tracers in the air. He's remarkably graceful considering he has barely any room to maneuver. Nathan makes his way through the shoulder-to-shoulder crowd, the humidity of the space causing his shirt to begin sticking to him.

He greets Remy with a quick peck, just to let him know he's there, then lets his boyfriend resume his set as the seductress onstage concludes her dance. Her show music fades out and house beats resume to cheers. Nathan steps to the edge of the dance floor and scans the crowd – he spots Annika, and Sid, and a few others chatting on the other side of the room. He sips his drink, tries to shake the image of burning corpses from his mind. He wants to settle into the groove of the party, and burning corpses really aren't the right mood. Maybe some conversation will be a good distraction. He's about to cross the floor again to join his campmates when someone tugs at the shoulder of his shirt.

"Nathan baby!" a voice shouts in his ear. "Come smoke with me."

Delilah. Good, maybe she can help make sense of what he experienced earlier. She is kind of psychic, after all. They step onto the sidewalk, the outside air cool and refreshing after the close, dank club, even though he'd only been in there a short while. He loves the vibe at the Stud, but spacious it is not.

Danny is alone on the Fish now, the group he had been entertaining having moved on – their laughter sounds from down the block. "Hey, you gonna share that?" he calls when he spies Delilah lighting a joint.

"Let's sit up top," she says. They all climb the ladder at the back of the vehicle that leads to the platform on the roof. They settle in, sitting cross-legged – this area is large enough for six to sit comfortably; a few more can squeeze together if everyone is standing. Sitting down as they are, the fins that rise at the top of the Fish keep them hidden from the street level. Delilah finishes lighting the joint, then passes it to Nathan. He feels her analyzing gaze on him as he puffs. "I'm sensing a vibe," she says while exhaling a plume of smoke up towards the sky. She waves a hand up and down, no doubt feeling his aura.

"Nothing gets by you, does it?" Nathan says as he passes the joint to Danny.

"A vibe?" Danny asks before taking a toke. Then, holding it in, he says, "What kind of vibe?" He blows smoke, sending tendrils curling up towards the stars, barely visible through the haze of the city lights.

As they continue to pass the joint back and forth, Nathan tells his friends about the visions he had while touching the cup, the fires, the storms, the dead stacked in the streets. "I saw your neighborhood get flooded," he says to Danny.

"Happens all the time." Danny shrugs. Due to it being built on top of what should be a marsh, parts of Danny's neighborhood flood whenever there are heavy rains, a state of affairs that is a nuisance, beyond inconvenient, but one to which the community has grown accustomed. Everyone who has lived in California for any length of time will not be terribly surprised by floods, or fires, or earthquakes. Danny's house, thankfully, is up a hill above the flood zone.

"But, like, really bad," Nathan presses. "Water-over-the-rooftops bad."

"Sounds apocalyptic." Danny doesn't really seem too put out by Nathan's account. This is all a vision, right? A vivid imagining? A hypothetical? Not reality.

"It sounds pretty wild to me," Delilah says. "Anything like that ever happen before?"

Nathan shakes his head. "You'd already know about it if it had. What do you suppose it means?"

"It sounds like a premonition. I've heard similar accounts of the kind of stuff you saw. Prophecies of the end of the world."

"So our man is a prophet now," Danny says with a chuckle. He puts a hand on Nathan's shoulder and gives him a gentle shake. "One more talent to add to his arsenal. Cooking, sewing, making high-tech doodads, and now predicting future tragedies."

For the second time tonight, Danny has made Nathan blush. "You really know how to make a guy feel special," Nathan says.

"It's too bad you're not a girl," Danny quips. "I'd steal you away from that DJ. DJs are trouble."

Nathan laughs. "Don't I know it."

Delilah offers up the last of the joint, but when there are no takers, she stubs it out on the metal of one of the guard-rails lining the deck's perimeter.

"So if Danny's right, I'm a prophet now?" Nathan asks, bringing the conversation back to his visions.

"Maybe something is opening up in you," Delilah says. "Do you have the cup now?"

Nathan shakes his head. "It's still at the gallery. I'll get it back after the exhibition closes."

"Is it that same cup I've seen? At your place, on the shelf? The jade one?"

"That's the one."

"Huh. It looks so unassuming."

"Truly powerful things don't need to be all showy." Danny offers up a bit of his usual stoner wisdom. "Tell us more about the visions."

Nathan is happy to oblige – he's still weirded out by the experience but is glad to share it with friends who don't judge. "The things I saw all felt different." It's fading now, but he can remember that the burning building and the burning city felt like history, and the storms and bodies and the burning ocean... well, that all felt like history too. "It all felt like somebody else's history. Or like history that hasn't happened yet." He can't explain himself better than that. And would it make any more sense even if he could?

"Well, show it to me when you get it back," Delilah says. "We'll do a ritual."

"You believe me? I don't sound crazy?"

Both of his friends laugh heartily.

"No, dude, you sound crazy," Danny says.

"Darling, of course you sound crazy," Delilah adds. "But crazy shit does happen in this world. And yeah, I believe you had some kind of experience." She turns to Danny. "Do you believe he had some kind of experience?"

He shrugs. "I remain agnostic on the matter. I'm willing to be convinced, though."

"Well, I will help you unpack it," Delilah says. "What are girlfriends for? But for now, let's dance."

The three climb down the ladder, Danny doing it facing outward which always freaks Nathan out. They head back inside together and join the crowd that shimmies and pulses in the embrace of the beats. Behind the decks, Remy has stripped his shirt off and beams out at the crowd, his people, one hand raised and bobbing in time with his head.

Danny follows Remy's lead and peels off his t-shirt, then whips it around in circles above his head as he whoops. His whooping starts a chain reaction, and suddenly everyone around them is whooping and hollering.

"Stop staring at your hot boyfriend and dance with me," Delilah says.

Nathan takes his friend's hand and puts all fiery visions out of his mind. He gets his groove on, and for this one blissful moment, it's the whole world.

8.

MAIDA

March 8, 2106
The Cow Palace, San Francisco-Daly City border

The world was tinted all orange on the day of my first Remediation and Reclamation shift in the area. The hints of smoke I picked up that night in North Beach had exploded into wildfires burning up north, and the particulates that resulted from the conflagration colored the very sky. The light was burnt like the forests and grasslands whose destruction it signaled and the world looked like some kind of sci-fi filter had been put over it, but what was even weirder was how everyone just went about their business, puttering along like everything was normal in their goggles and breathmasks. Like I did.

My assignment brought me to a place called the Cow Palace, located in the southeastern quadrant of the extended metropolitan area. It had once been a large arena on the border of San Francisco and a place called Daly City. The old structure still stood, though it was in a state of disrepair – the years had not been gentle. Large letters, tattered and faded and once red in color, by the looks of it, still spelled out the name of the place across the front. Scaffolding framed one side of the building; an effort to refurbish the structure was underway, though the project was somewhat controversial. Some thought the thing should have just been torn down. The building was surrounded by a large lot of empty pavement – parking, I guessed, from the old days. This area was a dumping site – unofficial – in the 2060s and 70s, and while some clean-up and remediation efforts had been made, there was more to do.

The air was full of flying stuff – barrels, rotting furniture, appliances, old-fashioned cars – all of it sorting itself in mid-air and loading itself onto the transports that would haul them to designated containment zones. Of course, it wasn't all moving and sorting itself; this was the doing of the team of telekinetics who were stationed at towers throughout the area. They were wearing their distinctive blue coveralls, and all of them moved through a set of flowing postures, their arms swaying and gesturing as if performing some kind of mysterious choreography or obscure martial art that involved circulating invisible energies. But they *were* circulating invisible energies, weren't they?

The Sorting Depot was set up in a large canvas tent – one of the kind the army of the former nation-state deployed. I recognized the design and structure from old history videos. Bins of stuff were stacked and lined up in one corner that occupied nearly a third of the space. I spotted utensils, dishware, clothing, toys, electronics. There were bins of smaller bins and other plastic containers. So much plastic! It was hard to fathom how much waste that culture produced. And seeing all this stuff and knowing that it was only a fraction of what was in this area, which was a fraction of what was in the world, brought up a sadness for the planet – and I must admit, anger and judgment for the Precursors. Why had they even wanted this stuff if it was just going to be tossed? What was the point of making everything disposable? I had to remind myself that all of this stuff did once belong to people who are long dead – and it might have been dumped because they died. There had been over eight billion people in the Precursor world. We're down to five billion now – the drastic population reduction being the result of multiple pandemics, environmental devastation, and war. All this stuff in this place once belonged to those long-lost people.

My job was to go through my bins and sort items that could still be of use – things like dishware, kitchen utensils, and tools – from that which was unsalvageable. I was also supposed to be on the lookout for rare items that may be of cultural or historic importance, and those items would later be sorted further by specialists – people like Bertrand. Old tech went through its own sorting cycle to see if rare minerals and metals could be stripped from it and used again. Heavy-duty work gloves were assigned as part of the standard safety protocol, but I would have worn them even if they weren't; it would have been overwhelming to get hits of the histories of so many random items passing through my hands and keeping up my defenses the entire time.

There wasn't a lot of chit-chat amongst the workers. It was eerie how quiet it was, made doubly so by the orange light coming in through the window panels. The silence was broken by the occasional static from a walkie-talkie carried by one of the foremen, the distant sound of trucks pulling in and out. We were all in our coveralls, head coverings, and safety glasses and masks – a uniform not very conducive to socializing, I suppose. But then, this work wasn't fun, and maybe it shouldn't have been.

This particular location was where the personnel of the Cultural Recovery Project were assigned, but there were folks from other organizations and administrative divisions also. Service at these centers was compulsory – a minimum of two days a month for the residents of most Administrative Regions. Here in Sierra Northshore, anyone who worked more shifts than their compulsory ones earned luxury credits. Due to that incentive, many people put in more time than the minimum requirement, and I had been doing it since I was in my early teens, before I ever went to the Academy. There are rogue places who reject the notion of collective responsibility outright – places like Arivada, for example, the region comprised of the former states of Arizona and Nevada – who seemed to make their mountains of trash and lack of care a point of pride. Those places were barely habitable, and contained the lowest population as a result, so at least there was some comfort knowing that such flagrant disregard wasn't exactly a mass movement. But, still...

Those of us who were not giant assholes dedicated some of our time to clean up the mess. We considered such labor penance for the sins of our ancestors, and part of our stewardship to make the planet better for the generations to come. Hard to imagine that was considered a radical idea once. It was fitting that doing such work was what earned us our luxuries while our regular work covered the basics.

In another corner of the tent was a pile of plastic baby heads of different sizes gazing out with vacant eyes, some with no eyes at all, their faces framed at odd angles by arms, legs, and torsos of various proportions and skin tones. Some of the heads had hair, some did not, some wore clothing, some looked just born. Well, just born and dirty with the grime of fifty years. There were dolls of adult figures too, dressed in doll-sized versions of contemporaneous fashions, some with mangled haircuts or scribbles on their faces. Some were decked out in outlandish garb, like characters from sci-fi and fantasy stories or superhero fables. They were all laid haphazardly in a pile, but the pile itself was clearly intentional. It looked like some sort of demented art project – a commentary on human existence, how we were all nothing but disposable dolls on the junkheap of history. Yikes. Never said I was an art critic.

I got to my station and confronted my bin of random household objects. There were a couple of picture frames with photos still in them. I couldn't help but wonder who these people had been, how they had died, how this happy picture of a couple and their baby and their dog ended up here. I was sorely tempted to pull a glove off and scan it. But I knew better than to get sucked in. I'd go down a rabbit-hole of sadness for people I never knew, not get my shit done, and deplete myself psionically. So I brought my attention only to the things in front of me with no thought as to their histories, with no thought other than Salvage or Dispose.

Nearly everything went into the Dispose bin, it turned out. I added a couple of baby dolls to the doll pile – why were there so many dolls? A couple of the other workers gave me nods of approval as I did so. I didn't really get what the doll pile was about, but it was clearly what they did here.

At mid-day break, I was making my way to the canteen for lunch when the room started spinning and a dizzy feeling of euphoria took me over. I knew these were not my feelings as the psychic echo I recognized as that of Nathan swirled together with the alarm and panic that were my organic feelings. What the fuck was happening?

I was on top of a vehicle, sitting in a small rectangular space illuminated by blue light that traces the silhouettes of what I think are meant to be the fins of a fish. The stars overhead danced their eternal dance. Someone was singing, badly. They finished, and then came applause and cheers.

"Nathan!" somebody called. *"Get down here! You're up!"*

I made my way down an angled ladder to the vehicle's lower level where a few people were sitting on the bench seats inside. Most of the people around were standing outside. They were all watching people do something called "karaoke," and it was Nathan's turn. My turn? Music started – a familiar beat, something I just heard – and I was me but also not me...

And then, a feeling of barely contained panic, heart pounding, adrenaline rushing, as several filthy girls rushed out of a dingey little room. And then someone grabbed me, covered my mouth as I struggled and tried to scream. And then fire. The same fire I saw before, the same building, the same doorway, the same burning city, the same smoke filling my nose, but the burn was so much stronger now, the sting and the stink of it, and I cried out –

I cried out, sat bolt-upright. I was on the ground. I don't remember getting on the ground.

"Take it easy, take it easy," a soothing voice said. "Here."

A water bottle was shoved in my hand, and I slipped its tube under my mask and drank from it greedily. My throat was so parched from the smoke and fire... wait. There had been no actual smoke and fire there where I was – just the one far away. Shit. This again.

"What was all that?" The woman who handed me the water asked. "The song, and the fire..."

"Telepath?" My voice was shaky, and smoke still assaulted my nose. Everything smelled like smoke. Looking around,

I half expected to see that a fire had broken out in some garbage pile. Then the orange sky reminded me. But no, it wasn't this present smoke – or was it? I was so confused.

"I didn't mean to pry," the woman said. "But you fainted, and you were giving off crazy echo in the psifield. I normally keep myself shielded, but whatever was going on with you was really intense and broke through, like somebody suddenly cranked the volume way up."

I nodded in understanding. Telepaths often used sound volume as an analogy for the experience of their abilities.

"I thought maybe you were like me and needed containment."

"It turns out I did need containment," I said. "But I'm not like you." At her puzzled eyes I added, "Psychometry."

"Oh." She looked and sounded surprised, then was clearly even more puzzled than before. "But you're not in contact with anything. Surely the uniform, the gloves –"

"No. It isn't any of this." That damn teacup flashed in my mind. Did my telepath helper pick up on it, or was she shielded up again?

"Does this happen a lot, with those of your discipline?"

"I've never heard of it happening before. I'm a pioneer, I guess."

She helped me to my feet. "You should probably see somebody about it."

"Yeah. I probably should."

The psion medicine specialist on site was there mostly for the benefit of the telekinetics. While he wasn't uninformed or completely inexperienced in my discipline, he had never encountered a case like mine. "The conventional wisdom is that psychometry is a hybrid of clairvoyance and claircognition," he said. That was nothing I didn't already know. He went on, "Others feel there's an element of telepathy to it. The fact that you seem to be experiencing moments in these subjects' lives from their perspective would seem to support that."

He paused, looked to be lost in thought for a moment. "Could there possibly be a connection to these subjects? Have you ever scanned something that belonged to a family member and had a similar experience?" So he was thinking along the same lines as Roan and Lorel.

I shook my head. My parents didn't really have very many personal possessions; there had been no family heirlooms or keepsakes when I was growing up. We barely knew any family history beyond my parents' parents, since record keeping in the dark years between the Collapse and the Bloom wasn't exactly rigorous. We moved around assigned housing a lot, which came with it furnishings and household items. This was pretty common for folks in the Service Corps. Even our clothes, for the most part, were Corps issued. Nothing was really *ours*; our things didn't *belong* to us in the same way, with the same depth, that the things I scanned had belonged to others.

Once it was determined that I wouldn't inadvertently impose my visions of the fiery past onto those around me – which I couldn't anyway because I wasn't a telepath like that – I was dismissed for the rest of the day and left to ponder this mystery on my own. I caught one of the earlier shuttles back to the city, but since I was feeling okay and wasn't expected at the lab, I took a streetcar to the New Embarcadero Waterway. This network of plazas and parks and ferry stations was relatively new construction, only about ten years old. The original Embarcadero had long been underwater, hence the current name of the place. Although, as I understood it, the place where I got off the streetcar was where something called Fisherman's Wharf used to be.

The haze and smoke had begun to clear and the weird orange light was gone; the sky was now a pretty standard overcast grey, with hints of yellow here and there. Those would pass soon too. Had the winds shifted or had progress been made getting the fires out? I knew from my Academy days that there were firefighting telekinetics stationed up north who were specially trained to use their abilities to contain the flames within force fields that they then sucked the air out of to snuff out the fires. They could quell the infernos in a fraction of the time that it took the old fashioned way, with sprayed chemicals and water. Considering that the sky was already returning to normal, I guessed those telekinetics must have been deployed.

Sea lions basked on their usual rocks, even though there was no sun at the moment. I remembered seeing them on that trip with my parents when I was little, and remembered thinking what lazy blobs those creatures were. And they were lumbering wads of blubber, it was true, but there was something endearing about them. A modest sort of dignity. They were rather simpleminded, according to the animal-adept telepaths who could connect with other mammals – that ability didn't cross over into other classes of creatures like birds and reptiles and insects.

Off in the distance, the bell-shaped central core of the Alcatraz desalination center glowed, even in the daylight. Boats cruised past the island's rocky face, their white sails fluttering in the bay breeze. The island's profile was different from what I had seen in pictures of the historic site. It was smaller, and the facility atop it now was curvy and bulbous, not blocky and square like the infamous prison that had once been.

A group of skaters on those boards adapted for the algae-powered lightrail path whooped and hollered as they glided by. Overhead, seagulls hovered and caught the wind, scavenging for scraps dropped by careless humans, though there were fewer of us now than there used to be. I wondered, not for the first time, what the experience of animals that lived in close proximity to humans had been over the past fifty years. They don't care about borders, or nation-states, or politics. They had adapted to changing environments many times over the course of the planet's life and had witnessed the rise and fall of multiple civilizations. Had the fabric of the birds' existence changed to the extent that humans' had? Somehow, I didn't think so.

A piece of historic pier was displayed alongside a plaque explaining the history of this area – a popular tourist attraction at one time. This particular bit of pier dated back to the late 1800s. I placed my palm on its rough wood. Would history sing for me? Public structures didn't resonate the same as personal items, but I still got impressions: of the millions of feet that had walked this pier during its useful life; of the storms it had weathered; of the silent witness it had borne to the very changing of the sea. Ships, dockworkers, hawkers of souvenirs and knickknacks and terrible food all flashed through my sight. And also, men kidnapped from Barbary Coast saloons and taverns and sent away as involuntary labor on foreign ships to foreign lands, girls taken from some of those very same foreign lands and brought here to serve. Yes, this pier had been the site and setting of all sorts of trade.

Li Nuan would have arrived here on a ship from China and landed on a pier very much like this one. I have not witnessed that moment of her past and I don't know how I'd handle it if I did, considering how much of her emotional state came through in what I did pick up. I'd like to think that I would have been defiant and rebellious had I been in her situation, but I also knew how defiance was beaten and tortured out of people, how the instinct for survival took hold, how people submitted and endured what they had to for the hope that liberation might one day be theirs. I wanted to believe I would be a fighter, that I wouldn't be broken, but what did I really know of such horror? I couldn't imagine the autonomy of my very body being taken away, being the property of another. The thought of it turned my stomach, and a flicker of the rage I had felt from Li Nuan burned through.

I pulled my hand away to shut off my channel to the past. In the present, the tree line of the Presidio rose in the north and the tops of the cypress trees swayed lightly in the bay breeze that was quickly clearing of smoke. It wasn't that far, I didn't think, so I decided to walk back to campus. The air had cleared some more, and I pulled off my goggles and breathmask and tucked them into my satchel as I walked. A chain of pylons painted the golden orange of California poppies hugged the shore, marking the former shoreline of the city. Some were far out into the water, while others were close to the promenade I was following. What remnants of the old culture might have remained under the water? What glimpses of the past might I have snagged from what lay drowned?

Distance was tricky, though, and the Presidio was much farther than it appeared, so it took me a lot longer to get back than I thought it would. Plus, the woods in my view were only the outer edge of the area, I neglected to factor in the rest of the walk to the staff house. My feet and legs ached mightily when I finally got back. Roan was out front, a tablet in hand, with which he was controlling his flock of drones. There were about a dozen of them buzzing all around, like the murmuration of some mutant bird. Their flight paths seemed random, but then they organized into a circular formation, then scattered apart again.

"Having fun with your little toys?" I asked, borrowing Lorel's term for them.

"Ha ha," he replied. "I'm working out some new patterns. Controlling a group of them takes some practice. Gotta keep the skills sharp."

I watched the things flitting about in the late afternoon light; the winds had clearly shifted, and the overcast haze was starting to break up, revealing patches of clear sky. The drones were rather mesmerizing to watch. "Do they just fly around?"

"These have cameras on them, so they can be used for surveillance," he explained. "They're used a lot to scope out inaccessible areas, to find paths for remediation crews, or to make observations of volcanic activity or fire paths. Things like that."

I watched for a couple more minutes, impressed by Roan's focus, then headed inside. Lorel was in the common room having tea and reading. She looked up at me with a warm smile. "How was your shift?"

"It ended early," I said. I told her about what happened, the repeat of the, as Roan dubbed it, "psychometric spasm" of the other night.

"I'm starting to think you should maybe take that whole situation a little more seriously." Her tone was scolding and not a little maternal.

"I am taking it seriously." I sounded more defensive than I meant to, but I didn't care.

"I mean actually seek some help. From somebody who knows about this stuff." She tapped her tablet, scrolled, then handed it to me. On the screen was an announcement of a lecture happening on campus later this week. A former instructor from the Academy. "You know her, right? Could she provide some insight?"

I nodded. Yes, she probably could.

9.

MAIDA

March 11, 2106
*Golden Gate Cultural Recovery Project, Presidio
Campus*

"Just checking in," Aviva said as she popped her head in my lab door. "Before the site visit. Are you all ready?" She walked in and looked around and I couldn't help but feel a little put out by the spontaneous inspection, although I wasn't sure why. The top official of our region, our head of state, was visiting, so of course she'd want to make sure everything under her purview was tip-top.

"I'm ready to discuss my work and answer any questions," I said. "And I'll tidy up a bit."

She walked over to my station where the time capsule contents were arrayed, pausing to look at the photos, some of which I had laid out as if they were comic book panels. "These folks look fun."

"They had a bit of fun together, from what I've gleaned."

She picked up the cup. "This is interesting," she said. She held it in both hands, rolled it a bit between her palms. "In with the rest of this stuff. There must be a story. Have you gotten to it yet?"

Have I! But I wasn't up for recounting everything going

on with it in that moment. "Just some preliminary notes. I have a deep dive planned."

She gazed at the cup as if she, too, perceived something within its deep green. "I look forward to hearing all about it." She set it back down, a curious expression on her face. I couldn't help but feel she knew more than she let on. "Well you seem ready to me. By the by, there's a seminar happening today you may be interested in."

"Sera Ri from Circle of the Eye? Yes, I'm planning on attending. I should get going, in fact."

"Yes, of course. Don't let me keep you. And besides, I need to finish my rounds. When you next see me, I will have our esteemed leader in tow."

The lunchtime seminar was happening in the main lecture hall. I grabbed a wrap from the commissary and brought it with me, since I knew I wouldn't have time to eat afterwards with the Assessor Prime's visit happening later. That telepath at the Reclamation Center told me to see somebody, as did Lorel, and I took their advice to heart.

The speaker was Sera Ri, one of my favorite instructors at the Academy. Her specialty was clairvoyance – with a precognitive element, rumor had it – but I had been a student in her meditation unit. Meditation was the basis for accessing and controlling all psionic abilities, across all disciplines, so it was no exaggeration to say her class was foundational for me, as it was for so many others.

After an introduction and welcoming applause, Sera stepped up to the podium dressed in her customary robes, her mane of wild white hair flowing down past her shoulders. "I'd like to talk to you about time," she began.

"Linear time is an illusion. Many of you may be familiar with this idea, especially if you are a psion trained at Circle of the Eye. But I state this for the benefit of those of you who may never have considered this notion. It is the base understanding from which the rest of this talk will stem. Within this understanding, past, present, and future exist simultaneously in the all-encompassing Now. It is our conscious perception, locked as it is in these machines of flesh and blood and bone and electricity, that is limited to the linear model. Does this mean outcomes of our actions are predetermined, that causality, itself, is an illusion? No; for just as light exists as both particle and wave until observed, so too does the future exist as a probability wave…"

The faces around me were enraptured – no surprise there. Sera had a way of discussing heady concepts as if she were sharing a great secret. She spiraled out from this opening in her usual poetic way, but I got distracted thinking about everything I had experienced over the past few days. Before I knew it, the talk was over. I made my way down, hoping to grab a moment with her, hoping for some insight. I wasn't the only one with that idea though, so I hung back as a small cluster gathered around her. I didn't want to discuss what I had to discuss in front of everybody, and I didn't want to hold up the line. Once the room was more or less cleared out, I approached.

Her face lit up when she saw me. "Maida." She greeted me warmly, offered a light, quick embrace. "So good to see you. Are you posted here? How is your psychometry developing?"

"It's been a lot, actually." I launched into an account of my experiences with the teacup.

She listened thoughtfully, barely moving but for a nod every so often. When I finished, she commented, "You weren't kidding about it being a lot."

"Any insight would be appreciated."

She gave me a look that I remembered from my time at the Academy – like she was about to drop some wisdom. "As you know, all time is now. That's a big part of how your ability works."

I nodded, impatient for something new, something I hadn't heard yet.

"But it isn't a flat circle, expanding ever outward, exactly. The forward motion that we experience in time isn't an arrow, as has been poetically expressed by thinkers and writers of the past. It moves more like a corkscrew, spiraling through creation." She spun one finger around in slow circles to illustrate the point.

"Is this a new model physicists have come up with?"

She chuckled. "No. This is my perception, from my own explorations. You can take it or leave it, but I think this concept will be instructive for you." She paused, as if waiting for my assent. I nodded and she continued.

"Along this spiraling path of time, there exist parallel moments at specific intervals. Decades. Centuries. Millennia. These time periods you are experiencing exist in such windows – the girl in 1906, the man a century later, and you a century beyond that. That's part of it. But I also suspect your friend is correct; there is likely a family connection. Telepaths and clairvoyants have particularly strong connections to those connected by blood, no matter how far removed. It would make sense for psychometrists to be the same, though I haven't encountered one who has reported such experiences until now."

Could she tell how much my brain was breaking at all of this? "That's all well and good, but if I get another flash without contact with the object, what should I do? I don't think I want to keep having episodes like that."

She considered this. "First, I'd work with a telepath on your shielding technique. You won't need to keep a barrier up all the time, I shouldn't think. But if or when another episode happens, you'll want to get one up quickly, to minimize distress to you. Second, try to glean from your visions what they want."

"What who wants?"

"These individuals you're experiencing."

I gawked at her, flummoxed. "What they want? Li Nuan and Nathan? But they're dead. They've been gone a long time. Surely, they've gotten what they want, or not, by now…?"

Sera smiled and shrugged. "Maybe they need a nudge from you."

"People long dead need a nudge from me… to get what they want in the past that's… passed?" I shook my head. Was she being deliberately mystifying or was I too dumb to get this?

"Time is confounding and paradoxical. History is being ever written."

"But the past is passed. It's done. It's settled."

"Is it?"

She gazed at me with a face full of patience and compassion. She had always been a great teacher. She seemed to understand that I needed something actionable in that moment. "A telepath may be able to help. I'm sure you know one."

There was that woman who helped me at the Reclamation Center, but I never got her name. The only other telepaths I knew were from the Academy. Were any of them here in San Francisco?

"I can find somebody."

"I've no doubt you will."

Coming from a clairvoyant with rumored precog-enhancement, that was both reassuring and a bit unnerving.

I got back to the lab about twenty minutes before the visitors were due to arrive. There was nothing really for me to do but wait – I only had one other batch of items aside from the time capsule, and those were all already arranged in their trays. The new batch was jewelry, and I did like the sparkle. Those baubles tempted me with the stories promised by their gleam, but I didn't want to be in the middle of scanning anything when the delegation arrived. I never much liked feeling like a show pony, the demonstration at Lorel's birthday the night I arrived notwithstanding. So I reviewed my log entries from earlier, highlighting items that merited a deeper dive, so that I would be doing something when the group showed up and not just sitting around.

Our visitor today, Julian Linstrom, was the third Assessor Prime since the establishment of the Sierra Northshore Regional Alliance, the area where we live that's comprised of what used to be Northern California, Washington, and Oregon in the former United States along with British Columbia, of what used to be Canada. When the Administrative Region was established – a term devised to reflect a more cooperative and holistic mindset behind the differentiation of territories than "nation-state" – the office of Assessor Prime was created to oversee the Assessor's Council. Each Assessor represented a different zone within the region, and the Assessor Prime was the chosen leader of the Council. In the Precursor model, the Assessor Prime might have been called President or Prime Minister. Even though I had always thought of myself as somebody not particularly impressed with titles, I had never been in the presence of someone as high up the leadership chain as the Assessor Prime, and I was surprised by my nervousness.

Finally, the door to the outer room opened, and overlapping voices echoed through the vaulted space as the delegation entered.

"This is our main artifact room," Aviva explained, "where retrieved items are catalogued and their histories discerned and recorded. Items remain in the holding room, where we just were, until they're ready for this step."

"What do you mean by 'discerned'?" asked the tall, fair-haired man I recognized from the newsfeeds – the man himself, Assessor Prime Julian Linstrom. He cut an imposing figure, given his height, and his gaze and attention felt sharp under a placid surface. He projected an air of ease, but something in his practiced calm put me on edge.

"Well, to answer your question, allow me to introduce the newest addition to our team, the psion, Maida Sun." She gestured to me with an open sweep of her arm as she guided the group into my lab.

"Hello," I said with an awkward wave. So dorky. How was I supposed to behave with individuals of high political and social import? I was annoyed with myself for being flustered by high status and position.

Aviva continued, "Maida possesses the talent of psychometry, which means she can psychically receive the histories of items that she touches. Her skill will prove invaluable in discerning the lives of these objects, and by extension, the culture that produced them."

"Fascinating." Linstrom met my eyes for a second before turning back to the others. "It gratifies me to know that the skills of all our citizens – even the most unusual – can be put to the great work of understanding the past and building our future."

I bristled a little bit at being classified as a "most unusual" citizen – although maybe he meant my skills? Either way, there was a tone of othering, despite the appreciative words, that bugged me. Still, I felt the need to say something. "I'm happy to be able to contribute." I addressed the group with this, not Linstrom himself. I flashed the friendliest smile I could muster as I looked from face to face.

"Have you discovered anything profound?" Linstrom asked.

Fire, terror, and escape rushed through me in a hot blaze. "I've only just begun my work here," I said. Then, gesturing to the spread on my lab table, I explained, "This batch of items was recovered from a private citizen's time capsule. A group of hedonists, from what I can tell so far. The group includes an artist of the time, possibly a musician."

"The hedonists fascinate me. So dedicated to their pleasure even as the world burned. I've always wondered if that behavior was full of naïve hope or bereft of any hope at all. Perhaps you can – what was the word Aviva used? 'Discern' the answer to that question." He smiled. It was a little creepy.

Just then, his watch slipped off his wrist and slid across the floor, stopping at my feet.

"Oh, not again," he sighed. "The clasp keeps coming loose. Antiques…"

I bent down to pick it up, and as soon as I touched it, the plans for something called Operation Golden Days flashed in my mind. There were blueprints titled *Psion Containment Terminus* – what looked like an expansive facility of some kind. It's what the Assessor was looking at before he left his office to come here. He was addressing a group, *"We'll round them up in the name of Regional Security."*

"Maida? My watch?"

His voice brought me out of the unexpected scan back to the room. "Oh... I'm sorry." I held the watch out. "It looks like the clasp broke."

There was a glint of curiosity in the Assessor's eye. "Did you... what's the word for what you do?"

"I call it scanning."

"Did you scan something, just now?" His eyes settled intensely on me, as if he were trying to peer into my brain.

I knew better than to ask about Operation Golden Days, and grasped at the other details that came to me. "The timepiece was made in Geneva, Switzerland, by watchmaker Patek Philippe and Company in 1927. It once belonged to Humphrey Bogart, a famous actor in motion pictures of that time. There was an oil tycoon after that... It was a birthday gift..." I grasped these bits out of the ether so I had something to say, but I wasn't that focused, so the watch's story was all a jumble. I continued holding it out and was relieved when he took it from me.

"I'll have to look up this actor you mentioned," he said. "Thank you for sharing what you do."

With that, some invisible signal was made, because the whole group seemed to understand at once that it was time to leave. Aviva gave me a nod as they headed out, and I got the distinct impression she would have stayed behind and asked me follow up questions were it not for the presence of the others.

The plans for the secret facility filled my mind. *Psion Containment Terminus.* I really didn't like the sound of that.

And then his words, *"We'll round them up in the name of Regional Security."* I didn't know what that was all about, but it really didn't sound like anything good.

I couldn't quite concentrate after the visit and turned what I picked up from Linstrom over and over in my mind. I made a stab at getting more work done, but focus eluded me. Tea would help, so I headed for the commissary. I wasn't having a productive day at all today, and I was glad we weren't closely monitored at work. I would have to make up for it, though. Maybe I'd stay late and work on that jewelry batch that just came in. But really, I knew there was more the cup had to tell me. I just wasn't quite ready yet. Maybe something ordinary and everyday like an herbal tea would help.

As I added honey to my drink – real honey! What a treat! – Aviva sidled up beside me with a tea of her own. "I've heard you've been having an intense time."

"Oh? Where'd you hear that?" Did she buy the lightness I forced into my voice?

"Our favorite technology expert."

Of course: Roan. The little busybody. I was annoyed, but I couldn't really be mad at him for looking out for me, and it wasn't as if I swore him to secrecy or anything.

"It has been a little overwhelming. There's an object that's… proven to be a lot. I've never experienced anything like it."

"Is it just that? Let's walk."

We left the commissary and Aviva guided us down a path through some cypress trees that were full of squawking parrots, their emerald-green bodies and red heads bright against the foliage. We walked by a section of Wood Line – a sculpture of eucalyptus branches created in the Precursor days by an artist named Andy Goldsworthy. It was being restored as part of the Cultural Recovery Project. The wind through the trees' twisty limbs sounded like the ocean – and of course, there was the actual ocean too; its steady wash was audible from where we were, but its expanse was still out of sight. A storm at sea raged in my mind and was gone again. My tea was sweet and hot, but it did nothing for the knot in my stomach.

"Let's sit." Aviva steered us to a bench at the side of the path, one of many such seats distributed throughout the forest intended to foster contemplation, according to the orientation materials. "I did notice a shift in your demeanor after the visit with the Assessor Prime and his delegation." She paused, then added, "After you touched his watch." Her amber eyes fixed on me with a penetrating gaze.

Before I knew it, the words tumbled out. I told her what I picked up from touching the Assessor's watch: the glimpse of the blueprint, Operation Golden Days. The words I heard him speak. Even my impression of his emotional state, confident and contemptuous. I told her all of it. "I don't know what to make of it."

But the truth was, I did have an inkling what to make of it; I just didn't want to face it. I couldn't believe such plans would be in the works in this day and age, not after the Bloom. Is the evolution of humankind just a myth we've told ourselves to make sense of the darkness of the past?

A storm gathered on Aviva's face after I told her what I saw and heard and felt. "What are you thinking?" I asked, not sure if I wanted to know.

"Do you have plans tonight?" She stood abruptly.

"No. Why?"

"Good. I would have asked you to cancel if you had. There are some people I'd like you to meet."

10.

LI NUAN

February 1, 1906
Chinatown, San Francisco

The man receiving the beating whimpers, one eye swollen shut and already turning purple. Blood dribbles from his mouth and nose as he begs for mercy. Li Nuan wonders if such is the fate that would have befallen her father had he not sold her to settle his debt. One of the two henchmen carrying out this punishment pulls the man's head up by the hair, his hand wrapped in the long queue. He gives Wu Jun a nod of acknowledgment as they walk past. Of course the Boss's men would all know each other. The other henchman does the beating.

The punished man is on his knees in front of the entrance to Boss Fong's gambling house. As Li Nuan understands it, such displays tended to not be carried out so openly. So if this beating is happening in full view of the gamblers at their mahjong tables, if it's being carried out in plain sight of the ghostly, hollow phantoms stumbling in and out of the opium parlor next door, of the patrons in the restaurant across the street, it could only be because the Boss wants it that way. The Boss wants everyone to see. What is the nature of this man's transgressions? He either owes money or he'd been caught cheating. Or both. In any case, this beating isn't only a punishment; it's a warning, as well.

Wu Jun seems to sense her distress. "Never mind that gutter dog," he says.

She feels sorry for him, but also wonders what act of stupidity could have earned him such treatment. Everyone knows what happens to those who cross Boss Fong – or any of the Tong leaders, for that matter. Everyone. The man taking this beating, pitiful as he is now, should have known better than to do whatever he did.

They walk quickly by this scene and make their way to the teashop. It's time to replenish supplies, and the Boss asked for rock sugar this time. Madam Bai likes it in her chrysanthemum tea. Were they involved? She put the question out of her mind. It doesn't matter. It's none of her business.

The old man was behind the counter and greeted her with his usual smile. "Tea for the Boss?" he asks. "And some ginger and preserved plums."

"And rock sugar," she adds.

"Go talk to Bao while I fill the order," the old man whispers.

She looks to a corner of the shop and spots Bao speaking with a very short woman, dressed in black. Her dress is in the style those Jesus women wear and her hair too. Who is she? Li Nuan walks over cautiously, checks that Wu Jun is still outside and not peeking in.

"This is Tye Leung," Bao says as she approaches. "She works at the Home up the hill. She helps girls escape…"

Li Nuan gasps, unable to contain her shock. She has heard that one of their own, a Chinese woman, helped girls escape the brothels and evade the Tongs. She stumbles, afraid to even be in the woman's presence. Despite Tye Leung's short stature – she must have been only four feet tall – she has an intimidating presence. Li Nuan has heard that this woman has taken up the white devils' religion.

"Do not be afraid," Tye Leung says. "And be calm or you will catch your guard's attention." She knows Wu Jun is around and what he's there for. Tye Leung explains that she works with the Jesus people – 'missionaries,' she calls them – and translated for them, to reach girls like her, to convey their stories to the white authorities. "We can help you escape. Help you make a better life."

"No." Li Nuan shakes her head. She shouldn't have this conversation; she shouldn't even think about this. She turns away as Bao calls after her. That Tye Leung woman says, "She isn't ready. Let her go."

Back at the counter, the old man says, "Take the help," as he hands the order over. Then, more loudly, likely for the benefit of the guard he knows is standing outside the shop, "Blessings upon Boss Fong."

The rest of the errands go by in a blur, and before she knows it, she is back in Boss Fong's home, performing her domestic duties before she has to report for her other work at the Lotus Pearl. Can she start going to another teashop? She doesn't want to see the old man or Bao again. She doesn't want to risk another meeting with that woman. How can she explain to the Boss why she needs to go to another shop to get his favorite tea when the Moon Goddess Teahouse was his? But she doesn't want to go back there. The offer of assistance, the prospect of escape, is too frightening to think about. It reminds her of the horror of her present circumstance, and without that reminder, she can just focus on the duties in front of her as they come up. She doesn't have to think about her situation, the same as all the other girls. It's all more bearable that way.

In moments like this, she thinks of home, but home is farther and farther away all the time. Guangdong Province fades more and more quickly from her mind as her time here in Gold Mountain drags on and on. For the first couple of years, she could call up memories of the village, of overhearing the gossip of adults as she collected water from the well, the smells of frying fish and boiling chickens, the smell of the dirt. Her parents' faces, her brother – the child they kept. The one they wanted. The one they loved.

She remembers that though they were poor, she was loved, or at least she thought so. She was part of a family. But was she really ever? When her father ran up his debts, she learned what her true value was: whatever price her father could get. She still doesn't know how much she'd been sold for. If she had been truly loved by her parents, could they have sold her so easily? All she knows is that her sale got him out of trouble – though she has come to learn that men like her father will always find trouble again. Men like her father, who end up selling their daughters to cover their debts, will sink into debt again. It isn't just one time, lesson learned. The fearful faces of desperate men that have come before Boss Fong, the ones she has seen over and over, have taught her that.

It is bitter knowledge she wishes she could give back. But give back to who? The fates? Kuan Yin? The god of the Jesus people? Can she go to one of the temples of Chinatown and light a clutch of joss sticks, and send everything she knows of the world up to Heaven, and empty her mind and her soul of all of it? Wipe herself clean?

How she wants to feel clean. When was the last time she was clean? When was the last time she was innocent?

To the Boss's spoiled son, to the Little Emperor, she is no innocent, and he won't leave her alone.

"How long can you keep your legs in the air?" he likes to ask with his face twisted and grotesque with his lust. There is no hiding his depraved nature – he always wears a demon face like that. "Do you get sore, down there? Does your jaw ache?"

Though her face flushes with shame, she keeps her head down and performs her duties as she is supposed to. Finally, those duties bring her to Boss Fong's parlor where he smokes and reads and takes meetings. The presence of his father is enough to keep the Little Emperor away.

"Is the boy bothering you?" Boss Fong doesn't look up from his newspaper.

She wants so badly to say yes, but it isn't her place to complain. Why is the Boss even asking? Surely, he knows what his son is like with her. Is the question a test? She answers with a quiet, "No. No bother." Her words are a betrayal of herself, and they hollow her out, leaving an empty, ragged feeling where her heart should be.

Do her parents know this is the life they were condemning her to when they sold her? Does her mother know or even think about her anymore? Did her mother know when she birthed a daughter that the girl's place in this world would be to simply exist as a ghost in a shell of a life that might have been? Not for the first time nor the last, she stifles her tears. They knew what her future would be. Did they truly believe that life here would be better than the life she would have led back in Guangdong Province? Married to some poor village boy and giving them grandchildren? A life like her own mother's? Or did they lie to themselves, too? She realizes, as despair eats up her insides, that they never cared about her future at all. She was simply the price they paid to secure their own futures.

She dusts, imagining that she wiped away her own debasement. She cleans the gold sycee and wonders how many of these she is worth. She gently wipes the figurine of Zhao Gongming, the God of Wealth, who apparently smiles down on Boss Fong, no matter his violence and the vices that make him his fortune. She dusts the wood carvings of the horse and the dragon. She dusts the books. The opium pipe, which she has heard the Boss mention more than once that he isn't stupid enough to use, though he likes to display the intricate detail of its carved length, its ivory bowl. She begins moving the jade tea set that the Boss likes displayed in the side cabinet when it isn't in service. The set itself has recently been cleaned, after the last tea with the managers of the gambling houses, but she needs to move it to clean the shelf it sits upon. She starts with the pot, then one cup, the next, the next –

Fire. Once again, fire engulfs her. But instead of overwhelming her vision and her senses like last time, the heat and smoke quickly fade. Time seems to run backward, and she sees the fire spread to Boss Fong's building from a neighboring building, she sees the rubble of the structures that fell during an earthquake. A date flashes in her mind: April 18th. There is a feeling of… Is it encouragement?

Be warned. Is that a voice? Now her mind's eye is filled with masses of people gathering in Portsmouth Square, in parks in other parts of the city she has never set foot in – some place called Presidio, some place called Dolores. She doesn't know these places, but the images come with the knowledge of what she is seeing. Her mind crowds with sooty faces, faces trying to look presentable still, even as the city lies in ruin. People line up for water, for bread. People organize to rebuild.

Then the images change – there is still fire, but this time it is forests that burn. Gigantic trees engulfed in flame as people and animals flee and roast. Houses turn to ash – enormous houses, rows and rows of them, and strange-looking wagons, and gigantic roads on pillars of stone abandoned to fire, to storms. Wind and rain lash the cities she sees, and enormous floods around the world tumble earth and buildings – impossible towers of glass. People lie dead in the streets – of war, of plague. *This is coming.* That voice again. Whose voice is it?

And then she is back to a cold and rainy February morning, back in Boss Fong's parlor in the back of his apartment. She glances over toward the Boss and he's sitting there, watching her over the top edge of his newspaper, his face puzzled.

"Something the matter with you?" he asks. "Losing your mind?"

She shakes her head. "No." What other answer does he expect? But maybe she really is losing her mind?

"No time for daydreams."

What she saw in her head just now was no daydream. Why is this happening, why is she seeing these things? She stares at the cup in her hand – this specific cup sparks the visions. It looks like the others in the set, but she knows it is this one in particular that causes her to see fire and smoke and ruin like she has never seen or contemplated. Why? Pondering such questions is another luxury she cannot afford. The date sticks in her mind, though: April 18th. Is something going to happen then?

"What do you know of the white devil woman?" Boss Fong asks suddenly. He has set his paper down in his lap and watches her with an intensity she finds unsettling. Why is he asking this? Had Wu Jun told him about the conversation in the teashop after all?

"I have heard she steals girls," Li Nuan says. She wants to say "rescues," but she knows the Boss will not take kindly to hearing it put that way. She also does not want him to think she believes any girls like her need to be rescued from anything.

"That is right," he says. He looks... thoughtful. It isn't a look she is accustomed to seeing on his face. "They hate us, you know. One day, not long after I first came here, a group of the white men ran around Chinatown destroying what they could. They smashed windows, they set fire to laundries, and temples, and the teashop that you go to. The white devils look down on us. The white devil woman and her associates, they steal our girls and make them follow their religion. They want to make our girls their servants. They want us all to serve them. They want us to believe as they do because they think the way they live is better than the way we live. They steal our girls to make us think we are wrong, to make us lose money, not because they care about the girls. I hope you know well enough to stay away."

"I know," she says. "She cannot be trusted. None of them can."

The Boss stares at her a second longer, as if judging how truthful she is being. He nods with a grunt, then goes back to his paper.

The doorbell rings, its alert clanging through the apartment and startling her from her reverie. The Boss looks up too, though he doesn't startle like she does. "It is Madam Bai," he announces. "For you."

She sets down the cup and her rag. Why would Madam Bai want to see her, much less make a special trip? She is due at the Lotus Pearl tonight anyway. But the Boss knew she was coming. They have plans for her. She walks down to the door, each step growing more and more leaden.

Madam Bai stands in the doorway, her head high and proud like she is some kind of noblewoman.

Li Nuan bows in deference to her superior, even though she'd have preferred to spit in her face.

"You are working upstairs tonight," the Madam says. "In the parlor house. Make sure you bathe yourself and wear this." She hands over a parcel.

Li Nuan guesses from Madam Bai's words and from the weight and feel of it that the parcel must be some kind of garment. "One of the other girls will give you some cosmetics and perfume when you arrive. Put some on before your first customer. Don't be late."

Li Nuan stares at Madam Bai's back as she walks away, disbelieving. Working the parlor house is a step up, of a sort, and the conditions are not as dirty and foul. But it means something else too: she will be serving white men tonight.

11.

NATHAN

July 5, 2006
SOMA District, San Francisco

Angry shouts greet Nathan as he arrives at the office. A group of about two dozen or so protestors circle the front of Phase Designworks's South of Market headquarters, chanting "End child slavery now!" and "Shame, Shame, Shame!" at everyone entering, at every passerby. There are signs, there are leaflets.

"Portal Technologies is evil and profiting off of the exploitation of children!" an angry man bellows, spraying spittle in Nathan's face with his vehemence. "Shame on Phase for working with child slavers!" He shoves a pamphlet into Nathan's hands, then resumes his chant of "No blood for tech! No blood for tech!"

What. The fuck?

Nathan presses his way through the crowd and enters the building with his heart racing. The receptionist meets his gaze apologetically, as if the hullabaloo out front were her fault. "I'm trying to get police down here," she says, her exasperation clear.

"Can you believe this shit?" Lili asks, greeting Nathan at his office door. "Those people are insane."

"What the hell is all that?" Nathan glances down at the pamphlet crumpled in his hand.

"Don't read that shit," Lili says. "Throw it away." She glares at him until he complies and chucks the crumpled pamphlet into his recycling bin.

"What is all that they're saying? About child slavery?"

Lili sighs. "They're saying the rare earth minerals that Portal Technologies needs for its devices are sourced from mines in the Congo. Children work those mines. Allegedly."

"You don't think it's true?"

Lili rolls her eyes. "I think activist types just want something to yell about. I hope that mob gets cleared out soon. How are we supposed to work like this?"

That's not an answer to his question, is it? He decides not to push. "It's not quite a mob."

"Oh, really?" She deploys that haughty, borderline contemptuous tone she uses when she thinks someone is being ridiculous. He's witnessed it directed at other people, but never at him before. "What's your threshold for mob?"

The question takes Nathan aback. He hadn't thought about it really. Fuck. He has shit to do, and now he's thinking about the definition of mobs. The chanting from the crowd outside can be heard, but it's distant, muffled. He can't make out any actual words – they could be chanting about anything. Peace in the Middle East. Save the whales. The name of their favorite pop idol.

"Anyway, it's worse at Portal HQ. There's an even bigger protest there."

"They'll say their piece and be out of here," Nathan says.

Lili huffs and walks away. He admires her talent and drive, and she is a fun after-work drinking buddy, but boy when she gets irritated, everyone around knows about it.

More than once he had been thankful to not be the target of her ire, and he finds being the target now disconcerting. He shuts his office door so he can better collect his thoughts and start his day. Delilah would suggest burning some sage to clear out the negative vibes, and part of him wishes he had some in his desk. It would probably be some kind of workplace violation if he did, though.

As is his habit, the first thing he does is open his email, and a priority message pings. It's from Kendal. Given the protest, no surprise.

To: All Employees
Fr: Kendal Jakes, VP

As you are no doubt aware, Phase Designworks and our client, Portal Technologies, have been targeted by radical activists. Please note that only authorized personnel may address the media or anyone seeking comment. Should any friends or family inquire about the situation, you may let them know that Phase is committed to equitable working conditions for all employees and contractors. Violation of this policy will result in disciplinary actions, up to and including termination. Thank you for your cooperation.

So that's the company line. Nathan's not surprised, but the mild disappointment he feels is surprising. What does he really expect his bosses to say or do? Anyway, he really should get to his work, but the pamphlet the activist guy shoved in his hand is nagging him. He plucks it out of the recycling bin where he'd tossed it at Lili's urging and begins reading.

The Democratic Republic of the Congo produces 53.8% of the world's cobalt, a rare earth mineral required for the production of lithium-ion batteries. These batteries are a crucial component of consumer electronic devices and electric vehicles – markets expected to grow exponentially in the coming years. The workforce of the so-called 'artisanal' mines that produce these minerals includes thousands of children as young as the age of seven, who work in life-threatening conditions...

The pamphlet contains citations from the International Labor Organization, Amnesty International, and UNICEF. He considers getting online and doing some research to check the veracity of these claims, but doing so from his work computer on company time is probably not the best idea, especially considering the directive from Kendal. Still, he can't shake the feeling that even if the numbers and statistics could be quibbled with, the general thrust of the accusations is valid. Nathan has never been much of an activist himself, but he doesn't dismiss these concerns out of hand the way Lili seems to. At the very least, he doesn't assume the protestors are only out to make trouble and grab attention for themselves. He takes them at their word that they give a shit about the matters they're protesting.

Still... even if these allegations are valid and true, what the hell is he supposed to do about it? And why has Phase been targeted? What have they done that...

Link. The Link is set to be a paradigm shifting device. Much of that potential is due to the tech that Portal brought for them to work with. And some is due to the design concepts sparked in his own imagination using his knowledge of what's possible. The form factor. The touch controls. A new type of glass. And a re-tooled power source, a next-generation lithium-ion battery. A battery for which demand will surge in the wake of the Link's release as competitors rush their own new products to market. All those batteries are going to need a lot of cobalt. And production must be ramping up because of the expected increase in demand, and so... child labor. Wait – what? No! Child labor isn't inevitable! Why did his mind automatically go to that?

He has never been confronted before with how conditioned he is to accepting atrocities as the cost of doing business, and the recognition of that thought pattern in himself shocks him. No, child labor is a thing of the past; it should be relegated to the bin of history. It is by no means an inevitability, a given – or it shouldn't be. But because it isn't inevitable, that means somebody made a choice to use it.

How much of this is on his employer and how much on the client? How much of it is on him? He isn't being called out specifically, but that angry man shoving this pamphlet at him did feel awfully personal. He's known the rechargeable batteries were sourced from a Chinese company, but he hasn't dug into where that company sourced their materials. And even if he had, would he have uncovered the information on this pamphlet? And what if he did uncover this information? What is he supposed to do about it? Stop the production of the most anticipated consumer device in years, and upon which their client company – their largest client by a lot – is banking its future?

He pulls the buzzing phone from his pocket and stares at it a moment before looking at the notification. What parts of this little thing were mined by child labor? Is every person who uses consumer electronic devices complicit in the exploitation of children? And for that matter, is anything he's wearing right now made in sweatshops? What about the computer on his desk? What about his desk? What about the carpet on his office floor? Is ethical consumption under Capitalism even possible? He spirals with these questions that he cannot begin to solve right at this very moment, and turns his attention to something reasonable to deal with: the text on his phone right now.

Delilah: *still on for tonight?*

They're supposed to work on cushions and other details for the Fish later.

He responds: *7 works*

            Remy's making dinner

Delilah: *:-)*

Then he tosses the phone onto his desk and stares at where it landed on the child labor pamphlet. He crumples the pamphlet up once more, tosses it back in recycling. Then he retrieves it from the bin and lays it on his desk, smoothing it out with the heel of his palm before slipping it into a drawer. He can't think about that stuff all day. He has work to do.

Nathan and Delilah tackle their crafting project in the cosmic playspace. That's what Remy calls the room where he has his mixing station set up and where they do yoga and calisthenics. Art featuring sacred geometry adorns the walls, along with a tapestry of the tree of life and a poster illustrating the chakras. Remy is into all that stuff; Nathan doesn't mind it. The sacred geometry is cool. He likes the lines.

Delilah and Danny had brought over all the cushions from the Fish – which is parked in front of Nathan and Remy's place and drawing the attention of neighborhood kids, whom Danny is outside entertaining with tales of its construction right now.

"This is the same stuff we're using inside the time machine," she comments as she pulls bolts of fabric from a large shopping bag. "It'll tie the different aspects of our camp together, don't you think? A unified aesthetic?"

"Sure," Nathan says, less than enthused.

"I figured mister hotshot designer would be into it." She sets the different fabrics beside the cushions they're intended for: purple and red velvet for the pillows and red and silver stretchy stuff for the flat cushions on the benches.

"No, it's good." The velvet purrs against his fingers as he strokes it. How long will this suppleness last? Out in the heat and the dryness and the dust? "I'm a little distracted."

"Tell me about it while we cut." She grabs a pair of fabric shears from the craft table. "I'll do the pillows, and you take the seats? And you can tell me what's up with you."

Nathan acquiesces to his friend, and as he begins marking the outline of the seat cushions with chalk on the back of the stretchy stuff, he tells her about the protest at work. And about the children in the mines.

"All right, I think I can see why you're stressed." She nods in understanding as she cuts pieces of red velvet. "Plus, you've got the weirdness with the teacup."

The teacup. In all the agitated excitement around the protest and accusations of child exploitation lobbed at his work, he'd forgotten about the visions of smoke and fire. Now, at the mention of the cup, phantom flames come roaring back in his mind. He pictures a mine on fire, incinerating the child workers in its infernal depths. He shuts his eyes tight.

"I haven't seen you like this before," Delilah says.

"Anxiety used to be much more of a thing with him," Remy says from the doorway, a dishrag slung over his shoulder. "Until I became his rock." He laughs at his own joke, and Nathan does appreciate the attempt to lighten the mood. Remy continues, "I didn't mean to interrupt. Dinner's ready."

Danny, having regaled the neighborhood youth with fish tales, joins them at the table where they continue the conversation as Remy serves up a lovely pork tenderloin with mashed potatoes and roasted vegetables. They go round and round about the challenges of ethical consumption, how nothing about the way society is set up at this juncture in history allows moral purity by anybody who participates in the world, by anyone not living off the grid, raising their own food with saved rainwater, powering their homes with solar and wind, who only wear second-hand clothes or make their own from textiles that they grow and weave themselves. There's a part of him that has always known this, and while he hasn't been living in denial, exactly, these are facts that he – along with everyone else in the developed world, it seems – could happily keep compartmentalized, completely segregated from his image of himself as an accomplished person, generally kind and not contributing to evil, and simply enjoying his life.

Has this self-image been so fragile all this time? That all it takes is one protest and some inconvenient facts to trigger an existential freak-out?

"Well, it seems to me you've got two choices," Danny offers. "Accept this is the way it is, that one result of the work you do leads to children in rare earth mineral mines, and that's the way of the world. Or you can do something about it. But don't complain and do nothing. That's the worst." Danny has been known to drop friends and girlfriends who spend a lot of time complaining about things in their lives without taking steps to change them. He has no patience for those who only complain and take no action. Nathan does not want to be one of those people Danny drops, not at all.

Delilah chimes in, "Even if you do something about it, somebody else will do the work you walk away from. You can't tell me there wouldn't be a line out the door of people who'd kill for your job."

"No, there would be a line." Nathan looks at his loved ones sitting around the table, their expressions stern, contemplative, puzzled.

"Have you spoken with your bosses about this?" Remy asks.

Nathan shakes his head. He hasn't raised the issue yet, having only learned about it all this morning, but he suspects none of the information about the mines is actually news to Kendal or Phase CEO Lamont Reeves. Lamont hails from a family that made their fortune in diamonds, after all. And not the newfangled kind grown in labs. No, his family wealth is based on the old-fashioned kind, the kind dug out of dirt and rock by, let's say, "exploited labor". He can't quite bring himself to use the word "slave." Even to himself.

"Well, we can't transform capitalism and the structure of society in one evening," Delilah says. "But we can maybe get some insight into your vision."

When it comes time to return to the cosmic playspace to do whatever they're going to do, Delilah banishes Remy and Danny from the room for being, in her view, "non-believers."

"Healthy skeptic," Remy protests.

"Agnostic," Danny says, repeating his take on the whole situation that he had shared that night at the Stud.

"Same-same," is Delilah's reply to that.

So the two men stay in the front room to smoke some weed and watch a movie while Nathan and Delilah set about communing with the teacup. Nathan pushes a pile of cushions aside to make room on the floor for the two of them to sit cross-legged, facing each other. The cup, wrapped in its silk, is still in the box the messenger had delivered it in.

"I've been afraid to touch it," Nathan confesses.

With a sharp look from the cup back to his face, Delilah communicates he should stop being such a wuss. He takes a breath, as if preparing for the cup to burn him, and pulls it out of its box, careful to keep a layer of silk between the jade and his fingertips. He sets it on the floor between them, and Delilah draws a circle of salt around it. Also set around them are crystals of different hues that he doesn't know the names of, but in which Delilah puts great stock. She considers herself a witchy woman, but whatever her practice is, it isn't formal so much as it is a hodgepodge of elements from different traditions she has read about. He always figured anyone who seriously practices witchcraft, or wicca or whatever, or anyone who seriously channels messages from the great beyond, would scoff at her dilettantism. But he doesn't really mind. He isn't sure he believes all this stuff himself, recent harrowing visions be damned.

Delilah invokes the cardinal directions and the "spirits of the center," and declares the circle a sacred space as she smudges them both with sage. "Please let Nathan learn what he must learn…" She repeats this over and over again while indicating with her eyes that he should pick up the cup.

Faintly, from down the hall, he hears Remy and Danny laughing at whatever it is they're watching. He pushes that noise aside, he pushes aside all thoughts of his work and the protestors, and focuses only on the cup. The jade is cool against his fingertips when he picks it up – not hot like he partially expected. No smoke, no fire. There's nothing like what had happened before. He looks over at Delilah, shrugs. He moves to set the cup down but holds back at the vehement shakes of her head as she cups her hands together, one on top of the other. Understanding her meaning, he continues to hold the cup in one hand and places his other hand over it.

Delilah increases the volume of her chanting, "Let Nathan learn what he must learn," over and over again. Finally, she raises one hand and smacks its open palm into the center of his forehead.

A warm tingling flows from Delilah's hand into a swirling spot in the center of his forehead – did she actually activate his third eye? – and flames lick around the periphery of his vision. Heat radiates from the fire, but it isn't overwhelming; rather, it's a warm glow at the outside of his awareness, sort of like warming his hands at a campfire, rather than plunging them into the heart of an inferno like before.

The fire fades and an image of a little girl enters his mind. He recognizes the girl's bangs and her pigtails and the coat she's wearing: his great-grandmother as a child. He'd seen the family photographs that his mom treasures. She isn't alone but is with an older woman who is passing her the cup. And then the fire comes roaring back, the cup sitting on a table along with the rest of the set it's a part of. The table gets broken by falling rubble, then it, too, goes up in flames. A hand grabs the cup, and he knows – he doesn't know how he knows, but he knows – that this is the hand of the older woman from before, only she's younger now. She's getting ready to run.

His eyes snap open as the vision fades away. He doesn't drop the cup this time, but keeps it cradled in his hand.

"What did you see?"

"My great-grandmother didn't bring this from China like my mom always said. Somebody gave it to her. Her mother. I never knew about her."

"Okay." Delilah nods approvingly. "Okay, that's something. That's some new information. Anything else?"

"Just this feeling..."

"A feeling of what?"

Nathan sifts through the emotions churning in him, tries to separate his own from what he had perceived of the female ancestors in his vision. It's a feeling of terror, and also a hope. A hope of what?

"Escape."

12.

MAIDA

March 11, 2106
Angel Island, San Francisco Bay

During the Bloom, the skies were all lit up in shades of blue and purple and green and pink. Some yellow shimmers in the daytime. I hadn't been born yet, but I've seen the footage. It must have been glorious in person. Mom said the Bloom was an interaction between our planet's atmosphere and the cosmic dust that infused the part of the galaxy our solar system was traversing at that time. In the clips I'd seen, it was a combination of a fireworks show and aurora borealis. Illuminated skies swathed in diaphanous colors all through the day and night, for a year. No accompanying explosions or anything – it was just silence and light. And after every day of the labor of remaking the world came the nights of people looking on in awe and reverence.

Some scientists had wanted to send satellites up to get samples and see just what all that stuff was, but the infrastructure for orbital launches wasn't functioning at that time, so that ambition never became a reality. The lightshow around the planet lasted for a solid year, at the end of which humanity was different. Psions appeared and reality shifted. The psions could be seen as a symptom of a change that began with the first sparks in the sky.

The history we'd been taught told us that the psion phenomenon began with telepaths – people all over suddenly hearing voices in their heads. At first, they – and everyone – freaked out. Then others appeared with different types of abilities and people freaked out even more, but then they got curious. Some folks could move things without touching them, while others could see things happening in faraway places and visit them with their minds, and still others could find lost things by concentrating on them – that's what Mom was like.

When my psychometry manifested, I'd been raised by and known another psion my whole life – my mother. I had freaked out at first, but then I grew excited. Besides, my parents had told me from the time I was little that I might bloom as a psion because Mom had. It wasn't until I went to my first school and revealed my status to strangers for the first time that I learned what the rest of the world was like. Some were curious and wanted to "test" my abilities. Others were afraid or envious. But one thing was for sure: I had stopped being just a person to all of them.

The Academy was the natural place to go; I was intrigued by the notion of deepening our understanding of our abilities and exploring applications, rather than stopping at maintaining basic control and rarely using the talent, as some psions chose to do. Besides, anybody who wanted to center their ability in their specialized vocation was required to graduate and receive full licensure before they could assume a post, and I knew that was what I wanted to do. My psionic talent is a tool I'd been given to help make the world better, a task we're all in together.

That's the path that led to me speeding across the bay on a boat called the Pelican – the name of a bird that doesn't exist anymore – with Aviva. The silhouettes of the desalination stations pulsed around the bay, solemn and stalwart. Their colored lights indicated which stage the process was in, but I liked to imagine they were force fields. What would they be defending against? Our own worst instincts, probably.

I was clearly Aviva's tag-along; the others all seemed to know each other. Were they all psions? Aviva had said we were going to some sort of gathering and that there'd be psions there. I'd been to such meetups before, but never one so clandestine as to take place on a deserted island across the dark bay at night. The shadow of Angel Island rushed at us as we zoomed towards it. A historic site was still maintained there, but it was minimally lit at that hour and most of the island lay in shadow.

The engine cut as we arrived, and once the boat was tied, I clambered up a ladder and onto a pier, then followed the others down a path towards the complex: a set of beige buildings, a couple of which looked old but well maintained. The central building was of newer construction but built in the style of the historic ones. This place had served as an immigration station in the early 1900s – ancient times in a foreign place to us now. We headed for one of the smaller structures, its name spotlit on the façade: *Community Hall*. Others ahead of us chattered and laughed amongst themselves, so I gathered that this meeting wasn't all that clandestine.

"Why are we meeting out here?" I asked Aviva who walked beside me.

"We're the only ones out here at this time, so we can be reasonably assured there aren't telepaths around. Except ours."

Okay, maybe it was that clandestine.

"Who's the 'we' in 'ours'?"

"You're about to know." A hint of mischief in her voice. She really was playing up the mystery, wasn't she? I kind of liked that.

We were the last ones through the door, and Aviva pulled it shut behind us. Most of the group – about a dozen or so – milled about a refreshment table in the lobby we had entered. On the wall just inside the lobby hung a map that showed the former shape of the island as it was in the year 2025. Less than one hundred years had passed, but about ninety meters of shoreline had become submerged in that time, bringing the water much closer to the building. That was true of everywhere close to the sea, of course.

The refreshment table beckoned – I didn't have time for dinner before heading out tonight, and I was hungry – but Aviva was drawing my attention to the other side of the space, where light spilled from another room into the end of a wide corridor. She hadn't brought me here to snack, so despite my grumbling belly, I followed her down the hall. The whole group wasn't heading this way though, just us two. We arrived at what looked like a conference room or all-purpose room; it was empty of furniture except for a circle of chairs in the center. More chairs and tables were folded up and tucked away around the perimeter.

"Hello, everyone," Aviva addressed the two others in the room with us. "So nice to see you, Del," she said to a person with long, white braids that hung down to their waist. On the lapel of their jacket, I spotted a pin in the shape of a symbol used by some nonbinary folks.

"Aviva," Del replied curtly. They looked me up and down. "And who is this?" There was a slight lilt in their voice – Scottish. And grew up overseas, from the sounds of it. I rarely ever met somebody not from the Federated Regions.

"This is Maida."

"I'm Kemp," said a dark-skinned man, who offered his hand. Old school. I shook it as we had learned in our Precursor Customs class at the Academy. Like Del, he seemed to be sizing me up. He looked really familiar, but I couldn't quite place him.

"This meeting of the Leadership Circle of the Golden Gate chapter of Circle of the Eye is now called to order." Aviva's tone was authoritative, and it was clear she was the one in charge here. "We are joined this evening by a special guest: Maida Sun, who works with me at the Cultural Recovery Project. Her gift is psychometry."

Polite nods from the other two as I looked from face to face. Did my confusion show? Because I was confused. Circle of the Eye was the training center for psions. But if Aviva was here and in charge...

"Are you a psion?"

Aviva nodded with a sly smile. "Telepath."

"Oh. Wow. Okay. Why –"

"I keep my status on a need-to-know basis. You didn't need to know before, but now you do."

Aviva's sudden appearances over the past week came to mind – her showing up randomly at my office just to "check in," her suddenly being there next to me at the commissary. Had she sensed something from me even if she wasn't probing my mind, exactly?

But before I could ask anything further, Kemp interjected, "Any developments on Rebecca?"

Aviva sighed and shook her head sadly.

"Do you mean Rebecca Morgan?" I asked.

The others all turned to look at me.

"What do you know about it?" Aviva asked.

"Lorel showed me the Missing Persons notice and said she was our Liaison Officer. That was the first and only thing I've heard about it. Did you all know her?"

"Knew *of* her," Del said with a glance at Aviva.

"We're not here to talk about Rebecca." Aviva's tone left no doubt that the conversation was shifting now. She turned to me. "Why don't you share with the others what you picked up from the Assessor Prime?"

I hadn't realized I would be the first order of business, but given what I saw... Yeah.

I told them everything – about the blueprints the Assessor was reviewing, Operation Golden Days. I told them what he said about *"...in the name of regional security."* Everybody's expression went dark at my account. Once I'd finished, a long silence followed.

Eventually, Kemp turned to Aviva. "That was a more fruitful gambit than I expected."

"Gambit...?" My glance bounced from him to Aviva as I tried in vain to discern what was up.

"Kemp is Cultural Advisor to the Assessor Prime," Aviva said, noticing my confusion. Did she pick up on it telepathically or just by observing me?

Now that she had identified Kemp, I recognized him; he was part of the delegation that visited campus. He raised his teacup in a sort of salute, then released it, bringing his hand away as the cup continued hovering. It slowly floated back down to his hand. A telekinetic.

"The Assessor Prime doesn't know of this particular talent of mine," he said with a coy smile.

"I asked Kemp to get something of the Assessor Prime's to a position where you would touch it," Aviva confessed.

"And I happened to know that watch clasp had been

giving him trouble for days, so it wouldn't have been suspicious if it broke again and slid over to you." He winked.

So that whole thing with the watch was intentional, set up by Aviva. I turned to her. "Did you know I'd see what I saw?" Dread crept up my spine like a spindly legged spider.

"I didn't know if you'd scan the watch or not. I know automatic response doesn't always happen and that you yourself are trained to shield against such occurrences. But I also know that sometimes they do happen, if there's enough emotional charge. I suspected you might see something like you did. I hoped I was wrong." She looked at her colleagues. "I wasn't wrong."

"It's not paranoia if they're really after you," Del said.

"Pithy as ever," Kemp quipped.

"A tiger can't change its stripes, luv."

"Okay, what is happening here?" My curiosity was burning up and I hoped my tone wasn't too impudent or demanding. But there was clearly backstory I wasn't getting.

Aviva sat more upright in her chair as all eyes turned to her. She raised her chin, a gesture that gave her a regal air that contrasted with her usual warm friendliness. "We have suspected for some time that there are those within the leadership of the Regional Administration Council of Assessors who are, shall we say, 'uncomfortable' with psions and the new structures emergent in human society. Those who wish to –"

Kemp burst in impatiently, "They want to bring us back to the madness of ecological abuse and sociopolitical marginalizations. The rule – the domination – of the few over the many. Oligarchy. The craven times. The decadent decline of empire. The height of folly. Call it what you want." He met Aviva's glance. "What? No point being diplomatic about it. We're still cleaning up the poison and trauma that culture left behind. There is no room for not calling it out for fear of being labeled strident and pedantic. It's the fucking planet we're talking about here. It's our species."

Aviva shook her head with an exasperated sigh. "You are arguing with people who are not here. In this room, we are in accord." She turned to me. "As incendiary as Kemp's comments are, he is correct. We call them Regressives, this secret cadre within the leadership. And it is our goal to stop whatever it is they plan."

"And what is it that they plan?"

"You've provided a glimpse. With what you gleaned from the Assessor. But we don't have the full picture."

"It comes clearer every day though, doesn't it?" Kemp asked.

Aviva turned to Del. "Speaking of things coming clearer. Any progress with you?"

Del shook their head and the beads at the end of their braids clicked together. "There are strong psychic shields all around Linstrom. I can't see past them. It's just a fog in the psifield."

Clairvoyant, with maybe a remote viewing specialty?

"Keep working on it."

"What made you suspect Linstrom?" I asked.

"He has expressed interest in regressive notions," Kemp explained. "In the form of seemingly innocuous comments or questions. He's wondered aloud if psions should be regulated. He has expressed a sympathetic attitude to the emerging Freedom Faction movement. He has made statements around the profit-making potential squandered by current practices around old-growth clear-cutting and fossil fuels. Things like 'we could have made a bundle on that in the old days.' And 'too bad responsible stewardship limits profitability,' accompanied by a fake laugh. So fake." He clearly found Linstrom distasteful.

He paused and must have registered my incredulous expression because he went on to add, "Yes, these are things he has actually said. I get the distinct impression he's been trying to assess my attitude in such matters. I've expressed my opposition to limiting the freedom of movement and autonomy of psions. He doesn't seem too impressed by that. Plus, he's been taking conferences with the Governor of the Arivada Autonomous Region. He's put together what he calls a working committee and has excluded known psions from this group. They are discussing Arivada's plans to privatize solar capture."

I gawked at him some more. "They want to privatize sunlight?"

Kemp shrugged. "There's nothing that sort of mindset doesn't want to own. Although, they would argue it isn't sunlight that's being privatized, but the means of processing it for the power grid." He rolled his eyes, "But considering they want to ban homemade and independent systems and implement a proprietary standardized system they control, I'd say it's a distinction without a difference. Particularly when infrastructure has been laid by others. From these tidbits, we have made an inference. It was only ever suspicion, however. This information you gleaned from his watch has clarified things." He looked at Aviva and Del rather pointedly. "Things are clarified, are they not?"

Grim silence was the others' only response.

"Can you get on the working committee, to capture some details?" Del asked.

A shake of the head. "There's no need for a Cultural Advisor in such matters. I couldn't rationalize that, as persuasive as I can be."

"We'll work this from another angle," Aviva said. "And we may need you to pretend to revise your opinion on the psion question." Then, back to me. "So that's what's going on. We're gathering information. We now know, thanks to you, that one goal is to contain psions – but is that part of some bigger plan? And it's not the kind of thing that Linstrom could spring on the world apropos of nothing. He may be waiting for someone to lose control of their ability. He's been pressing the Academy for more details on our training protocols. Where do you stand?"

The question took me aback; this was all a lot to take in, and I just came here to tell them what I saw. I wasn't expecting a call to – what? Resistance? The thought of challenging the Administration, the Assessor Prime and his allies, felt as heavy in my guts as the thought of challenging those proselytizers that night in North Beach. I was never a stand-up-and-fight kind of person. "Assessor Prime Linstrom gives me the creeps now," I said. I'd only been mildly intimidated before the glimpse into his psyche. "But I don't know about joining your rebel movement, or whatever this is."

"You've given us some useful insight," Aviva said. "Any further participation on your part should be set by your comfort level only." She paused, looked over at her colleagues. "But there is something else we do here." The look on her face was sly, an expression I was starting to get accustomed to from her. "We're a Linking circle," she continued. "Are you familiar?"

Del got up and went to the door, began waving people down the hall. I'd forgotten there were others having refreshments in the lobby. Their chatter got louder as they made their way down the corridor.

I'd heard about Linking while in my training unit at the Academy. It was a practice open to fully-trained psions and was intended to foster unity – soul to soul, heart to heart, mind to mind – by a telepathic and empathic connection. I'd never taken part in one but had been curious for a while. I nod in response to Aviva's question.

"We invite you to join us tonight. Otherwise, you may wait for us to finish in the lobby, or outside. Just not in this room." She sat back, her expression calm yet expectant.

What the hell was this night? I wasn't sure what to make of their spy games with the Assessor Prime, but Linking I had been curious about. More than curious – I'd felt a pull toward it ever since I'd heard about it. The idea of being connected with others so deeply while maintaining our own individuality sparked something in me: that yearning for oneness with humanity – grandiose and cheesy as that sounds. It was something I felt was possible; my psychometry connecting me with people's personal histories was just a glimpse, a taste. Linking sounded like the next step toward that bigger, deeper connection, but the sessions tended to not be advertised and open to drop-ins, instead taking place amongst curated groups. I had been invited to one during my last year at the Academy, right around the time I was preparing for my trials. I used prepping as an excuse to not go – I wanted no distractions – but truth be told, I was a little scared. I didn't know the person who invited me very well – and the others participating not at all – and I wasn't comfortable being witnessed in that way. I had regretted that choice ever since. I wanted to choose different this time.

"I'm in," I said. "For the Linking. Just to be clear."

Aviva smiled. "Understood."

The others joining the group had grabbed chairs from the stacks at the edge of the room, and we all shuffled to make space for them in the circle. Once the larger group was all settled, Aviva instructed us, "Everyone close your eyes."

"Do I have to do anything?"

"Just close your eyes and focus on your breath. Standard meditation."

I did as I was told and brought my attention to my breath, released the tangle of my thoughts. The Circle of the Eye didn't let students graduate until we could drop into theta state on command. So far, this was standard practice.

It started with a warm rush in my chest that flushed up my neck to my face. Then the top of my head tingled, with patches of heat at points where my psion training taught me my crown chakra and third eye lay.

open open open

The voice wasn't a voice, really, but a knowing that appeared in my mind, a presence gently asserting itself. Aviva. It wasn't like I heard her, exactly, but I did, soundless though her beckoning was.

My whole body flushed, and a warmth spread from my chest outward, up and past my head, out to my fingertips and down to my toes, and I felt them all – Aviva, Kemp, Del. I could feel the others as well, but the ones whose names I already knew were clearer to me. But soon, identities dissolved as my mind filled with golden light. It was their presence, in me. It was the light of all our presences aglow and linking up within the psifield. At the same time, I felt myself in them – myself reflected back to me by the others – the different versions of me that they saw. And then I felt all the different versions of the selves that the others witnessed reflected back to them, and all our selves refracted and joined. I didn't hear their thoughts, which surprised me. Was it because they were better at shielding their minds? I hadn't practiced that too much. Could they hear me?

release your conscious thoughts

A soft nudge from Aviva, which I somehow knew was just for me, a private ping in this collective experience. Swirls of color in my mind, then the swirls settled into a field of deep purple, and I saw the group of us floating in this field – a representation of water or just energy? Were we floating on our back, arranged in a circle, or were we weightless in boundless space? Yes. Our auras – our lightbodies? – glowed with gold light that was white at the outer edges. The field we floated in formed shapes and patterns, all of it in shades of purple. It was all the same color, yet patterns were discernible. We were all unified in the psifield.

And there was this feeling that came up in me – a rush of happy understanding that we were individual branches... No. Blossoms. We were individual blossoms springing forth from the same evolutionary branch – soul branch? We were individuals that were part of a whole, and I felt that wholeness inside me even as I felt I was a part of that wholeness, even as I was aware of myself, of me, of Maida, an individual bloom unfurling into this connectivity. Little bits of the others came through: Del's puzzlement, Kemp's passion, Aviva's focus. There were wisps of feeling from the others, the ones I didn't know: bits of worry about a daughter, and grief over a lost pet, and preoccupation with lab results, and wondering if the new bamboo will grow quickly enough to meet the next harvesting target, and who's the new girl (was the new girl me?) and, and, and... These flare-ups of individual concerns were fleeting, and soon there was just a gathering of calmed minds and Aviva's telepathic embrace containing us all. And in that embrace, I felt where others were coming from, and for a brief moment, I understood them. They were me and I was them. In that container I saw how our paths were joined, how my path, even, was joined with these others, no matter what I thought I wanted.

breathe

The instruction grounded the euphoric sense of connection, and the others drifted away from me, and I from them. Separation increased with each breath, and my awareness came back from whatever ether we had been drifting in, back into the solidity of my body. I was alone in my head again. My psychic self, separate unto itself once more. I opened my eyes, looked around at the group. As my gaze met that of each of the Leadership Circle – Del, Kemp, and Aviva – I knew that despite my words earlier, I was one of them now. And they knew it too.

13.

LI NUAN

February 1, 1906
Chinatown, San Francisco

The Boss and the Little Emperor have dinner out tonight, so Li Nuan doesn't have to cook. Is that on purpose? Does he know what her evening will be? Of course he knows; Madam Bai would never move her from the cribs to a parlor room without his permission.

The parcel she's been given is a cruel joke: a silk dress, a finer garment than she has ever before touched with her own hands. Yellow silk with delicate white and pink flowers embroidered on the bodice. What poor girl's labor is this? It's very fine – so much effort, such luxury as she has never seen, and for what? To present herself well to fetch a good husband? To serve tea to the Emperor? Or even to serve this city's leaders, the Mayor, the Police Chief? No, this dress is just to make herself pretty for the men who will enact their lusts upon her. Its luxury is a prison.

She sits on her cot and cries, taking care not to stain the silk with her tears. But she doesn't have time to indulge in sadness and hate for her situation. She has to get to work.

As promised, when she arrives at the Lotus Pearl, she is ushered upstairs to one of the other girls' rooms.

"Have you been crying, little sister?" the girl asks. "You must never cry in front of them."

She pushes Li Nuan down onto a bench in front of a vanity. "Have you used powder before?"

Li Nuan shakes her head, then the girl begins dabbing her face with a soft brush, smoothing out her skin tone in the flickering light of the lamp. Then she applies some rouge, some stain on her lips. Her "sister" then pulls a brush roughly through her hair and pins it up with a comb. Finally, she holds out a little jar of perfume. "Rub some on your wrists, and on your neck and your bosom."

"How old are you?" Li Nuan asks.

"Fourteen."

Even younger than her, and such an expert in this life. Li Nuan feels tears coming again but presses them down. She doesn't want to be chastised again by little sister. She applies the perfume as instructed, then marvels at the face looking back at her in the mirror. A pretty face, wearing cosmetics, in a nice silk dress. This is more luxury than she ever thought she would live to see, but then she remembers what she has to do for it. This isn't her whole life now, is it? This dress up? This is just for tonight; who knows if she would be put in the parlor rooms again. Tomorrow, she will be back to being housekeeper for the Boss, and then back down to the cribs. But maybe not if she performs well this evening. Is this now her ambition? To perform well enough to be kept in the nice part of the brothel? To be able to wear nice dresses and perfume? Oh, this is all a horrible show of some kind, a twisted version of the operas that used to come to the village, bearing the news from Beijing.

Madam Bai charges into the room. "Is she ready yet?"

"Ready," the other girl says.

"Let me see. Stand up."

Li Nuan stands for the Madam's inspection. "Fine, fine. Your customer is here." She holds the door open for Li Nuan, as if she were the servant and Li Nuan the mistress in her finery.

Madam Bai leads her to another room down the hall where a white man stands waiting. He turns around at their entrance, his face expectant.

"I present you Xiao mèi," ," Madam Bai says, using the Mandarin term for "little sister," as she pushes Li Nuan towards the man. "I leave you." She bows and makes her exit. Strange, watching her behave like a servant. Just as strange as hearing her speak English.

"Xiao Mei." The man repeats the name he's been given, trying out the foreign syllables on his tongue. Little Sister. What they are all called. Does he know what he is saying or even that there is a difference between Mandarin and Cantonese? She is sure he does not. "I'm Patrick. Do you speak English?"

Li Nuan shakes her head. "No English." She has been coached by Madam Bai on this question.

"I don't suppose it matters anyway. Come sit." He sits down on the room's small sofa and pats the seat beside him.

She obeys, taking a seat next to him, keeping her hands in her lap.

"Let's start with a drink," he says. On the table in front of him sits a bottle and two glasses. "I brought this stuff from France. It's called absinthe."

What is he talking about? This stuff he poured for her? She sniffs it; it reminds her of anise. He raises his glass, and she copies his gesture, laughing nervously. Is she doing this right? She doesn't want to drink it, but he is drinking it, and he seems to expect it of her. She is there to please, and maybe if she draws out this drinking ritual, it will delay whatever he wants next. It tastes simultaneously of anise and grass, and is warm going down. Her senses flutter with the first whisper of intoxication.

"You're so pretty," Patrick says. "Your kind are all so pretty. So delicate." He raises a hand and strokes her cheek with the back of his fingers.

What is this? None of the others have ever touched her this way, so softly.

"I like how demure your kind is," he goes on. "The ladies over in North Beach are too bawdy for my liking." He downs his drink, pours himself another. He doesn't offer her any more, but she doesn't want more anyway. He leans back, pushes his crotch forward and she sees a prominent bulge is there, and it is growing. "Why don't you take care of this for me?"

She doesn't understand his words, but she grasps his meaning. After setting her glass back down on the table, she begins undoing his pants. His engorged manhood springs forth, surprisingly pink. She has never seen such a thing in her life, and tries to keep her shock from showing on her face. She can't risk insulting him.

He raises his hips and slides his pants down, pushes them down to his ankles. "Go on," he says, jutting his chin at his member as he leans back on the sofa.

She begins by stroking it, and it is hot in her hands. Her two hands together don't cover the whole thing, to her astonishment. She thinks it will hurt going in. Maybe she can finish him with just her hands; some men, that's all they want.

He hisses with pleasure, tilts his head back as she runs her hands up and down his shaft. This goes on for a couple of minutes until he pulls his head back up and looks into her eyes. His face is different now. The open friendliness from earlier has been replaced by something dark and hungry. "Kiss it for me," he says, his voice deeper than it was before.

She understands this meaning too, and does as he asks. Then he pushes down on her head, and she knows to use her mouth and tongue. This is the thing they wanted most often. As she performs her task, he gropes at her breasts, undoing the knotted silk buttons on the bodice that contains them. She helps him open the flap, and bares herself to him.

"So small," he whispers, cupping her in his hot palms.

She wants to smack his hands away and run out of the room screaming, but she can't do that. Not without incurring the wrath of Madam Bai and Boss Fong. What would they do to her if she did? She lets him continue to grope her as her breath grows heavy. She is disgusted, but he seems to take her heavier breathing as passion. Or at least a performance of it.

He sits up and pulls her up suddenly with his hands in her armpits. He then throws her face down onto the sofa as he positions himself behind her. He pushes her dress up, his hands on the back of her thighs, on her buttocks. No. No! He presses himself against her, throbbing.

She struggles. *"Um ho, um ho..."* she says in Cantonese. *"Don't don't..."*

"I don't know your chink language," he says hoarsely as he presses her down into the sofa, as he presses his hardness insistently between her buttocks.

No. She will not let him enter her this way. Down there. No. Hot tears of rage rise to her eyes as she keeps saying no in her useless tongue. He reaches one of his hands down to his member to get it at the angle he wants while the other hand shifts onto the sofa to bear his weight and maintain his balance. His bare wrist is right there in front of her face now, and without a thought, she bites down hard, breaking skin, drawing blood.

He yowls in pain and surprise, springing up away from her.

"Bitch!" he cries as he grabs a handful of her hair, pulling her head back. "Filthy whore!" His spittle spatters her face as he bellows.

She doesn't have to understand his words to know what he thinks of her.

The door burst open and Madam Bai storms in. "What is the matter? What is wrong –" Her eyes open wide as she takes in the scene before her.

"This little bitch bit me!" He holds up his wrist and flashes the angry red oval of Li Nuan's bite, his pants pooled around his ankles, stiff member still bobbing up and down.

"So sorry, so sorry," Madam Bai says, flustered. "I help you. Get medic…"

"To hell with this place!" He gets his pants back up, tucks himself away, then pulls out a kerchief and presses it to his wrist. "If that whore is diseased –"

"No disease, no disease," Madam Bai says urgently. "We clean you, we clean…" She ushers the customer to the door while shooting Li Nuan a look that is dark with thunder.

Li Nuan buttons up her dress, wipes the iron taste of the man's blood from her lips. She goes to the door, not sure what she should do, when one of the guards steps in her way. "Come with me." He brings her to Madam Bai's office and orders her to wait.

She paces the room, frantic, and tries not to think about the man's rage after she bit him, tries not to think about what he wanted to do to her. Oh, what has she done? What has she brought upon herself? She thinks of the welts on a poor girl's back, a man's swollen face as he's beaten in the street, a severed finger in a pool of blood. She should have submitted. She should have just gone away in her mind and let that man do as he would. She doesn't know how much time has passed when Madam Bai finally joins her.

"Why did you do that?" the Madam demands.

"He wanted to put it…" Li Nuan can't bring herself to say the words.

"Where? Where did he want to put it? Surely no place you haven't already taken a man?"

Li Nuan shakes her head, "Not the usual place." She hates that she is crying in front of the Madam, yet again, but she cannot hold it back any longer. "In…back…"

Madam Bai smirks. "In your bunghole? Yes, some men like that. It is your job to provide whatever service they seek. What is the matter with you?" She goes to a cabinet behind her desk and pulls out a switch.

"He threatened to go to the police because of you," Madam Bai says. "Hard enough to keep them away without you causing trouble. The Boss will not be happy. This will cost us. It will take a good bribe to fix this. You will have to take care of a lot more chickens to pay it off."

"I'm sorry," Li Nuan says, "I couldn't –"

"Stop being such a baby and know what you are!" The Madam screeches as she smacks the switch down hard on the desk. "Bend over and pull up your dress."

"What?" Dread makes a pit of her stomach and cold sweat breaks out across her brow. "Please. No. I didn't mean to –"

"You didn't mean to what?" Madam Bai's voice drips with disdain. "Not accept that you are a whore with one job to do, and that is to give men the pleasure they pay for? Bend over now or I will have four guards hold you down and Boss Fong will do this himself. You will like that even less; I promise you."

Tears streak her face, and she doesn't care about staining the dress now. She does as she is told and braces herself. Why? Why is this life so wretched?

She cries out with the first smack of the switch.

"You must learn to be a good girl," Madam Bai says.

"I will be good, I will be good," Li Nuan pleads through her tears. "Please."

"You will say anything to avoid a beating. But it must be done."

Another smack stings across her rear, and a long-simmering anger breaks within her. Li Nuan whirls around, one hand balled into a fist, and she strikes Madam Bai across the jaw. The Madam cries out, stumbles back, drops the switch. "You ugly little dog!"

Li Nuan picks up the switch and runs to the door. Heart pounding and breathless, she quickly orients herself and dashes for the door to the alley. One of the guards sees her and looks puzzled at first, then quickly understands the situation.

"Stop her!" Madam Bai calls from her office door.

Li Nuan swings with all her might as she runs, brings the switch across the approaching guard's face, leaving an angry red lash. "My eye!" he cries as he stumbles backwards into a wall. Down the hall she runs before dashing though the door to the alley. The street is damp from a light rain, and her feet send mud spattering as every step carries her further away. She doesn't look back toward the angry shouts coming from the Lotus Pearl.

She runs for the large brick building up the hill, the house where the Jesus people live. The house where girls like her seek refuge. She runs up the hill, lungs and legs and feet aching. She runs as if a demon from hell chases her, intent to devour her soul, if she even has a soul. She runs from the Madam, from Boss Fong, from the Little Emperor, from Wu Jun and the other guards. She runs from the other girls like her, girls too afraid to run, girls cowed into submission to their fates. She is never going to be one of them ever again. She runs toward the house that looks like a fortress. The sign out front reads *Occidental Mission Home for Girls*.

She pounds on the heavy wood door, pounds and pounds and pounds. A familiar face answers – the woman named Tye Leung, whom she met at the teahouse just this morning. It feels like another lifetime now.

"Help me!" she cries, then collapses in the tiny woman's arms.

14.

NATHAN

August 23, 2006
Richmond District, San Francisco

An ever-so-slight pang of guilt tugs at Nathan when he arrives at his parents' house. They only live four miles away from his and Remy's flat, but it's a world away in this city, which has a way of warping time and space within its borders. The guilt stems from the fact that they hardly ever visit. But visiting is a two-way street, isn't it? Reaching out goes both ways? Lack for lack doesn't mean anyone is at fault, does it? Or maybe everyone, equally. Ever since getting those crazy visions off the teacup, he's been wanting to talk to his mother about it; what he pieced together from the visions didn't quite jive with the story she'd told him and his brother when they were growing up. And who is this mysterious ancestor? A great-great-grandmother his mother never mentioned? He had wanted to speak with her sooner than now, but had to wait for his parents to get back from a cruise and European vacation and decompress from the trip, and then for his mother to find time in her schedule.

"Nathan. My second born but first to call. Hello."

"Mother." He greets her with a peck on one cheek, clasps her shoulders. *Don't let her make this a competition.*

She stands aside, holds the door open and waves him in. The first order of business is to take off his shoes in the foyer and put on a pair of guest slippers. After that, he follows her up the stairs lined with photos of her as the Swan Queen, as Giselle, as Juliet, from her days with the Ballet. When rising star Elsa Lee-Zhao still danced the leads. Before she became a mother, as she constantly reminded Nathan and his brother Robert all throughout their childhoods.

At the top of the stairs, he sees that she's laid out a tea service on the dining room table, where formal guests are served. He takes this as confirmation of something he has long understood about their relationship: that he is held in the same esteem as a professional colleague, or book club person, or neighborhood association member. Respected, but with no intimacy. No closeness.

He feels the same, but is that because he'd been taught to feel that way? Did he simply learn by her example? With Remy, with his friends, he's come to experience closeness. But here, in this house, he follows his mother's lead.

They take their seats, and he accepts a cup of tea. She likes pu-erh, but he likes chrysanthemum. Which will she be serving? Jasmine green. A compromise.

Nathan shakes his head. Why has his inner narration turned this into a sit-down between rival politicians or gang-bosses all of a sudden? Gang-bosses? Where did that notion come from?

"Your brother and his wife are expecting," she says.

"I heard. Robert told me. Are you excited for another grandchild?" He hadn't meant the question as a dig or insult or indictment of her age, but he can tell from the way she briefly winces that his mother takes it like that.

She recovers quickly. "Overjoyed. I knew this was my destiny when I gave up my career for children. I hope I'm not still alive to see great-grandchildren." She removes the covers from a dish of candied dates, and another of preserved plums still in their paper wrappers, and a plate of coconut-filled pastries – his favorite. Well, that's thoughtful. "You said you had a family matter to discuss."

From his pocket, Nathan pulls the teacup. He sets it down on the table between them, lets the yellow silk fall as it may, petals settling around a blossom of jade.

She casts a glance at the cup, then meets his eyes once more. "What about it?"

"Why did you pass it on to me?"

She shrugs. "It's traditional to pass it to a girl, but I have no daughter, and you were second born. Common sense, really."

Nathan takes a breath. "Why are you like this?"

They glare at each other, raising an invisible glacier higher and higher. She looks away. Then, without meeting his eyes, "Was that all you wanted to know?"

"You told me and Robert that our great-grandmother brought it from China. But she didn't, did she? She got it from somebody who was here already." He pauses, having named the family lie out loud. "Our family has been here longer than the 1930s, haven't we?"

"Why are you asking this?" She meets his eyes now, and her expression is the softest he has seen from her in a long time. What is this look? Is it... humility?

"You're going to think I'm crazy." He looks down at his hands, wonders if he really is going to share all this. Then he launches into an account of the visions he's experienced.

She takes in his story with a minimum of reaction, just nods. After a moment of silence punctuated only by his sips of tea, his chewing of a coconut tart, she replies. "It is as she predicted."

Nathan's cheeks flush hot. He feels disembodied, like he is suddenly watching somebody else have this conversation with his mother. "What do you mean, 'as she predicted'? As who predicted?"

"Your great-great-grandmother, Chan Li Nuan. She died when I was fourteen. But before she died – just two months before she died – she told me that she fought for that cup. She told me the cup meant freedom. She told me someone in the family will eventually see the truth. But my mother told me that Li Nuan was crazed with dementia and remembered things all wrong. She told me her mother – your great-grandmother – brought it from China. But my mother knew the truth and couldn't face it. Li Nuan said she would accept the truth one day, that our family would. But mother never did, and I –" Her voice catches, and for a second Nathan thinks his mother might cry.

She composes herself and continues, "I never did either. Even though I believed it. Believe it." Tears well up in her eyes, a sight Nathan hasn't witnessed since he came out as gay.

"And what is this truth?" Nathan asks, his voice quiet, barely above a whisper.

"Your great-great-grandmother Chan Li Nuan was a freed slave – sex… slave. She was brought here to California, to America, against her will. She escaped that life. She saved the cup from a fire, and for her, it represented freedom. When she took her freedom. She handed it down to the eldest girl in the family, and so it went, until me. Until you."

Nathan sits back, lets the words absorb and metabolize. "Why have you never told us any of that?"

"Tell you what? That this heirloom was brought into the family by a whore?" She sits back, an astonished look sweeping over her face, as if her own vitriol has surprised her. "It's a shameful thing to talk about. 'Sex work', it's called now, but it was just being a whore back when I was coming up."

"And not a proper backstory for a prima ballerina." Nathan wants to be angry, but finds he just isn't. He is mostly just tired and sad. His female ancestor was sex-trafficked; the products he designs rely on child slave labor. How is the world so fucked up?

"I had a chance to make a mark in culture," his mother says. "At a time when women of our heritage were mostly overlooked. I had to take it. It was my own liberation."

"But if you don't share the true history that led to that liberation, is it really anything at all?"

"It was something to me!" She slams her hand down on the table, jostling the tea in front of her, spilling some onto the white tablecloth. "You think an aspiring world class ballet company would have put the descendant of a Chinatown brothel girl on their stage?"

"The San Francisco Ballet is world-class."

"It is now, but it wasn't then."

"Whatever. Not being public about it is one thing, but you kept the true story even from us, from me and Robert."

His mother lets out a sob, crumples her cloth napkin and brings it up to her face. "You're right, you're right. I'm sorry I kept it from you. I was just so ashamed of the history. But now you know." She pauses, meets Nathan's eyes across the table, and her face softens. "A vision, you say?"

Nathan nods. "Of a fire. Lots of fires, actually. Crazy stuff."

"Like it's the end of the world? Are there floods and famines and wars and plagues and dead bodies in the street in these visions?"

All the hairs on Nathan's body stand up along with goose-pimples at this inquiry. "Yes. How did you know that?"

His mother smiles, a sad smile, mostly for herself, it seems. "Li Nuan told me about visions she used to get when holding the cup. I was very young – maybe eight or nine. I remember my mother telling her I was too young to hear about all of that. I never forgot it, though. But I did come to tell myself she was old and senile and demented. It was easier to believe that than her visions of a terrible future coming for all of humanity. Maybe the ghost of your great-great-grandmother Li Nuan lives in the cup."

"That would be fucking terrible."

"Language. But you're right. That would be fucking terrible." She laughs, and the glacier between them thaws ever so slightly.

"Maybe somebody could make a ballet about it," Nathan says, appreciating that the mood is lightening up, just a little.

His mother smiles at that. "I'll get Helgi to choreograph something just for me." She refers to Helgi Tómasson, the current artistic director of the Ballet, though not who she danced under. "I'll come out of retirement for it. *The Jade Teacup*. It will be the show of the season." She takes a sip of tea, and her dancer's grace is evident even in that simple motion.

"I'm glad I know all this."

"I am too," she says with a nod. "It feels lighter, doesn't it?"

Nathan has to agree; the truth, no matter how heavy, does lighten the spirit by some strange alchemy. But as he thinks about his family history, what his great-great-grandmother must have gone through, he can't keep his mind from turning to the protests against his work. The alleged child slavery used in the mining operations that are so crucial to the batteries of the products he designed. The circle of exploitation just goes round and round, doesn't it? Can it be broken, that cycle? *Just don't exploit people.* The sentiment seems hopelessly naïve, and at the same time, it could not be a simpler notion. Is it really so hard to not exploit people?

"I have an appointment to get to," his mother says. "Otherwise, I'd take you to lunch."

Nathan can't remember the last time he and his mother went to lunch. He rises from his chair and gathers the silk around the cup before tucking it back into his pocket. "Thanks for telling me about the teacup. And about Li Nuan."

"I hope it helps with your visions, or whatever is happening with you."

"You don't seem too surprised about any of that."

"I've had weird psychic experiences too," she says. "Stories for another day. Oh, and take some pastries with you. You're too skinny."

When Nathan gets to the office for the afternoon, he begins researching the history of the brothels and female enslavement in Chinatown during the Gold Rush and Barbary Coast eras of the city. He learns how some girls were sold by their families, while others were brought to California from China under false pretenses. How they were lured by promises of good jobs and good husbands that didn't exist. The girls were forced to sign these documents they couldn't read. They looked like contracts that made it seem as if the girls were voluntarily working for these people. Mostly men, but some of the brothels were run by women. Members of the police force were in on it, as well as members of the Board of Supervisors. Together, they used city authority to help protect this trade, and for their efforts, as is the way of such things, they received a cut. He'd had no idea about any of it, just like he'd had no idea about the child labor in the mines. How sheltered is he?

A knock on the door breaks him out of his contemplation. It's Sally, a junior member of his team. She's clearly been crying.

"Hey, Sally. Something the matter?"

"I've been fired," she reports. "I... I just wanted to thank you for believing in me and giving me a shot –" She burst into tears again.

"Fired?" She's a promising talent, and did good work on the Link project. He had planned on recommending her for a raise at her next performance evaluation. "What happened? Come in, sit down."

He ushers her into the office and closes the door. She doesn't sit, though, just stands in the middle of the room holding a banker's box of her personal effects.

"Who fired you? For what reason?"

"Kendal," she says. "I... Okay, this might have been a stupid thing to do. But I joined one of the demonstrations. Against Portal. Over the weekend, so I was off the clock. But somebody at Portal recognized me from the meetings and told her." Sally is supporting staff and was present at all the ideation and update meetings with the client for the Link project. Anyone on the Portal team would have noticed her over the course of several meetings.

"They can't fire you for that!"

"Kendal said that publicly opposing the products of our clients is a breach of trust and counter to the good of the company." She lets out a sound that's somewhere between a laugh and a grunt. "She also said that I violated the directive about speaking out on this topic."

Nathan recalls an earlier email from Kendal.

Sally continues, "But that directive only addressed talking to the media, which I didn't do. And I was at the demonstration as myself, not as a representative of the company. Anyway... Maybe I should have known better. But I just couldn't let it go. Those kids."

Nathan admires Sally's bravery in standing up for her beliefs against an obvious wrong, an obvious injustice. He also thinks that yes, she should have been smarter. He won't be protesting anytime soon – does that make him smarter? Or just a coward? But this thought doesn't make him feel smarter or better about himself in any way.

"I'll talk to her," he says. "See if I can smooth this over."

"Don't get yourself in trouble. I'll be fine. I already have an interview with a social-media start-up. I just wanted to say good-bye and thank you for giving me my first real job."

He looks at his staffer with admiration. She seems to be accepting the situation with grace, and if she can do so, he can as well. "Okay, Sally. Take care of yourself. I'm happy to give you a glowing recommendation."

She nods at that. They hug awkwardly, then she takes her leave.

What the fuck?

He opens the drawer of his desk where he'd put the pamphlet he got from the protestor. He reads the stats again, then looks up the mining company. There's a pledge on their website that they will "do better" to ensure safe working conditions, and that they are "looking into" the child slavery allegations. Not a denial, which for corporations like this is tantamount to an admission.

His inbox pings, and he glances over at his monitor with annoyance, but the urgent tag catches his eye along with three capital, bolded letters: NDA. What the hell is this? He opens the latest missive from Kendal.

Date: August 23, 2006

To: All Employees
Fr: Kendal Jakes, VP

Attached, please find a Nondisclosure Agreement for your signature. As you know, Phase Designworks and our client, Portal Technologies, are under attack by radical activists.
No employees may make public statements or take public action in support of these activists. No employees may relay details of our work or the supply chain and production details of any project for any client. Print and sign the attached document stating that you agree to these terms, or submit your resignation to HR. Thank you for your cooperation.

Leaning back in his chair, Nathan covers his face with his hands and lets out a deep sigh. Just what is he a part of? He has a nice office, an impressive title, an influential role in the development of high-end consumer gizmos. Something that taps into his design skills, that pays well, that carries with it prestige and a "cool" factor. But none of that changes the fact that at a base level, what all of this is built on is the exploitation of workers, of children. Any number of children was too many. And the material those kids mined was the key to the power source for this whole enterprise he's just an incidental part of, no matter his title and salary and the design-magazine coolness of it all.

He walks across the buzzing open-floor workspace to Kendal's office. She looks up when he appears in her doorway, her annoyed expression softening when she sees it's her star designer.

"Nathan. What can I do for you?"

"I wanted to talk to you about the NDA. And my team member Sally. And the protests."

"Yes. Sally. Going to a protest was foolish. I already let everyone know that termination was on the table for public statements. And attending a protest counts, even if she didn't get on a megaphone herself, as I explained to her. Whether or not she was on company time."

Nathan sighs. He sees that it's futile to argue for Sally, who is already moving on anyway. "And the child slavery?"

"That has nothing to do with us." Kendal's expression morphs back into a scowl. "Those activists are ridiculous. Completely out of touch with how the world works."

"But it's all true," Nathan presses. "About the child labor. The child slavery. In the cobalt mines."

Kendal removes the glasses Nathan is pretty sure she wears just for show, and rubs her eyes. "All of that is quite a few degrees of separation from us," she says. "And what do you suggest we do? Drop our most lucrative account? What good would that do? Some other company will get Portal's business, and Portal will be buying up that cobalt anyway. Many other companies need those minerals as well – so those mining operations will be happening regardless of what we do, or even what Portal does. As for the children, maybe a few get in through the cracks, which is unfortunate, but it isn't our job to police child labor around the world. A huge chunk of our business would grind to a halt if we insisted on verified ethically sourced materials at every step of the supply chain, which again, we do not control. This is the way of the world we live in, Nathan. A world that pays this company, and you, quite handsomely for what we do."

"I just don't feel good about it," Nathan says. "Benefiting from such questionable practices. I feel culpable."

"Does existing in our society make you feel culpable?" Kendal asks, her face growing even sterner as her nostrils flare. "You have a lithium-ion powered device in your pocket right now, do you not? Your clothes – your shoes – do you know for a fact that none of it was made in sweatshops? That none of it passed under a child worker's hands? What about the fact that some of our clients have divisions that make weapons for the military? Does that bother you too? I'm sorry, Nathan –" She pauses, as if intentionally stifling a tirade she can feel building. She places her hands on her desk, and visibly gathers her composure.

"Look," she continues. "You're brilliant. You do fabulous work. I love and respect you. But this line of thinking will get you nowhere. Like it or not, this is the world, and it always has been. I'm sorry if these protests have opened your eyes to something you didn't know before but – I'll be frank here – maybe you didn't want to know. I suggest you get right with it and focus on your job. Which you're amazing at."

Fire from another chapter of history sears through Nathan's mind. He can see he's getting nowhere with Kendal, that nothing he can say – that no amount of data the activists brought forward – will budge her. But what did he really expect, anyway? She's just doing her job. And he has his.

He has his.

She changes the subject. "You're out starting next week, aren't you? Going to Burning Man?"

He nods. "We leave tomorrow."

"Enjoy the party."

With that, she turns her attention to her monitor, and he's dismissed. He makes his way back to his own office, a sullen mood descending upon him with each step. Cheers and shouts of "Happy Birthday" burst from one corner of the common work area – oh, right, it's Lili's birthday today. He should probably be at the celebration, but the sinking feeling that Kendal leaves him with drains all want of joy from him.

He has an amazing, comfortable life that he never thought twice about before now, that he always thought he'd earned and built himself with hard work and dedication and skill. Which he did. But there is so much invisible labor and invisible support that makes his whole life possible. Not just his – all his friends, his colleagues. Everybody. He is lucky, and he knows it. But the cost of that luck – the cost to others – was never something he considered until now. He doesn't like it. And yes, guilt fills him, branching out from his center into every part of him, heavy and cold. But just what the hell is he supposed to do about it?

15.

MAIDA

March 12, 2106
The Presidio, San Francisco

Roan, Lorel, and Bertrand were hanging out in the common room when I got back to the staff house after working late at the lab. Needing a break from the time capsule batch, I had turned my attention to that jewelry I'd laid out before the Assessor Prime's visit and was so caught up I didn't realize the time until my stomach growled at me to put something in it. When I walked in, it looked like they were trying to watch a streaming story on the main monitor, but it kept getting interrupted by clips of Roan being silly – making faces in a bathroom mirror, describing the minute details of random items in his office, doing a silly dance somewhere on campus.

"Cut it out." Lorel smacked Roan with a pillow.

"It was cute at first, but now it's bothersome," Bertrand said.

"What's going on?" I asked, though I wasn't sure I wanted to know.

"I'm demonstrating the latest feat of my genius," Roan said as he held up a compact, square-shaped device. It was a simple-looking thing, a couple of small dials and a large red button. "It's called a signal transducer," he explained.

"And it is getting tiresome," Lorel said. "Or maybe that's just the user."

Roan ignored her barb. "It blocks the output of all screens and monitors within a fifty-foot radius and replaces it with what's streaming from the device it's paired with. In this case, my node."

"That's cool," I said. "But why?"

Roan shrugged. "This is an example of what's known as 'security apparatus tech –'"

"Spy gizmos," Lorel translated helpfully into regular person terms.

Roan didn't miss a beat. "The device was created for use by American and British intelligence agencies back in the 2040s, right before the dissolution of the United States began. This specimen was recovered at a former military base. I don't know if it ever was actually deployed in the field. I'm happy to have met the challenge of getting it to work again."

"And using it to annoy your friends is such a useful, productive application." Bertrand really cranked up the snide on that one. I liked him. I liked all of them, actually.

It was then that I noticed there were remnants of supper on the table – some grains, some greens, some roasted fennel and protein cake along with a plate of lavash.

"Oh my god, I'm starving." I dashed over to the table and grabbed a plate and a piece of lavash and started fixing myself a wrap.

"You were out late last night," Lorel said. "What were you up to? Hot date?"

I laughed. "I don't date."

"Oh. Good to know."

"You were out clubbing!" Roan said enthusiastically.

"It's not the twentieth century anymore," Bertrand said.

The three of them looked at me expectantly, awaiting an answer. They were my only friends at this point, so of course they were curious when I didn't come home until after they'd all gone to bed. If I wasn't hanging with them, what was I doing? Plus they knew I didn't know anybody in town.

I decided to share. "Have you ever heard of Linking circles?"

"I have!" Bertrand exclaimed. "It's when a group of psions are telepathically linked together in a group mind. Right?"

"It's not exactly a group mind," I explained. All their eyes widened, bright with interest. I told them all about my experience. Aviva had asked me not to share what I gleaned from the Assessor Prime, but she said nothing about keeping the Linking a secret. I didn't mention that it was Aviva who brought me to it and led the proceedings – let them think I was plugged into the mysterious psion network. Which I guess I was.

"That sounds so cool," Lorel said. "I want to go to one."

"I'll invite you as my guest," I said. Lorel beamed, and that made me happy.

"We've been waiting for you," Roan said. He held his face all serious to go with the ominous tone, then busted out laughing. "The conversion of those music files is complete. We wanted you to be here for the debut. I guess it isn't technically a debut since this music is a hundred years old and probably played at that party in those pictures – you know what I mean."

A little music sounded like a good distraction. Roan got his tablet at the ready and looked at me expectantly.

"Let's go," I said. "Play the music, maestro."

He tapped his tablet and skittering beats crinkled out of the sound system. In short order, heavier percussion sounds took over, and a thick bass line.

"What are we listening to, exactly?" Bertrand asked.

"This would be 'Awaken Beat Collective Sunrise Party, BRC 2006 by DJ Aspect," Roan informed us.

"I don't know what any of that means." Bertrand shook his head.

"Enlighten him," Lorel urged, nudging my arm.

I pulled my tablet from the satchel still slung across me and pulled up the photos I logged from the time capsule. I swiped to the picture of the bare-chested man with headphones standing behind what I now understood was sound mixing equipment. "Pretty sure this is DJ Aspect." I hand the tablet over.

Within a second of glancing at the photo, Bertrand commented, "Oh, he's cute." He continued swiping through the pictures, Roan and Lorel peeking over his shoulders.

"Nathan is in these pictures, right?" Lorel asked.

I nodded, took the tablet back. I swiped to a sweet shot of Nathan and DJ Aspect together, both of them looking deliriously happy in the sun, a flat desert landscape behind them, black hills in the distance. "Him." I tapped his face.

"You've seen him in your visions?" asked Bertrand.

"I both see him and see through his perspective. He and DJ Aspect were a couple. 'Awaken Beat Collective' was a group that DJ Aspect belonged to. They put on parties and events, from what I can gather. The 'BRC' referenced in the title of this music stands for 'Black Rock City,' which was the name of the temporary city erected during an annual festival called Burning Man. So named because the event took place in the Black Rock Desert of what was then Nevada."

"So the site of this event was in the Arivada Autonomous Region?" Bertrand was incredulous at this information. "I bet the fundamentalists love that."

"I doubt they even know," Lorel said. "They don't care about history or culture. They've made that clear."

"This style of music was called Techno," Roan said, seemingly eager to change the subject. "Or maybe it's Trance. I'm unclear on the difference. But both were popular among the hedonists of the era, and it seems, at this event."

"His actual name wasn't 'DJ Aspect,' was it?" Bertrand asked.

"He was called Remy," I answered. "Short for Jeremy."

Lorel had checked out of the conversation and was moving in time to the music with her eyes closed. "It is a little monotonous," she said without opening them, "but I kind of like it – ooh…"

The music shifted suddenly, the pounding rhythms dropping off as a sound I could only describe as twinkling took over, along with a female sounding voice vocalizing without words. There was a yearning in the voice, in the melody, that touched me. Also, it was familiar, and I realized I caught some of this exact music in one of my psychometric flashes to Nathan's time. Then a rising, tense chord sounded and buzzed in our bones, then the beats crashed again.

"I think this music was intended to foster a sense of euphoria," Roan said. "It was probably complemented by psychoactive substances."

"Did you glean that from your cultural inquiry of the past?" Bertrand asked. I wasn't looking at him, but I could hear his smirk.

"It is my specialty." Roan gave us a little bow. "I know it's yours, too, but I go a little deeper than names and dates."

"Fighting words!" Bertrand exclaimed.

Are they flirting? I think they might be flirting.

Just then, one of the other staff house inhabitants, a woman I didn't know all that well named Marta, rushed in. "Put on the news bulletin now!" she exclaimed as she frantically waved her hands at the monitor.

Roan stopped the music and activated the monitor.

The footage was of a scene in chaos: the smoking wreckage of a derailment, survivors being treated by emergency personnel, a few body bags. It was the Northshore High Speed Rail, the bullet train that connected Vancouver and San Francisco. From what was in the shot, I couldn't tell where they were, but the crawl at the bottom of the screen indicated this happened outside Portland.

"A radical group calling itself PsiSupreme is claiming responsibility for the attack," the newscaster said. "This radical movement advocates for so-called 'psion supremacy' and holds as its mission the promotion of psion dominance over society and culture…"

The report droned on. The tear-streaked faces of witnesses filled the screen as they were interviewed in turn. But I had stopped hearing anything, and the room, my friends, the house – all of it was suddenly far away. Something had tilted in the world. With a sinking feeling, I realized this was the opening the Assessor Prime needed for his plans. His words echoed in my mind: we can round them up in the name of regional security. Had he been waiting for this? Had he… had he planned this?

I didn't trust him, and I didn't trust this event nor the account of it. We all continued staring at the screen as the reporter rambled on about "unprecedented violence" and "disregard for human life" and a "return to the barbarism of the late Precursor era."

Lorel grabbed my hand and gave it a squeeze. I could see fear in her eyes, and I knew she must have seen it in mine. I was numb. Everything good in my life – my personal fulfilment in my new posting, making new friends, the untangling of the personal mystery of the teacup – it all faded into the background. This news we were watching pointed at something dark and unnamed, some shapeless shadow rising to swallow us all.

16.

MAIDA

March 13, 2106
Angel Island, San Francisco Bay

"He is faking this," declared Del. "What the Precursors called a 'false flag operation.' PsiSupreme is just a name Linstrom and the media are throwing around. There is nothing behind this but manufactured fear. It's despicable."

"Surely people will see through this sham?" I said. We were back on Angel Island, back in the circle in that meeting room.

"Sweet child," Kemp said. "Of course they won't. Even here, in the Sierra Northshore Regional Alliance, where the good work of the psion community is most well-known, there are those who don't trust us. A minority, to be sure, but they fear just this very thing the media is feeding them. This attack, and the narrative being spun around it, is intended to encourage those fears. That mentality is even more prevalent in other regions, and some, like Arivada, have zero tolerance for psions within their borders."

"There are already calls to create a public registry," Aviva said. "The Circle of the Eye has received a request for a full log and the records of all its students, going back to its founding."

"It's not like the existence of psions has been a secret," Del said. "They're acting like we just appeared and began taking over all of a sudden. This is just rabble rousing. Creating the illusion there's something to fear. Utter bullshit."

"All it takes to reshape the world, to turn people against each other, is a well-devised lie." Kemp sat back in his seat, arms crossed, his face a scowling mask of barely contained fury and frustration. "History has demonstrated that time and time again. We like to think that in this post-Bloom world, humans have evolved past this. But maybe that's been nothing but a comforting delusion all this time."

"I don't believe that." The others all looked at me after I blurted this out, and I didn't really have a back-up statement or evidence to lay out to support my case. But it was true. I didn't believe that the progress human society had made since the Bloom was a delusion. Maybe our evolution wasn't complete; maybe we were still on a journey to greater enlightenment, or whatever; maybe the journey only ends with extinction. But by and large, our society had moved beyond the era of extractive capital and mindless consumption and factional hatreds. But fear of the unknown was hardwired into us, and maybe it always would be. It was instinctual, after all – self-preservation. But where was the line between rational self-preservation and paranoid aggression?

"I'm with Maida," Aviva said with a reassuring look my way. "I don't think the notion that the world, that people, have evolved is delusional. But there are always snakes in the garden."

"Are they part of a healthy ecosystem?" Del snarked. "Or an invasive species? Maybe we should lop their heads off."

"That's exactly the sort of rabble being roused against us," Aviva noted.

"But we're not actually attacking anyone!" Del exclaimed.

"And we need to prove that," Aviva countered. "Not just declare it."

"How do we prove a negative?" Del's tone is barbed, and they're clearly directing their frustration over what was happening at the wrong people. But I can't blame them, really.

"We don't," Aviva replied calmly. "But somebody did attack, and blamed it on our community. No doubt there will be more. We have to pull the veil back on that."

"Well, we better do it before they round us up in those pens that Maida saw." Del shot me a look like they thought I was somehow responsible for the Assessor Prime's plans, as opposed to merely reporting what I saw. It was the first time this meeting that anybody referenced what I picked up from Julian Linstrom's watch. Operation Golden Days. But it was the monster in the room, it was the storm gathering over our heads that nobody had directly acknowledged yet.

"The only calls for such actions have come from Linstrom's political allies," Kemp said, bringing the conversation back to the immediate situation. "The so-called Freedom Faction. They were ready with statements as soon as the attack was reported. This was clearly all coordinated."

Del scoffed. "Has there been another word more co-opted than 'freedom'? Freedom to be dicks. Freedom to dismiss the humanity of others. Freedom to force constraints and limit lives and codify bigotry. That's what they mean by 'freedom.' Fucking assholes."

Or maybe it was freedom from shame. Maybe people like the Freedom Faction knew how they were mistreating people, how they have mistreated people, how they want to mistreat people. And rather than face up to themselves and their actions, they shifted the blame onto their targets. Their victims. The lowly ones that bore the marks of their cruelty. Maybe they knew, deep down, that they were wrong, but they didn't want to be wrong because being wrong is shameful and weak. Maybe it was that feeling that they actually wanted freedom from, but they made it about something outside themselves and imagined their own oppression. There's an old saying my dad used to like to pull out: "We don't see the world as it is, we see the world as we are." Maybe they so easily believed that others wanted to dominate and suppress them because what they want is to dominate those they've decided are their enemies, and they can't imagine anybody not wanting the same.

"Still, there are those who will see reason," Aviva said, as if Del hadn't just gone on a rant. Her voice was sonorous and reassuring. "We mustn't lose faith in them."

"Faith won't protect us from whatever is coming," Kemp said. "We need action."

"Faith may accomplish more than you realize." Aviva's calm in the face of what was happening, in the face of Del's and Kemp's agitation, was impressive. "But point taken. And since you're so keen on action, I have a task for you, should you choose to undertake it."

Kemp arched an eyebrow. "Go on."

"We need to know Linstrom's next moves. Indicate you're sympathetic to his ideas. That you oppose the actions of this alleged supremacy group. Make him believe you believe it, that this attack has swayed you. Try to get close. Get included in the meetings or listen in somehow. Doesn't matter to me. But we need to know."

Kemp's expression grew somber and he nodded, accepting the assignment.

"I'll keep trying too," Del said. "Maybe some of his close associates aren't as psychically defended as Linstrom himself."

It was true that Del's remote viewing ability could be useful here. Did they hear what was being said in the room or only see what was happening? I'd always been curious about that, but judging from their mood, now was clearly not the time to ask.

Aviva continued, "In the meantime, keep performing your duties at the top of your abilities. Be proud of who you are."

With that, she asked Del to call in the others gathered in the lobby. Aviva had put a call out for an emergency Linking circle, thinking that people may be craving community at this time. She said that in times of challenge, our community holding fast to our ideals and traditions was paramount, and the Linking circle was one such tradition. The mood was uneasy as everybody came in – not surprising, really, considering the blame for a terrorist attack was being laid at the feet of our community. There weren't as many here as last night, only eight of us total. She settled everyone down with the opening breathing exercise and meditation, but the actual Linking was a loop of anxiety. It was somehow reassuring to know that none of us were alone in our feelings, in our fear of what might come down the pike, of what would become of all of this. When it ended, there was a feeling of solidarity, but no reassurance or calm, not at all like the Linking the previous night. Funny, how much can change in a day.

She cast one of her beatific smiles around the circle. And with that, we all understood that the meeting was adjourned.

Aviva caught up with me as we put our chairs away. "Lorel mentioned you're having some intense experiences."

Everyone was telling Aviva my business – first Roan, now Lorel. I knew they were looking out for me, but it was a little off-putting. At the same time, it was a relief to have people know what was going on with me. To have support, even if I didn't directly ask for it myself. Luckily, I was emotionally mature enough to receive that support when offered. Ha ha.

"Can't you just read it in my mind?"

"I could, but I don't want to. I never go into someone's mind without prior consent unless it's an emergency or defensive measure. If someone is troubled, I'd rather they tell me about it with their words. So, tell me."

I told her about the visions that started with my contact with the cup, told her what I had gleaned of Li Nuan and Nathan's lives. Told her about the psychometric spasms. "I'd just like to not be ambushed by visions of fire and destruction at random. You're a telepath – can you help me?"

"The most I could do is help calm your mind and close off the visions. But I could only do that if I was with you during an episode, and I'm pretty sure neither of us wants me to be with you around the clock every day."

I laughed. "Not that I don't like you or anything…"

She laughed too. "I do know another telepath that may be able to help you in a… deeper way. Are you free tomorrow night?"

I nodded.

"I'd like to bring you to a conclave."

"What's that?"

"Meet me at the Marina at sunset tomorrow," she said. "And you'll find out. A boat called Epifania. Bring the teacup."

* * *

When I got back to the house, loud, rough music was blaring in the common room, and several folks sat around making placards.

"What are you listening to?" I asked Roan.

"It's a style of music called 'Heavy Metal,'" he explained. "Its adherents were called 'metalheads.' I unlocked a big trove of old music today, on some very well-preserved servers. We're kind of cycling through different genres."

"This music makes me want to shake my head like this," Lorel said and demonstrated a thrashing sort of motion, flinging her long hair back and forth and back and forth.

"Change it!" Bertrand bellowed from across the room. "I've had enough of this stuff!"

Roan acceded to the request and tapped his tablet. The music changed to something much softer and more melodic.

"Is this that Taylor person?" Lorel asked. "I like her too, even if I don't get all the references."

"Who's this Taylor person?"

"Her name was Taylor Swift," Roan explained. "She was a massively famous pop singer who was active from the early two thousands right up to the beginning of the Collapse. Her debut album – that's what they called collections of songs – was released a hundred years ago. She had a long, rather illustrious, career as far as I can tell. Right up until precursor society fell apart.

"It's her picture in the dictionary when you look up 'popstar,'" Lorel informed us.

"I'll take your word for it," I replied. This Taylor person's voice was pleasant enough. Much less processed than that other singer we listened to, and the melody carried a distinct sweetness and comfort. "I think I like pop music."

"As long as it's not that metal stuff," Bertrand said as he walked over to us. "What do you think?" He held up a placard that read PSIONS ARE PEOPLE, the bottom of which was taken up by a sketch of two brains with wavy lines connecting them.

"What's all this?" Looking around, I saw that everyone was making signs along those lines, declaring the humanity of psions. FREEDOM FACTION = FASCISM read a couple of the other ones.

"Those Freedom Faction lunatics are staging a demonstration at the Sub-Regional Administration Headquarters in a few days," Lorel explained. "We're counter-protesting. You should come."

"I think Freedom Faction has a point," said a man I didn't know.

He was sitting on the couch, having a drink, and he was notably not participating in the sign making.

"Daveed, come on," his friend said. The friend was making a sign – somebody from the house that I don't know really well. Troy, I think?

"No, really," Daveed said forcefully. "I mean, what's to stop these psion supremacists from attacking again?"

Something snapped.

"There is no psion supremacy movement," I said, my face flushing. As much as I hated confrontation, I hated disinformation even more. In school and at the Academy, we studied ways in which disinformation was used by political movements in the Precursor era, and while it was no doubt effective and brilliant in its way, the thought of swamping people's minds with lies in order to manifest an agenda turned my stomach and got my blood boiling. Making a world that is just and where all are free didn't require lies. Lies were only needed to suppress and control, and this psion supremacy nonsense was such a lie, and Linstrom wanted to leverage it to take away the autonomy of people like me, and I could not let that stand. So I forced my words out through my rising discomfort, which I was afraid showed in my burning cheeks, in my sweaty palms and pounding heart.

"Oh, I suppose you're going to say this is all made up?" Daveed's tone was mocking, and it made me a little crazy.

He wouldn't stop. "I heard they have secret meetings that normal people aren't part of. What do they do? What do they talk about? And if they didn't attack the train, who did it, then? And why?"

I couldn't say what I knew – what I'd seen. What Aviva and the others suspect of the Assessor Prime. Not yet, not until we have solid evidence. "Who benefits from spreading this story? Ask yourself that question."

"You sound conspiracy addled," Daveed sneered. What an utter tool. "Fucking psions were always suspect if you ask me. Nobody should be able to do that shit."

"You're just jealous," Lorel said. She cast me a sympathetic glance.

"Are you one of them?"

"She isn't, but I am." This conversation was pressing my buttons, and I no longer had patience for it. The words tumbled out before I even realized what I was saying.

Daveed looked at me like I had sprouted another head.

His bewilderment was so annoying that I couldn't fight the urge to fuck with him. "So shut your face, or I'm going to use my telepathy and fry your pathetic little excuse for a brain." I knew taunting him was not really the best move, but I couldn't help myself. And of course, I was no telepath, but he didn't know that. To drive the point home, I put a couple of fingers to my temple and reached my other hand out towards his face. It was a move I'd seen in superhero movies from the last century. Lorel guffawed.

He leapt off the couch. "I think I should go."

"That would be a good idea." It was a struggle keeping the tremble out of my voice. If I had telekinesis, he'd have been defenestrated already. If there were such a thing as pyrokinesis, he'd be ablaze.

"I'll walk you out," Troy said, standing up. He shot me a look and shook his head, but he didn't hide the half-smile on his face.

"I'm not sure that was the best move to calm frayed nerves," Roan said once Daveed was gone.

"Other people's frayed nerves are not my responsibility." I wasn't sure where this bravado was coming from, but it felt good, and I was going to ride it for as long as it went. "I can't help it if people are fucking stupid."

"Well there are those that seem intent on making their stupidity your problem."

Roan was right, of course. And to be totally honest, I knew damn well it wasn't annoyance or impatience that made me talk to Daveed that way. It was fear. Not his, but my own.

17.

MAIDA

March 14, 2106
East Shore Marina, San Francisco

The ship called Epifania was docked at the end of the pier Aviva directed me to. It was smaller than I'd expected – really more of a boat than a proper ship. It was elegant in its lines, a classic looking seafaring vessel from a world gone by. There were clearly newer parts built upon the original frame, and the hull looked newly re-skinned with carbon fiber. The stern of the ship and the portholes there looked antique and original. The name of the ship and "San Francisco" were spelled out in brass letters. It reminded me of an old storybook my father read to me when I was little. About pirates.

Aviva was sitting on the deck along with a couple of others, including Del. She waved as I climbed on board, then introduced me to her companions. Del and I greeted each other with nods. "Did you bring the cup?"

"I have it." I patted the lump it made in my satchel.

"Excellent," she said. She threw a warm glance at someone behind me. I turned to see a short, white-bearded man coming up from the ship's lower level.

"Felix," he said, offering his hand.

"Felix is the captain of this fine vessel," Aviva said.

"Should I call you Captain Felix?"

He laughed. "Felix is fine. I don't stand on formalities." He looked around, gave a signal to a young woman named Blythe, who hopped off Epifania and began untying the boat's lines from its moorings on the pier.

"So, what exactly is a conclave?" I asked, taking a seat beside Aviva.

"You didn't tell her what she's in for?" Del asked, sounding amused.

"I find surprise enriches the experience," Aviva answered, clearly attempting to foster an air of mystery around the proceedings. I got the feeling Aviva liked keeping secrets because she liked revealing them.

I looked around; around the top deck sat Aviva, Del, Blythe, Felix, a young man named Ruben, and me. "Is this everyone? 'Conclave' makes it sound like it would be a bigger thing."

"We're meeting the others."

"Is Kemp coming?"

"He's attending to our business with Assessor Prime Linstrom."

Del gives a sly side-eye to Ruben, who was looking out at other boats on the water, and I understood. He wasn't in on it. Whatever it was.

Epifania's sails were down, and we motored out of the Marina and into the Bay. The air smelled faintly of smoke – again – and the late afternoon sky was overcast – again – gray-white from the combination of fog and distant wildfire. It was dull and kind of depressing like this. I realized we'd be out on the water during sunset and lamented not being able to see it because of the clouds and the haze. But then, this wasn't an outing for sightseeing, was it?

I noticed that we were heading for the Golden Gate Bridge. "We're going out on the ocean?"

"We sure are," Del said. "Heading up the coast to Point Reyes."

My pulse quickened. I'd been on boats before. There was that one time, on this very Bay, on that childhood trip. I'd also been on plenty of riverboats due to Dad's work, and we spent some time visiting lakes as well. But I'd never been on the ocean before.

A couple of seagulls glided beside us, then peeled off just as we hit the nearest edge of the bridge. Overhead, the lightrail that crossed the span sang past us. The clear, pinging tone it left in its wake faded northward with the train. The breeze had a bite to it, and I pulled my hood up against the chill – the air was so different out on the water than it was back on shore. Everyone seemed to be in a contemplative space as we crossed the entry into the bay then tacked starboard – which I believed meant right. Then we were out on the open sea.

Nobody aboard seemed to be in the mood for talking. I looked around at my companions, and they all sat staring out at the water towards the gray line of the horizon or else toward the shore. Just what was this 'conclave' thing? Whatever it was, it seemed to be a solemn sort of affair.

"I could use some water," I said to Aviva. "Is there any...?"

"Down below. Cooler in the galley."

I stood shakily, caught my balance, lost my balance again. I made my way into the cockpit where Felix and Blythe were stationed.

"Water?"

"With me," Felix said, beckoning me to follow. He let Blythe take over the steering of the ship. He rubbed a wooden fixture by the wheel as he stepped away - a compass. His gray eyes twinkled in his weathered face as he met my gaze. He led me down the stairs to the cabin below deck. I was unsteady on my feet and felt like I was learning to walk again – or really drunk.

"You'll get your sea legs soon enough," he said. "It'll be easier once we anchor."

I nodded; not sure I believed him.

"Aviva tells me you can read the psychic history of objects," Felix said.

"That's right. I call it scanning." We had paused at the bottom of the steps – the railing of the short staircase was finely carved, polished wood of a ruddy hue. It was surprisingly nice, like the grand staircase of a grand home, only miniature.

"Ever scanned a boat before?"

I shook my head.

"Would you mind scanning this ol' gal?" Felix asked.

"Not at all."

"We have some time before we arrive." He handed me a bottle of water.

I took a couple of sips and looked around. The stairs weren't the only part that was wood; the floors, the interior walls, built-in bookshelves, even – all made of wood. It smelled like wood down here in the cabin, and it smelled old. We stood in what looked like a condensed living room. Through one door, I saw a bunk and a tiny bathroom on the other side of it. We were right by a kitchen – the galley, I think they're called on boats – complete with an eating nook comprised of a built-in bench and small table. It was all so cozy, and it looked like a comfortable home.

"Do you live here?" I asked.

"I do. I dock at the Marina when I'm down this way. I'm up at Vancouver Island a lot."

"Do you have a house on land, too, or just this?"

"Just my sweet and sturdy Epifania. I don't much like living on land. I grew up on an arkship."

The arkships were self-sustaining communities, small cities built on huge floating platforms deployed throughout the world's oceans in the years leading up to the Collapse. A couple of them were still operational and upgraded with more current technology. I'd never been aboard one, but I saw one from afar once.

"I've never met anybody who's lived on one."

"People who figure out a place there stay, and others, like me, head on out and see what's going on in the rest of the world. Not as many of us head out as stay put."

"Why do you want me to do the reading down here?"

"This is the heart of her. What better place?"

This man was clearly bonded to this vessel. I found it endearing.

I looked around the small living room we stood in – there was a couch and an easy chair beside the built-in bookshelf, a couple of end tables, and a cabinet which looked like it housed a radio, over which hung a monitor. I decided that sitting on the floor in the center of the space made the most sense. "Can we roll up that rug? I'd like to be in direct contact with the floorboards."

He got up and rolled up the thin rug, put it aside, and sat down on the edge of the chair, looking eager. I removed my satchel that contained the cup – I didn't want another psychically loaded object on me while I was scanning a different one. I got down cross-legged on the floor, took a breath, and closed my eyes. The boat swayed gently. I'd never scanned anything this large before, but my ability wasn't like telekinesis, where the size of the thing would make a difference in how I handled it. I placed my palms flat on the floor and asked the past to open to me.

1979, Taiwan. The year and place this boat was built by the Chao Brothers, though it was designed by somebody named John Perry. It didn't have a name yet. Shipped across the Pacific on a much larger transport ship. Received by her first owner, a music producer in Los Angeles named Al Rossi, who dubbed her the Interlude. He took her out around Catalina Island a lot, but not much else. In 1989, Al sold her to John and Lilian Kirk of Long Beach, who renamed her Copperfield. They were attorneys. There were many trips as far south as Santa Barbara and as far north as Salt Spring Island. The next owners were another couple, Mark Firestone and Bruce Wang – an architect and a chef, respectively – who acquired her in 2001 and brought her up to this area, to a place that existed before the Collapse, called Sausalito. When Bruce died, Mark sold her in 2017 to another couple: Davis and Amber Roth of San Francisco, collectively known as DnA to all their friends. They rechristened her Epifania and installed the brass lettering on her stern. They undertook many journeys up and down the west coast of North America, and also to the Gulf of Mexico. They frequently hosted friends on board, much more than the previous owners had. Epifania was in their possession until 2037. Then things got fuzzy. Somebody named Elias took care of her until the early 2040s. Then she was in drydock and remained there through the years of the Collapse. Work had probably been intended, but the chaos the world descended into meant that work never happened, and she sat forgotten for years. Nothing came through for that period of time – just a dull fog in the psifield, in my mind. Shortly after the Bloom, young Felix salvaged her, saving as much as he could of the original structure and replacing the rest.

The information came to me in a steady stream, during which I whispered bits of it to myself. When I came out of the trance, Felix was watching me intently. I reported what I'd gleaned. "The years of the Collapse are usually fuzzy," I told him when I was done. "No matter what the object is."

"Is there some sort of cosmic explanation for why that is?"

"The prevailing theory is that the world was in such a state of psychic flux then, when it was unclear which way the shape of reality would go, that the psychic window we look through is fogged up in that time. It's an imperfect metaphor, but we can only talk about it metaphorically. The metaphysics of it all are a little beyond me, to be honest. It makes intuitive sense, though."

"So I'm the sixth owner?" Felix counted on his fingers just to be sure.

"Elias feels like he was more of a temporary caretaker than an owner, per se. But he's in the psychic record."

Blythe's voice crackled through on a radio. *"We've arrived."*

I slung my satchel back on, then we headed up. Other boats had also arrived – I counted six, including Epifania. It appeared that each boat had deployed a floating platform, and they'd all been linked together to form a ring that floated in the loose circle formation the boats had anchored in. The outer edge of the platform was lined with thick, tubular foam.

"What is all this?" I asked Aviva.

"Preparations for the conclave."

Folks from the other boats began climbing down the ladders on their respective vessels... *Wait...* "We're not getting down on that platform are we?"

"We are," Del said. They smirked at my astonishment. "Don't worry about not having your sea legs; we'll be lying down the whole time."

The daylight was fading, and all the boats had put lights on – strings of amber lights all around their decks, some spiraling up their masts, even, like twinkling constellations.

"Let's go," Aviva said. "We're ready."

"Don't we need lifejackets or anything?" Nobody I could see gathering on the floating platform was wearing one.

"Trust is part of the process," Aviva said. "After you."

With trepidation, I climbed down the ladder on the side of the boat and stepped onto the platform which bobbed under my feet. "Isn't Felix coming down?" I asked when I saw that he was staying aboard Epifania, though Blythe had come down with us.

"He's nul-psi," she said. "They're not part of this."

The platforms were made of a translucent material – not fully transparent, but not fully opaque, either. Everyone laid down on their backs and arranged themselves in a circle with their heads at the center.

"She's coming," Aviva said.

"Who's coming?" I asked, more and more bewildered with each passing moment.

"Grandmother."

Aviva's response didn't clarify my confusion even a little bit, but she didn't need to say anything more, because I felt her. A massive presence in the psifield made itself known in my sensing, and then I saw her. I saw Grandmother. Through the translucence of the platform, an enormous shadow moved below us. My heart pounded at the enormity of the clearly alive being that dwarfed us all.

"Get yourself down," Aviva urged, "And take out the cup."

As I sat, the whale surfaced, as gently as such a large creature can, and emitted a plume of spray from her blowhole. I made eye contact with her for a second before she went under again. She saw me – she definitely saw me. I was pretty sure she was a blue whale, the largest creature on Earth. Holy shit, humans are puny things.

"Place the cup over your heart," Aviva instructed, and I did as she said, resting the cup on my chest as I lay down. I was laying between Del and Aviva and took each of their hands. Aviva gave a reassuring squeeze as I closed my eyes.

I got it: the conclave was a Linking Circle, only the telepath linking us this time was this whale. Like I did the other times on Angel Island, I dropped into theta state. There was the familiar call to *open open open,* only it wasn't words in my mind, exactly. It was a feeling, and a presence. An enormous eye peered into me from beneath the sea, and I sensed the pulse of a heart that was bigger than my whole body. This heart, this life thrummed in the psifield, thrummed with connection – itself to our minds, our minds to our hearts, our minds and hearts to the sea. In my inner Sight, the heart beat with warm, ruddy light. I felt the flow of blood through an enormous body, weightless in the embrace of the ocean. A flush of warmth accompanied familiar tingles at my third eye and crown chakras, then my body dissolved – just faded away. Or at least I wasn't aware of it anymore.

Grandmother floated below us, and through the telepathic connection, I could tell she held herself vertical in the way some whales oriented themselves to sleep. And I guessed it was a kind of sleep she slipped into now, that all of us did. She floated at the center of the circle the rest of us had made of our bodies, of our minds.

A golden thread wove between us, mind to mind, heart to heart, soul to soul. I was aware of my breath, my pulse, but I was equally aware of the pulse and the hearts of the others in the circle. I was my own self, but also a part of this group. We were each of us individuals, but also we were one. We were not only part of this circle, but part of the sea, and the land, and the air. Every creature, every person, was part of one thing, and that thing was the world. In my mind, we were all in the water with Grandmother, floating as she floated, as her kind floated when they dreamed.

And then the water wasn't water anymore, but a nameless space, full of ribbons of stars, full of whirling galaxies, full of worlds we didn't know. Each of us there was a world unto ourselves, even as together we made one world. And the merging of worlds was a beautiful thing, a communion. In the old-world religions, angels served as intermediaries between divine intelligence and humanity, and it struck me with a bolt of clarity that Grandmother, her kind, the mammals of the sea, served as angels for us: intermediaries between the earthly and the divine. These beings were intermediaries between ourselves and our Selves, and they always had been. And as ever, so many of us didn't bother to listen and learn. The Bloom opened a door for greater connection, and we were only now figuring it out.

In Grandmother's heart sang a grief as large as the ocean. A grief for her home waters, for the world that she had been born into, for the species and living places lost to the frenzy of domination that had consumed us, us humans, for so long. Grandmother was over a century old, a century that had witnessed the final spasms of a world that could no longer sustain itself. But her heart also held a hope – no, a faith – that healing could take place.

you are an open wound

Grandmother's voice, her psychic presence, rang through me with all the years of her existence and eons of existence beyond either of us. Her voice, her mind, her heart rang through me deep as the sea. Only, hers wasn't a "voice" exactly, and the message wasn't in human words, yet I knew what she meant.

your very Self is a portal through time

all time is now

you connect every now such is your gift

Fire and billowing ash, swirling lights and fireworks, a false euphoria masking guilt and fear: it all swirled through me

you seek liberation this is liberation

No, it's them in the past, I thought back.

tell them of the world you know, the world they make of their Now

A highlights reel of tragedies and turmoil swept through my mind: earthquake and fire and wars and disasters and plagues and eco-collapse. Nearly half the population gone. The world falling to chaos before order started to make a comeback, barely, and then the Bloom. Psions awakened, and the work of healing the world began. Our history, their future. *Be warned.*

I was connected to Grandmother, and I was connected to the others in this circle, but I was also connected to Li Nuan and to Nathan. We all, everyone in this circle, right at that moment, were connected to those two figures in the teacup's story. And the history we all knew was a thread woven into the energetic matrix of the cup. All time was now. This thread was a message, supercharged by our communion with this being that loomed below us, this mind and heart of the sea.

My voice now, transmitting through the cup, through time: *Seize freedom. Change the world.* I sent these words into the past, to Li Nuan and to Nathan. Did they receive them? Do they?

Grandmother woke, and we all woke with her. Swells of gratitude rippled from us to her. From her – was it love? It was a deeper love than I'd ever felt. It encompassed everything. Grandmother dove away. Was that a goodbye in her wake? And because there was still a wisp of a connection between us, Grandmother's knowledge of her coming days became our knowledge too: soon, she would be whalefall. She wanted us to know this. Her aged body was going to cease, and it would no longer be hers, for she was going to leave it to swim in another kind of sea. It was a transition she welcomed without fear.

The circle was open, the Linking closed, and everyone lay still as we all came back to ourselves. My eyes were wet with tears, and I clutched the teacup at my chest – my hands and the teacup itself were hot. I didn't remember releasing the hands I had held before we started. I didn't remember taking hold of the cup. But I could feel how it had transformed, or maybe I was tripping, but I got the feeling those visions of fire wouldn't bother me anymore unless I intentionally called them forth. There was a golden halo around the cup, like the shining thread that connected us during the Linking. Hallucination, or no? It didn't matter, did it?

I sat up slowly, still clutching the cup, and everyone was looking at me.

"They taught us how to Link, didn't they? The whales."

Aviva nodded. "Their telepaths to our telepaths. When the Bloom happened, human minds were not the only ones affected."

I took her words in. There were telepaths who could communicate with animals so why had it not dawned on me that the animals could communicate with them? With us? Was I really that anthropocentric? And why wasn't this knowledge of whales more widespread, at least among psions?

As if reading my mind – was she? – Aviva said, "We keep knowledge of communion with whales limited. To keep mass pilgrimages at bay." After a pause, "What about your people in the past? Do you think they got the transmission?"

A thread had been stitched into the fabric of the teacup's story. Did they catch it, in their time? Had they, have they? Shouldn't the world feel different?

A patch of clouds cleared overhead, and the stars that had been there all this time shone through.

18.

LI NUAN

April 12, 1906
Chinatown, San Francisco

In a house with bars over the windows, freedom doesn't feel so free. It's only a sliver of a comfort to know that the bars are intended to keep their would-be captors out, not to keep the girls in. Sometimes, when Li Nuan peers through a window, through the bars enclosing it, she sees Wu Jun glaring from across the street, or the other one – the one who now wears an eyepatch. Then she's glad for the bars. Strange, how they provide both protection and imprisonment. Those things aren't one and the same, are they?

Over the past two months, she has settled into a new daily routine. The girls rise at seven in the morning and begin their day with prayers. Then, after breakfast, housework. It's a strange thing, doing such work in the company of others, without the Boss's dreadful son lusting after her. Later in the day, they receive schooling – proper education! They learn sewing and other subjects, such as reading and arithmetic. Geography, too, which seems cruel to Li Nuan – why should they learn about places they will never be able to go to? After lessons, Li Nuan and a few others work in the kitchen to prepare dinner. While the housework and the cooking were part of her previous duties in her previous situation, making dinner for this household feels like much less of a burden than doing it for the Boss and his son. They all eat dinner together, another pleasing experience. At night, they pray some more – so much praying – then go to bed.

This is the new rhythm of her days. It doesn't feel more free than her life before – she still must submit to a schedule and tasks others set before her – but there are no beatings. There is no Little Emperor bothering her every day. There are no disgusting acts she must perform on disgusting men in the filthy cribs. Her days are still not her own, but she prefers living this way to what she had before. With the boss, she performed her work to avoid beatings. But here, she is contributing to a collective effort of keeping girls like her free from the brothels. Having that purpose is a saving grace.

The so-called "Oriental Room" is her least favorite part of the house. It is furnished Chinese style; everything from the furniture to the vases and statuettes are "authentic," a word used by Miss Cameron when bringing visitors by. It supposedly provides a taste of home-culture for the girls, so it is said. But Tye Leung – whom Miss Cameron, the headmistress of the house, calls Tiny – explains it is really for the benefit of would-be benefactors who liked seeing a bit of the exotic. It seems the Jesus women expected them to love this room and the things in it, and Li Nuan goes along out of politeness and a sense of obligation – if pretending to love that room is the price of no longer being Boss Fong's captive flower, then she will pay it.

But it's accepting their religion that is the true price. She has to submit to Bible lessons, and attending church, and learning to sing hymns. She hates that Boss Fong had been right about this. She doesn't particularly believe these Bible stories, but she knows how to pretend. A part of her wishes she could truly believe, but she just doesn't. She has seen the sorts of things this god of theirs allows to happen in the world. But she does owe what freedom she has to adherents of this religion, so it is only right that she should go along. She doesn't want to be cast back out. Nobody has ever said she would be or could be, but the threat lay beneath the show of kindness and compassion.

Li Nuan had only been at the Home for a few days when she witnessed her first attacks. At the front door, back door, and in one of the first-floor windows, fires had been set. They were put out quickly with no real damage done other than scorch marks on the bricks. On another night, bricks and stones had been hurled at the windows. One got between the bars and sent a web of cracks through the glass. One of the other girls, Mei Ling, explains that windows had been smashed before, and that is why the bars were installed. The Tongs, Mei Ling says, don't like that these white devil Jesus women were stealing their property.

The scorn of the Tongs was most heaped upon the leader of the women, the one in charge of the house, the one named Donaldina Cameron. They hoot and holler and whistle at her whenever she steps foot outside. They call her "whore" and "devil" in Cantonese, and she pretends not to understand, even though she does. Tye Leung says that Miss Cameron isn't fluent in Cantonese, but she knows some words. She knows those words.

Just like in her previous circumstance, Li Nuan cannot leave the house unaccompanied. But unlike Boss Fong's house, the precaution here is not to make sure that she won't run, but to assure she is not captured again. Wu Jun and Eyepatch are not the only Tong underlings who keep the threat of attack and kidnapping simmering; there are several men who hang about the corner across the street, a couple she recognizes from around Chinatown who work for other bosses. They are sure to be near when it's time to go to market.

Only Tye Leung has no fear. She is only a few years older than Li Nuan but carries herself with more confidence and seems older. Unlike the other girls, she had been born in San Francisco and was never captive in the brothels. Her father worked in a shoe store – but still, she was sold as a domestic servant. She had sought refuge at the Home to escape an arranged marriage to an older man.

The police would turn a blind eye – most of them – if one of the girls were snatched, but if something were to happen to Tye Leung, they would have to care. They would have to do something. So the girls are always accompanied to market and to church, sometimes by Tye Leung, sometimes by white women volunteers, whom the men of Chinatown would stare at, but didn't dare approach.

Visitors to the house arrive in a steady stream: missionaries from other cities, politicians, wealthy women from whom Miss Cameron would request financial contributions to continue the work of rescue. The girls are summoned to perform for these visits – sometimes woken up and pulled from bed, even – to recite Bible verses or sing hymns. It is a different way of earning their keep, a different sort of performance. It is also during these visits that Li Nuan comes to understand that the conversion of the girls to their religion is the main reason the home receives any support at all. Freeing girls from that wretched existence in the cribs isn't enough to justify the work. Freedom for its own sake means nothing to them. She intensely dislikes these women. If justice and freedom are their true concern, what does it matter if the girls believe in their Bible? Still, it's better here than where she came from.

February turns to March, then passes into April. The date Li Nuan received in her last vision, April 18th, draws closer, and with it, a rising sense of anticipation. What is going to happen? Can such devastation as she saw really take place? There is an earthquake and fire – these she knows to be coming soon. But the teacup had shown her other fires besides that one – places she had never seen before engulfed by inferno, looking like visions of Hell itself. And storms, and floods, and famine, and diseases, too.

She understands these are visions of the future, and they match some of what she is learning in Bible study. Revelation. But what is she supposed to do about any of that? What is she supposed to do about the end of days? Such an end might one day come, but she doesn't think that day is now. She doesn't really know where this conviction comes from. It seems to be in her bones. But this April date... that is something else. Should she warn everyone? Will they think she is mad and cast her back out onto the street, back to the Boss and Madam Bai?

She says nothing about any of it to anyone.

One day, in preparation for a visit from a group Miss Cameron hopes to secure a large donation from, the girls are rehearsing "Amazing Grace" around the piano in the room that serves as a chapel when the police come. They all know from the intensity, the fury, behind the pounding on the front door that this isn't some social call; this isn't someone like them seeking help.

"We must scatter," Tye Leung instructs. She exchanges knowing looks with Miss Cameron, who takes her time going to the door.

The girls have clearly been through this before and know just where to go. Many of them head down into the basement where they can hide in the shadowed corners, behind shelves and sacks of rice. A few of the girls are under the legal protection of the home, on record with the white authorities as being such, and they take to the bedrooms, sit on their beds with their Bibles.

Li Nuan isn't sure where to go and looks around in confusion and rising panic. Mei Ling grabs her hand and pulls her towards the back of the house. "Keep quiet," the girl hisses as they run out a back door with two others into the alley. They dash down a set of dark steps into a neighbor's storage room, where they hide among barrels of wine. The neighbor, a white man, gives them a stern nod before he closes and locks the door. Though this dark, cramped room serves as refuge in this moment, it feels more like a cage.

"Some of the police work for the Tongs," Mei Ling whispers. "They come to take girls back to the brothels. They come every few months. Sometimes they accuse one of the girls of stealing jewelry or money and have a report from her owner. They know it's a lie."

"How do we know this man won't give us up?" Li Nuan whispers back.

"He is one of the Jesus people," Mei Ling says. "His parents worked to free the Black slaves. We can trust him."

"Shhhh," one of the other girls admonishes them. "Keep quiet. Get under the cloth."

They are hidden behind a stack of barrels covered with burlap, crouched under the loose folds.

"Mornin', Jack," a man's voice says. "You seen any of them China girls come by?"

"Not a one," says another man. Li Nuan guesses this is Jack whose room they hide in now.

"Not that I don't believe a God-fearing Christian such as yourself, but you wouldn't mind if I had a look, would you?"

"Be my guest," Jack says. The jingle of his keys sound through the door, and Li Nuan gets the distinct impression Jack is making a show of finding the right key. Finally, the lock clicks and the door slides open. "Nothing but barrels."

"How's the wine business going?" the first man – obviously a police officer – asks. His steps echo as he goes down the stairs, and then he is in the room. Under the burlap, the girls grip each other's hands and hold their breath.

"Pretty good, pretty good," Jack says. "I think it's a good vintage this year. The Zinfandel, especially."

"Well, I will have to have some with the wife sometime."

A call comes from down the alley, from the direction of the Home, too far away to make out the words. The police officer's steps head back up the stairs, then outside. "Clear!" he calls. Then, "Thank you for your cooperation, Jack."

"God be with you," Jack says, closing the door back up.

They stay crouched under the cloth for several more minutes, barely breathing for fear the officer will suddenly come back, that his leaving is just a ruse to lure them out. Eventually, the door opens and Jack calls, "You can come out now."

The girls all climb out from behind the rack of barrels. They exit and head back to the house. Li Nuan takes the opportunity to use some of her new English. "Thank you."

"May the Lord protect you and bless you," Jack says. There is only kindness in his eyes. No pity.

Everyone gathers in the common room when they get back, and Tye Leung performs a headcount. "We all made it," she says when she's done.

"Have girls really been taken from here?" Li Nuan asks.

"A few," Mei Ling says. "Two from the house during raids, but a couple were grabbed on the street."

That members of the police force and some of the city's government officials allow the brothels to hold girls captive – using legal trickery and paperwork, if she understands correctly – infuriates Li Nuan. What kind of world is this? What kind of god do these women worship that allows this to happen? How is "faith" supposed to help them out of the horror they lived?

The day returns to normal surprisingly quickly. There is no more singing of "Amazing Grace," but some of the girls settle into quiet Bible study while others work on embroidering the kerchiefs that are sold to raise funds for the house.

Li Nuan is on kitchen duty when the headmistress, Donaldina Cameron herself, summons her to her office. Li Nuan follows Tye Leung up the stairs to the study on the third floor, a room to which few of the girls ever go. The walk there reminds her of being called to Boss Fong's parlor, to Madam Bai's office. "Am I in trouble?" she asks in Cantonese.

"No trouble, no trouble," Tye Leung answers in English. Then, back to Cantonese. "We need your help."

Help? What can she do to help?

Miss Cameron sits at a small desk in the cramped room when they arrive. Li Nuan had thought the headmistress's office would be a grander affair than this. She is Boss here, after all.

"How have you been finding life here?" she asks, with a glance at Tye Leung, who interprets.

"It is a good life," Li Nuan answers in Cantonese, also looking at the interpreter. There is an English word she has recently learned that sums up how she feels about the refuge she has received: "Grateful."

"That warms my heart," Miss Cameron says. "I am hoping that you can help us help others like you." She then speaks a lot of English, which Tye Leung dutifully translates.

As she understands it, Miss Cameron wants to carry out a raid of her own, and break free the girls of the Lotus Pearl. Tye Leung explains that they have carried out similar operations before.

"You know the building, you know the schedules," Miss Cameron says through Tye Leung. "And the girls there know you. You can convince them to come with us. Can you help us?"

Li Nuan remembers the fast-approaching date: April 18th. She flashes on the visions she received from that teacup in Boss Fong's parlor – the earthquake, the fires. "Before April 18th morning," she says with her limited English. "Best time. I help."

19.

NATHAN

August 31, 2006
Black Rock City, Nevada

"Welcome to the yesterday of tomorrow, today." Delilah opens the flap of the Time Machine and grins at her own silly pun, to the consternation of the very stoned hippie boy who is their latest passenger. The young man's hair is braided, and his lean torso is bare and coated in a fine layer of the alkali dust that makes everyone look beautiful in the late afternoon light. He wears a diaphanous piece of fabric tied around his waist, but it's sheer, so everything shows through – he's basically naked with a little sparkle over his dick. He smells like patchouli and his own natural musk.

Despite himself, Nathan is a little enamored, even though he doesn't typically like his men this crusty. But it's Thursday of Burning Man, and since he got in on an early arrival pass to set up their official theme camp, he's already been in the desert for six days and is feeling a little punchy at this point.

The hippie dude lets out a chuckle. "Because today is tomorrow's yesterday. Like tomorrow, when we talk about yesterday, we'll mean today... I get it."

After their passenger shares this tremendous revelation, Nathan looks him in the eye. Yup: dilated. Very, very dilated. "Be here now," Nathan says sagely. He wishes he had a beard to stroke.

"Another satisfied customer," Delilah says as she and Nathan watch the lad shuffle away.

"It's been a big hit," Nathan says. The Time Machine has indeed been a popular attraction, drawing in curious passersby all week. Danny had the bright idea of setting up a misting station at the exit, so as folks complete their experience, they get a cool fan-generated breeze along with a light spray of water infused with lavender essential oil. Just the right touch.

Delilah flips the OPEN sign to NOPE. The sky blazes towards sunset, and the crew of the camp has planned a group dinner before setting out on the Fish for the night's adventures – the start of them, anyway. "I'm gonna go get pretty," she says and scampers off to her tent.

One of their campmates brought an Italian ice machine, and Nathan scoops up a tumbler of crushed ice, then fixes himself a mint julep at the bar, which is really just a collection of liquors in a milk crate back in a shady section of the Quonset hut. Delilah had prepared a batch of simple syrup as well as fresh mint, which they keep in one of the coolers. Having such a beverage in the heat of the day in the middle of nowhere really is a treat. Simple creature comforts are luxuries out here.

But then, even creature comforts they take for granted back home are luxuries to somebody, somewhere, aren't they? Nathan sips the cold, minty, bourbon sweetness of his drink and tries to push thoughts of reality away, but he can't help it. The last conversation he'd had with Kendal, the day Sally got fired, sticks in his craw, and he can't help worrying it over and over in his mind. Plus, he'd had to enter his and Remy's camp expenses into the spreadsheet the group used to track costs – fabric and sound cables for the Fish, supplementary lighting for the camp – and he was astonished at the many thousands of dollars they'd spent collectively. And that figure didn't even include people's personal fuel, gear, costuming, and whatever else they brought out here. The current budget isn't really much more than what they've spent in the past, but somehow, in light of what's happening at work, in light of the things the cup has shown him, it all hits different this time. This event has always been a balm to his soul – for the wild flowering of human creativity, for the community, for the quality time with his friends, for the glimpse of another kind of reality humans can make.

Yet none of this would even be possible were it not for the capitalist consumer culture all of this is rooted in: the camping gear, the bikes, the packaged food, the booze, the fuel, the port-o-potties... *Stop.* He shakes these thoughts away and slurps down his drink so quickly he gets a bit of brain freeze. He fixes himself another. He doesn't like drinking that much out here in the heat and the dryness and the elevation, but these mint juleps are just too good. Good enough to distract from the train of thought starting to take over. Almost. He vows to stay present and worry about consumerism and the state of the world when this party is over. He's already out here after all; why spoil a good time?

Remy and Danny and a couple of the others are spending this later part of the afternoon cleaning up the Fish. Their efforts could well turn out to be an exercise in futility due to the inevitable dust storms, but the forecast they'd gotten for this evening was that it will be clear with low wind, and Danny wants the Fish to shine. And shine she does – one of the amphetamine-fueled campmates spent the day polishing every individual scale on the outside of the Fish to gleaming perfection. Hundreds of scales, hours of time. Nathan keeps clear of speedy drugs, but when he sees the results of the work, he can maybe see the appeal. Still not for him, though. He's seen what it does to people.

"She looks great," he says, giving Remy a kiss.

"Hey, Nathan, mind shaking out the cushions?" Danny asks. He points at the cushions, which have been removed from the vehicle and lay in a haphazard pile close by.

Nathan sets down his drink and begins beating dust clouds out of all the pillows that he and Delilah had pulled an all-nighter to get done in time. It was a bit of a drag at the time, but then he reflects on how lucky he is to be in his thirties and still having fun with his friends. He knows that isn't the reality for everyone his age. He wishes it could be. The world would probably be a better place if everybody could just have more fun with their friends. But would the world be better because of the fun, or would the fun be possible because the world was better?

Danny comes up to Nathan as he finishes freshening up the cushions and sweeping out the floor of the lower level of the Fish, even though that seems pointless considering the environment they're in.

"You've been awesome," Danny says. He stands bare-chested, a sarong that he got in Bali at some yoga retreat tied around his waist. Dusty goggles sit atop his forehead, and his hair is highly textured in the way white people's hair gets out here, which Nathan, to his consternation, always envied.

"Well, I think you're awesome."

"Seriously, dude," Danny goes on. "You've always worked really hard to contribute to the camp, and I just want you to know I see you."

"Thanks for saying that. You're pretty swell for a straight guy."

Danny pulls him into a tight bear hug then, the rug of his body hair rubbing into Nathan's own bare chest. It's kind of sexy, even though Nathan doesn't think about Danny that way.

"You're awesome, buddy," Danny says. "It's not just the drugs talking."

After dinner, Nathan and Remy do a quick body-wipe bath in their tent. There is a communal camping shower set up, but Nathan always found using it to be more trouble than it's worth. Instead, he and Remy have stocked up on packets of those thick body-wipes intended for use by folks who've had surgeries and can't bathe in water while healing. Those things are perfect for camping. He can't help but wonder if people like him, buying up this product for a purpose for which it is not intended, ever caused shortages for people who *did* need it for the purpose for which it *was* intended. *Fuck. Don't think about that shit. Not now. Later.*

Although it's just the two of them, Nathan and Remy are in a nine-person tent, one that has a space high enough to stand up in. Their sleeping area consists of a queen-sized air mattress topped with a feather bed and duvet, and there's room to have a small sitting area with inflatable furniture and a rack of their outfits in a makeshift dressing room.

"You are such a princess," Remy had said when Nathan first revealed his plans for this setup. Nathan had laughed it off at the time, but now he can only imagine the squalor the kids forced to work in the cobalt mines must live in.

And how this festival setup of his and Remy's, that isn't even their regular home, this party place, is probably more comfortable than whatever those children have to endure. Holy shit, he cannot stay on this all night.

The vibe is electric when everyone gathers at the Fish. Twilight has descended, and the early stars wink on overhead. This is Nathan's favorite time, as the heat and bright clarity of the day shifts into magic and mystery and more comfortable temperatures. It's a liminal space, and that is the space of creativity and revelation. Everyone is dolled up in sexy, sparkly outfits right out of an alien rave except for one of the new guys, who looks more like a wizard from a fantasy novel about gay elf centurions, or something. This contingent of the camp is heading out to the deep playa together, and Remy and a couple of others from the Awaken Beat Collective will be spinning their own little dance party away from the big sound camps.

A separate contingent is playing Follow the Virgin – the virgin tonight being Tim, the guy who made the delicious curry they all had for supper earlier. It's a game that consists of experienced members of the camp letting a first timer dictate to the group where they are going and what they are doing throughout the night. Nathan bids them good journey, then hops aboard the Fish as she sets out across the desert.

He rides shotgun with Danny driving and sips some water through the tube of his hydration pack as they roll slowly down the dusty streets towards the Man, which stands at the center of the circle that is the footprint of the city. The speed limit is five miles per hour, so as not to break up the ground too much, and to be mindful of all the thousands of people walking or on bikes, often oblivious to traffic due to some form of intoxication or all the thumping sounds and blinky and shiny everywhere, or both. It's slow going, but by no means boring. Pounding beats drift through the air from the parties erupting all around, and they somehow don't sound discordant but merge into a coherent pulse – the rhythm of this crazy beautiful city at night. Colored lights spin and blink and whir like a rainbow exploded and dripped candy-colored bits of itself everywhere. During the day, the event feels like a large camp-out art festival in the desert. But at night, it really feels like a city. A city alive with its own strange culture that centers creative expression, revelation, and hedonism.

But as fun as it is, and as good for the spirits of the participants as it can be, what is the carbon footprint of the event? How sustainable is this?

"What you thinkin'?" Danny asks with a glance over to Nathan. He's put a vest on over his otherwise naked torso, and he now wears a top hat with a big peacock feather coming off of it, and his eyes are circled with glitter. Laughter erupts from the passenger area behind them; it sounds like Annika is sharing some bawdy story about a hook-up she had last year.

Nathan is well aware he's in a downer of a headspace but decides to be real with his friend. "I'm thinking about all the fossil fuels required to make this event happen and get everybody out here. All the consumption everybody out here takes part in for the sake of our party. All the while, kids are slaving away in mines for the benefit of our shiny devices –"

"Oh, you're on that trip again." Danny shakes his head. "I get why all that upsets you. Really, I do…" He taps the brakes, lets a group of young women in this year's trendy bikini-top, booty shorts, and fuzzy legwarmers look cross our path.

"But?" Nathan braces for the pushback.

"You gotta put up or shut up, my man."

The Fish has cleared the Esplanade, the main drag and inner-most street of the city. She's heading across open playa now.

"What do you mean?"

"I get that you have this new awareness, or whatever, because of what you've learned about the products you design and what it takes to make them. And I get you're all caught up in the overconsumption that existing in our culture requires. But angst-ing about it and complaining about it don't do any goddamn thing. So I challenge you, Nathan: either do something or shut up about it."

Okay, wow. Nathan flushes with embarrassment – shame? – at being called out, but he sees that his embarrassment is mostly rooted in the acknowledgment that his friend is right. There is no integrity or pride to be had in just being a whiner. Is he becoming a whiner? He doesn't really want the answer to that question. "I'm just not sure what to do," Nathan says. "But you're right."

"Do you know what permaculture is?" Danny asks, while adjusting the volume of the music in the passenger part of the Fish while also navigating the weaving, blinking bicycles and pedestrians that surround them.

"Isn't it like, organic farming, or something?"

"Kind of. It's a philosophy of working with nature rather than against nature or trying to control it. There are principles that can be applied to farming, sure, but also to building, resource management, land stewardship. It's a holistic way of living with the earth. I met these folks earlier this week who're starting up a course back in San Francisco that starts at the end of September. I'm gonna do the course. Why don't you do it with me? It might not become your thing, but I bet the stuff we'll learn will help point you in the right direction. Might help you figure out what your thing is."

That... that sounds like a good idea, actually. A manageable, tangible step in the face of overwhelm. "All right, Danny," Nathan says. "I accept your challenge and your invitation."

"Shake." Danny holds out a hand and Nathan shakes it firmly.

"Is there any topic you don't know something about?" Nathan asks.

"Shit tons. But if you don't learn about stuff you don't already know about, what are you even doing in life? That's my philosophy."

"You are a wise man, Danny Gobo."

"I have my moments."

Danny has stopped the Fish beside an art installation: the one called Serpent Mother, built by an artist collective known as Flaming Lotus Girls. She is an enormous, metallic, skeletal snake, spiraling around her egg. Plumes of fire light up each vertebra as well as the jaw. Even though they're a good distance away, Nathan feels the heat when bursts are fired along her body. Not for the first time, he marvels at the creativity and ingenuity of the community this event gathers.

The guest riders on the Fish all hop off while those in the inner circle gather in the back passenger area.

"Does everybody who's partaking have a cup?" Delilah asks the group. She's pulled out a thermos, which Nathan knows contains her psychedelic brew.

From a side pocket of his hydration pack, he pulls out the teacup. He hadn't thought of bringing it until Delilah shared her plan for this special beverage. Then he realized he had to; how could he not?

"Cool cup." Annika shimmers beside him. "Jade?"

He passes it to her and watches as she turns it over in her hands. "Yeah. Family heirloom."

"Will Delilah's magic potion put you in touch with your ancestors?" She smells faintly of something floral, and her body glitter sparkles in the mood lighting – color-shifting LED strips.

"I dunno. Maybe. Not sure I want it to, though." He thinks of fire. Is it an echo of his visions? Probably not – this event features fire everywhere, after all. Big ones, little ones, at random intervals.

Everyone holds out their cups as Delilah pours. "I invite you to set an intention for this trip," she says. "Don't feel you have to, though." Once she's made sure everyone has their portion, she raises her own cup. "May the Mother bless your journey."

The class he has agreed to take with Danny is a step, but Nathan still ponders the bigger question: *What should I do?*

He drinks down his tea, struggling not to gag on the strong, slightly bitter mushroomy flavor, which Delilah has tried valiantly to disguise with herbs. Then he squeezes some water out of his hydration pack, swirls it around in the cup, and drinks that down before putting the cup away.

They hang out at the Serpent Mother for a little while before moving on. Yes, the plan is to have a dance party out in the deep playa, but they appear on no schedule and are on their own timetable. Off in the distance, Nathan spots the one-hundred-foot-tall sunflower and its accompanying flytrap. They're built on cranes so they're mobile and extendable, but this far away, their underlying structure isn't discernible and they're simply monster blossoms of light rendered tiny in the flat expanse.

The Fish stops again in an area of open space, so that she is the main attraction at this little patch of desert, and Danny lets everyone know she'll be parked here for a while. They all clamber off, and from the top deck, Remy begins spinning his set. The groove he puts out attracts passersby, and soon the Fish is surrounded by blissed-out dancers, and a ring of their blinking bicycles is laid down on the ground all around them. Nathan looks up at his boyfriend, admires his stylishness, his coolness, his hotness. Remy spots him from his perch and blows him a kiss.

Nathan's knees begin feeling rubbery, his tell-tale sign that he's coming onto his trip. He joins Delilah and Annika and Mason, who appeared from somewhere, and that girl Sugar Bunny they met the other night who had spotted the Fish and came running over. Together, they dance under the singing stars and stomp joyously in the dust.

A crew of firedancers has rolled up and is entrancing the crowd with their whirling rushes of flame, their fit leather-clad bodies, the captivating patterns they spin. The fiery mandalas unfurl right out of the air, danced into being by these magical creatures. Nathan looks around at the glory of it all, taking in not just the crowd around the Fish, but beyond and beyond and beyond. Everyone here at this event, in this city that will be gone in a week, a month, is a part of this thing that they came out here to build and do and be together every year. Whatever this thing is, one thing is sure: something from deep inside humanity's psyche is being expressed in all of this, some collective yearning. Something ineffable. It's with these thoughts that Nathan realizes he's tripping hard.

"They're gonna burn the Belgian Waffle," somebody says.

The enormous installation is formally titled "Uchronia," but everybody calls it the Belgian Waffle because its surface texture looks like a waffle and it was built by a crew of Belgians with a shipment of wood imported from Canada. That's the rumor, anyway. It's the big art hit of the Burn this year. Nearly everyone Nathan runs into, nearly every stranger he had struck up a conversation with throughout the week, brings it up eventually. "Have you seen the Waffle? Isn't it amazing?"

Its interior is a cavernous, fluid space that feels a bit like a cathedral, in the sense that the grandeur of the space inspires a quiet kind of awe. It's open space inside, and he doesn't really know how tall it is at its highest point, but it has to be a few stories, at least. He's pretty sure the three-story building he and Remy live in could fit inside easily with room to spare. The whole thing is constructed of thousands of two-by-fours, and it blows his mind that such linear things such as two-by-fours can, en masse, create a form so curvaceous. He had hoped to visit it again, but if it's about to burn, that chance is gone.

"Let's go," Delilah says, grabbing his hand. "Do you have your water?"

He runs his thumbs under the straps of the pack on his back, then sips from the tube to make sure. "Yes."

They begin walking toward the Waffle. Nathan looks back at the Fish, to seal its place in his memory, but then sets that goal aside. She's going to be parked for a while, and anyway, she has such a distinctive silhouette that he can spot her from across the playa.

"How are you feeling?" Delilah asks.

"Flying pretty good." That he can reply surprises him a bit; in his mind, his access to words seems far away.

A substantial crowd has gathered, ready for the spectacle. Nathan had wanted to see this – had felt a pull toward this from the moment that stranger back at the Fish said it was burning. But now that he stands in front of this grand sculpture... installation... thing, a disquiet settles over him. The same disquiet plaguing him all week, all day. Consumption, unsustainable and built on exploited labor. He tries to shake it off, not wanting his trip to go to a dark place. He focuses on the joy of being out here with his friends, of sharing this experience with one of his closest people at his side. He casts a glance skyward: the stars are out in full force now. Even though there are lights and fires all around Black Rock City, there is nowhere near the level of light pollution that exists back in San Francisco.

Holy shit, this entire world is just a drop in an ocean.

Cheers erupt as the first flames lick out from the interior of the wooden structure. For a moment, it looks like an enormous cactus in this desert, blooming with fire. And then the fire spreads – quickly – and soon the whole thing is ablaze, the entire shape of it, the silhouette that had dominated this part of the playa all week, is engulfed. The two-by-fours it's built of are black lines haunting the flames. They stick out every which way in a pattern that is both chaotic and organized. The roar of the fire drowns out the beats thumping in the night – no small feat, considering – and Nathan feels the heat of it even standing twenty, thirty, forty feet away. He's not sure how far away he and Delilah stand, actually. He's normally good at judging distances, but not when he's tripping.

Before too long, the top of the Waffle caves in, and the rest of it starts falling in on itself, to thunderous applause from the gathered crowd.

Houses.

Nathan thinks of houses. How many houses could all those two-by-fours build? All that lumber burning for the delight of this crowd could have housed how many? Other fires flash in his mind now: a building in Chinatown, forests, whole cities. The visions the cup had bestowed swarm his inner sight now, not just with conflagrations, but with storms, too, apocalyptic water, decimating tides. He knows these are visions of the future; he knows the cup is transmitting these images, this knowledge, from some future point in time. *This is what's coming.* So says the voice in the cup. Is it the voice of some future holder of the cup? It doesn't matter, really, who it is. What matters is the message. *This devastation is coming, but it doesn't have to be this bad.*

He thinks of the ocean. A whale.

Enraptured faces all around – just a few hundred gathered here of the tens of thousands attending the event as a whole. Again, he thinks of all the resources expended to make this happen – oh, he has gone through this litany before, and he doesn't want to again. This event is a grand endeavor, and one he loves, but then he once more thinks of the children in the mines. How can anybody party like this when others must live like that?

A veil draws back in Nathan's mind, and he can no longer simply enjoy the beauty and the rapture of it all. The visions the cup has given him, what he has learned about his work, sheds new light on all of it. Now all he can think about is waste.

"I'm gonna walk."

Delilah doesn't question it when Nathan informs her of this, just nods. They've partied enough together that she knows he sometimes needs to grab some solitude at some point in the night. He heads away from the burning Waffle and the now even more enormous crowd it had gathered. He passes the Fish, which hasn't moved since they parked, just like Danny promised, though everything around her has shifted. The firedancers are gone, but the music is still going, and people are still dancing. A jellyfish has pulled up beside her and billows gossamer ribbons beneath a translucent, color-shifting canopy. He walks beyond the Temple – the structure built at the midnight point of the clock that the circle of the city forms. It's a space designated for honoring the dead, whether that be loved ones that have passed on or phases of life that are ending. The mood is quiet and contemplative and somber, and Nathan feels more at home here than in the revelry he has escaped. But he doesn't want to stop here, and keeps walking, right on up to the trash fence.

The fence is set up around the farthest perimeter of the event and is intended to catch any stray bits of litter – MOOP, it's called: Matter Out Of Place. The fence is to prevent any bits of moop from being carried out into the open desert by wind. Nathan stands at this farthest most boundary of Black Rock City, the party going off behind him. He feels like matter out of place right now. He turns his back on the lights and the flames and the beats and the beautiful people and looks out at the open expanse of the wild desert beyond.

Oh, what the hell is he doing with his life? He slips off his pack and pulls the teacup out from the pocket. It's dark where he stands, no lights but for the blinky things he wears on his vest, and the twinkles of the few other people out this far. The cup is heavier than he remembers it being. The green of the jade is just black shadow, but there's a shimmering, golden glow around it. He grips it tightly, and the visions it had given him echo in his mind along with the chants of angry protestors. There is a voice in it now, a golden thread in the cup's energy that he hadn't picked up before. It tells him stories about the future. It tells him to change the world.

Shadow wreaths the desert, gives way to the curved and broken backs of the black hills, whose silhouettes interrupt the whirling dance of the Milky Way. This is as much solitude as he's going to get out here.

Visions of the future. A history of exploitation in his family. His work benefiting from the exploitation of others. What is his purpose? Such are the patterns and questions of his life. He gazes out at the night and maps his life to the distant constellations, and he looks for a path among them.

20.

MAIDA

March 17, 2106
City Hall, San Francisco

I stood close with Lorel, Roan and Bertrand in our own little cluster in the midst of the throng that had gathered for the Assessor Prime's address. We were gathered in the plaza in front of a building called City Hall, a structure still in use as a seat of civic leadership after having survived multiple civic uprisings over the past eighty years. These days, it functioned as SubRegional Administrative Hub for the Southern Quadrant of the Region, which like the other SubRegional Administrative Hubs, served as central office for the Assessor Prime when he was in the area. It was a building out of time: grand and ostentatious in a way that really wasn't done anymore. A remnant of a world that was, like the pyramids, or dinosaur bones.

The plaza had been updated over the years with seating and shade, along with biofeatures that allowed rainwater to sink into the ground. One half of the space was taken up by neat rows of atmospheric water generators, their fine mesh pulling moisture out of the air and pooling it in cisterns. Most of the area in view had once been nothing but pavement and lawn. What a silly way to design public space, but whether or not anyone nowadays would call what was done "design," I didn't know.

Even though the features of the place reflected the current world, the footprint was still what it had been in the Precursor days. The space dwarfed the crowd, and it was as large a crowd as I had ever seen. If it hadn't been for all the terrible things that have happened over the past seventy-five years or so, this space might well have been packed. But that world wasn't this world.

The mood of the crowd simmered on the verge of unruly, and I didn't need to be a telepath to pick up on the antipathy of the Freedom Faction contingent. And given how much I could feel it, it must have been so much worse for actual telepaths.

REGULATE THEM was a common message on the placards of the anti-psion crowd. *ROUND THEM UP* was another.

Nothing like getting blamed for an act of terror to unite people against a community, huh? Was I naïve to ever have believed that humans had evolved beyond this sort of thing?

"We cannot allow these freaks and their unnatural abilities to replace us!" some red-faced instigator bellowed into a bullhorn. Where did he get a bullhorn?

The Assessor Prime exited the building with his aides and strode with purpose to the podium set up at the top of the City Hall steps. Kemp stood among them, and he did not look happy.

"Fellow citizens," the Assessor began. "As you know, our compatriots in Portland have been targeted in an immoral and unprovoked attack by radical extremists –"

"All psions are radical!" somebody yelled, and murmurs of agreement percolated amongst the Freedom Faction side of the crowd.

Linstrom put on an appropriate expression of concern – I wasn't convinced – and raised his hands to settle everyone down. "While there are those among the psion community who feel their abilities put them above the law, and above non-psions, we cannot assume those attitudes are widespread."

What the fuck was he talking about? I had never encountered psions with that mindset. Ever. Academy graduates took an oath to serve humanity. I trusted Del's clairvoyance and claircognizance and believed the accusation of psions being behind the bombing to be false, but that didn't matter if people believed it, which the Freedom Faction community seemed primed to do. Just make up a story about the enemy and tell them to be afraid. Was that really all it took? I also noticed he used the term "non-psions" rather than "nul-psis".

"That being said, until those responsible for Portland are apprehended, the public use of psionic abilities will be restricted…"

Cries of disbelief arose from the folks close to me and my friends, while the Freedom Faction side cheered and applauded this news.

"Any psion who uses their abilities outside of officially assigned environmental remediation and specialized vocation duties will be detained. We encourage you, psion and non-psion alike, to report any psionic activity you bear witness to, whether in private or in public, that is not directly related to work duties. You can submit reports via the Civic Services Request widget on your nodes. In the meantime, the Circle of the Eye Academy is cooperating with Regional Administration in our efforts to identify the culprits behind the attack. We hope that all psions will follow their lead in the spirit of cooperation. I'd like to –"

A small object flew out of the crowd toward the Assessor – a bottle. I could see what it was clearly when it stopped a foot or so from the Assessor's head and hovered there. The entire crowd was quiet as the bottle captured everyone's attention. Then it dropped and shattered and broke the hushed silence. Something else shattered too: the peace that was far more fragile than anybody realized.

"It was one of them!" the man with the bullhorn bellowed.

What stupidity. Surely everyone saw that it was telekinesis that stopped the bottle from striking Linstrom. But it quickly became clear that I was the stupid one for thinking anybody would use a lick of sense. Soon, bottles and stones were being hurled at everyone carrying a propsion sign. Some telekinetic in the crowd – maybe more than one – got a shield up, and the objects hurled at us bounced off an invisible barrier above our heads. Then a voice in my head: *get out of there.* I recognized Aviva's telepathic voice, but I didn't see her anywhere.

"We should go," I said to my friends as the crowd began dispersing every which way. No argument from them. We dropped our signs and ran away from the security detail who were going after people with billy clubs and stun guns.

Nobody came after us once we cleared the plaza; security had been minimal, more personal protection for the Assessor than crowd control. There hadn't been riots or need for riot police since the Bloom, at least not here in this region. There hadn't been uprisings since the world settled into this new normal, when humanity, for the first time, had become united in common cause – mostly, a few hold-out territories notwithstanding. Or at least we all thought we'd been united. That was all changing now. Who would benefit from breaking that unity?

We made it back to campus and headed straight for the staff house. It suddenly felt like the only safe place to go, but that was ridiculous – I was being paranoid, right? The scene that unfolded at the Assessor's address was already on the newsfeeds by the time we got back. A couple of others from the house threw dirty looks my way – was I imagining that? – and got up and left the room when we arrived.

"Psion activists attack the Assessor Prime and his supporters during his remarks on the recent attack by a radical faction…"

I tuned out the rest of the newscaster's words as I stared at the screen in disbelief. The footage had been edited to look like all those bottles and stones had been raised telekinetically, then thrown at the Freedom Faction activists. Clips of Freedom Faction members bleeding from head wounds filled the screen.

"They just went crazy," a witness said in an interview. It was the man with the bullhorn. *"The Assessor made a reasonable request to limit the public use of psionic abilities, and they went crazy. It's obvious psions are unstable people…"*

"Turn that shit off," I said. My heart pounded and blood rushed in my ears. My breath grew rapid and shallow and out of my control, and I burst into a sweat – my brow, under my arms. The room closed in, the world closed in, and my vision narrowed to a tight circle right in front of me. It was still on. The bullshit was still broadcasting. "Turn it off!" I screamed as I waved my arms, frantically failing to make the off gesture. Roan took care of it with a sweep of hand and clutch of fist.

"Sit down and breathe." Lorel spoke softly and rubbed my back gently as she guided me down onto the sofa.

"We see what they're doing," Bertrand said. "We were there with you. We are with you."

"They're so clearly misrepresenting what happened," Roan said. "I don't get why, though. What's the objective?"

"It's not surprising, really," Lorel said. "It's how they would be if they had abilities. The supremacist attitude, the being above the law thing. They can't imagine that anybody would not be that way."

Aviva had sworn me to secrecy, but given what was happening... fuck that. I told my friends about Operation Golden Days, about what I gleaned from the Assessor Prime's watch that day, about the Regressive movement within Regional leadership. "Whatever they're planning, it's happening now," I said, wrapping up my account.

They all looked grim, but none of them said the psion group's suspicions were crazy. I'd probably have lost it if any of them pulled some "there must be a reasonable explanation" crap. I couldn't keep the defeat out of my voice, though. It had barely begun, whatever all this was, and I was already feeling defeated. Was I weak? Or did I not know how to fight because I haven't had to before? Because I hadn't dared to before?

Meet me at the front gate, Aviva's telepathic voice intoned in my mind.

This was going to take some getting used to. "I have to go."

Everyone looked at me quizzically as I got up to leave.

"Aviva called." I tapped the side of my head.

She was at the gate with a waiting transit pod when I got there. I climbed in after her, and we set off in the direction of the central city. "Where are we going?"

"To speak with a friend who works in Regional Administration. He's a senior Clerk, not an Assessor, but he's respected by them and knows a couple of them personally. Things are getting out of hand, and we have to share what we know."

We didn't speak the rest of the way and arrived a short while later at a residential tower on Market Street. The top of the tower was aswirl with haze – the fog rolling in, illuminated by the tower's lighting. The vertical gardens of the building's exterior terraces curled with green life, flourishing with leaves straining against the vines and branches that held them as they soaked in the mists of evening.

We took the elevator up to a 20th floor apartment and were welcomed by a scholarly looking man wearing thick, black-framed glasses. He had one of those faces of indeterminate age – he could have been thirty-five or fifty-five. He and Aviva greeted each other with quick pecks on the cheek.

"It's been too long," he said. "Not since that time in the Sierras."

"That was indeed a time," Aviva replied, and the two shared a private chuckle.

He ushered us into a well-appointed apartment – he must have been high up in the administration indeed to be assigned such nice living quarters. The floors were slate, punctuated by sumptuous looking area rugs, and the fixtures were all fine-lined and sleek. He brought us to a living room where the furniture looked like it had never been sat on.

"This is Oliver," Aviva said once we were seated. "Maida, here, is assigned to the Cultural Recovery Project."

"Ah," Oliver said. "Discipline?"

"Psychometry."

"Well that only makes sense, doesn't it? Tea? Something stronger?"

Aviva shook her head. "This isn't a social call. We have information. We believe the attack on the train in Portland and the violence at today's event were perpetrated by the Assessor Prime and his regressive allies in the Administration."

Oliver lifted his eyebrows in obvious disbelief. It seemed like maybe only his respect for Aviva drove him to ask a follow-up question instead of dismissing her assertions out of hand. "What makes you think that?"

Aviva turned to me. "Maida, would you open your mind to Oliver and share with him what you gleaned from the Assessor?"

Oliver was another telepath, then. Part of me had wondered why Aviva brought me along when she could just tell her friend what she knew herself. But I saw that it was so he could bear witness to my firsthand experience himself; she didn't want to leave any room for ambiguity, to leave openings for "are you sure she saw what she saw?" lines of questioning.

"Sure." I met Oliver's eyes. Though his expression was friendly, his eyes sized me up. "Do what you need to do."

"Just think back to the moment of contact," he instructed me.

I did as he asked, thought up that day in the lab, Linstrom and his delegation on their site visit. I recalled the watch breaking, how I picked it up, what I saw when I touched it. I wasn't just remembering it, though. In Oliver's telepathic embrace, we were in the memory, together, reliving it. Witnessing it as if we were in that moment, right then and there. We were back in that room with Aviva and Linstrom and his people, and now Oliver was there too, beside me, watching. I've had memories telepathically extracted before, and it had always consisted of a vivid remembrance and then a fading away. This way was different. This way, there was an intruder in the memory, somebody who hadn't actually been there was there now. This was my first taste of this mode of telepathy, and I didn't much like it. Or maybe his true, psychic self didn't match his outside persona.

He may have picked up on these thoughts; there was a jab of annoyance from him that smoothed away quickly. Then, he was out of my head, and I was back in the living room in his swank twentieth-floor apartment, sitting across from him, both of us in our physical bodies.

"This is rather alarming," Oliver said. "And it's in line with some concerns my colleagues have raised. You were right to bring this to my attention." He stood up. "Now."

Now what? I was confused at first, but then it all became quite clear. Black-clad security personnel poured in from an adjacent room and from the foyer where we entered. A couple of them aimed firearms at us while the others brandished stunsticks, blue sparks sizzling at their tips. We were surrounded. Aviva rose slowly to her feet, and I followed her lead.

"Oliver...?" She threw him a wounded look. A look that said whatever affection there had been between them was gone. "Maida, go out the front door, turn right, and run towards the window at the end of the hall. Go now."

I stood stock still, not sure if I had heard her right, but then she shot me a look, and I took off. None of the security people tried to stop me, and I realized they seemed to be frozen against their will. I had to squeeze myself between two of them blocking the door, watching my own face slide across the mirrored surface of one of their visors as I did so. I could have sworn I felt his eyes on me.

Aviva apologized to somebody, and then her quick footsteps sounded as she caught up with me in the hallway. She wasn't alone. One of the security people ran alongside her. They pulled their firearm and aimed it at the glass we charged towards. From the apartment, sudden yells and a rush of feet. I looked over my shoulder and they appeared in the hallway, tumbling out of the apartment after us.

The security person who ran with us fired several rounds at the glass, shattering it. "Just jump!" they yelled as they charged to the window then through it as the glass flew outward, into the foggy night.

No fucking way, was what I thought, but then Aviva was in my head with, *it'll be fine just keep running.* And then I was at the edge of a long fall ringed by broken glass, then I was in the air, then I was falling. I looked up to see the other guards get to the edge of the obliterated window and stop.

It was all a blur – that heart-in-the-throat feeling as I went out the window and dropped. My heart pounded and raced in my ribcage, trying to bust out of this crazy person's body, what the fuck. Just as quickly as I noticed my hair whipping around my face, it had stopped, whipped back, and then we were no longer falling but flying over the street. There was a rushing feeling of exhilaration, and then I thought my brain might explode from all this input – the running, the jumping, the falling, the flying, and now the gliding towards the open side door of a van racing down the street. The psifield around us buzzed, and I could feel it: the telekinetic emanation of whoever was carrying us through the air. It was that of the person in the van – familiar. Who was it? Then, suddenly we were in the van and the door slammed closed behind us as we raced down Market Street.

Kemp greeted us – it was him that brought us to safety and had us from the moment we leapt out the window.

"How did…" I looked from Aviva to Kemp to the security person. I looked around the van like it might have been an illusion. Back to Aviva.

She started to explain, "I was concerned Oliver might be compromised –"

The security person cut her off. "If by compromised you mean on the wrong team betraying all of psion-kind." They pulled off the visored helmet – it was Del.

"I thought something like this was a possibility," Aviva continued. "I had hoped not, hoped that my trust in my friend – who I thought was a friend – wasn't misplaced. But clearly, it was. In any case, I thought there should be an exit plan."

"We coordinated telepathically, courtesy of Aviva," Kemp explained in response to my unexpressed need for clarity.

"And I serve Administration Security," Del said. "Or I did, anyway. I think maybe I'm fired now."

They all had a laugh.

I thought back to our previous meetings and realized I never did find out what Del's occupation was. That the Security division would utilize those who can remote view made sense, but where would those folks stand now that Linstrom was making this anti-psion play?

"And speaking of not going back to work…" Aviva turned to me.

If Oliver wanted to take me into custody, which appeared to be the case, he would send a squad to detain me at the staff house. He knew where I worked, and it would be easy to find my housing assignment. I didn't have anywhere to go, and a sharp panicky feeling rose up inside me like bile. I struggled to keep my composure; I didn't want to lose it in front of these folks, who seemed to be taking our recent actions in stride.

"So I'm the only one that still has a job, hmm?" Kemp asked with just a hint of a smile. Glad somebody could be lighthearted during all this.

"We'll drop you off somewhere safe." Aviva patted my hand and I returned the little squeeze she gave.

After several more minutes, we stopped. I was let off at a familiar marina, and I understood.

"I will reach out telepathically," Aviva said before we parted ways. "Lay low for now."

I walked out to the only slip I'd been to here. Felix waved from Epifania's deck as I approached. "Aviva tells me you might be staying a while."

"For a little bit, it looks like," I said. I'd have plenty of time to get my sea legs now.

21.

MAIDA

March 19, 2106
East Shore Marina, San Francisco

Community Garden North Beach. Tonight.

The note the messenger dropped off was to the point and unsigned. I knew who sent it as soon as I touched it – Lorel knew that I would. I'd asked Aviva to let my friends know I was safe. I guess Lorel must have deduced my likely location; I had told her about the conclave and being aboard Epifania.

"You're sure it's not a trick?" Felix asked. We were having a light breakfast of melon and tea on Epifania's deck. It had been nice, waking up on the water and spending the day on board the boat at the marina or out on the bay. For a second, I thought I could get used to being on the run if it entailed hanging out on a nice boat all day. Something told me this idyll was not going to last.

I got more than just who sent the note from touching it: I also sensed her concern for me and couldn't help but find it endearing. So this is what making friends was like. "Yeah, I'm sure."

I understood Felix's worry: we were keeping an eye on the newsfeeds, and our faces were all over them. *PSION FUGITIVES* scrolled across the chyron below our stern expressions. I could tell from the background that they used my staff ID pic, but they edited my smile away and made me look all stoic and serious. Our names, too, were in the report: *Maida Sun, Aviva Martinez, Del McPherson.*

"Members of the extremist PsiSupreme organization attacked Regional Administration Officer Oliver Shulamith at his San Francisco home Tuesday evening." There was a shot of the broken window of Oliver's Market Street building.

"These deranged, violent activists made a daring escape, leaping from the twentieth floor, then getting to safety via telekinesis. This bold strike demonstrates the tactical advantage such individuals have over conventional security personnel."

Cut to a security officer being interviewed. *"After the attempt on Mr. Shulamith's life, the three attackers blew out this window and jumped. They were aided by at least one other unidentified person, who drove the getaway vehicle. We unfortunately were unable to get security footage of the escape. These psions should be considered armed and dangerous."*

"Armed and dangerous, huh?" Felix asked. I appreciated his attempt at finding the humor in the situation, but it didn't really alleviate the overwhelming sense of fuckedness that was making my insides feel full of fire and lead – a hot, dead weight.

Had security personnel showed up at the staff house looking for me? I had to assume they had. Did they come before or after Lorel heard from Aviva? Were my friends good liars? Roan and Bertrand: them, I could see handling questioning well. Lorel, though? Her big brown eyes were far too sincere.

We were docked at the Tiburon pier, but Felix assured me we'd be back to the city in time for me to meet up with my friends. After watching the irritatingly skewed news, Felix set off to deal with an errand – new parts for the bilge pump. From what I was picking up just from my brief time aboard, living on a boat meant being in a constant state of maintenance, just non-stop fixing things. While I was alone on board, I spent some time in meditation on the back deck. Afterwards, some tea seemed like a good idea. On my way down to the galley, I grabbed the banister to swing myself around when a scene from the past life of Epifania splashed brightly in my mind.

Images etched themselves onto the psifield and took over my vision. There was a group of laughing people gathered around the eating nook. It was the owners known as DnA, the couple who purchased the boat in 2017, and some of their friends. And then I saw him at the table, one of the friends. He was older and a little thicker than I was used to seeing him, but there was no doubt: it was Nathan, and it was eleven years beyond the time period I'd seen him in with the cup. But it was definitely him. Older, and maybe a little wiser, too? He looked it, anyway. In his eyes. He had a beard now. I touched the table lightly, warmed by knowing Nathan had once sat here, when Epifania was part of a different community's life. Or maybe branches of the same community after all, along far-flung stretches of time.

How did Epifania know to show me that scene in particular? Of all the moments in the boat's life, how did she know to reveal that one? Because it did feel like the objects I scanned had interior lives of their own, that they were aware of the memories they held. I just happened to be able to witness them too. Or maybe, because I'd encountered Nathan in the psychometric psifield before, his vibration was in me. And since he had also been in this physical space once upon a time, that memory I just witnessed resonated with the wispy trace of his presence.

The memory was gone as quickly as it arose, but I felt down to the choral singing of my cells how this space at the heart of Epifania had nurtured friendships and deep connections in its warm, woody embrace. I was so grateful to encounter a space like this, because they were rare, and because if we found ourselves in such a space, that must mean we were at a juncture in our lives where we were in need of and receiving community support.

The gate to the community garden and food forest was open, and the lights strung up around it cast a warm, comfortable glow. But comfort ultimately always came down to an internal state, didn't it? As inviting and lovely as this space was, I found myself on edge, despite the cozy warmth of the paper lanterns illuminating a path towards the center of the plaza ringed by agave plants and a small grouping of cabaret tables and chairs. I made sure to keep my hood up, and the caution felt both absurd and necessary.

"You're probably safe here," Bertrand said when I joined them.

"Can't be too careful."

Lorel grabbed me a drink from the refreshment cart – a soda with a few drops of the local variety of bitters, made with only herbs grown in this garden.

"Are you sure you weren't followed?" Roan asked.

I answered with a flush of panic, "I don't think so..." I looked around furtively before I got that he was being lighthearted and probably referencing some old spy movie. I also realized that my looking around the way I just did probably looked more suspicious than anything.

"No – It's all right…" he said, his expression letting me know that he realized he shouldn't joke about that sort of thing.

Lorel and I embraced, and Bertrand gave me a side hug. Roan reached his hand across the table and gave mine a squeeze.

"What the hell happened?" Lorel started in. "Aviva said you were safe but nothing about what happened –"

"–we figured you didn't really try to kill that guy," Roan said, referring to the news.

I told them everything about what happened at Oliver's apartment, why we'd gone there, that he'd been a friend of Aviva's that betrayed us, and finally the details of how we escaped. It was harrowing when it happened, but I had to admit I appreciated watching my friends' faces as I shared the now-exhilarating-and-not-at-all-terrifying tale. Should I have felt guilty about my enjoyment of telling the story? We all made it, and if we couldn't take time to share triumphs – and narrowly escaping detention with a twenty-story leap into nothingness counted as one for sure – if we couldn't appreciate small moments of pleasure and connection, then what the hell was even the point?

"I can't believe this is happening, and that people are falling for it." Of all of us, Bertrand, the history nerd among us – well, we were all kind of history nerds in our own way, but he was the nerdiest – certainly would have known about all the times this sort of thing had happened before. But we all really believed that after the Bloom we were one unified, enlightened people. And maybe that was true for most of us, but as we were seeing, all it took was a small party of aggrieved liars to derail progress.

"When do you think they'll start implementing the other plans?" Lorel was hesitant in her question, which was unlike her. She clearly didn't want to speak the horror into existence. "The containment zones. Or detention centers. Whatever they're calling them."

"Not until after the next major attack."

"You think there will be another one?" Roan asked.

"I think we can count on it." Aviva and the others were busy trying to ascertain further specifics of the Assessor's plans. Had they had any luck?

"So you're really in it now, huh?" Lorel looked at me with those big brown eyes.

What was there to say? Despite my misgivings, despite how I thought of myself as a pacifist, I was in the thick of it. Jumping out windows and all. Lorel seemed to perceive everything my silence suggested and just nodded before I said anything.

"What do you need from us?" Bertrand asked.

"You haven't seen me. You don't know where I am. I'm probably not going to stay with the boat much longer, so soon you really won't know. Be careful if you go to any more protests. I hope the project doesn't fall too far behind with me gone."

"There will be plenty of artifacts and stories to record when you get back," Roan said.

"And you will be back," Lorel added.

We said our goodbyes, and almost immediately, Aviva called me in my head.

Across the street. Poetry.

The Ferlinghetti Center for Precursor Literature glowed on the other side of the parkway. I crossed the plaza where a small group was playing music like that beat-driven, electronic stuff by DJ Aspect. They were spinning colorful lights, weaving whirling patterns in the air. The patterns and the music made me think of Nathan and his friends.

The receptionist greeted me as I entered. Since paper books were no longer a consumer item, the legendary bookstore City Lights Books that had occupied this space for over a hundred years had many years ago been transformed into a literary center and library. I had come here with my mother on that childhood trip.

I headed up a narrow flight of creaky stairs to the poetry room.

Grab a book and sit down.

"What?"

Grab a book and sit down, and don't speak out loud. Just think what you want to say.

I did as Aviva instructed, even though I was comprehending nothing. I grabbed a volume from the shelf closest to me. *An Atlas of the Difficult World,* by Adrienne Rich. I didn't know this one, not that I was well-versed in late twentieth century poetry.

I settled into a corner seat and opened the book...

And suddenly I was in an office. A wall lined with books, and another filled with old photographs and maps.

Aviva: *This is a psychic recreation of my office.*

The detail was uncanny, and it really felt like I was there.

Me: *This is all in my mind?*

Kemp: *It's in all of our minds.*

I looked over and saw that Kemp and Del were also present. Present in this psychic space, not physically where I was. What a trip.

Me: *Why this place?*

Aviva: *We improvised based on your current location. I would have preferred that you weren't in public, but this is our only window of time with all of us. At least there, you can sit by yourself and not talk to anyone and not look out of place.*

Me: *How did you know where I was?*

Del: *I can see you. But not in a creepy way.*

Kemp: *I've learned another attack is being planned for next week, but I don't know exactly when and I don't know the target.*

Me: *Okay. How can I help?*

Aviva: *We're going to need you to scan something in the next couple of days. Be prepared to drop whatever you're doing and go where I tell you. I'm letting you know now, so you can expect it. And please stay on land; don't go sailing with Epifania if Felix decides to get out on the water.*

Me: *All right. What's the end goal here?*

Aviva: *To reveal to the world that Linstrom was behind the attack.* She looked at me – or her telepathic projection was looking at my telepathic projection. This was so weird. *Maida, I sense you have something on your mind.*

Me: *Will revealing Linstrom's nefarious doings be enough?*

Del: *Enough for what?*

Me: *To stop the psion hate that's being stoked? We know Linstrom's doing it to serve his own agenda – whatever it is. But the fact that such sentiment could be so easily stoked indicates there was mistrust to be exploited, doesn't it? How do we address that? Using our talents in service of our communities doesn't seem to be enough.*

Aviva: *What do you suppose would be enough?*

Me: *What if Linking Circles were open to everyone?* As soon as I thought it, I sensed a tension rise among the others.

Kemp: *The nul-psis aren't ready for that.*

Me: *And we're the ones who gatekeep that?*

Del: *Of course we are, who else?*

Aviva: *I think your notion is coming from a good place, but it isn't realistic.*

Me: *Why not? That connection – that communion – highlights our common humanity and shared connection to the planet, which nul-psis are also a part of. There are already rumors out there that we have secret meetings and are plotting a takeover – that's why the Freedom Faction is so quickly gaining ground. Continuing to shut them out will only reinforce those beliefs –*

Kemp: *You know damn well that's not what we're doing in the circles –*

Me: *But nul-psis don't know that! All they see is that we have these gatherings they're excluded from for no good reason.*

Del: *There's plenty of reason. Our psionic awakenings are a realm of experience they can never understand.*

Me: *You're sounding like a supremacist.* Del looked shocked that I thought such a thing. Good. *And maybe if they were included, they would have a greater understanding. Maybe it's our duty to spread understanding.*

I could hardly believe I was thinking these things. In that telepathic space, I wasn't as aware of my body, so all the usual physical discomforts that came upon me when I challenged or confronted anyone weren't bothering me. Maybe because we were communicating with the speed and immediacy of thought, there was no time for my fear to censor my words. I kind of liked it.

Aviva: *We are not going to decide this right now. Thank you for your suggestion, Maida. Be alert for further instruction.*

They were gone. The office was gone. The telepathic transmission cut off with a blink, and I was back in the poetry reading room at the Ferlinghetti Center. I couldn't shake the feeling that they were still all together in Aviva's psychic office, talking about me. About what a naïve fool I was to suggest such a thing. I knew I wasn't being naïve, though; I knew I was right.

After slipping the book of poems back in its place on the shelf, I made my way out.

"See you again!" the receptionist called out cheerily.

I set myself in the direction of the Epifania, and couldn't help but feel like I had crossed some invisible line.

22.

LI NUAN

April 17, 1906
Chinatown, San Francisco

"Why do you insist it must be done late at night on April 17th?" Tye Leung asks after Li Nuan agrees to help with the operation.

"You will think I am crazy."

"Tell me." Tye Leung gives no indication as to whether or not she thinks Li Nuan is crazy, and she makes no promises.

There is nothing to do but tell the truth. "There will be an earthquake early in the morning on April 18th. Big one. And then fires will come. I..." How can she explain getting visions from a teacup? "I had a prophetic dream." She flushes with the half-truth, but a dream will be easier to believe.

"The Lord has sent you a sign to help the mission," Tye Leung says, putting her hands together in prayer and raising them to Heaven. "Oh, thank you, Lord."

Li Nuan knows this isn't the case – she knows from her contact with the cup that the vision it showed her was some message from the future, from someone for whom all of this is in the past. But she doesn't know how she knows that.

She just knows. Is that faith? Is it the same faith that Tye Leung and Miss Cameron and the ministers at the church preach about? Whatever the case, it is probably better to just let Tye Leung believe as she believes.

Miss Cameron seems doubtful when the reason for the choice of date is explained, but she trusts Tye Leung. When she asks for how foreknowledge of the quake can help, Li Nuan explains as Tye Leung translates: "After the quake, the Boss and Madam Bai can gather the girls together, and in the chaos, we will not be able to get to them and get them away. We will lose our chance for a long time. So we get the girls out before the quake. And after the quake, the Boss and his men will have other concerns, and with the chaos in the city that I see coming, it will be harder for them to come after us."

Miss Cameron seems to accept this but still has doubts. Li Nuan doesn't care; Miss Cameron doesn't have to believe her completely, or even at all. She just needs to agree to the plan. And anyway, the operation is happening quake or no quake, so if it happens as Li Nuan says, her reasoning is sound, and if no quake happens, it doesn't matter because they are still doing what they were going to do anyway.

It's clear at the planning session that Miss Cameron and Tye Leung have done this sort of thing before. Li Nuan had heard the rumors, of course – the rumors about the white woman, who the newspapers called "The Angry Angel of Chinatown," storming brothels and setting the flowers free. But she had always thought those stories were exaggerations, that hatchet-wielding women and men could not possibly storm the Tong's territory and free the girls. Now she knows the stories are true, and here she is with the Angry Angel herself, helping her forge a brazen plan.

They will gain entry through the Lotus Pearl's front door and roof. A path across the rooftops that connected the brothel to a laundry the next street over had been worked out. Miss Cameron will lead the rooftop charge herself, hatchet in hand. Her team will access the roof by climbing up the laundry's fire escape. Then they will break into the roof access door on the Lotus Pearl's building and get the girls in the upper-level parlor rooms out that way. The laundry is under the control of one of Boss Fong's rivals, but its manager is sympathetic to the cause of freeing the girls and the larger goal of ridding Chinatown of the Tongs.

Li Nuan joins Tye Leung with the street-level group. There are nine total for the operation: four on the rooftops and five on the street. The five include two flying squad officers from the Police Department. The flying squad officers are trained to quell riots, Miss Cameron had explained. And just as some on the Police force accepted bribes to help the trade in girls, there were others who helped to stop it. What a strange thing, for the authorities to not be of one mind. Tye Leung is a hatchet wielder for the street group, along with a man named Dennis who is the husband of one of the American church ladies who volunteered at the Home. The policemen have firearms. Li Nuan and the church lady, Beatrice, will remain unarmed. Their job is to corral the girls, and the thinking is that they will be less frightening if they weren't swinging hatchets themselves.

From across the street, Li Nuan watches the roof of the building for a signal from the rooftop team. It's nighttime, but the gas streetlights cast enough light that she can just make out the edge of the roof above it. When Mei Ling appears and waves, Li Nuan signals Tye Leung, who pulls her hatchet out from under her skirts and lets out a battle cry and charges the entrance of the Lotus Pearl, hatchet swinging, as the others all storm in behind her. Li Nuan runs across the street and joins them, breathless and buzzing.

The few guards that are on duty are there to keep the girls and customers in line more than to defend the place from attackers, so they are unprepared for the onslaught and jump and duck away from the swinging hatchets. One of the guards pulls a firearm and aims it right at Li Nuan's face. She wasn't expecting to greet her death this night, this way, but so be it – she is shocked at how calm she is in the face of such a fate – then a shot thunders in her ears. One of the policemen behind her had fired – it strikes the guard targeting her in the shoulder, and he drops his weapon. The second guard, armed only with a knife, drops it and throws his hands up. Li Nuan catches all this in a flash as she runs past the scene. She'd expected the guards to fight to the bitter end, but she doubts that they're paid enough to make taking hatchet wounds and gunshots worth it. Also, they are outnumbered.

She dashes to the basement level. There is no time to process and absorb anything happening – just move, move, move, run, run, run. As the hatchet wielders hold the guards at bay, she dashes in among the cribs, and the familiar oily scent of the dim lamps that carved shadows in the dank space fills her nose and makes her queasy, and her time down here comes rushing back. But there is no time for terrible memories.

"Time to go!" she cries, in Cantonese, at the stunned faces of the girls. "Follow me to be free of this. Come! Come now!"

The male customers protest and curse at them but don't put up a fight. This isn't the first time such a raid has happened, though it is the first time here. Some of these men have probably witnessed something similar elsewhere. Some of them pull up their pants or cover their lustful parts with their hands, but a couple of them actually continue to pleasure themselves, their faces twisted and grotesque in the flickering light as their hands move furiously over their crotches. Li Nuan wants to hit them but holds back. This isn't about these men, and she and the others have to get the girls out as quickly as possible.

Beatrice leads the girls up the stairs to a door that opens onto the back alley. She gives Li Nuan a nod and a determined look that says, *I am with you.*

"Fai, fai di la," the church lady says in American-accented Cantonese. It is one of the words and phrases Tye Leung thought important enough for their allies to know. *Quickly. Hurry up.*

Li Nuan dashes down the corridor, heart pounding at the thought of running into a guard or Madam Bai. She heads for the room where the girls sleep. Dennis smashes down the door she points out and the smell of shit and sweat and unwashed bodies and despair assaults them both. The look of pity and disgust that takes over Dennis's face will haunt her for years afterward. But right now, in this moment, a pair of girls cower and cry in the squalor they have been forced into.

"We are helping you get free," Li Nuan tells them in Cantonese. "Come now. Come quick!" Sounds of confusion echo from upstairs, screams and roars and the thud of hatchets in wood. The girls in the parlor rooms have been reached and now they must be heading for the roof – their footsteps rumble through the stairwell. She ushers the girls out of the room, down the hall, to the door that opens onto the alley. One of the policemen holds the door as they exit – the girls, then Beatrice, then Dennis, then Li Nuan.

But before she had taken just a couple of steps, the policeman grabs her from behind, one arm locked around her while the other hand holds a cloth to her face, covering her mouth and nose.

"I have you, lassie," he says in the accent Tye Leung had once told her was *Irish*. "I've got you for the Boss."

And then the world goes dark.

When Li Nuan wakes, she is bound and gagged in a room she recognizes as the Little Emperor's bedroom in Boss Fong's apartment. She has cleaned this room many times and knows each floorboard, each corner. She is slumped on the floor, her hands tied to the bedframe, ankles bound together. What time is it? How long until the earthquake? The bedframe screeches sharply as she tugs at her bonds, willing the rope to break. It doesn't. Letting out a breath of frustration, she gives the bed a shove, sending it scraping across the floor again.

The Little Emperor enters then, lantern in hand. "You're awake," he says as he crouches in front of her. "It's about time." He smiles as he cups her face in his hands. He licks his lips. "You're not so tough without the white devils, are you? And have you learned you cannot trust them? That police officer is more loyal to bribes than he was to you."

She jerks her head back to avoid his touch, but then he grabs her by the hair and snarls. "Father will beat you for what you've done. You cost us eight girls tonight. That is lost income, plus they will be expensive to replace if we cannot get them back. So much trouble from such a pretty little thing."

He sounds almost impressed. "And Madam Bai may want to get in a few strikes also." He laughs. "And Father might just let me keep you, as a reward for capturing the wayward flower. But I am not sure you are worth keeping, after being so much bother. The best thing might be to beat you and leave you to die in the street like the foul thing you are. But I might as well have some fun with you before you receive the punishment you have earned."

He pulls the gag from her mouth. "You're going to need your little mouth to pleasure me."

"Monster," she curses him. "I will bite it off if you bring it near me."

He slaps her with the back of his hand, so hard she tastes blood in her mouth and her eyes are full of white stars. He stands and begins undoing his pants. "You don't talk to me like that, you filthy whore. Who do you think you are? Did that white witch convince you that you matter? That you are a person deserving of dignity?" He grabs her face by the chin and tilts it up at him, squeezing hard. "You are property. You are worth nothing but what pathetic men are willing to pay for you. But my father owns you, and that makes you mine, and I don't have to pay. I can just take." He pulls himself out of his pants. "If I feel any teeth, I will make your pretty face not so pretty anymore."

23.

NATHAN

September 3 - 4, 2006
Lake Tahoe, California

Breaking down camp and packing it all up is grueling as always. A few of the crew decide to skip the Temple burn of Sunday night, feeling ready to head back to the reality that includes indoor plumbing, hot showers, dust free beds, and all-you-can-eat prime rib buffets sooner rather than later. The Temple burn had long been Nathan's favorite, but he had never done the early entry thing before this year. And with those extra days on the front end, he's feeling crispy and ready to get the hell off the playa by Sunday morning. Not to mention, where once he had seen beauty and resilience and a fun sort of challenge, now all he can see is self-indulgent wastefulness and every human in sight diving headfirst into apocalypse.

He had even stayed sober Saturday night – Burn night – so Sunday would be less painful. He hadn't been able to convince the others to join him in that experience, however. Experiencing the orgiastic release and revelry of Saturday night at Burning Man stone cold sober had been trippy in its own way. After his revelation the other night, he just couldn't get into the big party in the same way as he had previous years. The fireworks annoyed rather than dazzled, and as the Man ignited, burned, and finally fell into a blazing heap, all he could think about was carbon emissions and depleted resources. He didn't hold the others back from their fun, though, at least he hoped not.

But come Sunday, he isn't the only one ready to leave. He and Remy break down their area, then help break down most of the group infrastructure – some of it will be left for those staying into Monday. After the dismantling of camp and loading of the trucks, he undertakes his favorite part: mooping. Matter Out Of Place is, of course, Burner culture's term for litter, and mooping is the cleaning up of that litter. Anything that isn't playa dust is picked up and put into bags to be hauled away by the group. Food scraps, stray bottle caps, anything plastic, fallen sequins or rhinestones, a crumb of a cookie, a ziptie – so many random bits. He walks his designated area in a grid pattern and picks up every stray bit of anything that isn't desert dust.

"Leave no trace" is a primary tenet of the event, and it's one that Nathan has always taken seriously. Haul it in, haul it out. The idea is that once the party was over and all the people gone, there would be no evidence that anything had even happened out here. There are those attendees that flout that guideline and leave behind tents, or bicycles, or bags of garbage. Of course there are. These are humans, after all. But most participants do their part responsibly.

As sunset approaches, they finally finish. Nathan, Remy, Mason, Delilah, Annika, and Danny all leave before dark, then spend three hours in exodus – the term for the line to get offsite and onto the highway – and then they drive through the night. There had been a thought to stop at a buffet in Reno, but the group collectively decides to push through to Mason's Lake Tahoe place where in the wintertime some of the gang go skiing. Danny and Annika pilot the Fish while Nathan and Remy follow in one of the box trucks, and Delilah and Mason take Mason's SUV.

There isn't much traffic at this hour, so keeping the caravan together isn't hard. To keep awake, Nathan and Remy drive with the windows down and the wind blowing, and they keep the techno pumping. They finally arrive in the early morning hours. After taking their first showers in ten days, Nathan and Remy collapse in bed in the guest room they usually take, and fall asleep snuggled up in the pre-dawn light.

When Nathan finally gets up, it's close to noon, and he's cotton-mouthed and fuzzy-headed. It's only the smells of bacon and coffee that motivate him to rise. He finds the others having brunch in the kitchen. They have no right to be as lively as they are.

"Try this," Delilah says as she shoves a piece of bacon dipped in chocolate in his mouth.

"We're heading to the lake later," Danny says. "After we give the vehicles a rinse. You down?"

"Sure." Nathan gratefully accepts the coffee that Remy hands him – his boyfriend knows just how he likes it. They have a couple of days here, and he's open to just going with the flow and having no agenda. But in the back of his mind, he's aware of a bigger issue: he has the rest of his life to figure out.

They give the vehicles a cursory rinse – a more thorough cleaning will come later – then unload Mason's SUV and pile in. He drives them to his favorite spot on the lake, where the water is clear and blue and cold. After a quick dip, Nathan and Remy sit on a big, sun-warmed rock and share a spliff.

"You've been in a funk since Thursday night," Remy says.

Nathan takes a toke, coughs – there's more tobacco in it than he expected. After a couple of silent passes and tokes, he says, "I don't think I'm going again."

"Going where?"

"The Burn. What we just did. I think that was my last time."

"Wait. What? It was that bad?" Remy's voice squeaks with surprise. "Why? I mean, I know it's a lot of work –"

"It's not that." Nathan sighs. "You know how I told you about the visions I got from the cup?"

"You mean all that apocalypse stuff? What about it?"

Nathan hadn't shared his mushroom tea experience with anybody since it happened, and he sees that now is the time. "Drinking the tea from that cup might not have been the best idea. But, well, I saw some things that night. Not hallucinations – revelations, more like. I'd had these thoughts all day… Well, ever since the protests at the office, really, and then it came to a head at the Waffle burn…" He tells Remy all about what he'd been thinking that night, the waste he saw, the visions of global catastrophe. He explains how in light of what the cup showed him of the future, he just can't in good conscience participate in the event any longer. As he speaks, he feels both sure of his convictions and also like a crazy person. He's making a big decision like this based on psychic visions from a teacup? Really?

"You believe those visions are real?" Remy has donned his cloak of skepticism. He likes to do that to feel smart. "Like, really real?"

"Yes. Really real. I think what I've received from the cup is a warning. About this path we're on as a society. And Burning Man is like – I don't know – like all of it in microcosm. The beautifully social and creative parts, and the ugly wasteful parts too. Anyway, when I held the teacup while I was standing out at the trash fence, it felt like somebody was talking to me. From the future."

"That's a big, weird-ass assumption that might be a hallucination to base such a huge life change on."

"I don't know if not going to Burning Man anymore is that huge a life change, really. In the grand scope of things."

Nathan knows this might be hard for Remy to hear. So much of their lives, so much of their relationship, revolved around being Burners together, and taking part in this community, in the creativity and the parties. In the annual pilgrimage to the playa. The whole thing had become an organizing principle of their lives. What would they be, together, without all of that in common?

"I'll still go to off-playa stuff," Nathan says. "But the big thing in the desert – I just don't think I can do it after what I've seen and what I've felt and thought. That bell can't be unrung, you know?"

"Are you sure you're not letting the situation at work color your judgment a little? Like whether you go to Burning Man or not is something you can control, but you still gotta work for an industry that uses child labor?"

Oh, that fucking NDA. No doubt Kendal will expect him to sign it as soon as he gets back.

"Are you signing it?" Remy asks, as if reading his mind. "And staying gainfully employed? Or are you gonna blow that shit up too?"

"I'm not blowing anything up..." Okay. Remy's taken aback by this decision. Nathan did just spring it on him, from Remy's perspective, out of nowhere. He can let the snide tone go. "I don't know how to do anything else. And

Kendal's right. Look behind the scenes at pretty much any tech product and there's bound to be somebody being exploited somewhere." Fuck! What the hell are we doing in this world?

"I don't know what I'm going to do," Nathan finally says.

The gang leaves the lake after a couple of hours, then they stop by a market to grab provisions for the evening. Once back at Mason's place, Delilah whips up a batch of sangria while Danny mans the grill. After dinner, Mason pulls out a mirrored tray and sets it on the coffee table in the living room. "All right," he declares. "Leftovers. Let's see what ya got."

Everyone tosses out their leftover party supplies, which amounts to a few tabs of acid, a handful of mushrooms, some MDMA, some ketamine, some coke. Danny and Mason go for the coke, while Annika and Delilah each pop a couple of mushroom caps and also dip into the MDMA.

"A little hippie flip, huh?" Remy teases.

"Just a little itty-bitty flip," Annika says with a laugh. "Takes the edge off, you know."

Nathan and Remy each do a dab of MDMA, but Nathan isn't up for much more than that. Remy checks in with him before doing more himself, in accordance with their longstanding relationship rule: you can fuck whoever you want, but don't you dare do drugs without me. They have stuck by it these few years of couplehood. It hasn't been that difficult. They snuggled up on the couch, grooving to the music Mason put on, and they all shared their highlights from the week. Everyone agreed Sugar Bunny was a joy.

"She was definitely my favorite new person," Danny says.

"You two made a love connection, huh?" Mason teases.

"A gentleman doesn't kiss and tell."

"So why aren't you telling, then?" Remy asks to everyone's laughter. "Oh, hey, she gave me this," he adds, and pulls a small clay tablet from his pocket. "It says 'a dreamer.'"

"Oh, is that from the wheel of fortune thing?" Delilah asks. "Let me see." The group passes the tablet around.

"I got one too," Annika says. "But I lost it. It's probably in my shit somewhere. I hope it's not moop."

"What did yours say?" Delilah asks.

"A skeptic."

"Remy should have gotten that one," Nathan says without really meaning to. They exchange looks, but Nathan can tell Remy is taking it in stride – the drugs maybe helped – and they remain snuggled up.

"I think a healthy skepticism should be maintained in all things," Remy says. "Gotta keep the bullshit at bay."

Danny cuts himself another fat line while speaking. "Bullshit is the currency of the day." He nods in his usual sage-like way for dramatic effect before going on. "Everyone wants to sell you some."

"Wouldn't that make bullshit the product, and not the currency?" Mason asks.

"Shut up," Danny counters profoundly. "I don't have to make sense."

"All this talk about currency and product…" Annika shakes her head and runs her fingers through her hair. "It's like all our minds are colonized by capitalism."

"It's the water we swim in," Remy says. "We're like… consumer fish."

"Okay this is getting too serious." Danny stands with purpose, ready to lighten the mood or proclaim another keen insight. Maybe both.

"You're the one that said bullshit was currency, or whatever," Mason points out.

"And I regret it." Danny walks to the center of the living room and raises a glass. "We've got good drugs, good tunes, and good friends. Let's..."

Everyone leans forward, anticipating more party wisdom from Danny Gobo. His hand goes to his chest, and a look of confusion sweeps across his face. Then he collapses – just falls straight to the floor. His dropped sangria spills across the white rug in a red wave.

"Danny!" Mason yells, leaping to his feet and rushing to where Danny lay. He turns their friend over. "Shit, he's not breathing. Shit shit shit –"

"I know CPR!" Annika cries and leaps into action. "Somebody call 911."

Nathan dials, frantic, as Annika begins tending to their friend. Something cracks as she performs the first round of compressions. Whatever buzz Nathan had been feeling has evaporated. Funny how a crisis can sober you up real quick.

"What's your emergency?"

"Our friend collapsed..." Nathan says. But even as the words leave his mouth, even as Annika performs emergency measures, he knows in his own still-beating heart, that Danny is gone.

24.

MAIDA

March 21, 2106
East Shore Marina, San Francisco

"Why are you helping us?"

We had taken to leaving the newsfeeds off over breakfast. I didn't want to see all our faces on screen coupled with the twisted-up story anymore. The silence allowed space for conversation, and provided an opportunity for me to ask Felix something I had been wanting to ask.

A rare seriousness came over him before he answered. "A telekinetic saved my life once. On the arkship where I grew up. A crane broke, and this big pallet of steel pipes hanging above me was falling. I would have been smashed to jelly if she hadn't been there. And, on top of that, my mother heard voices. At first, she thought maybe she was telepathic, but it turned out they weren't real voices. She was just old-fashioned psychotic with auditory hallucinations that told her to hurt people and burn things. But a telepath helped sort her out. Another time, my father was lost at sea after getting caught in a storm while out on a fishing expedition. A clairvoyant found his boat and saved him and his crew. Psions have helped my family in major ways throughout my life. So for me, people like you are a blessing in this world, and nothing to fear. And I know I'm not the only one with stories like that."

I saw Felix through a new lens of appreciation. People like him were blessings in the world too. People willing to put themselves out to help others, even those not like them.

A familiar psionic tickle in my brain. Aviva: *We've got something. Can you get to Dolores Park in an hour?*

Yes.

Obscure your face.

I've seen the news.

I let Felix know I had an errand to run.

"We'll be here," he said, then went back to tinkering. He was always tinkering with something on board. "Be careful."

I didn't have many options in the way of disguise, so I tied up my hair, pulled on a light hoodie, and donned a pair of Felix's sunglasses. It wasn't much, but it was what I had to work with. I was just thankful that the Sierra Northshore Regional Alliance didn't engage in surveillance state activities like some other regions – if there had been security cams everywhere, I'd have been screwed. Would that change in light of the psion threat? We couldn't let it get to that. Would I still do the mission even if there was security everywhere? I wanted to believe I would.

I hopped the nearest lightrail – only about a block away – and headed for the Mission District. Daylighted creeks glinted in the afternoon sun as the tram made its way along its designated path through the city – living, flowing water where asphalt and concrete used to be. I wondered what the precursor residents of the city would make of it now. Someone wearing translucent wings stood above the arc of a footbridge, arms out against the wings' multihued glimmer, as if they were blessing the watershed.

As I disembarked at the Mission Dolores station, I heard from Aviva: *Southwest corner. Bench at the top.*

I kicked off my shoes and walked up the slope, my bare feet on cool grass. As I walked, scenes from the park's life played out in the psifield: ghosts in feathered headdresses danced on the grass – phantoms of the Yelamu Ohlone Tribe who once lived on this land. Then, as they faded, Spanish priests in fine vestments appeared, carrying golden crosses and imposing themselves on the land and the people here. The priests faded, and graves bearing monuments carved with Hebrew sprang from the ground, mourners weeping or looking contemplative by an oddly whimsical fountain. And then the cemetery was closed and gone, the graves fading out with the emergence of tents housing earthquake refugees, horse-drawn wagons here and there. Then, leisurely folk in rapidly shifting fashion styles flickered in and out – flying discs tossed about, brightly colored hoops glinted in the sun, political actions and festivals taking up the hillside with throngs of activists and celebrants, banners fluttering. Bands jammed, poets and activists chanted; so many causes and pleas for equality and justice rushed by. This hillside practically shone with all the collective prayers of centuries. Fields of scantily clad people sunned themselves. Happy dogs ran about. Ice cream and ganja treats sold. A playground came and went. Picnics and barbeques and birthdays and memorials. All the eras of this park fluttered through my sight, a palimpsest of the life of the city, year overwriting year, generation over generation, century over century.

Had Li Nuan or any of her community taken refuge here after the disaster? Probably not, since the Chinese community was more segregated at that time. Had Nathan and his friends ever spent nice, sunny days here? I hadn't gleaned anything like that, but my guess would be yes, they did. They seemed like the kind of people who did that sort of thing.

And this day, it served as a spot for a clandestine meeting of activists, or subversives, or rebels, or whatever the hell we were, working out a nefarious scheme by a political leader. I wondered how many of those had happened here as well. In two hundred years, this can't have been the first clandestine meeting.

Who am I meeting? Del or Kemp?

Someone from Freedom Faction. He's helping us.

Okay, my nervousness ramped up a little with that information. Maybe it was a good thing Aviva didn't divulge that before I came out here. I spotted the bench I was supposed to go to; nobody was there at the moment. The park was well populated, though I wouldn't have called it crowded. Still, a fair amount of people lounged on the grass, as they do. The day was clear, and it was warmer at the park than at the marina. I took a seat with my hood pulled up, sunglasses on. Did this attempt at going incognito work, or did it look way conspicuous? I took down my hood but left the sunglasses on. I wished I'd thought to bring an e-book or tablet or something to look at. Instead, I took in the vista: all of downtown could be seen from that spot, and a bit of the bay beyond. It was too bad I didn't have a picture of the old skyline, before some of the towers were dismantled and the parts repurposed. It would have been fun to compare and contrast.

Aviva, I thought into the psifield. I didn't know if I could really call her that way. I was no telepath, so would she pick up my signal if she wasn't tuning into me already? Or did she pick up whenever somebody thought at her? I didn't know how that part worked. But then, I was on a mission, so wouldn't she have been paying attention? *Aviva.*

He's close. His name's Victor.

After a couple of minutes, a dark-haired man, also wearing sunglasses, sat down on the other end of the bench.

"Maida."

"Victor?"

He didn't say anything. Could I look at him? Should I? He didn't look over, so I didn't either. This was so weird.

He pulled something from his inside jacket pocket and slid it across the bench. I grabbed it, took a look. A pair of eyeglasses in a hard case.

"I hope you can do something with those. I've got to get them back to the office in thirty minutes."

I'll see what you see.

I was about to ask who he got these from, but I didn't have to bother. I'd know in a second. After removing the glasses from their case, I clasped my hands around them and focused. Threads of awareness reached out from me and back into me within the psifield, and the circuit brought knowledge: Robert Patrick Fisk owned these glasses. He oversaw a wastewater processing plant in the city. He was also a Captain in the Freedom Faction organization, and came into possession of these glasses in–

We don't need to know all that. Can you direct your scan?

I've never really tried that–

Try it now

There was a rush of data: frames were vintage, made in the 2050s by a company called Optical Prime, which disappeared during the Collapse. Salvaged in a site recovery in the 2090s. Lenses crafted five years ago, specifically for Mr. Fisk who has an astigmatism. I let the data rush through my mind. History flowed right through me.

What have you seen, what have you seen, what have you seen, I thought to myself – and to Aviva, too, I guess, since she was in my head. A wisp, a tendril, of Aviva's telepathic link, and I felt her grasping the question I was thinking and… directing it? A rush of images: a little girl running up to hug him, a distressed-looking woman – his wife, Abigail – as they argued in a kitchen. An inspection of the Living Machines that were the basis of the waste treatment he oversaw. And then a meeting, with Oliver Shulamith addressing a group. There was a white board that had four circles drawn on it in black marker. They were numbered one through four, and lines were drawn from two of them to a square labeled "Target 1."

The stream of images stopped.

Is there more?

I focused, but all I picked up were flashes of whoever owned these glasses before they were the property of Robert Patrick Fisk. Somebody named Greg, who worked in financial services –

Okay. Thank you.

I put the glasses back in the case and slid them back across the bench.

"Is that it?" He sounded surprised.

"It all happens in my head." I cast a glance his way and saw that he was looking over at me now too.

"Wow," he whispered, mostly to himself, I think.

"Why are you doing this?"

He let out a sigh. "My sister is a psion. My twin sister, she's telekinetic. I don't believe the stories they're feeding us about the community, and, well, she's my sister."

I nodded my understanding.

He pockets the glasses case and stands. "Good luck with everything."

I watched him head down the hill and gave it a couple of minutes before I got up to make my own way out of the park. I was probably being paranoid, taking cloak-and-dagger spy-business secret meetings in the park will bring that out in a person I guess. But before I made it down the hill to the lightrail stop, a black vehicle with dark windows pulled up in front of Victor. Two men dressed like the security detail at Oliver's apartment grabbed him and shoved him into the back. That wasn't good.

One of them spotted me – he was looking in my direction and speaking into a comm device. Fuck.

Aviva!

You're tense. What's wrong.

Security people grabbed Victor. They've spotted me. I had turned around and was heading back up the hill as quickly as I could without running. I chanced a look back and saw they were following. I ran.

I'll have Del keep an eye on you.

That was reassuring, but it didn't really help me in the moment. But what else could Aviva do, anyway? Where even was she? I got to a pedestrian bridge that crossed over the lightrail tracks and came out on a street that ran perpendicular to where those guys grabbed Victor. Crossing it, I planned on ducking into the neighborhood streets. And after that, I didn't know what. Hide behind somebody's compost bin? Maybe I could find an unlocked tool shed or garage?

Just as I thought I might have had a shot at evading these guys, another one of those black vehicles rounded the corner, headed out of the street I was shooting for. As I turned to head the other way, the other one approached from the other direction. I turned back towards the footbridge as two security personnel stepped off of it. Shit. I was surrounded.

Stopping in the middle of the street, I put my hands up, which seemed like the thing to do.

"I think there's a big misunderstanding here –"

Something sharp pinched me and I looked down to see a dart sticking out of my chest. The whole world wavered and blurred and I fell to my knees, to the street. The masked men closed in around me as my sight narrowed to a tight aperture, then it closed up and everything went black.

25.

LI NUAN

April 18, 1906
Chinatown, San Francisco

A church bell rings five times from some place in a foreign part of the city she has never been. The sky begins to lighten with the first hints of approaching dawn, and Li Nuan knows that soon the ground will shake. When she hears the Boss rise, she coughs loudly and struggles against her bonds, scraping the bed against the floor. The Little Emperor, still snoring in the bed, doesn't rouse at all. As she had hoped would happen, Boss Fong opens the door to see what the racket is. He pauses, startled, in the doorway when he sees her tied to his son's bed.

Then his face darkens. "Treacherous dog," he spits out. He crosses the room to shake his son awake. "Get up and bring her to the parlor." His voice is low and heavy.

Little Emperor slides out of bed and glares down at her. "Don't be any trouble."

When they reach the parlor, Li Nuan is surprised to see Madam Bai present. The Madam rushes over at the sight of her and slaps her across the face.

"You ungrateful wretch." She wears only a dressing gown after a night, no doubt, of pleasuring the Boss, yet she is no less imperious in her bearing. "We were moving you up to the parlor rooms! Who do you think you are?"

"Bai Ying," the Boss says and snaps his fingers.

Madam Bai responds immediately to the snap. From the tea set on the table, she pours him a cup as he takes a seat in his favorite chair. So the Madam isn't above making tea. Li Nuan knows she must have prepared it – who else, the Boss himself? She almost laughs at the absurdity of the thought. The Boss waves Li Nuan over. She obeys, wondering how close it is now. The sun isn't up yet, though it looks like the streetlamps are going out. The room is lit by a couple of kerosene lanterns in addition to the gaslights, and candles send shadows flickering across the Boss and Madam Bai like whispers of ghosts.

Madam Bai hands the Boss his tea, then stands beside his seat as she gathers her robe tighter around herself.

"You have cost me dearly," Boss Fong says. "You and the white witch. I should drag you down to the alley and cut your throat and leave you out with the trash. I should drag you through the streets to let everyone in Chinatown know the cost of crossing me. But I think binding you to my son for the rest of your useful years will be better. Maybe you can birth some girls to replace the ones you stole."

Disgust roils inside her and a curse burns on her tongue. But the sky outside grows ever lighter, and a charge has come into the air, causing the hairs on the back of her neck and the fine hairs on her arms to stand up. The disaster the cup foretold approaches.

"How would you like to punish her for her terrible behavior?" Boss Fong asks with a glance at his son, who is standing a few steps behind her.

"Whip her," Little Emperor says. Li Nuan recognizes the lust in his voice.

He isn't done. "After the skin is whipped off her back, we burn down that white witch's house and all our stolen girls."

"I wish to be there for that," Madam Bai says, her face gleeful.

"Why are you smiling?" Boss Fong asks with a scowl at Li Nuan.

A hint of a smile does indeed curl her lips. "Because it is your house that will fall –"

She hasn't finished speaking when the floor shakes. Then it shakes harder, and a rumble fills the air, and a wave moves through the building. Li Nuan is shaken to her knees and watches in wonder and fear as the walls and the floors ripple with the quake. A chunk of ceiling above Boss Fong breaks off and falls, and from behind her, Little Emperor's cry of alarm followed by a loud crash. Madam Bai has ducked under the table and cowers there, whimpering. Li Nuan crouches on the floor, huddled over with her hands over her head. After what feels like an eternity, but which Li Nuan understands is only several seconds, the shaking stops.

Madam Bai crawls over to Boss Fong, while the Little Emperor reaches for help from under the bookshelf that had fallen over onto him. "Help me," he says.

"Li Nuan!" Madam Bai cries, "The Boss is alive! Help me get this rubble off of him!"

She looks around at these people, who, moments ago, had been ready to whip her and enslave her, and are now asking for her help. Who do they think she is? Who do they think they are? The flames of the candles and the lanterns call her. She dashes over to the table, grabs a lantern, then hurls it at the floor where it smashes in front of Little Emperor in a burst of fire and glass. Oily flame spreads across the floor, hungry for vengeance as he cries out.

Madam Bai screams. "Crazy whore! What are you doing?"

Li Nuan grabs the other lantern and sends it flying to Madam Bai's feet, where another blossom of flame erupts to life.

"Getting away from you," Li Nuan answers. "You can burn."

Madam Bai's screams grow even more shrill as she spins, dropping her burning robe to the floor so that she stands disheveled and naked. The smell of singed hair fills the room. The Boss is unconscious in his chair, half-buried by the bits of fallen ceiling, and Li Nuan wishes he were awake to be afraid and to hurt.

The teacup, the one that told her this day would come, seems to glow with its own internal light, a golden halo surrounding the deep-green stone. Voices whisper out of it, telling her the cup is hers, telling her to seize it like she is seizing her freedom. She grabs it, clutches it in her hand as she dashes for the door. Madam Bai runs after her, screeching, incoherent, and claws at her clothes. The floor shakes again with another tremor as Li Nuan fights her off, bats at her face, slaps her hands away. She presses her back towards the two pools of fire that are about to merge into one. They step past Little Emperor's burnt form under the bookshelf – he is perfectly still as he quietly burns.

Madam Bai keeps screaming, but Li Nuan is calm, the calmest she has ever felt, as she gets the Madam right to the edge of the fire, then she sticks a foot out behind one of Madam Bai's ankles and gives the woman a hard shove, sending her stumbling backward into the burning pool of kerosene upon the ignited floorboards. The woman's screams don't faze her in the least. It is merely the sound of justice.

Li Nuan closes the door behind her and twists the key in the lock, leaving it in the keyhole. As she runs down the stairs, an explosion rocks the building from the upper level, and a bloom of flame comes roaring at her. One of the pipes that fuels the gaslamps must have been broken by the quake. She hurls herself out the door and into the street just as an explosion blasts out the windows into a rain of shards. The ground rumbles some more, but not as strongly this time. When it stops, Li Nuan gets to her feet, brushes herself off, still clutching the teacup. The building that had been her prison burns. She looks around at the crumbled structures all around her. She knows from her vision that, soon, it will all burn.

She heads down the street, her steps surprisingly light as she walks in the direction of the Home. She hopes everyone there is safe. After she'd gone a couple of blocks, someone calls, "Li Nuan! Li Nuan!" It's a familiar voice she hasn't heard in a while.

She turns to see Bao running over to her from the teashop. "You're all right?"

She nods. "Your father?" She looks over Bao's shoulder and sees the old man, blinking and confused in the dusty air.

"I go home," she says, pointing in the direction of the Mission Home.

Bao's face softens as he nods his understanding. "Be safe." He turns and rejoins his father.

People spill out into the streets, stagger about in sleeping clothes, some barely dressed at all, some in their coats and bare feet. They all blink at each other, at the falling city, as they stumble into whatever awaits them next.

The ground rumbles again.

She expects to find a scene of chaos at the Home, but when she reaches it, it's surprisingly intact. In fact, she doesn't see any damage at all. The girls have gathered outside and are mostly calm and orderly under Tye Leung's command. Miss Cameron spots her approaching up the hill and clasps her hands together. Then Li Nuan is caught up in a tight embrace.

"I was so worried," Miss Cameron says. "Come join the others."

Li Nuan walks over, exchanging a look of acknowledgement with Mei Ling who is busy corralling a few of the younger girls. Tye Leung walks up to her and takes her hand.

"They tried to take you again," she says. "That policeman was dirty."

"They won't take any girls ever again," Li Nuan says. She doesn't say more, but in Tye Leung's eyes and in the nod the tiny woman gives her, Li Nuan sees understanding.

Miss Cameron comes over to them. "We can allow the girls to grab a few things, but we must find a place to go. Li Nuan, can you help with some of the younger ones?"

Li Nuan nods, happy to help. Despite the chaos and destruction, she feels the calmest she has felt in years. The past is rubble and flame, and the future beckons.

"What's that?" Tye Leung asks, looking down at Li Nuan's hand.

Li Nuan holds up the teacup. "It is mine."

26.

NATHAN

October 6, 2006
SOMA District, San Francisco

He thought at first that he would miss this office, but now that the last of his stuff is all packed, he doesn't really think he will. He actually can't wait to get out of here, to walk away and never look back. But there are the niceties to get through. He owes at least that much to his soon-to-be-former colleagues. After the visions he got from the cup, after the realizations he had at the Burn, he's come to understand that if he were to continue in his current career, he would not be living a life of integrity. He would be making the easy decision: to keep making bank even knowing the horrific, hidden costs.

Besides, he knows he doesn't want to sign that NDA; it amounted to a legally binding promise to never speak of the inhumane practices upon which their sector is based, and the thought of making such a promise repulsed him. He could never live with himself. And he imagined that Danny would be disappointed in him, knowing what he knows and still making the choice to shut up and go on like everything is just fine. The only other option Kendal left him was to hand in his resignation. So he did. Is he scared and freaking out about what he will do next? Fuck yes. But he's got savings, and Remy still makes good money, and he has some time to figure out his next chapter. It's scary, this step, but it's right. He wants to be the kind of person that's brave enough to do the right thing, even if it's hard.

Lili sits in the chair behind the desk, arms crossed. She looks so annoyed. "I can't believe you're walking away from this. You are absolutely brilliant, with an even more brilliant future ahead of you. And you're casting it aside all because of some vision you had at fucking Burning Man?"

"It's been building for a while, Lili," he says. "And if you'd been paying attention, you'd know that."

She looks offended, but he really doesn't give a fuck. She's a work friend, not a friend-friend, and her callousness towards the revelation of child labor being so key to keeping their enterprise running showed him who she is.

"What are you going to do now? Save the allegedly endangered environment?"

He wishes he could help her see what he sees of what's coming – and he has no doubt that what the cup has shown him really is their future. He is more certain than ever that those visions had been a warning, and were intended as such. In his mind, the Belgian Waffle burns. In his mind, patches of fire light up the ocean. This entire culture of consumption and waste is heading toward disaster, disaster still far enough away, as measured by human lifetimes and product cycles, to be seen as the distant SciFi Future. But it isn't, really. Maybe not tomorrow, but certainly by the time he's an old man, things are going to be more starkly clear, and the generation after that, and the one after that, are going to have to deal with the reckoning. Sorry, younger people. Sorry we fucked it up.

"I don't know yet," he says. Lili continues glaring at him from what had been his desk. He's donated his entire bonus from the Link project to the International Initiative on Exploitative Child Labor, the NGO founded in 1998 dedicated to eliminating the worst abuses. It's a good start, but he wants to do more than give money to causes. He wants to use his skills and experience to help make the world better – he just hasn't worked out the specifics yet. But he has faith it will come to him. The permaculture course he agreed to take with Danny started last weekend, and he's into it so far. But he's only been through the first weekend, so it's too soon to say what kind of impact it will have on him, but he holds out hope it might provide a sign-post for him to follow. He doesn't want to tell Lili about it, though – such a course would be way too hippie for her jaded urbanity, and he's had enough of her judgment.

"Well, if you're done packing it up, will you deign to join us for a toast?" Lili gets up and strides to the door. "You're still the best designer this company ever had, despite your newfound global conscience. You still deserve a toast for all you've accomplished here."

The common area is decorated for a party, with streamers and balloons. It's all meant to be a colorful celebration, but all Nathan can see now is waste. Yes, it all looks lovely now, but it's also all destined for a landfill. He appreciates the effort made on his behalf, made by his colleagues to show they will miss him, that they appreciate him, but it's all so weird now. The bell can't be unrung.

Someone shoves a plastic cup of champagne in his hand.

"Attention, please." Kendal doesn't even have to raise her voice much to capture the attention of the room. The chatter around the office quiets as she raises her cup. "Nathan, your contributions to this company have helped us earn the reputation for innovative, elegant, and groundbreaking design that we enjoy, and that brings us top-notch – and top paying – clients. I have long admired your work ethic, your insight, and your creative mind. We are going to miss you around here, and I know a couple of our major clients are going to miss you too. I know that whatever you decide to do, you will be spectacular. And I hope you find whatever... purpose... it is that you're looking for. Here's to you, Nathan."

Cheers all around, applause.

Nathan smiles, waves, sips his champagne. This is all very sweet, and he is touched by this display. At the same time, it feels a little like going through the motions of a life that isn't his anymore. It feels a little empty, and he can't wait to get out of here.

The cove is sheltered from the wind by the surrounding cliffs, and the moon hangs high and bright. Out at the Burn, Remy had made the acquaintance of a band of firedancers called Solar Flare – they were the group that came and spun by the Fish the night of the mushroom tea. Someone from that group invited the Fish crew to join in their full moon gathering on the beach by the Sutro Baths ruins. Delilah had pointed out that the moon was a sliver shy of full tonight, but somebody from Solar Flare explained that some of the crew had a gig on the actual full moon night, so they were doing their jam the night before.

The Baths had been a recreational attraction for San Franciscans in the late 1800s, and featured swimming pools, restaurants, and hosted concerts. It had a capacity of ten thousand people – Nathan pictures a gigantic day spa and thinks such a thing would be pretty cool to have today. But now all that's left of that place are concrete ruins.

The path they take – Nathan and Remy are following one of the Solar Flare crew – entails walking along a narrow path of rough concrete that's probably the remnants of one of the pools. On one side, the ruins still hold water – a tidal pool, essentially – while on the other, a barrier of rocks lay between them and the crashing tide. Nathan had heard about incidents of people being swept off the rocks and drowned. He isn't sure that they absolutely had to take this particular path to the cove, but it's certainly scenic and mysterious. It's like they're adventurers on a quest. The path is narrow, and walking it, Nathan understands why they were advised to bring headlamps.

He'd seen firedancers before, of course. They're a pretty consistent presence at the parties and festivals that Remy plays, which are a central feature of their lives. But until now, they'd always been background eye candy. He watches this crew as they carefully set up the area where they keep their fuel and dip their wicks – which he's learned are made of Kevlar. They also keep at the ready the black drop cloths they used for putting out unfortunate accidental ignitions of clothing or hair or skin.

This group has choreographed routines and had performed a "fire opera," called Oedipus Sex, out on the playa this year, which he is now sad to have missed. It's always been impossible to catch everything that happened out there. He admires the skill and grace and creativity, mesmerized by the fiery trails made by their props as they spin and whirl. Once again, thoughts of wastefulness preoccupy him. These folks dip their wicks in white gas, the same type of fuel that he and Remy use for their camping stove. But here, the fuel isn't being burnt for any practical purpose – it's just pretty.

"You can't go through the rest of your life thinking this way," Remy had chastised him in the middle of Trader Joe's when he'd been going off about the wastefulness of every item within his gaze, all the unnecessary packaging. "You're going to make yourself crazy. What are you going to do, live in a cave and subsist on lichen and burn only foraged deadwood for fuel and drink your own piss?"

He had a point. And Nathan supposes that whatever amount of fuel the global community of firedancers burns for their art is a drop in the bucket compared to the needs of mass amounts of private cars, air travel, energy production, plastic production, and so on and so on. The problem is systemic and needs to be solved on the level of industry and global economy, not on the level of a group of friends practicing their artform on a beach.

Somebody from the Solar Flare crew named Pixie passes him a flask.

"I hear you quit your soul-killing corporate job," she says.

"Basically, yeah." Funny how total strangers perceive a person's deeply personal situation from the outside. He takes a swig – whiskey – and hands it back.

"Here's to ya." She raises the flask to him before taking a sip herself.

As the firespinners take a break, Nathan and Remy stand at the water's edge, looking out at the ocean.

"Someday, this will be gone," Remy says. "Like those baths are gone, just ruins now. Eventually, the ruins will be gone, and our buildings now will become new ruins. This cove we're in is accessible only at low tide, but one day it's always going to be high tide. It will be an even higher tide."

Nathan giggles. "How high are *you* right now?"

"I've been reading up on global warming. It seemed like I should know about what these visions of yours have told you. Some people on the internet think it's fake."

"Some people on the internet are fucking morons." Though he's being snarky, Nathan is touched that Remy has taken the time to learn about something important to him, something about what he's going through.

"Last burn!" somebody calls out.

Whoops and hollers echo across the moonlit beach and against the cliff that rises behind them. The mood is light – joyful, even. One by one, balls of flame ignite, like little stars waking up.

27.

MAIDA

March 22, 2106
Occluded Location, San Francisco

I woke up in a gray room, laid out on a cold and hard metal shelf – which I think was supposed to be a bunk. A toilet stood in the corner with no privacy barrier around it of any kind. The heavy steel door confirmed I was a prisoner here. But where was here? A secret lab? The blueprints of the facility I gleaned from Linstrom flashed through my mind and I sat bolt upright; was I there, in whatever that place was? The detention center? How long had I been unconscious?

I looked around, tried to quell rising panic. The gray brick walls were lined with a fine silver mesh that caught the harsh, white, institutional lighting. It twinkled, and I'd have thought it was pretty if I wasn't locked up. I wanted to touch it, but I had no idea what it was or what it did, so I held back.

There was a panel at the bottom of the door, which I supposed was how they'd feed me – assuming that they did. I got to my feet slowly – whatever it was they shot me with still had me feeling groggy, but fear was starting to bring some sharpness back to my senses.

Aviva…?

Nothing. Which was just what I expected. With my palms on the slab I rested on, I reached out with my psychometric sense – maybe I could get a clue as to where I was if I knew the ownership of this room, these fixtures. But I got nothing. It wasn't just that I didn't get a hit off the furniture; I didn't feel my psychometric sense at all. The psifield just wasn't there, or else my connection was severed, a possibility I didn't want to entertain. *Shit hell damn fuck.* I took a couple of deep breaths to still the anxiety burbling up in my gut.

"Hello?" I kicked at the door.

A walkie-talkie crackled on the other side. "She's awake," somebody said. So they had me locked up and posted a guard right outside the door. I was almost flattered.

There was no window and no clock, so I had no idea what time it was, where I was, or if it was even the same day as when they grabbed me. But the guard outside just let somebody know I was awake, so I expected to have some company sooner rather than later. I sat back down.

The silver mesh that lined the walls and ceiling of the room caught my eye again. What was that stuff? I reached out, tried to sense it through the psifield. Again, nothing at all. I brought my fingers even closer to it and a strange repelling sensation pressed against my fingertips – a similar feeling to trying to push magnets of the same charge together. That repelling force. I pressed through and touched the mesh and gasped. An intense feeling swept through me from my hand – not painful, exactly, but it felt like the psifield was being inverted inside me; it felt like my psychometric sense was being sucked out through my skin.

I pulled my hand away, surprised by the panic that swelled within me, and the – was it fear of loss? When my ability first manifested, it freaked me out, but then I got used to it, and while I never would have said I *loved* it, it was a part of me. But being cut off from it in this room, that moment just now of feeling like the mesh could have taken it from me for good, I wasn't prepared for how bereft I would be without it. I looked at the sparkly mesh again, feeling like it was a live thing that could pounce at any moment. No, I didn't like that stuff, not at all.

A few minutes later, the door beeped and swung open, and in strode Linstrom.

Wow, the man at the top himself, here to see me in my cell. I really was flattered.

"Maida, was it?" The door remained opened behind him, and two guards stood just outside, batons drawn and at the ready.

"Assessor Prime," I began, hoping that a show of deference and acknowledgment of his position would get me – I didn't know. Something. Some sort of consideration. "I think there's been a misunderstanding –"

"I'm sure you do." He smiled a smile that I knew was not intended to be reassuring. "That day when I visited the Presidio campus and came to your work area. You picked up my watch." He raised a hand and pulled his sleeve back, showing me the timepiece, as if to remind me. Like I needed reminding. "What did you see?"

"Oh... I don't remember all the details. It was made in Switzerland... It had been owned by a famous actor..."

"That's not what I mean." His voice took on a hard edge, not that he had been super friendly before.

"I'm not sure what you're getting at." Continuing to plead ignorance seemed the way to go, but deep down, I knew it was futile. "I could scan it again –"

"You'd like that, wouldn't you? So you can get a further peek into my business? Tell me what you saw that day in your lab. I do have means of extracting the information, which I assure you will be far less pleasant than this polite conversation we're having."

All right. He clearly knew anyway. "Operation Golden Days."

"Now we're getting somewhere. What do you know about it?"

I shook my head. "Just that there's something called 'Operation Golden Days.' There was a glimpse of blueprints that included a Psion Holding... Terminus? I think was the word? I didn't know what to make of it. That's all I know, that's all I saw. I mean..." I wasn't sure whether or not to share my speculation about it.

"Go on," he prompted. His eyes were a pale blue that reminded me of pictures I'd seen of arctic ice. They looked just as cold and unforgiving as that ice would be if it still existed and I were suddenly transported there, naked, and had to survive.

"I infer that Operation Golden Days involves rounding up psions and holding them at that facility. The one I saw the blueprints for. But that's all. I didn't scan anything about the purpose or timeline or details of the plan. It was just a quick flash. I swear."

"And you've obviously shared this with your boss? With Aviva?

I nodded.

"And what did you glean from the object that Victor Lee brought for you to scan? The eyeglasses owned by Robert Patrick Fisk?"

"Nothing important," I lied. "An inspection of a wastewater treatment facility, a glimpse of his daughter. An argument with his wife." I left out the battle plans. I left out that I knew Fisk was involved with Freedom Faction. "I'm not sure why I was given something of his to scan. Who is he?"

Linstrom stared me down, no doubt assessing my sincerity. "Aviva didn't inform you of that when you met with her?"

I shook my head. "She just told me where to go and who to meet."

"How imperious. I always thought her nurturing Earth Mother persona was just a front."

Somehow, that Linstrom would make a snide, disparaging remark about Aviva surprised me. He clearly was a creep with a dark agenda, but he never struck me as petty.

One of the guards interrupted. "The lab is ready."

Lab? I didn't like the sound of that.

Linstrom signaled the guards with a nod. "Let's go."

The guards came in and grabbed me by the arms. I didn't struggle much. "What's happening? Where are you taking me?"

"Don't put up a fight and it will go much easier for you."

Okay, I really didn't like the sound of that. I'd been trying to keep up a brave front, but fear surged through me in that moment. "I don't know anything else, I swear."

Linstrom led us out of the room and down a short corridor, at the end of which was another guarded door. The cell I was in seemed to be the only one. The only one down this hall, at least.

A by-now familiar presence was suddenly in my head grabbing my attention. *What's happening?*

Aviva? Where have you been?

I couldn't reach you before, you were occluded. What's going on?

I don't know, I was in a cell and they're bringing me somewhere else.

After a couple of turns and an elevator ride up two floors, we arrived at a lab. A couple of technicians in lab coats were at monitors, along with a woman in business dress who just stood there, stock still, and giving off a really weird vibe. She was familiar, but I couldn't place it.

Be prepared to do what I tell you.

What the fuck? *All right.*

I was pressed into a reclining chair, and the technicians strapped my wrists to the armrests and also restrained my legs at my ankles. Not for the first time since I woke up here, panic swelled in me, but this time I had Aviva in my head, so I felt less alone.

"My associate, here," Linstrom gestured to the woman in the suit, "is a telepath. She's going to do a little probe of your mind, to see if there's anything you haven't told me." He raised a hand to silence me as I began to protest. "Not that I doubt you've been anything but truthful. But it's possible there are details that you didn't notice or think to report that she will be able to perceive. After which, she will wipe from your mind everything you scanned from my watch and Mr. Fisk's eyewear."

"Telepaths can do that?" I looked at the woman. "You can do that?"

She looked down at me dispassionately, her gaze empty. Two things struck me at once: one was that she was not operating under her own volition – she was an automaton. Or had been made into one, because the second thing that struck me was that I recognized her: from the missing persons notice Lorel showed me at our first lunch together. The missing Liaison Officer that Aviva was worried about – Rebecca Morgan. Linstrom had her in his custody and was somehow controlling her and making her do his bidding. His own personal pet telepath.

"Such mind wipes are a more aggressive application of the ability than is taught at Circle of the Eye Academy," Linstrom said. "Which goes to show that your alma mater doesn't really encourage the full development of psionic potential as they claim. In fact, they steer you away from the most powerful possibilities."

Realization dawned. "You're not really anti-psion, are you? You want to round us up to use our abilities for your own ends."

"And you're not even a telepath!" Linstrom exclaimed. "And no, I am not opposed to psionic abilities. I am, however, opposed to people with such abilities running about free to do as they please. For a community who demands full personal autonomy, a lot of your own leadership seems afraid of your powers. Or talents, as I believe some of you say? In any case, what I propose will allow psions to use the full extent of their abilities. Push you to their very limits, not hold yourselves back as the Academy trains you to do. All in service of me and my allies, of course. We can't have you doing as you will. In any case, I will have my telepath here wipe this insight too."

Oh my god, what a condescending prick.

Stall him if you can.

"Wait – so why did you have to bring me to this lab? Why couldn't this be done in the cell?"

"The mesh in that room neutralizes psionic abilities. This procedure we have planned for you requires telepathy, so you, and my telepath here, can't be in there. Allowing the possibility that Aviva will contact you telepathically is a risk we simply must take." He stared into my eyes, practically willing me to confess Aviva and I were telepathically linked that very moment.

The mesh was freaky and interesting, but it didn't feel like the time to get into it. But I needed to stall him some more. "So you're going to wipe my mind and then? What? Keep me in that cell? Make me work for you too? I would never." I struggled against my restraints even though I knew it wouldn't do anything.

"What you would or would not do is irrelevant. You think Rebecca here is doing this of her own free will?" He snapped his fingers and barked at one of the technicians, "Bring me a chip."

The technician walked over with a square of some kind of clear material, on top of which rested a small black and silver circle, with hair-thin filaments coming out of its circumference. "This chip, implanted into the minds of psions – and regular humans, too, I suppose – keeps you docile. Makes sure you don't use your abilities until ordered to do so." He laughed. "Yes, that look of horror that just came over you, that's what I wanted to see. I'm only telling this to you so that the knowledge that your kind will soon be enslaved to me will horrify you. And, of course, this whole conversation will be erased from your memory, but I do hope some of that dread you feel will linger and haunt you." He dismissed the technician with a wave.

"Is that what you've done to Rebecca? Is..." I'd felt anxiety and panic and a general sense of unease since coming to in that cell, but this was the first time I actually felt afraid. The thought of my will and my very mind not being my own, being taken over... Linstrom was right. It was horrific. "Is that what you're going to do to me? Is that thing going in my head?"

"Your particular ability is interesting, to be sure, but of limited tactical advantage. Telepaths, telekinetics, and clairvoyants are more what I'm looking for. The best and strongest will be enlisted to my cause, the rest eliminated."

Limited tactical advantage. Yet I had glimpsed Operation Golden Days, the blueprints, the attack plan for whatever they're attacking. But I didn't argue. "Why are you doing this? To what end? So you can build your own private psion army and install yourself as dictator of all the regions?"

He just stared at me with a frozen smile.

"Oh my god, is that really your plan?"

A light over my face is turned on, and I squinted my eyes against its blazing glare.

"You are possessed of keen insight," Linstrom went on. "There may be use for you yet. Perhaps as an inspector or investigator of some kind. Perhaps you can help flush out those who would work against me."

"I don't want to work for you. I don't want to be part of your... your regime, or whatever."

"She didn't either." He cast a glance at Rebecca, who stood idly by, awaiting her instructions. She seemed like no more than a household appliance in this state. He continued, "Not all of your kind are as self-interested as Oliver Shulamith, who is more than willing to cooperate as long as he is rewarded with a position of privilege and authority. We expect most of you will be like Rebecca, here, unwilling to use your abilities to oppress your own kind. Luckily for us, we have developed the neural implant to encourage compliance."

Linstrom turned to Rebecca. "Dig up anything she knows about our plans, then wipe her memory." He stepped aside.

Rebecca stepped up to the chair where I was restrained and put her hands on the sides of my face, looking into my eyes. Her look was blank, and I swore I would never let that happen to me. "You don't have to do this," I said to that empty stare, hoping I could reach some part of her.

"She does have to, though," Linstrom said. "Because I told her to."

Scan her

What?

Scan her now!

I'd never scanned a person before, but I was willing to try. I had also never scanned anything without using my hands, but technically, all that was required was contact with the object and my skin. I was just used to using my hands. What choice did I have, anyway? I could already feel the tendrils of her telepathic probe, weird buzzing threads that were invasive in a way that Aviva's gentle immersion was not. Before she could get any farther into my mind, I initiated a scan – what a relief to feel the psifield again. The chair was manufactured in – No! Not that! I lifted my hands off the chair so that the only bits of my skin touching anything were the parts of my face in contact with her hands. I tried again. I experienced a tingling warmth in my hands whenever I scanned anything, and I tried to bring that feeling to my face, imagined the skin of my face tingling in that same way.

The psifield opened up: Rebecca Morgan, born in San Jose in 2068, became the property of Golden Days Holding Company in December 2105 when – a surge of light in my mind, not pain, exactly, but a sustained vibration, and a long, high-pitched tone sounded in my ears. Rebecca let go of my face, stumbled back a couple of steps and blinked.

"What is it?" Linstrom asked. "What's wrong?"

"Bastard," Rebecca said quietly. She looked up, and Linstrom, the guards, and the technicians all appeared frozen in place. "Release her," she said to one of the technicians, who walked over to me and undid my restraints. He seemed to be in some sort of trance, and I realized Rebecca must be telepathically controlling him. Was that any better than the chip Linstrom put in her head? It was not the time for pondering ethical conundrums, however.

Leave this room and go left, there's a stairwell at the end of the hall. Go all the way to the bottom and out the fire exit. Go now before the alarm.

Without really pausing to think about it, I did as Aviva told me. I grabbed one of the guard's stun guns, just in case.

"I'll hold them," Rebecca said. "Aviva's let me know what's happening. Go!"

I wanted to ask how she was doing, how she came under Linstrom's control, but there wasn't time for any of that. "Thank you," I said, and ran.

As I approached the door to the stairwell, another lab-coated technician spotted me.

"Hey!" he called.

I hesitated for a second. I'd never shot anybody before, not even to stun, but the guy had pulled out one of those blue spark-sticks like Administration Security uses, and the look on his face said he'd like nothing more than to hurt me, so I fired. The capsule sizzled with blue electricity as it discharged, arcing in the space between me and my target. He dropped to the floor.

"Sorry," I said before dashing into the stairwell and sprinting down the stairs. I was on the seventh floor and made it down to the third by the time the alarms started to blare. Did that mean they took Rebecca out? What was going to happen to her? I knew what position she held, but there was more to who she was, wasn't there?

You'll get your answers, just get out.

I didn't stop to ponder these questions, just focused on getting the hell away from this place. Finally, I reached the ground floor and pushed open the fire exit door, ignoring the warning that the alarm would sound. Alarms were already going off, what's another one? I ran out the door, not knowing where I was going to end up, and found myself in an alley where a car was waiting. Roan was behind the wheel.

"Get in!" he yelled, and he didn't have to tell me twice.

28.

MAIDA

"So, who's Rebecca? I mean, I knew she was the Project's Liaison Officer in Regional Administration, but there's more to it, isn't there?"

Roan and I had made our way to a little house in Bernal Heights, where Aviva and Del had been hiding out. It was a currently unassigned residence in the housing inventory managed by the Cultural Recovery Project, but the record hadn't been updated to show that the previous occupants had been reassigned, so the two had been squatting. The neighborhood was a lush area, with full trees and bright gardens. From outside, the caws of the crows that kept watch over the neighborhood could be heard. They were clearly having their own meeting.

"Rebecca Morgan was an Adept at Circle of the Eye Academy," Aviva explained as she held court in an easy chair. "Adept" was the title for students at the Academy who wished to become instructors there. "She is one of the strongest telepaths we at the Academy had ever encountered. I considered her my protégée. But she had a far more militant view of our abilities and of our place

298

in the world. Not exactly a supremacist in the way that Freedom Faction portrays us, but moving in that direction. She wanted to develop more... shall we say, aggressive, applications of telepathy."

"Like mindwiping," I offered. I could still feel her hands on my face, the beginnings of her mind probe.

"And mind control. Of a sort. She had no qualms about using her abilities to make people like her. Fall in love with her, even. Do whatever she wanted."

"Sounds like a lovely person," Roan said. He'd taken a seat in the corner, as if he was trying to stay out of the way, though he clearly wasn't hesitant to chime in.

"Oh, she could be charming, even without her mind tricks." Aviva looked away thoughtfully. "But her goals were incompatible with the tenets and philosophy of the Academy, and we parted ways."

"You mean she was expelled."

Aviva smirked. "Yes. She went off into the world. I had heard she'd gone to work for Regional Administration, so imagine my surprise when she became the new Liaison Officer for the Project. She had requested the assignment, I'm told. I have no doubt it was so that she could become my boss, after her time at the Academy was cut short by me. When I saw through Del's sight that she was in the room with you and tried to reach her, I couldn't. That's when I realized that she herself was under some kind of control. The psifield around her was distorted."

"And you can connect with people at a distance once you've connected at close range," Roan said. He knew firsthand, apparently. Del kept their Sight on me after I was grabbed at Dolores Park. And Aviva, wanting to send someone familiar to me but not to security, recruited Roan, with whom she had shared a telepathic connection with at some point before I arrived for this post. And I needed to get that story some time. But first, a question of motivations.

"I don't get Rebecca," I said. "From what you've said, it sounds like how she wanted to use telepathy is in line with how Linstrom wants to use it. So why did she have to be controlled by this implant when Oliver didn't?"

"You've said the key phrase," Aviva answered. "You said, 'with how Linstrom wants to use it.' Linstrom wants to use our talents to serve his agenda. Rebecca would only have been interested in serving her own, or what she would view as best for the psion community in general. She found Linstrom loathsome, for other reasons, and using her ability to help him would have been anathema to her. Oliver, on the other hand, has turned out to lack that kind of personal integrity. As long as he got his comfortable home and maintained a place of privilege, he would do as the powers that be asked. In this case, Linstrom and the Regressives."

"The control mechanism is that implant Linstrom showed Maida," Del reported. "After Maida left the lab, I kept part of my focus –"

"I'm sorry," Roan interjected. "*Part* of your focus?"

"When I'm in my sight I can perceive multiple areas at once." Del sounded peevish, and I could tell they were making an effort to be patient with Roan since he helped us. "Anyway, once what was happening in the lab was discovered, reinforcements arrived and Rebecca was stunned. Then I saw one of the lab techs attach some sort of device to the back of her head." Del indicated a spot at the base of the skull. "They performed some kind of recalibration. My guess is to undo whatever it was that Maida did."

"It would appear Rebecca is a trial run for this new technology that can compel psions to serve him," Aviva observed. "Also, there is the matter of the mesh in your holding cell –"

"There was definitely a barrier there," Del said. "The psifield was warped. Completely occluded."

"It was scary," I said. "It was like that stuff was sucking my ability out of me." That feeling of something that was a deep part of myself being taken came back to me, along with queasiness at the idea. Revulsion.

"So he wants to turn all psions into his personal legion," Roan said.

"And kill the ones that he deems not powerful enough," I added. "Don't forget that part."

"And kill the ones he doesn't want. And then install himself as what... King? Emperor? The Assessor Most Prime?"

"With obedience and rule enforced by his superpowered army." Del shook their head in disgust. "He wasn't wrong about psionic abilities being used to oppress people. It just isn't the psions who want to do the oppressing."

"And it isn't just our region," Aviva said. "Remember, he's holding secret meetings with leadership from other territories and administrative zones as well."

"You think he wants to be the dictator of... what? The continent?"

Aviva shrugged, an oddly casual gesture to make in response to something so momentous as the conquering of a continent. "Or as much of it as he can grab."

Roan was continuing to piece things together. "And meanwhile, he's whipping up fear of psions among the rest of the population to justify the detention of citizens. And to get people to report on their own communities."

I couldn't help but wonder how much good could have been done if Linstrom directed his obvious talent for planning and logistics to something more positive. But there was something else I was wondering too. "How did you know my scanning Rebecca would work?" I asked Aviva.

Again with the shrug. "I didn't know for sure that it would. It was an educated guess. The reason why psychometry doesn't work on people is because people are self-possessed. No person has been owned by another for a long, long time. But it occurred to me, in the moment, that if Rebecca was under Linstrom's mental control, if her personal agency was compromised, then she was, essentially, objectified. Thus, she might scan as an object. She is, in a very real sense, Linstrom's property. He claimed ownership the moment the thing in her head was put in her head."

"So why would my scanning of her break the control she was under?"

"That control and that possession of a mind, of a consciousness, is an unnatural state of affairs. I had hoped that the use of your ability would have a disruptive effect. Sort of like a reset of the psifield around her. It might not have worked. I was improvising. Good to know it does, though. For next time."

Next time? Of course there would be a next time, how could I think otherwise.

"Well it seems she's back under his control," Del said. "From what I saw of the lab. She's occluded again."

Aviva sighed dejectedly. "I can't reach her telepathically any longer, either."

A knock at the door froze everyone in the room.

"It's Kemp," Aviva said.

Del answered the door and Kemp rushed in, buzzing with urgency. "It's the desalination array," he said. "That's the target."

"Why didn't you reach out telepathically?" Del asked.

It was Aviva who answered, "Because after our little escapade today, Linstrom now has Rebecca monitoring telepathic communications with people in his office."

"There's something to be said for old-fashioned, in-person conversations," Kemp said.

"When are the attacks scheduled?" Aviva asked.

"Day after tomorrow. On World Water Day."

Del laughed. "Of course."

Kemp spotted Roan, sitting quietly in the corner. "Who is this?"

Roan introduced himself. "I'm a friend of Maida's."

"He broke me out of psion jail," I added. "Well it was a group effort, really, but he drove the getaway car."

Kemp arched a brow in that way he does. "I clearly missed some goings-on." He made a shooing gesture, and I slid over, then he squeezed onto the sofa with me and Del.

I filled him in on my capture and what I discovered while in custody. He furrowed his brow and nodded as he took it in. Once I told him everything, he said, "There have been whispers in the Council that Linstrom is planning a coup. I had no idea plans were this far along."

"Well it begins with stirring up public mistrust – even hatred – against psions," Aviva said. "Del, start planning our countermoves. It's time to –" She stopped talking, and her eyes went far away for a second. "We have company." She gets to her feet while looking at Kemp. "You were followed."

A look of dismay takes over Kemp's face. "I'm sorry. I was careful –"

Aviva held up a hand. "It's not your fault. But we need to get out of here." Then, suddenly, "Get away from the window!"

Del, Roan, Kemp, and I all leaped forward, away from the window we'd been sitting in front of. An object shattered the glass and landed on the floor. Gas began seeping from it, and Kemp immediately held out a hand, encompassing it within a telekinetic field. He lobbed it back outside with a flick of his wrist. "Sedative grenade," he said. "Would've put us all to sleep."

"Kemp Redmond and all other occupants, come out with your hands up."

Aviva looked at Kemp, "Come with me. The rest of you, get to the car." She looked over at Roan. "Are you ready to drive again?"

"Yes," he replied. "Whatever you need."

Then she and Kemp walked out the door.

"Hands where we –" The voice of the security officer cut off and I knew Aviva was in his head.

We dashed out the door. Several security personnel had drawn their weapons and were aiming at Aviva and Kemp. A couple of others were out of her eyeline, and thus protected from her telepathic freeze. They fired when they saw us head to the car, but nothing reached us. I could tell from his focus and the look of concentration on his face that Kemp had used his telekinesis to catch the projectiles, which he directed back at the men who fired.

Aviva was backing up to the car, which Roan had already gotten started. From out of one of the Administration Authority vehicles stepped a familiar figure: Rebecca. Her focus was on Aviva, whose hand went to her head as she let out a grunt. The officers she'd been holding in her telepathic thrall were freed and began firing once more. Kemp stopped the projectiles – it looked like they were using stunners and not bullets – and sent Rebecca flying backwards, slamming her into the vehicle she'd come out of.

Aviva ran over and got in the car. "Come on!" she yelled at Kemp.

He let out a roar that frankly surprised me – he never appeared to have that kind of aggression in him – and sent five of the officers flying backwards. He spun and dashed toward us when another shot sounded, along with the sizzle of its stun charge. He was struck in the back, and surprise swept over his face as he said "Go." Then he fell to the ground.

"Go now!" Aviva ordered Roan and we went taking off.

"Fuck fuck fuck." Del pounded their knees, freaked out and frustrated. "They got him."

"He's still alive," Aviva said in an attempt to reassure. "They were using stunners. They wanted to bring us in alive, not kill us."

"But now they know Kemp is a telekinetic," Del said. "Do you think Linstrom is going to be pleased to find out one of his senior staff is a secret psion? That'll really add fuel to the fire. It'll drive support to Freedom Faction."

"He'll have use for telekinetics," I said. "He told me." The idea of Kemp being controlled like Rebecca was not a pleasant one, especially now that I had borne witness to what he could do, which was a lot more than levitating a cup.

"We'll worry about that only if we have to," Aviva said. "And besides, we have a way to counter that mind-control technology now." She threw me a pointed look.

"Where am I going?" Roan asked. We were speeding through a residential area, taking tight curves on narrow streets that wound downhill.

"Head south," Aviva said. "Towards the McLaren Preserve."

29.

MAIDA

March 22, 2106
Portola District, San Francisco

Sera Ri stood outside a modest-sized geodesic dome as we pulled up. We had gone to her home in the southern part of the city, near the McLaren Preserve, a sprawling nature preserve that, like Dolores and Golden Gate Parks, had been dedicated park land since well before the Collapse. Sera's home was right beside feral land – it may as well have been her backyard.

"Welcome. Come in, come in." She ushered us into a soaring internal space full of plants and large tapestries bearing sacred geometry designs. The space seemed larger on the inside than it should be, from looking at it from the outside.

"Good to see you again, Maida," she said as I walked in. "You have found the telepath who could help you, I see." Her eyes twinkled with mischief.

I remembered that the last time we spoke, after her lecture on campus, she had advised me to find a telepath to help me with the visions from the teacup. She had known, of course, that Aviva was a telepath, but I hadn't known that yet. I appreciated that she'd kept her colleague's confidence. Was that what Aviva and Sera were? Colleagues? "Nice to see you again too," I replied. "Too bad we're on the run from the authorities."

She laughed at that, then led us to a large table, upon which rested a plate of sandwiches, a pitcher of water, and another of some sort of juice.

"You put this spread together fast," I commented.

"Oh I saw you coming. Please help yourselves to refreshment and make yourselves comfortable. You're all on quite an adventure, aren't you?"

"That's a nice way of saying 'hunted by a power-hungry psycho'," Roan quipped.

Sera chuckled at that. "Yes. Well." She cast him a curious look. "You're nul-psi."

He nodded ruefully at that. "I am. I've never particularly wished I were a psion until getting caught up in all this."

"Why do you wish you were a psion now?"

Although it was Sera who asked this question, everyone turned to look at him, awaiting his reply.

I would have felt self-conscious with the whole room's attention on me, but it didn't seem to faze Roan at all. "So I can contribute more to this effort. I don't like being useless."

"You have not been useless," I said emphatically. "You helped me escape Linstrom."

Surprise lit up Sera's eyes when she turned to me. "You were in custody?"

We all took seats around the table and I told Sera all about my experience. Then Aviva filled in the details of the events at the house in Bernal Heights that brought us here, to her doorstep. She had previously let Sera know we needed a place to lie low, but not why.

"So the operation is due to take place the day after tomorrow," Sera reiterated. She and Aviva locked eyes. "We need to mobilize the special operations team."

"Special Operations Team?" I asked. The more this all went on, the more layers peeled back.

"It's time to tell them," Sera said, still holding Aviva's gaze. I couldn't shake the feeling they were having a telepathic exchange right there in front of us, a conversation not spoken aloud.

Aviva took a deep breath. "I was just getting to this part when we were interrupted by Linstrom's goons back at the house. The Circle of the Eye Academy has trained an elite team of psions in paramilitary operations. Just in case a thing like what is happening now happened. We'd hoped we'd never have to mobilize in this way, but here we are."

Okay, wow, this was news. I was about to ask why this wasn't more common knowledge, but I didn't really need to. If knowledge of the existence of a special ops team of psions was widely known, a movement like Freedom Faction would have happened much sooner than now, and probably be even more hostile. If that were possible.

Aviva turned to me. "You already know two of them."

I already know two... The escape from Oliver's apartment came to mind. I turned to Del. "You," I said. "And Kemp." The way Kemp caught us as we jumped from the high rise – the idea to even do that in the first place. The way Kemp handled the security team that came to apprehend us in Bernal Heights. It all made sense now.

Del smiled and gave me spirit fingers from across the table.

"Do you think maybe Linstrom has learned about this team?" I asked. "And that's why he's doing what he's been doing?"

"It's possible," Sera said. "But I don't think so. And even if he does know, I'm sure it isn't his primary motivation. Are you aware of Linstrom's family history?"

I shook my head.

Sera continued. "'Linstrom' is his mother's family name. He uses it to obfuscate that his father's family name is Johannen. Have you heard of the Johannen family?"

"They were the family that owned Global Standard Petrochemical," Roan answered. "One of the largest oil companies of the Precursor era. They were the most adamant opponents to the shift to sustainable energy in the years between the start of the Collapse and the Bloom. They owned the last functioning drilling operations and refineries, not to mention nuclear plants and fresh water sources."

"That's correct," Sera said. "The family only relinquished their holdings due to sanctions imposed by the Assessors Administration Council when it was formed to govern the Sierra Northshore Regional Alliance. There has long been suspicion that members of the family were simply biding their time to reassert dominance. Julian Linstrom, it seems, is the one who has taken up that mantle."

"And he's figured out a way to do that with the use of psions," Del said, shaking their head. "Just when I truly believed society had moved on from all of that."

"Society has moved on," Sera said. "A relatively small group of holdouts has not. And they want to get everyone else under their yoke."

"They can try." Aviva's voice was steel – I'd never heard her sound so grave and threatening.

"Are we safe here?" Roan asked. "We're under the impression Rebecca is the only psion he's got control of right now, but what if he has a remote viewer or clairvoyant? Wouldn't they be able to find us?"

"Remote viewing doesn't work like that," Del explained. "Yes, we are able to perceive what is happening in distant locations, but we need to know what location to focus on. The only way a remote viewer would be able to watch us here, would be for them to already know that we were here. Plus they would have to know where 'here' was – they'd need to know this place or at least the coordinates or address."

"How were you able to find me in Linstrom's facility?" I asked.

"I tracked you. I kept my Sight on you throughout your whole meeting with Victor. When they knocked you out and put you in that vehicle, I kept my Sight on the vehicle as it made its way to the building downtown where they held you."

"Won't a clairvoyant be able to find us?" Roan asked.

Aviva shook her head. "Clairvoyance works in an unrestricted way with objects. With people, a clairvoyant would only be able to locate someone that wants to be found. Someone lost in the woods for example. The will of the target has an effect on the psifield. Someone who wishes not to be found by such means, won't be."

"There is a workaround to that," Sera added. "A clairvoyant could search for an object they know is on the person. An article of clothing, or a piece of jewelry, for example. But they'd have to know the specific thing they were looking for, and the person would have to have it on them."

"So we're as hidden as it's possible for us to be right now," Aviva said with a glance to Roan. "Don't worry."

"What about Kemp?" I asked. "Linstrom has him now, and he's got a telepath that can probe his mind. What if he finds out about this team?"

"That is a concern," Aviva said. "But Kemp is trained in resisting telepathic probes. He doesn't know the locations of the other team members, though he does know who they are. He doesn't know where we are now, and he has never been here." She looked to Sera as if for confirmation and was answered with a nod. She continued, "Our risk of Linstrom learning everything from Kemp isn't zero, but it is mitigated as much as possible. I'm more worried about Kemp being controlled the way Rebecca is. He is a formidable telekinetic." She locked eyes with me. "But we have a way to counter that if it happens. Don't we?"

I nodded. I never thought my ability would be a counter to anything, but there we were.

Sera stood. "Aviva, Del. We have some work to do. You two make yourself at home."

The three of them left the room and headed through an arched doorway on the other side of the dome.

"I bet Lorel and Bertrand are freaking out right now," Roan said. "I left them all in a tizzy. But when Aviva telepathically calls, you answer."

"About that... if Aviva can connect with you at a distance –"

Roan understood what I was getting at. "She's been in my mind before. I had a bad fall a couple of years ago. I fell out of a tree."

"What were you doing up a tree?"

He blushed. "One of my drones got stuck and I climbed up to get it. I was just learning how to fly them then, and my control wasn't the best. It wasn't even that high up. But on the way down, I fell and hit my head. I was in a coma for a month. I wasn't getting better, and in a last-ditch effort, Aviva connected with me and brought me back to consciousness. It was wild. She guided me through a maze of my memories. It took hours but it didn't seem that long while it was happening."

"You remember it all?"

"I do. She hasn't ever connected telepathically with me again. Until she yelled at me to grab a car and go get you from that place. That was wild too, because she was also connected to... Del. Is that their name? And I knew where to go based on their clairvoyance. The image of the building was in my mind, along with knowledge of where it was. It was like I got a taste of what it's like being a psion."

I helped myself to another sandwich – I was starving – and poured some juice. Some kind of berry. "How are you doing with all this?"

"I could ask you the same thing." He took the top piece of bread off the sandwich he had grabbed and ate the middle parts one piece at a time with his fingers. "You part of this special operations team now?"

"I have no idea. I doubt it. Maybe as the psychometric consultant. I don't know how useful I'd be at, you know, special operations. Basic operations I can barely handle."

"Don't sell yourself short. It was your ability that alerted everyone that Linstrom had some kind of secret plan going on in the first place, wasn't it?"

He did have a point. "Did you like it? The taste of being a psion when you swooped in to save me?"

He let out a honking laugh at that. "I wouldn't go that far. I did think it would be cool to have telekinesis when I was a kid. But then I met some psions. Telepaths and telekinetics. And I don't know... The mental discipline involved to not lose control seems like a lot. Having to be focused like that all the time so you don't hurt somebody or get overwhelmed with other people's thoughts. I think I'd find it exhausting. Is it like that for you?"

"Not really. Sometimes when I touch stuff, I get a hit. But that's rare and it's usually antiques. Most of the time I have to focus in order to use my ability, not to shut it out. There was a guy in my class who got hits off of everything he touched. He resorted to wearing gloves all the time. So I'm lucky, I guess. Even if it's not the most powerful talent, compared to what the others can do." I pictured Kemp deflecting ballistics, Del watching events unfold far away, Aviva communing with whales and hosting meetings in her psychic office with all attendees in different places, in their own minds.

"Your ability would be really cool for a historian. I haven't met anyone else that had it."

"Psychometry is one of the rarer talents. Basic clairvoyance is the most common, then clairsentience and claircognizance, which are sometimes what people call 'intuition.' Next common are telepathy and telekinesis, which seem to occur at equal rates. And then remote viewing, which is a version of clairvoyance, and then psychometry. Remote viewing with precognition is the rarest."

"Does it feel special, to be one of the rare ones among the rare ones?"

When my ability first manifested, I could mostly keep it to myself. It wasn't like telekinesis where things would just start flying around, or telepaths who tended to either completely freak out or go catatonic before they learned to control it. With me, it was mostly quiet flashes of stories, glimpses into the lives the objects that pinged my psychometric sense were once part of. But one day, I touched a ring that had been worn by somebody who drowned, and the panic, the inability to breathe, overwhelmed me. I was twelve, and that was when the kids at school discovered what I was. Some were curious, but others kept their distance after that. Even though the psionic talents had been documented and categorized by then, some kids were still afraid I'd invade their minds or make their heads explode. So I learned to keep to myself. Then, at the Academy, I felt free to be open about my status with other psions, but I also felt inferior watching the telekinetic students practice, or being practiced on by telepaths – consensually, of course. I spent a lot of time wishing that I either had a flashier talent or that I was normal. Instead, I felt like a weirdo, but a boring one. It was having teachers like Sera that helped me get over that.

I was so lost in my thoughts I realized Roan was still watching me, waiting for a response. "Not really," I said finally. "It's just who and what I am."

We talked a bit more, about this and that. Anything to get our minds off the situation, which right then, in that very moment, we couldn't exactly do anything about. After a while, Roan lay down on the sofa, and I went out onto the back porch and settled into one of the lounge chairs and looked up at the stars while coyotes howled in the hills. It was a relief to have a second to not be running for my life or thinking about conspiracies.

The park whose boundary met the edge of Sera's back garden was a dark forest full of woodland creatures. Did Li Nuan or Nathan ever visit this place? This location was six miles from where Li Nuan lived – nearly as far as two places within San Francisco could be from each other, and it was unlikely a Chinese slave girl would have had any reason to come here. Plus, I didn't think it was a public park yet, in her time. Could she have visited in the time outside of the period of her life I could witness? Not impossible, but unlikely. What about Nathan? Were any of the parties he liked to go to held at this place? Was this place as wild back then as it was these days?

Aviva took a seat beside me. "The team will be arriving here tomorrow," she informed me. "We'll prep a battle plan then."

I nodded. Tomorrow would be a big day. And now I sat in the yesterday of tomorrow, today. I smiled at the memory of Nathan witnessing Delilah's joy at her art project idea. But there was something I'd been wanting to talk to Aviva about. "What do you remember of the changes?"

Even though her face was partially in shadow, I could sense her expression going far away as she thought back to that time. "I was a child when the Collapse began."

Grief and sadness infused her words. "I didn't really understand at first, what was happening. I remembered people dying of the heat, and cities being lost beneath waves. I remember strange diseases. My parents tried to keep the worst images on the news from me, but I remember seeing footage of pus-filled rashes, and people bleeding from orifices when their organs liquefied, and going mad, like rabid animals. People just shot their neighbors in the head when they began exhibiting symptoms, and that was considered a kindness. The mad thing is, it probably was. Then wars broke out, for food and water. I remember the United States splitting up, and then the Canadian Provinces had their rift. And then the regional alliances formed. But I was a kid through all of that, and it was background noise, stuff grown-ups got upset by and had heated arguments about. It was the world, the only world I knew, but I remember having a sense that it wasn't right.

"My family were nomads, and we finally settled up north, in Eureka, when I was eleven. And then the Bloom happened. The first auroras appeared on February 12th, 2072. I had just turned twenty, and was still living in the homesteading community where I grew up. The skies were astounding, full of the most beautiful light, all the time. And the lights didn't go away, not for a whole year. After the lights appeared, you could feel the shift happening, in the culture. And it wasn't just lights in the sky; there was an energy, too. But people kept dying, of course. Between the weird diseases, and the droughts and famines, and the heat waves, and the rising tides swallowing communities, and the extreme storms, and the civil wars in North America and other wars happening abroad, billions had died. There had been a real danger of a nuclear exchange with Russia and China. Many thought we were at the end of days, and it didn't really seem all that far-fetched, considering. But then the Bloom happened, and the auroras cradled the Earth as we buried our dead. After all that beauty and that horror, humanity came out the other side different than we had been."

"Do you think Linstrom can really undo all of that with his plans?"

She was quiet for a minute. "It's possible. We'd be fools to think it wasn't. That urge for dominion, the impulse to use hate to gain power: it seems hardwired in us. But I firmly believe we are overcoming it, generation by generation, century by century. The Bloom kicked that process into high gear for a while. It was a miracle – or maybe a part of a cycle. Just as the Earth revolves around the sun, our entire solar system revolves around the center of the galaxy – a journey that takes two-hundred fifty million years. Who's to say a Bloom hasn't happened before and knowledge of it has been lost in the span of time? But though the phenomenon of the illuminated skies happened thirty-four years ago, the Bloom is still happening, right now. And we are it. And we are not going to let that light go out. We can't."

Grandmother comes to mind – not either of my human grandmothers: the whale. Part of keeping that light alive is the Linking Circles, the conclave with those minds of the sea. "What about opening linking to nul-psis?" I asked. I was unsure if I should really bring up this topic again, given Aviva's previous reaction, but I had to. The idea compelled me. "Wouldn't that go a long way to spreading the illumination, to not letting the light go out?"

Aviva visibly stiffens at this suggestion, just like she and the others did when I first brought up this idea during that telepathic meeting in her psychic office.

"I know you mean well," Aviva said, "But that is not a possibility I wish to entertain."

"Why? Is it true that nul-psi brains can't handle the signal or whatever?" That assertion seemed dubious to me, considering nul-psis could handle telepathic communication. Even more so after hearing about how Aviva helped Roan come out of that coma.

She sighed. "No. That's not true at all, but it's a misperception that's useful to us. We psions have put ourselves in service of society as a whole already. And still, we are sometimes met with suspicion – as current events demonstrate. We need to keep something for ourselves, for community bonding, for our own spiritual nourishment. To maintain something of psionic culture. I believe that keeping Linking within the community is the best and most unobtrusive way of doing that."

"But doesn't keeping it so exclusive when it needn't be just reinforce this supremacy idea –"

"Maida." Her tone was sharp and chastising, and I immediately shut up. "This is not something we're going to talk about now."

Feeling scolded, I didn't say anything else. But in my heart, I knew she was wrong.

30.

LI NUAN

May 14, 1912
Chinatown, San Francisco

"Lo Paw," Bao says to Li Nuan, using the Cantonese word for "wife." He holds their daughter Emily by the waist as she struggles to break free of his grip, wanting to chase after one of the neighborhood cats. The cat pauses in its dash down the street, looks over its shoulder as if daring the girl to follow. Emily squeals in her father's arms. "Help me control this wild girl."

Li Nuan laughs at the sight of her husband and daughter and the cat mocking them. Who is more in control?

"You finish the lanterns, then," Li Nuan says as she climbs down a step ladder. They're preparing the teashop for a celebration: today is the day Tye Leung from the Presbyterian Mission Home becomes the first Chinese American woman to vote in the United States, with a vote cast in the presidential primary election. Women did not have the vote in all of the United States, but here in California, they were allowed the vote as of last year. Some say Tye Leung is not only the first Chinese woman to vote in America, but the first one to vote in the whole world. Li Nuan can believe that; she has experienced Tye Leung's force of will for herself. She takes the girl from Bao and brings her into the shop, leaving her husband to hang the rest of the lanterns around the door.

Tye Leung had not wanted a fuss made over her vote, but she had gone to such lengths to prepare – reading about the candidates, and learning about new laws – that Li Nuan felt some acknowledgment should be made for the accomplishment, plus all she has done for Chinatown. Miss Cameron agreed and persuaded Tiny, as she has called Tye Leung for years, to participate. Li Nuan and Bao consider it an honor to host at their teahouse, a new structure built during the reconstruction of Chinatown. The old Moon Goddess had survived the quake in '06, a few places had, but then the fire came and devoured it all and left only ash. Nothing that stands in Chinatown now stood then. It was as if the neighborhood started over again – truly risen from the ashes. Like the whole city has.

But this gathering is not about remembrance of the past, it is a celebration of today and the future. Li Nuan cannot imagine a greater leap forward than Tye Leung going from child bride to first Chinese woman voter – to vote for President is a great responsibility, and to be allowed to have a vote is a high form of freedom, isn't it? What is it like? To study the men who want the job of leading a nation and making a choice? Li Nuan can't imagine voting herself, and doesn't think she will ever be granted that privilege. Tye Leung was born here, so her situation is different. She is different than any other woman Li Nuan has ever known – like a typhoon in that little body.

She sets her daughter down with some nervousness; who knows what havoc the little one could make of the back counter? But Li Nuan wants to light a couple of joss sticks at the altar. Zhao Gongming, god of fortune, presides regally from his alcove in the back wall. At his feet sits a jade teacup resting upon a swatch of yellow silk. Li Nuan considers it her talisman, and she keeps it on the altar because she loves this life that freedom brought her, and the cup is a reminder that one cannot sit and wait and hope for freedom to be given; it must be fought for and seized. She is grateful for the god of fortune's blessings: the love of the teashop boy and having a daughter she will never sell to anyone, and now helping her husband run their teahouse. The cup will go to her daughter one day, and then to her granddaughter, and so on. She doesn't really understand how she knows there will be multiple generations of daughters after her. The knowledge is just there in her head.

Also in her head are the visions the cup had bestowed: the storms and floods and fires and famines and death. But also some kind of flowering, the sky radiant with colors like she has never seen. All of that is a warning, foreknowledge just like the date of the earthquake. But she still doesn't understand what she is supposed to do about any of it. The cup had given her another message, too: to make the world better. She doesn't know what she can do to stop famines and floods, but she can help make her corner of the world better. To that end, she continues to work with Miss Cameron and helps girls get out of the brothels, which many had hoped would disappear after the wreckage of 1906, but that was a hope in vain. Men will always be plagued by their hungers, it seems. Men will always want to own and dominate. Maybe one day, things will be different. Maybe.

The Tongs give Li Nuan and her husband a wide berth – they don't even approach them for protection money. The word on the street is that Li Nuan is a witch who destroyed the Boss and his bastard and mistress with the sheer power of her wrath. Some say she called upon demons to enact her wickedness – as if she were the wicked one! If there were demons in that room that morning, she wasn't one of them. But the story of her smiting them with magic – "smite" is a word she learned from Miss Cameron – isn't that far from the truth, really, as the knowledge of the earthquake and fire did come through the cup. And if that isn't some kind of magic, what is it? It is not magic Li Nuan has any control over, but nobody needs to know that. Let them be afraid of her. She prefers that to how they looked at her before.

A commotion at the door draws her attention: Tye Leung arriving to much fanfare on the street. People – men and women both – cheer and wave as she enters the shop.

"We are having a celebration," Bao informs the crowd. "Yum cha, yum cha." Tea and dim sum, who can resist?

People begin piling into the shop and Emily squeals and claps, walking from table to table and chattering in a mix of Cantonese and English. There is a stir as someone new arrives. Li Nuan turns to see Miss Cameron and a couple of the church ladies and their husbands, including Beatrice and Dennis.

"We couldn't stay away," Miss Cameron says. She and the others greet Tye Leung warmly. "Won't you say a few words?" Miss Cameron asks in English.

Somebody else, someone from the neighborhood asks, "What was it like?" in Cantonese.

The crowd hushes and all eyes turn to Tye Leung. She is the smallest adult in the room – only two-year-old Emily is smaller – yet is the largest presence in the moment.

"Very ordinary," she says in Cantonese. "The action is very ordinary. Just marking a paper and putting it in a box. Simple. But for me to be allowed to do it, the steps that led to that moment, was not so simple. This is a big day but also a small step. We must work for all women everywhere to be able to vote, and we must work for we Chinese to be seen as people who can contribute to this society in America. There is more work to do. Today is just one step. We must not let this go to our heads."

When she finishes, she turns to Miss Cameron and the other white Americans and repeats what she just said in English.

"Well said," Miss Cameron says. "I am proud of you."

One of the neighborhood ladies is entertaining little Emily while Li Nuan helps Bao serve. As she brings tea and dumplings to Miss Cameron's party, Miss Cameron says, "We are planning another operation. Two nights from now."

Li Nuan smiles as she sets down a cup and pours. "I will help."

31.

NATHAN

October 15, 2006
Potrero Hill, San Francisco

Today, they're making bricks out of mud and straw. Technically, the stuff is called clay slip, but to Nathan it's just mud. To his surprise, he enjoys the feel of it on his hands. The permaculture course that he'd promised to take with Danny is in its natural building section, and the class today is working on a cob house – cob being a natural building material composed of earth, sand, and straw. The structure is an Accessory Dwelling Unit in the backlot of some rich person's house. This person had purchased the lot the house is on, as well as an adjoining lot. This structure is intended to serve as a guest house/party hang out. Nathan would rather have been working on something that would be an actual home for someone, but this type of construction isn't legal for residential use – they can't have running water or electricity, per the current rules. But still, he appreciates that this person wants a structure made of sustainable, natural materials, even if it is a glorified clubhouse for his friends to party in.

The material is fireproof and resilient against seismic activity, and Nathan wonders why such construction isn't more common in California. Probably a host of reasons related to who can profit how much from it. He doesn't like this cynicism that has descended on him in recent months and hopes he can shake it. It's going to take some effort; but things psychologically and emotionally are already shifting within him. He can feel it.

The making of the cob had been a fun affair – much to Nathan's astonishment. It involved the class getting barefoot and rolling up their pants and mixing the stuff by stomping on it in large basins. Cob includes sand in the mix, whereas the stuff called slip is just clay and water. At first, he wasn't sure he'd enjoy getting his hands dirty, but it turns out he really does enjoy it.

Other members of the class are packing the timber frame, and slip will be used to coat those walls. Nathan and a few others are making bricks out of the slip and straw mixture, which will be used for internal, non-load-bearing walls and half-walls that will define some of the spaces inside the structure. He finishes packing a set of molds and looks around the worksite as he takes a breather. There are about thirty or so people in the class, and smiles and laughter abound as everyone goes about the work. A group of barefoot men brings a batch of cob closer to the structure on a heavy blue tarp, and people begin filling the forms with their hands while others pack them down with sticks. One of the things he appreciates about this process is how community-oriented it is, which was always the element of Burning Man he loved most. He wonders if such a structure could be built using playa dust?

It's been a mind-bending few weeks since the Burn and Danny's passing. On the first day of this course, when everyone sat in a big circle and introduced themselves, Nathan shared what his past work had been, and how he was looking for a way to live more sustainably and drive the culture in that direction. But then he mentioned, "a friend of mine convinced me to take this class" and he broke down. Not really the first impression he wanted to make, blubbering and grief-stricken, but everyone was so kind to him afterwards.

Since then, he's learned about how weeds are an indicator of what the soil is lacking, he's helped build garden beds and learned how to propagate seeds, he's shoveled goat shit for fertilizer, and now a practicum in natural building techniques. There are upcoming classes on design principles, designing structures that work in concert with local ecology and not only minimize human impact, but help nature regenerate. He's really looking forward to that material. This is all way more granola-crunchy than he ever thought he'd be when he was the version of himself working out gadget designs in his cloistered tech tower, but something in him is waking up, and he wants to nurture whatever it is, bring it to full bloom and fruition.

But the biggest lesson he has learned about himself: he isn't interested in merely stopping the things he doesn't want to see in the world, such as forced child labor and environmental degradation and injustices against marginalized communities. He believes in those causes and supports those communities – sure, of course. But he has always been a designer and maker of things, and he's more interested in bringing into being and helping to build a world he does want, rather than simply stopping a world he doesn't. Progress requires both approaches, but not everybody can do everything. In his soul, he is a designer, a maker and builder, and those have to be the guiding principles of his life now. He wants to make them so. And in the community of this class, he's finding like-minded folks and is starting to feel like maybe he has a shot at figuring this out.

At every class, Danny crosses his mind. Danny's been coming up in conversation a lot since they all got back from the Burn – of course he has. How could he not? He was so integral to the group. Remy has agreed to take possession of the Fish, which means it's now going to be even more a part of their lives than it had been. It would be in honor of Danny, keeping that thing going. Taking this class is in honor of Danny too – rising to the challenge that Danny had presented him that night on the playa. Put up or shut up. A wash of gratitude brings tears to Nathan's eyes, not for the first time. Gratitude that he has the ability to choose his life path. Gratitude that he had a friend like Danny to push him toward the discomfort that change requires.

"You okay?" a classmate asks. A woman named Tamara who's about his age and always smelled of weed and sandalwood. "Thinking about your friend?"

Nathan laughs and wipes his eyes with a non-muddy patch of forearm. "I'm not usually this emotional."

"Losing someone is always tough," she says. "Help me demold some bricks?"

He nods and follows her to a batch of bricks that have dried enough that they can be removed from the mold, which will then be ready to accept a new batch.

"You're a designer of some kind, if I remember right?" she asks.

"That's right. I designed gadgets. MP3 players, cell phones, remote controls. A couple of medical devices."

"Give me your email before we leave today. I have a job posting that might interest you."

Nathan agrees.

Once they get the bricks out of the molds, they add them to the pile that waits for their turn to be placed.

Then they prep the empty frame to refill with more of the slip-straw mixture.

"Tell me about your friend," Tamara says.

I wouldn't be here if not for him, thinks Nathan. Burning Man promoted a gift economy, and this class was Danny's last gift to him.

"His name was Danny," Nathan begins. "He convinced me to take this class. He could be gruff but was really a big ol' teddy bear. He drove a big fish..."

32.

MAIDA

March 23, 2106
Portola District, San Francisco

The seven other members of Del and Kemp's team arrived at the same time in different vehicles. They greeted one another with clasped hands and embraces, but the seriousness of the situation was drawn on each of their faces and their moods were dour. This was not a reunion of old friends, but a team with a mission. Aside from Del and Kemp, the other members of the team were Ani, a clairvoyant; the telepaths Rafe, Kirkpatrick, and Marlon; and the telekinetics Tilda, Jon, and Wei. Aviva briefed them on everything that had happened from the moment I touched the Assessor's watch to our escape from the Bernal Heights house. After that briefing, it was determined that the first step should be to locate Kemp – not for the sake of a rescue – but to see if any of Linstrom's logistics might be discerned.

Del took a seat and dropped into trance. Aviva explained that Del was first perceiving the facility where I was held in case Kemp was also brought there.

After a few minutes, Del came back to regular consciousness. "I don't see him. There's the same warp in the psifield around that one area of the building; it must be all lined with the mesh that Maida told us about. We're not getting what we need that way."

Because Kemp may have been unconscious or fitted with the same implant that Rebecca had been, or contained within neutralizing mesh, a different tactic was undertaken. It involved Aviva telepathically bridging Ani with Del. Once the link was established, Ani stated clearly, "With my Sight, I seek the Circled Eye of Kemp Redmond." Then it was her turn to go into trance.

To serve as a sort of beacon through the psifield, the whole team had the same tattoo: a haloed eye encircled. It was a symbol of bonding, yes, but it was also a means for the clairvoyant to locate her teammates in case they were incapacitated. The tattoo was something the subject possessed, so it could be searched for when the subject was closed off.

Only a couple of minutes elapsed before Ani said, "I have him."

Via the telepathic bridge, Del received the location and focused their vision on the place Ani indicated.

"He's undergoing a procedure," Del reported. Their voice sounded far away, distorted, not quite their own.

Even though I wasn't connected to them, I knew everyone's stomachs dropped just as mine did. "Undergoing a procedure" could only mean that he would soon be a puppet of Linstrom's just like Rebecca. So now the Assessor Prime had both a telepath and a telekinetic under his control.

"They're quick sealing the incision," Del continued. "I'll keep watching."

"I can't reach him," Aviva said. It seemed like she had stopped bridging Ani and herself to Del. "This won't help us."

"And Linstrom obviously doesn't want to be found," Ani said. "But I could try again?"

"Do it," Aviva commanded.

Ani slipped into trance again, this time saying, "With my Sight I seek Assessor Prime Julian Linstrom."

We waited for a tense few minutes before Ani opened her eyes. "Occlusion," she reported to everybody's disappointment. "Just a cloud in the psifield. A blur."

"What about his watch?" I offered. "Ani, you just found Kemp with his tattoo. Searching for an object on the person is a workaround to the person not wanting to be found, right? Linstrom always wears that watch."

"It's worth a try," Aviva said.

Once again, Ani slipped into trance. "With my Sight I seek the watch of Assessor Prime Julian Linstrom."

Another tense few minutes passed, and once again, Ani opened her eyes. She shook her head. The disappointment in the room was palpable.

"He must be using Rebecca to reinforce the occlusion around him," Aviva said. "That's what I would do, anyway."

There had to be a way through the occlusion. Even just a thread. Even just a string of connection... The image of Nathan aboard Epifania came to mind – a resonant string plucked, the same subject through space and time. I thought of how Aviva can contact at a distance once contact up close was made – did it work similarly with my ability?

"I have an idea," I said, more timidly than I meant to. I was definitely the novice here, offering up an idea to far more seasoned colleagues. They all looked at me, and before I had a chance to proclaim my idea stupid, I shared it. "I've previously scanned Linstrom's watch. I could maybe... I don't know. Call up the feeling of it? Connect with the vibration of it and see if that can be a thread to him through the psifield?"

Ani raised her eyebrows in a way that reminded me of Kemp. Poor Kemp. "Have you done that before?"

"No. But it could be worth a shot?"

Aviva nodded emphatically. "Let's try."

I joined the circle they sat in. We all closed our eyes and dropped to theta state. Then, a familiar buzz of connection, and I felt us all together in my head, and at the same time I felt how they all felt everyone else's head in their heads. It wasn't as disorienting as it sounded.

Do your thing, Aviva transmitted.

Ani said once more, "With my Sight I seek the watch of Assessor Prime Julian Linstrom."

In my own mind, I brought myself back to that day in the lab, when the clasp on Linstrom's watch broke. It slid across the floor and I picked it up... and it felt... what? What did it feel like? Come on... there was the leather wristband, it was soft and warm from Linstrom's wrist. The watch had been heavier than I expected, its face intricately etched. There was no string being plucked yet, no resonance in the psifield. What else, what else? Oh, yes: the hands. The minute hand and second hand, such finely curved, tapered arrows at the end of their delicate arms. The vibrating string I was hunting for was close, I could almost feel it, but it was just out of my perception.

Aviva's focus rested on me then, gentle, like a soft psychic massage. She was helping me tease out more layers of the memory, and yes – another sense memory came, so vivid: the smell of clay and dirt. The smell of old things and wood. Humphrey Bogart.

A vibrating thread tickled my inner sight, tingled at my third eye. The thread was alight, an effervescent gold strand in the waveforms that make the world, and it led me – led all of us, our minds joined together – on a winding way all the way to a boathouse. I felt through our connection that Ani was impressed, Aviva proud, and Del all business. They focused the location, and together we observed Linstrom addressing a group of twelve men. There was a map of the Bay Area, with targets clearly marked, the desalination facilities at Alcatraz, Treasure Island, and Alameda. We pieced together that the men were divided into three squads, with each team assigned one of the targets.

There were cases stacked behind Linstrom, and he opened one to show his men: explosives. The cases were distributed among the teams. Linstrom flipped the board over, and the standard design that all the desalination plants were built to was displayed. He pointed out the intake and outflow pipelines – the parts of the facilities that drew in the salt water from the bay and pushed out the desalinated water to the reservoirs onshore.

Del: *They are setting the explosives tonight, and they'll be detonated tomorrow, when Linstrom gives his World Water Day address at the New Embarcadero Plaza.*

Aviva: *That's enough.*

She released the bridge, and my mind was off on its own again, disconnected from the others.

"Nice work," Aviva said to me while Del gave a wordless nod of approval. That made me feel good – Del struck me upon first meeting them to be a hard one to impress.

"That technique will have to be added to the curriculum," Ani said. "The Maida technique."

I blushed at the attention and validation. I didn't mind it, though.

Then it was back to business. "We strike at their launch point before they set out," Ani said.

"No." Aviva met Ani's surprised eyes and shook her head. "We need to catch them in the act. Otherwise, they can spin it as us attacking them to serve our agenda. They can claim they gathered at the boathouse for any innocuous reason – preparing for inspections, water testing, anything. They could even spin the presence of the explosives somehow. We need to show they mean harm. We need to catch them in the act."

"Have any idea how we do that?"

"We let them carry out their mission, and ambush them at their targets."

"Should we alert Administration Security?" I asked. "Call in a tip or something?"

"It's safe to assume that Security is in Linstrom's pocket," Aviva replied. "Even if not every member of Security is on board with his agenda, he will no doubt get an alert – maybe not even as a warning, just as standard protocol, given his position. Surprise is our best option."

"It's too bad we can't transmit or record what I witness in my sight," Del said.

"There actually is a way we can do that," I said.

They all turned to look at me and I met Aviva's eyes. "Roan."

She caught my meaning with a smile. "And his little toys."

33.

MAIDA

March 24, 2106
New Embarcadero Waterway, San Francisco

I waited for the crowd to, well, actually be a crowd, before I
slipped myself among them. It would have been all too easy
to spot me otherwise. I was back in a hood and sunglasses
combo – only a nice satin one and not a sweatshirt this time.
I had raided Sera's wardrobe for this get-up, and she also
provided me with a wig – a curly blonde one so it couldn't
be any more different from my own straight black hair. At
a casual glance, I might have passed for an older Pacific
Heights-dwelling, high-status person. Looking so not-me
was the point. It was a warm morning, of course, but I kept
it all on because I had to.

The Alcatraz desalination plant was smoking in the
distance – I wouldn't have been surprised if they kept the
wreckage there intentionally smoldering for the visual to
go along with the spin Freedom Faction had put on the
previous night's fucked up plan.

"One of them tried to control our minds," stated the man on
the big screen behind the podium. *"My colleague shot that
one. Then a telekinetic threw us into the water, and then used their
ability to throw the bomb at the pipeline juncture."*

They were such fucking liars. But they knew that, right? They must have known on some level that their cause was not just if they had to make up lies to get people to accede to their plans. I wasn't too terribly confident in their levels of self-awareness, though. And also, I didn't think they cared about actual justice. Simon Pertkin, the interviewee, was a software engineer who had no business being at a desalination facility, much less late at night, and was a member of Freedom Faction. But that's not what was being reported. Nobody was even asking him what he was doing there in the first place.

It had started off well. Roan set up a viewing station at Sera's place where Sera and I could watch the proceedings. Aviva was with us but had linked telepathically to the teams and was observing that way. A couple of large monitors displayed the feed from each of Roan's drones, twelve in total, plus the body cams that each of the Circle of the Eye team members wore. We recorded the footage onto hard drives – footage we pulled an all-nighter cutting together for later this morning. Roan himself was aboard the Epifania, which had anchored out in the bay at a point central to the three targets. Epifania had also brought each of our teams to the targets ahead of Linstrom's men's arrival – the telekinetics floated them to shore so there would be no boats to hide or indication that anybody else was there.

We captured footage of the Freedom Faction teams departing the boathouse as Linstrom watched from the dock. We captured footage of Linstrom's men arriving, beaching their boats, then scuttling up the rocky shores to the places where the pipelines connected to the filters at the sides of the buildings. Our teams were there, waiting to ambush. Bright lights blazed on, Linstrom's men raised their hands to shield their eyes from the glare – the same scene played out at the three locations simultaneously.

It went according to plan at first, Linstrom's men all frozen, held in thrall by the telepath on each of our teams. The masks they'd been wearing were pulled off, revealing their faces – one of the members of the Alcatraz group was Robert Patrick Fisk.

Del narrated what was happening as leader of the Alameda team: *"These men are Freedom Faction, and they are attempting to destroy the desalination plants and blame psions for the destruction."* They took the case from Fisk's hands and opened it on camera, revealing the explosive devices. A similar scene played out with the Treasure Island group: the reveal of the faces, the reveal of the explosives. The Freedom Faction men were stunned and bound as part of the plan – the original plan – which was to drop them off at Administration Security HQ along with copies of the footage.

The Alcatraz Team, however, ran into trouble. The recordings captured the sound of a stunner discharge, and the Freedom Faction men were released from their thrall and began yelling *"Freaks!"* and *"psiscum!"* More garbled yelling came from the monitors, more discharges sounded and sparked brightly as they were deflected by the telekinetic on our team. Two of the men levitated off the ground and flew out into the water.

The third member, however, the one with the explosives, broke free of the group and ran towards the pipeline junction. The telekinetic, Wei, reached out a hand to stop him, then there was the loud pop of a firearm and Wei let out a gasp before falling to the ground; his bodycam then transmitted a close-up of rocks. From the drone footage, we could see that he had been shot by a guard who'd come down out of the building. Either the telepathic hold on the guard had slipped or the team didn't know the guard was there, but it didn't matter. The Freedom Faction man had reached the pipeline junction and yelled something unintelligible before hurtling the case. From three different angles, Sera and I watched the explosion on the monitors. The pipelines ruptured in fire and burst with water as their contents depressurized and released – thousands of gallons, tens of thousands, maybe more.

News of the "brazen attack on one of the Region's major desalination operations" was all over the feeds and, predictably, were being shown on the giant screens set up for Linstrom's World Water Day speech, which he had refused to cancel because he "would not be cowed by terrorists."

And there I was, the morning after our foiled counter-operation, at the plaza before Linstrom's speech, watching newsreel footage of the aftermath at the Alcatraz facility while the island itself continued smoking out in the water behind the screens. The Freedom Faction men that had been flung into the water were presented as security personnel who attempted to foil the psion terrorists' plot to cripple the region's water supply.

Linstrom was on the screen now: *"This attack demonstrates the dire need for a registration and public identification process for all psions. Any links to the PsiSupreme organization must be investigated. This cowardly act demonstrates the contempt psions have for regular people and cannot be allowed to go unpunished."*

The signal transducer Roan gave me was heavy in my pocket, and I ran my fingers over it, resisting the urge to press the damn button right then and there. The device was paired to a tablet that Bertrand had on him, and when I did finally activate it, it would interrupt the signal of all screens within a fifty-foot radius and replace it with the footage from the drones and the bodycams. I inched my way closer to the front of the audience. I didn't want to be in the front row, but I did need to make sure I was close enough so the screens at the back of the stage were within the signal radius. Operating this device was more in Roan's purview, but he was occupied with the piloting of the drones, which were dispersed over the crowd at a high enough altitude to not be obtrusive. Since I had to be in a close enough position to disrupt Rebecca's and Kemp's implants, it made most sense for me to have it.

I wasn't the only one from Circle of the Eye, of course. The others spread out around the plaza, blending into the crowd. Some might say we were being furtive and secretive - were we proving Freedom Faction's point? I couldn't believe I was even wondering that – it was so insidious how negative messaging of one's own community could be so easily internalized. We were not the ones pulling off these attacks, we were not the ones who wanted to use our abilities to dominate the region; that would be the man that Freedom Faction was holding up as a hero. And we were going to expose him.

I was paired with a telekinetic named Tilda, who kept a reasonable distance. We were acting like we didn't know each other at all, but she was close enough that she could help me if I needed it. Wei, the telekinetic that was shot, wasn't there. It hadn't been a stunner used on him, but an old-fashioned bullet. His condition was serious, but he was expected to make a full recovery. The others were all there, though. Aviva stayed at the back of the audience and had us all linked. Lorel and Bertrand were back there with her, livestreaming this event from their devices. And Bertrand also had the tablet with our footage. The event was being streamed through official channels, but there was no telling if the official stream would mysteriously cut off or be doctored once we took action. So Lorel and Bertrand, my trusty nul-psi friends, were there for insurance, essentially.

Through the telepathic link, I sensed the others' trepidation, their alertness, their anticipation of none-of-us-knew-what. I had to admit, I was a little scared of the crowd, especially on account of what they thought psions did. I hoped the others weren't judging me for it.

Musicians were playing now, entertaining the gathering audience. The music selection was unexpectedly lively, given that Alcatraz still smoked in the background. This event was normally a celebration of the region's waterworks, an example of how cooperation helped our society address a crucial matter of survival: the ongoing drought in the region that settled in during the second half of the twenty-first century, the water shortage that desalination was one part of solving. But this time, the usual celebration had been replaced by a collective mood that was agitated and somber, despite the musicians' best efforts.

Linstrom finally took the stage, to enthusiastic applause. It went on for a while, him smiling and waving at everyone. I could see in his eyes that he loved this adulation – or maybe I was getting a whisper of perception from one of the telepaths.

He held up his hands and the crowd hushed immediately. "My fellow citizens. Twenty-five years ago, the first desalination facility on Alcatraz was established. It marked the beginning of the regeneration of the San Francisco Bay Area, homebase for the Golden Gate Maritime Preservation Area and the Golden Gate Cultural Recovery Projects, the major civic projects seeking to restore the ecology and recover the lost history of this area and its people – of all of us. It was deemed fitting that Alcatraz, once the site of an infamous prison, had been selected for a new purpose: the production of potable water to counter the drought, itself a kind of prison that limited the scope of human endeavor, and of the area's ability to support incoming migrants who wished to come and contribute to the work here.

"But now, unscrupulous individuals have sought to put us back in that prison, to once again impose limitations on humans. Those individuals are the psion community, who after the so-called "Bloom" event of 2072 began appearing in our midst…"

He paused to allow the boos to rise before continuing. "At first, these abilities seemed a godsend, a boon to humanity. At first, psions put their abilities to work, assisting restoration and clean-up efforts, assisting community members to find lost things and people, assisting with the piecing together of our history, so fragmented by the years of the Collapse. But as we see, assisting us as a part of our communities is no longer enough, and they now seek dominance –"

"Liar!" I called out. I felt the surprise of my team – I surprised myself – and a collective *what the hell are you doing* rippled through the telepathic net that connected us. It was one voice with echoes of individuals. That wasn't the cue, I was supposed to wait for Aviva's signal, but I just couldn't let Linstrom's lies stand. They could not go unchallenged.

It's time, I transmitted. Aviva had reserved the right to make the call as to when to deploy our footage, but surely she trusted my instincts, or else why allow me the responsibility of the task? I knew in my bones that Linstrom would have this crowd on his side more than he already did if he got to the rousing and inspirational "we must stand together as non-psions" part of his speech that was no doubt coming.

An interruption was more unbalancing. There was no time to second guess, anyway – I activated the transducer and the screens behind the Assessor Prime were taken up by the drone footage of the operation carried out by his men.

Hope you're right about this.

There was Linstrom standing on the dock, seeing his men off. There were the boats landing, the men carrying the cases. Some of the footage was sped up, and there were cuts from different angles, but it was clear what was happening.

Murmurs of confusion rippled through the crowd, and Linstrom's face was a frozen mask of fake calm.

Okay he's off-kilter; that's good, right?

"You were the one behind Portland and last night!" I yelled, I screamed. "There is no PsiSupreme organization. You made it all up!"

A crawl at the bottom of the video let viewers know the uncut footage was available at para.site.linstrom. Nodes were pulled out of pockets all around me.

Linstrom signaled someone to cut the screens, to no avail – all thanks to Roan for his little gadget working its magic. Or maybe we should thank the former intelligence agencies of the United States and the United Kingdom.

But then, the screens tore asunder, sending sparks sizzling into the air. Pieces of hyperpixel displays and cables and fabric and circuitry rent in all directions. Kemp hovered in the space behind the ragged fragments.

Shit.

He's mind-controlled.

Thought he might be.

People began screaming as large chunks of screen and shards of their former frames flew into the crowd, A/V turned to shrapnel by Kemp's possessed mind. Vehicles parked at the edge of the plaza levitated high into the air and hurled themselves down towards the deck of the plaza. *A bloom of sparks as the cars impact* – I was seeing both with my physical eyes and with my mind's eye what the others saw.

"You see! You see!" Linstrom cried from the stage. "Even now they attack us!"

But the vehicles didn't impact in physical reality – I pushed the sparks, somebody's wild imagining, from my mind and saw only what was in front of me: the vehicles frozen mid-air, with people ducking, clutching each other, huddled against what they must have thought was an inevitable crushing. The vehicles didn't move, and Maida – I – could feel a ripple of the telekinesis the one named Jon emitted, a resisting force against Kemp's assault.

No telepathy on the nul-psis – non-consensual mental intrusions will not go over well in the current climate.

And so the telepaths set themselves to helping people to safety and attempting to calm them with just spoken words. Ani, the clairvoyant, joined that effort. Del was someplace a bit removed from the fray so that they could be in trance and have a bird's eye view of the whole thing. The knowledge of what they perceived rippled through the telepathic connection but didn't overwhelm. It was like another layer of awareness that added dimension to what I saw with my own eyes.

I locked eyes with Tilda – we both had known this circumstance was a possibility. The knowledge of what to do was in our joined mind, and just as we were about to make our move, a mind-splitting jolt of pain tore through our collective mind with white spots and stars blooming in our eyes. Screams burst out all around us as people clutched their heads and fell to their knees. They clawed at themselves, rolled around on the ground and wailed.

Meanwhile, for us, the pain subsided as the joint shielding – *"interlaced," we call the technique* – of our telepaths nullified the psychic blast.

Beside Linstrom now on stage stood Rebecca.

That mind-blast trick hurts.

Rafe and Marlon turned their telepathic attention to her. They had disconnected from the rest of us but were joined with each other. Her assault stopped, and she seemed to be locked in psionic battle with the two of them as one.

Kemp had levitated himself over the stage and was ripping it apart with telekinesis – tearing up the banisters, the Boards of the deck.

Can't pierce the psiblocks.

People flew over the edge of the deck and fell into the swales below. But then his attention turned, and his berserker assault on the crowd stopped. He was now facing the water.

The seawall.

He was going to breach the seawall. If that happened, this sector of the city would flood and a whole swath of it would be lost. Homes and resources and lives and livelihoods would be drowned where they stood. Where they thought they were safe. I caught Tilda's eye, and we agreed: *go now.*

Her telekinetic hold enveloped me, and Maida – I, we, this body – floated off the ground. The understanding of how almost coalesced in our mind, then we flew upwards at Kemp, whose back was to us as he faced the Seawall and the Bay. We slammed into him, piggy-backed him, and wrapped hands around his face and head. We scanned. I scanned.

He writhed, tried to shake this body off. We struggled to hold on as we hovered twenty feet or so in the air.

Kemp Isaiah Redmond, born January 10, 2061. Became property of Golden Days Holding Co – white light, images flood – *a childhood in a planned community being the only Black child on the playground a ribbon for spelling a birthday cake flying a kite rickety ancient thing being good at math making friends with a fox* – *Kemp.*

Kemp.

Kemp stopped fighting us – me – and the difference in his body, in the energy he gave off, was palpable. I slipped off his back, still hovering in mid-air, courtesy of Tilda.

"Rebecca next," he said and gave me a push.

I glided down to Rebecca and scanned her for the second time. It was easier this time, like her real self was just below the influence of the implant. All it needed was a crack to break through.

Rafe and Marlon released her. The telepathic group-chat ended, and the Circle of the Eye members assisted the bystanders. As soon as Tilda set me back on the ground, I looked for Lorel and Bertrand, and caught sight of Linstrom. I wasn't the only one.

The Assessor Prime had made it to his car, but so had others. People were shouting, "Was that real?" and "Did you lie?" and demanding answers as his security kept the simmering crowd back with stunsticks. Lorel had gotten close and attempted to interrogate him as Bertrand filmed. Security kept pressing them back, but Bertrand kept repeating over and over, "Why not talk to us if you have nothing to hide?"

At the same time, Lorel chanted, "We just want your side of it, sir."

"I have no comment at this time," Linstrom said, as he tried to get into the backseat of his official transport, to get behind the black glass. But the door slammed shut, seemingly of its own accord. Linstrom tried the door handle again, to no avail.

"You're not going anywhere."

I knew who had spoken even before I turned and saw Kemp approaching, with Rebecca close behind.

The crowd parted to let them through – they had all just witnessed what these two were capable of.

"He put neural implants into us and was controlling our minds," Kemp declared to the crowd. "Controlled our minds with technology, not telepathy."

Linstrom scoffed. "That's preposterous."

"He abducted me back in December," Rebecca said. "Rebecca Morgan. You can check the missing person notice. You can check my schedule as the Liaison Officer for the Cultural Recovery Project and see that my last appointment was a meeting with him, after which I went missing. We need surgery to remove the implants, but we both have scars."

Kemp and Rebecca both turned the backs of their necks out, and Bertrand got up close with his device zooming in on the incisions the installation of the implants had left.

It looked like some people had found the missing persons alert for Rebecca.

"Tell us the truth!" somebody bellowed.

"I know Simon Pertkin!" somebody else called out. "One of the men interviewed about Alcatraz. He's my neighbor and I know he's Freedom Faction. We've argued about it. He doesn't work security like that news story claimed. So that's a lie right there."

Murmurs bubbled up all around us and Linstrom looked panicked. Then he plastered on that look of fake calm and smiled, though he was clearly ill at ease. "This is all a misunderstanding. Psionic trickery, no doubt. The truth will come out."

"You're right about that," I said.

Linstrom looked startled to see me there. I forgot I still had the blonde wig on. I pulled it off.

Kemp had apparently released the telekinetic hold on the car door because Linstrom tried it again and it opened.

"Let him leave," Rebecca said to the crowd. "He can leave this place, but he won't evade accountability."

"We have the implants in our heads that will soon be removed," Kemp said.

"We have all the footage from last night," Lorel said.

"We know where your secret lab is," I said. "So you're right, Assessor. The truth will come out. And when it does, I think your political life will be over."

He looked shaken, and the petty part of me relished that; it meant he knew I was right. He got into his transport and it drove away, the crowd now booing as he left.

I turned to Rebecca. "Why didn't you make him tell the truth?"

"We can't give him any leeway to say that a telepath forced him to say anything. There will be court proceedings to come out of this, and there is a solid case against him. You were correct when you told him his political career will be over. I suspect it already is with the footage you've released." She paused, looked at me intently. "I sense you have something you want to ask me."

She was right. I did have something to ask. "Oliver Shulamith chose to work with Linstrom. From what Aviva has said, you believe in more aggressive applications of psionic abilities, including telepathy. So why didn't you work with him too, of your own accord? He seems to want to use our powers in that same way."

"Linstrom wants to use psionic talents in the same manner I do, yes. But not for the same purpose. I believe developing such uses are necessary to defend psion autonomy, of our bodies, lives, and minds. I have no wish to subjugate anyone. But to have our minds and talents leashed to a political leader's agenda to control our kind? No. I would never abide that."

Freed from the influence of the neural implant, Rebecca spoke with a confidence and surety that I admired, even found a little intimidating. She had a presence that commanded respect. I thought maybe I could learn something from that.

"That was so crazy," Lorel gushed as she and Bertrand came over to me. "Watching you up there in the air with Kemp."

"I didn't know psions could do all that." Bertrand sounded surprised, taken aback, shaken as he looked around at the destruction Kemp had caused.

"It wasn't a psion doing that," I said. "It was somebody using power he didn't understand for his own gain."

A drone dropped down from above and its light blinked rapidly. I gave it a wave. "Hi, Roan." Lorel and Bertrand joined in and waved too, the three of us clustered together like we were taking a group photo. The drone took off, headed back to wherever Roan was stationed.

"What happens next?" Lorel asked.

I looked out at the wrecked plaza, the smashed vehicles, the glass and bits of staging and hyperpixel screen everywhere. People that had been thrown off the plaza were telekinetically lifted up from where they had fallen as other members of the Circle of the Eye squad tended to folks who needed assistance. What happens next?

"Fuck if I know."

34.

LI NUAN

October 11, 1954
Richmond District, San Francisco

Li Nuan takes great delight in watching little Elsa leap and twirl around the living room.

"Tai Po, Tai Po, watch!" the little girl demands before she spins around on one foot while she holds the other foot against her knee. "That's called a pirouette! I'm going to get good at it. I'm going to practice and practice."

"Yes, yes," Li Nuan replies with her limited English. "You good, you good."

Elsa's mother Doris, Li Nuan's granddaughter, says in Cantonese, "Don't encourage her. The whites will never let one of us dance their dance." Then, in English, "Ballet." Is that scorn or envy in her voice?

"They accepted her as a student, didn't they?" The conversation is back in Cantonese.

"Because we pay."

"They are not afraid you are Communists."

"We are not Communists." Doris stiffens at the mention of the word, of the crazed politics that had taken over their country of origin. But she was born here, and she doesn't agree with the radicals over there.

Li Nuan understands that to some white Americans, the fact that her daughter, her granddaughter, and her great-granddaughter were born here doesn't matter. That agreeing or disagreeing with Communists doesn't matter. Americans would look at their faces and think they see the enemy. She is not naïve. But she also knows it will not always be this way. The Japanese were locked away during the war and now they were not.

Doris watches Elsa dance. Li Nuan knows her granddaughter's heart, and she knows that Doris is afraid to hope. But hope is still there.

"The dancing is good exercise," Doris says. "It will teach her grace. It will teach her to carry herself. But she thinks she can be a ballerina. She thinks she can be a swan."

"Maybe she can."

"Po Po."

Li Nuan knows her granddaughter thinks of her as a strange and silly old woman.

"The world changes," Li Nuan says. "Slowly and then all at once." She watches little Elsa. She remembers girls that age being brought to the brothels, and now here this little one is, dancing in her family home, cherished by her parents, cherished by generations, going to school, learning ballet. Prejudice is not gone from the world, of course not. But the people who shed it like dead skin grow in number. More people are willing to get to know others not like themselves, to see their shared humanity, to learn. In the future, there will only be more people like that. She believes it.

Doris sighs. She knows what her grandmother is like.

"Can I see it?" Li Nuan asks.

Doris gets up, walks over to the treasure box on the shelf, opens it reverently and fetches an item from its sandalwood scented interior. She walks back over with a small bundle of yellow silk.

Li Nuan takes the bundle, feels the weight of it in her hand. The silk had been from a dress she'd been given to wear a long time ago. It had not been a happy occasion. She cut that dress up, used the fabric for different things. This little swatch is the only piece left in her possession – well, the possession of the family, anyway. She unties the ribbon and the silk spills away to reveal the teacup. She touches it, but there are no more visions. There hadn't been any since the earthquake and the fire; it's as if a window that had been open is now closed.

Back in 1942, in honor of her years of service to the women and girls of Chinatown, the place once known as the Occidental Mission Home for Girls, then the Presbyterian Home, was renamed Cameron House, after Miss Cameron. Li Nuan, who had been working with Miss Cameron for years at that point, teaching cooking and sewing and assisting with rescues, was there. She and Bao and Emily and fourteen-year-old Doris were all there for the ceremony. Li Nuan is so proud to be part of the history of that place, even though it had been terrible circumstances that brought her there.

The cup brings it all back every time she holds it. Though the visions no longer come, she remembers them, but some details have faded over the years. Was it simply the city burning that she had seen, or were there bigger and more terrible fires? Fires that have not yet come? The burning forests and the storms, all those other, horrible things. The images had once been so clear, almost as if she lived through those things, but now they are faded dreams. She had always believed she had been given a warning, but it was a warning she could not understand, about a world that hadn't yet arrived. So she focuses on what she can do to make her world better. She still volunteers at Cameron House, still helping to save girls. There are always more to save.

"You always look sad when you hold the cup," little Elsa says.

"Sad and happy," Li Nuan replies in English. "No happy." She has to remind herself that *happy* means something more than *not sad*. "Proud."

"That makes no sense," Elsa says. "Proud of what?"

Li Nuan smiles. This is what girlhood is supposed to be like. Asking questions of elders. Dancing in the family home.

"Why is it so special?" Elsa asks. She grabs the cup, turns it over in her small hands.

Li Nuan exchanges a look with Doris.

"When you're older," Doris says. "We'll tell you all about it when you're older."

35.

NATHAN

Danny's house isn't big enough to contain all his friends, so the Celebration of Life is being held at Glen Canyon Park. There had been a formal funeral that the family arranged, but Danny's friends know that he'd want to be sent off into the great unknown mysteries of the afterlife with a party.

"Golden Gate and Dolores get all the glory," Danny had often said. "But Glen Canyon and McLaren are where it's at." He'd always maintained that the southern part of the city got short shrift, including – maybe most especially – its parks.

The Fish is present and parked on Bosworth, its sound system bumping with the last playlist that Danny had made, "PlayaTrek 2006." It was what he'd played on the way to the Burn to get stoked. Some members of the Solar Flare crew are present, spinning non-burning versions of their props that feature shiny ribbons on the things called poi, and sparkly tape on the hoops. It's nice that they came, even though a couple of them had only just met Danny this last Burn. But people fell in love with him quick like that.

There's a table loaded with food; Delilah made Danny's favorite chocolate chip pancakes. Remy baked Danny's favorite cherry pie. Annika whipped up a batch of some

352

awfully sweet beverage called Pixie Piss, which had been the signature cocktail of a bar called Doctor Bombay's that Danny had loved. It closed years ago. Nathan, too, made a favorite dish of Danny's. Whenever there was a potluck, Danny would ask him, "Are you bringing Asian Brown Sauce Chicken?" Nathan himself named it that and Danny quickly adopted it. The memory of his friend asking for Asian Brown Sauce Chicken brings tears to Nathan's eyes.

"Remy mentioned you have an interview coming up for a new job," Annika says as she and Nathan graze the refreshments.

It feels a little weird to be talking about something like that at a memorial, even if it is in the form of a party. But Danny would have been the first to acknowledge that life goes on. "I'm taking this permaculture class Danny and I were supposed to take together," he explains. "And somebody in the class sent a job posting my way for a new start-up called Ecology Design Workshop. They're developing sustainable materials and methods to make things like household items and textiles, and are recruiting for a design lead. I figured I'd go for it. They called me for an interview the day after I emailed my resumé, so I guess my professional background intrigued them."

"Right on," Annika says. "Good for you."

An altar has been set up – Annika and Delilah had worked on it together. Nathan joins Remy in front of it, linking up their arms. The altar is draped with red cloth and festooned with marigolds. There are pictures of Danny from childhood, through his teen years, his studly twenties.

"I can't believe how ripped he was," Remy says as he gazes adoringly at a shirtless photo of their departed friend. The Danny they knew, the thirty-something-edging-close-to-forty version, was a little thicker and a little paunchier than the lean young man in the picture.

"Would you have gone for him?" Nathan asks.

"I never liked wasting my time with the straight ones," Remy says. "But I would've blown him if he asked."

"Same." They share a laugh for a moment before they start crying again.

There are also photos of Danny's first couple of Burns, 2002 and 2003. Holding his arms up in front of the Man. Straddling his fake-fur-covered bike. A few pictures of the workshop where the Fish was created. Pictures of him with nieces and nephews. A graduation.

Sugar Bunny had come up from San Diego for this, and she stands now at the altar, holding a stick of nag champa and crying softly to herself. She and Danny hooked up on the playa and had exchanged contact information, and she had hopes. "I know it might not have gone anywhere, and even if it did, it might not have lasted." She pulls off her sunglasses and wipes her tears. "I'm not saying he was the one. But there was a spark. I was looking forward to seeing where it was gonna go."

Delilah, standing close by, gasps.

Nathan, Remy, and Sugar Bunny all look over at her.

"It's nothing," she says, waving it off. "It's inappropriate."

"Danny liked inappropriate," Nathan says.

Delilah looks at Sugar Bunny. "I just realized you're the last person he hooked up with."

Sugar Bunny looks shocked for a moment, and Nathan fears that she might burst into tears again, but instead she laughs. Uproariously. "Well at least it was a good one." She looks contemplative for a second. "I'm glad I didn't know I would be his last going into it. That would have made things awkward. Entirely too much pressure." She starts crying again.

As if to distract herself or everyone else from her tears, she asks, "What's that?" and points at the altar.

Along with the flowers and the photos sits a cylinder.

"That's a time capsule," Nathan says.

A quizzical look comes over her. "About Danny?"

"Not about him, but for him, for sure," Nathan explains. "Danny talked about doing a time capsule project with the crew for the longest time."

"When I first met him a few years ago, he was talking about it," Remy says. "He was convinced we were doing it that year."

"He was talking about it before then, even," Nathan goes on. "It was one of those things that was talked about forever but never followed up on. So I figured now was a good time. So that time capsule is capturing a little bit of this day when his friends say goodbye."

"Oh," Sugar Bunny says. "I wish I knew to bring something."

"It doesn't have to be anything super deep. Just something about today."

"Well in that case…" She tosses her sunglasses into the time capsule. Then she unclips her hair and tosses in the feathered hairclip too.

"Why those things?"

"Those were the only things I was wearing when I met him."

No further questions.

The time capsule isn't intended to only contain memories of Danny – the act of making it was the tribute. No, they all wanted to mark their time together as this friend group, acknowledge the different facets of the community that surrounded him. Each of them had been drawn into the orbit of Danny and his weird Fish car, and the bacchanal in the desert that had such a hold over them, and the music they all love to lose and find themselves in. It's a glimpse of, *this is how we live now.* Annika had put in a couple of her tiny paintings, and Remy put in the little clay tablet thing that Sugar Bunny had given him, since "a dreamer" suited Danny. He also added a thumbdrive of his mixes. Delilah put in a bunch of pictures from this year's Burn. A man pushing a shopping cart who looks like he maybe lives in the park at least some of the time tosses in a busted-up flip-phone with a quiet, "That dude used to give me socks."

Nathan pulls the teacup in its silk covering out of his pocket. He opens it up, admires how the green stone catches the sun. It has been in his family for generations, passed down from daughter to daughter, until him. And he knows he won't be having any kids, and his brother and his wife just had their second boy and have said they aren't having any more. He doesn't see a future where there would be a daughter to pass it to, and giving it to one of his nephews doesn't feel right. But there is something else, too.

That night out on the playa, out by the trash fence, when he had stronger visions than ever of ecological catastrophes and a planet in turmoil, he could have sworn the cup glowed with a golden light. Granted, he had drunk a potent brew of hallucinogenic mushrooms, but other things that night hadn't glowed with golden light. He had seen threads of connection, but connection to what and to whom, he couldn't say. But the threads had reached him from the future. The visions they brought him were of a coming storm. He's certain of that.

There have been no more visions after that night. The visions freaked him out, but now that they aren't happening anymore, he misses them. It feels like a channel that had been open is now closed.

He has a tickle of what Delilah would call intuition about the golden light, the threads, the cup. If he holds onto it, who would he pass it onto? If he holds onto it, wouldn't it just be lost in the detritus of life? And then where would it go when he died? He intended to live to a ripe old age, but heirs are unlikely. Sure, he could donate it to the historical society, or something, but given the visions he had, he doesn't know if it would make it through all that. But here is this time capsule that's going to be buried in Danny's garden. A bit of this time, six years into the twenty-first century, the now, preserved. He knows somebody will find it – maybe even the person who sent him those visions through time.

It's a crazy idea, yet it feels so right. He doesn't know how he knows. He just knows. So he wraps the cup once more in its silk, he puts it into the time capsule, and he gives it to the future.

34.

MAIDA

June 22, 2106
The Presidio, San Francisco

Jade teacup, Qing Dynasty China, circa 1860
uncovered in the Islais Cove Preservation Area, 2106

This cup is the only surviving piece of a tea set carved by the artisan Jing Yu, based in Beijing. Such sets were commissioned by the Emperor, and often gifted to visiting dignitaries or high-ranking officials. The set this particular cup was part of was gifted to a merchant named Fong Yu Chun, who then passed it onto his son, Fong Lin Chun. Lin Chun brought the set with him when he emigrated to San Francisco in 1890. He later adopted the English name Lincoln Fong, but was known in the Chinatown community as Boss Fong.

During the 1906 earthquake and fire that levelled the city, the cup was rescued from Fong's home by Chan Li Nuan, an indentured servant, who took that moment to seize her freedom. Li Nuan would later go on to work with the missionary Donaldina Cameron, noted for her work in rescuing young women and girls from indentured servitude and sex slavery in Chinatown.

The cup would later be passed along through multiple generations of Li Nuan's descendants, finally landing with her great-great-grandson Nathan Zhao, a noted environmental activist of the early-to-mid twenty-first century who was a founding member of the Pacific Permaculture Network, one of the key entities that would eventually become the basis for the Sierra Northshore Regional Alliance.

This cup is a testament to the extraordinary history witnessed by ordinary things.

– *Maida Sun, Staff Psychometrist*

The cup rests on its splash of yellow silk, arranged so that the pink and white blossoms embroidered on it curve around its base. It's on its own pedestal, a pinlight illuminating the brilliant green. The exhibit includes many other items, including an entire section on Burning Man, which seems to be a more popular event with inhabitants of the region than we first realized. Included in that section are the photos of Nathan and his friends, along with many other items from other people found at other sites. I can hear music by DJ Aspect playing in that part of the gallery as Roan tests the sound.

The cup's label isn't the only one I've written – I've scanned nearly half the items here – but it's the one that means the most to me. There are so many details left out of the public facing history of the cup, like the exact provenance: Li Nuan claimed ownership when she took it from Boss Fong and passed it to her daughter Emily (Nathan's great-grandmother), who passed it to Doris (Nathan's grandmother), who passed it to Elsa (Nathan's

mother) who passed it to him, who placed it in the time
capsule opened by Bertrand five months ago.

And how am I connected? Why was it that I had such
strong glimpses of Li Nuan and Nathan's lives in particular?
Aviva's best guess is that it's because Li Nuan and Nathan
were the first and last members of my family to possess it,
and as such, formed a kind of psychic circuit that I tapped
into when I scanned it. So, yes, Roan's initial intuition
proved correct, that I was connected to Nathan and Li Nuan
by lineage. My great-grandfather was Nathan's nephew
Jason, who was born in 2006.

This knowledge of the family tree might never have been
broken, were it not for the Collapse and everything that
followed. And it might not have been recovered, were it not
for my ability and my friend's research prowess. Funny, the
ebb and flow of people and stories and objects through time.
How fortunate we are when lost things come back around,
and broken stories are made whole again.

I have Bertrand to thank for this knowledge. We had all
been curious about Nathan after he put the cup into the time
capsule – it was no longer his at that point, since the act of
placing it into the capsule relinquished his ownership. Thus,
I couldn't scan anything about him beyond that moment
in time when he placed the cup into the cylinder at Danny
Gobo's memorial party. It was during his research, based on
what details I had gleaned from my scans, that Bertrand
discovered what Nathan had gone on to do later in his life.
Who he had become.

I never knew my grandparents – three died before I was
born, and my mother's mother died when I was an infant.
So going from knowing nothing of my heritage beyond
my parents to now knowing this history going back two

hundred years, going back to before the Bloom and before the Collapse – well, it's a trip. I can scan the histories of things I touch, catch the moments in time anchored by objects, but I myself had always been free-floating, unconnected to anything. And now I feel connected; now I know where I come from, and I'm proud of my ancestors.

The record shows Donaldina Cameron rescued approximately three thousand girls over the course of her career, and Li Nuan was part of that. And Nathan's revelation that night at Burning Man was the first step to him joining in with the environmental and social justice movements that led to the shape of the society we live in now. He'd gone on to found the Pacific Permaculture Network, an organization dedicated to sustainability and Earth-renewing practices that spearheaded the formation of the regional alliance that eventually became the society we live in now, at least in this region. He had participated in anti-racism and queer liberation movements – there were a couple of news articles that Bertrand had found that quoted him. I wish I had something else of his to learn more, but the cup and the historical tidbits Bertrand dug up are all there is. Not for the first time since all this began, tears come to my eyes.

"He was like a madman," Felix says, eyes wide and hands flying over an imaginary console. "Watching everything happening all at once." He's recounting the night of the attacks on the desalination plants, what it was like watching Roan command his fleet. His swarm. His little toys.

"I didn't want to miss anything," Roan says. "It was all too important."

"History was being made, all right," Felix says. "Can't believe I had a front-row seat."

We're aboard Epifania, anchored at a spot near Tiburon. Me, Roan, Lorel, and Bertrand. We're all up on the deck with Felix, taking in the late afternoon sun. The way it sparkles on the water is blinding. We're the first to arrive and are waiting for the others to get here.

Felix is right, though: history was made that night. Citing the footage of those attacks and the events of World Water Day, the Assessors Administration Council of the Sierra Northshore Regional Alliance, by a unanimous vote, removed Julian Linstrom as Assessor Prime. He faces charges of conspiring to subvert the authority of the Council, ceding unapproved concessions to rival regions, domestic terrorism, and abuse of civil liberties. His co-conspirators, such as Oliver Shulamith and Robert Patrick Fisk, have also been arrested and charged.

Rebecca and Kemp are key witnesses, and the domestic terrorism and public endangerment charges against them have been dropped after the extent of Linstrom's mind-control implant was determined. I, too, will be testifying about my scan of Linstrom's watch and my interrogation by him when I was held at the downtown facility. The trial doesn't begin for another few weeks, but I'm ready for it.

"So are you going to be part of this special ops team now?" Bertrand asks. "Have you and Roan been called to duty, service, and adventure?"

"I'm not a psion," Roan protests.

"Yes," Lorel says, "but if watching old spy adventure movies has taught us anything, it's that every team needs their techy gadget guy. That's you."

"I don't know how useful my talent would be on a team like that," I say.

They all turn towards me, staring in disbelief.

"You're the one who freed your mind-controlled teammates with your ability," Bertrand reminds me.

"I saw you flying around at World Water Day," Lorel adds.

"But I wasn't flying by my own power. Although, I guess I can come in handy to free people from mind-control, but that's pretty niche. And who's going to try that shit again?"

"You discovered Linstrom's plan," Roan reminds me.

"Oh, oh!" Felix exclaims excitedly. "And weren't you summoned to scan something from one of the Freedom Faction guys? To reveal even more of their nefarious plot?"

I have to concede these things are true. "Maybe I could be an on-call consultant or something. A specialist."

Felix's mention of Freedom Faction reminds me of an uncomfortable fact: Although the organization has disavowed Linstrom, they have continued their anti-psion crusade. "Sure, psions might not intend harm," goes their argument, "but what about the next power-mad Assessor who wants to use them as weapons of mass destruction? What then?"

They were a "movement" created entirely by Linstrom, but witnessing the ideology take off even though he's been discredited, and seeing the organization and his followers continue without him, is unsettling. To say the least.

"They're deranged," Del has said of them. "Some people just don't know who they are without somebody to hate. It's like they're nobodies without their prejudice. I thought we were past that bullshit by now. Maybe I'm the deranged one."

Del's point is a little harsh, maybe, but judging solely by the words and actions of Freedom Faction, I can't really argue against it.

"What we're doing now is a step in the right direction," I say to my gathered friends. They all seem excited, but I can also tell that they think I'm perhaps being a little idealistic.

One thing is clear in the aftermath of Linstrom: mistrust – or at least wariness – of psions has been let loose. Or maybe it's always been there, simmering below the surface, but nobody dared say anything until someone like Linstrom gave them permission. In any case, what's that saying? The bell can't be unrung. Linstrom the man may be discredited, but his words and actions awakened something real. There were plenty of people who bought into his plans, after all. Neuroscientists developed that chip. Somebody created that mesh. As far as we know, Oliver Shulamith was the only psion that willingly co-operated, but Linstrom was right: there would have been more willing to sell out their own community to put themselves in positions of privilege and power.

"Linking can heal us," I had pleaded with Aviva once the dust settled and Linstrom was formally removed from office. "I mean us specifically, but also us as a people. Us as a society. We need to let nul-psis into the circles. If they experience it, if they connect with us, they'll know there's no reason to be afraid. Plus, look at how Roan, Lorel, and Bertrand helped us through all of this. And Felix, too. They're not psions, yet they still helped. Doesn't that kind of participation in our struggle entitle them to another kind of participation as well?"

Sera agreed with me. I think maybe that's what finally swayed Aviva more than anything I argued. But maybe my points did make a bit of difference with her. Unlike the previous conclave I attended, which was all psions, this one includes nul-psis. It's a sort of trial run, and only nul-psis known personally by a psion who has previously attended are invited. My hope – and I think Sera's hope too – is that these will be open to the wider public eventually. The only way to counter the attitudes ignited by Linstrom and his ilk is fostering understanding. No matter what kind of laws and policies are passed, that's always going to be the most effective way to counter prejudice. And maybe that's the only way we'll evolve too.

Other boats have arrived as we've been talking; I recognize a couple of them from the first time I did this. Aviva arrives on a large tugboat called the Hindeloopen – like Epifania, another well-preserved vessel from the precursor world, but much larger than Epifania. The deck is crowded with people, perhaps forty or so. From the deck, Del and Kemp wave hello, and I wave back. There's something nice about greeting each other at a distance the old-fashioned way, without us all talking in each other's heads.

In short order, the platform is deployed – a much bigger one than the last one I saw.

"No lifejackets?" Lorel asks with alarm in her voice as she stands on the deck, staring down Epifania's ladder.

"Trust is part of the process." I try to put on a mysterious air, but it clearly doesn't work, because my friends just laugh.

"Why exactly are we on this platform in the middle of the water?" Roan asks as we get settled.

I haven't told them about the other members of the circle. They soon arrive.

It's a whole pod of them this time, not just one, and not just one species. I spot a blue whale, humpbacks, and grays – I think maybe a dozen of them in total.

"Holy shit," Roan whispers beside me.

"Oh my god oh my god oh my god," Lorel chants.

"Wow." Bertrand just stares at the beings circling us now, releasing plumes of spray from their blowholes.

"Everyone lay back," Aviva instructs us.

The whales themselves have formed a circle around us and assume the vertical position they take when sleeping and trancing.

Aviva offers further instruction: "If this is your first time, just take several deep breaths –" *and relax and keep your mind as clear as possible.*

That familiar tingle in my head and in my chest starts, letting me know the process of connection has begun.

Open, open, open.

Warmth spreads from my core throughout my body, all the way to my fingers and toes. In the connection, I know my friends are experiencing the same physical sensations, I know all of us here are feeling our hearts pound, are feeling the same anticipation. I'm aware of myself, in my own mind, but I am just part of a chain that links us all on this platform. Just.

Then, the realm below the surface of the water asserts itself with ripples of light that dance in my mind. The breeze across my skin whispers into my awareness, along with the water's warm embrace, which I know is not coming from me, but the beings below us and around us. I'd have thought it would feel cold, but it doesn't – not to them. I see myself joined to the others by a golden thread of thought, of emotion. Of spirit. The whales, too, are connected to each other by a golden thread. They're joined to all of us on the platform and we to them.

A whisper of grief: the blue whale that is the actual leader of this Linking is the offspring of Grandmother, whom I'd met before. Grandmother has passed as she told us she would, her body now decaying on the ocean floor and feeding so much new life, as her spirit swims among the stars and galaxies – dervishes of time, whirlpools of existence. Grandmother had been long-lived, a hundred years old, born the same year my great-grandfather was born, born the year of Nathan's life that I witnessed in the cup.

Tears flow, but are they my tears, are they my friends' tears, are they the tears of the other people here that I don't know, are they the tears of the whales, flowing out of those enormous eyes and melding with the sea? Yes yes yes.

Whalesong in our minds now, and the grief doesn't last. The grief moves on, passes through us as it must, and leaves peace behind. The golden threads of our beings encircle us, and the threads of the whales' beings encircle them, and they weave together into a net that holds us all. In the pulses and the harmonies and the eerie, haunted tones of their song, we understand the song is connection, we feel the song in our flesh and bone.

For all the differences in our material vessels, we are the same spirit-stuff, the spark of life, the blaze of consciousness. We have a duty to it, don't we? To do more than consume, to do more than our chores and our jobs. How much more can we heal this world? How much more beauty can we make? How much more gratitude can we pour out into the sea of our existence, the roiling in and out tidal cycles of our lives?

We feel it all, and we, here, now, feel each other feeling it. We are individuals but part of a whole, like petals on a flower or leaves on a tree. Threads in a weave, angels singing in an endless sea.

The song is over. The circle is open. I come back into myself, into my body, my breath, my mind. My tear-streaked face. People all around are sobbing. My friends and I sit up and embrace. We've taken in this song of connection, we've received this transmission. We are, each of us, part of this world no matter who we think we are, who we hate or fear or love. I know, and I know my friends know, that we've got no choice but to move forward and make this world together.

The whales circle around us before diving away. One of them, Grandmother's offspring – *Luna* is her name – surfaces on her side, waves a fin at us. She's saying farewell for now. She's saying *see you next time*.

ACKNOWLEDGMENTS

This story is deeply inspired by the cultural, social, and historic preservation work undertaken by these San Francisco nonprofit organizations: Cameron House, Burning Man, Chinese Culture Foundation, Chinese Historical Society of America.

My deep gratitude to:

• Amy Collins, my brave and patient agent;

• The Angry Robot Team especially: Desola Coker, Gemma Creffield, Caroline Lambe, Amy Portsmouth, Sarah O'Flaherty, and of course the fearless leader of the Robot team, Eleanor Teasdale;

• Early readers Kara Owens and Sarah J. Daley, and also Mitzi, of Paul and Mitzi, who were regulars at the Java Jive Café where I worked in Chicago in the 1990s, who I was friendly with for a while. Mitzi read the first draft and told me that it needed development, but the important thing was I got it down, and she was right. We lost touch ages ago, but Hi, Mitzi! I finally did it;

• Annalee Newitz pointed the way to resources that helped me figure out some stuff about the landscape of future San Francisco;

• The WMC, Transpatial Tavern and Bay Area Speculative Fiction Creators Discord groups;

- The Writers Grotto, San Francisco;
- Dominique Debucquoy-Dodley and the Burning Man Project for kind permission to set part of this story in Black Rock City;
- The crews of Camp Run Amok, Solar Flare and Salon Soleil and especially Jack Brady for instigating the creation of the Fish whose gifts continue to ripple out over twenty years later;
- Dave and Allison Shuttleworth for friendship and warm hospitality aboard the Epifania and on the playa over the years;
- The Flaming Lotus Girls for the creation of Serpent Mother, and the Uchronia creators;
- Julia Flynn Siler, whose book *The White Devil's Daughters* was invaluable in helping me get a feel for the day-to-day life of the girls rescued from the brothels, as well as some key dates related to the work of Donaldina Cameron in Chinatown;
- And finally, for my Marty, who for more than thirty years, has not let me give up on my dream.

Chapter One

After an hour scoping out the waves of tourists flowing in and out of the terminal, Jes spots what he's been waiting for: a clueless human clearly on his first trip away from Indra. One of those who are completely unaware of their surroundings, of the possibility of ruffians in their midst. The man fumbles with a bag as the holographic stripe of the pass pokes out of his slacks, winking at every passerby. A quick bump of shoulders and a swipe so delicate it barely happens, and Jes has a ticket off this miserable hell world also known as his home planet.

Overhead, glass panels set within the vaulted arches stream with rainbow-stained light. Holographic displays glow in amber, green and blue, destinations and launch times scrolling over their sleek surfaces. Travelers of multiple species, but mostly human and Rijala, move through the atrium as if performing some kind of obscure choreography. Jes casts his eyes about looking for orderlies but there's no sign of them. The spaceport is clear.

A Bezan girl behind the ticketing counter returns his smile, both of them performing the expected expressions of friendliness. "Slip and return to Opale Lunar Station, please." He looks into the camera set in the counter – he wants to make sure he's recorded making this transaction.

"Opale! Are you going for the Mudraessa Festival?" the ticketing agent asks. Her eyes are wide and gem-toned, a brilliant cerulean blue, deepened by the violet-to-purple tones of her skin. Her hair is pulled back, but maintains the characteristic phosphorescence of Bezan hair.

"Yes…" He scans her uniform for her name-tag, "Alys. I love opera in all its forms. Ever since I was little. I've never heard Mudraessa, of course, since the Asuna don't allow it off-world. It's supposed to be the most perfect. That's what everyone says. I can't wait to listen with my own ears." Jes can't stand opera, but in the moment he's quite certain that whoever he's pretending to be loves it deeply. Jes's mother and father wouldn't stop going on about the festival after they attended that one time, but he's glad he retained some tidbit to deploy now. He decides he doesn't want to think about them though, and fidgets with the strap of the satchel on his shoulder.

"Well, you must be thrilled to have gotten lucky in the lottery. The Asuna are so restrictive about off-worlders on Opale."

"Yes, I'm very lucky."

She arches an eyebrow as she proceeds with the transaction. With his empathic sense, he susses mainly indifference – he's one of many such transactions today and she doesn't really care, however well she fakes it.

"Node?"

He hands over the sleek palm-curved pebble of glass; she takes it and slips it into a groove on the surface of her workstation. Jes's buddy in town helped him get the alias – a favor banked for all the locks picked and safes cracked over the months they ran together before the Institute got him.

"You're all set," Alys says.

"Thanks." He takes the node back and slips it into his pocket.

On his way to the gate, the blazing white of orderly uniforms sets panic alarms pinging in his head. *Shit…* Jes looks around wildly for the nearest exit, heart pounding, sweat prickling at his skin.

No wait, he breathes. *Not them. Just a couple wearing matching white outfits.*

Jes exhales relief. Flashes of his past come to him without warning – the orderlies at the Institute, stunning him, shocking him, injecting him. All to make him weak and compliant. The pain. So much pain...

Jes shakes his head to clear his mind. How long will people wearing all white set him off?

At the departure gate he scans his node. With a beep and a flash of green light, he's registered boarded. He heads toward the boarding ramp, then spins on his heels, bringing a hand to his forehead in fake befuddlement. His pulse quickens as it always does when he's about to lie.

"I left my briefcase at the cafe!" he exclaims to the no nonsense Rijala gate attendant. It's the first thing that comes to mind, despite the fact that he doesn't look like the briefcase-carrying type. "Can I just run and get it? It won't take long."

"We depart in ten minutes," she says flatly without looking at him. She tucks a stray lock of hair behind her ear and smiles at the next passenger, simultaneously welcoming them and abruptly dismissing him.

Her disdain for Jes pokes like bony fingers. He can't tell if she's annoyed by him being a forgetful passenger, or if it's because his typically Rijalen blue-white hair and silver eyes combined with his human-toned, deep-tan skin makes his mixed heritage obvious. Rijala don't like hybrids much, but are always just short of being outright discriminatory.

"I'll be quick," he promises, despite the fact that she is no longer listening. His heart pounds like it did when he busted his way out of the Institute, but nobody is chasing him this time. He wipes his sweaty palms on his trouser legs as he walks away, then tosses the node into the first waste bin he walks by. The decoy alias has served its purpose. He's on his way to Opale, as far as anybody tracking him is concerned.

From the satchel on his shoulder, he pulls out the cape he acquired from one of the vendors in the bazaar outside the spaceport. It's made of green satin rimmed with gold – gaudy trying to look classy. It's a much more ridiculous thing than he'd normally wear, which is entirely the point.

The cape slips lightly over his shoulders, and he delights in the fake luxury of it, the aspiring glamor. He puts up the hood as he scans a destination board. He takes out the purloined all-travel pass; the rounded edges are smooth against his fingertips as he worries it. He can disappear on any world within the 9-Star Congress now. So… where?

He is tempted by a trip to Indra, but the Institute staff already know about his fondness for that world. It would definitely be the first place they'd think to look once they figure out he's not on Opale. Maybe a place that's the farthest away then? What star system would that be?

Vashtar. The principal world there is Lora, the other human world. Jes has met people from there before, and he didn't like them. They were polite, friendly even, but a strange aggression simmered under their surface. It rubbed roughly against his empathic sense, like sandpaper. It could have been down to the specific individuals he met, but his grandmother had warned him that they were like that; humans born there, who grew up without connection to Indra, come off that way. Though there are multiple species there, it's dominated by humans with this vibe. So – not there.

Also in the system is the notorious so-called pleasure moon, Persephone-9. That far-flung hunk of rock bears the most decadent reputation in the galaxy. The moon is truly a multispecies panoply as no single species dominates the mostly transient population there. The mix of his empathic sense and sexual aversion, however, would likely make being there uncomfortable at times. But, he reasons, that would be preferable to the harshness of Lora and maybe it would be easier to blend into the background in a place like that. Jes nods with his decision.

When he arrives at the departure gate for Port Ruby Station, he smiles to himself – with his cape, he fits right in. Of course the passengers traveling to a place famous for hedonism would be a colorful crowd! He can suss the general, collective feeling of the group: happy, buzzing anticipation. A lovey-dovey kind of vibe. He flips a panel of his cape over one shoulder in imitation of a Bezan dandy ahead of him in line – is this how these things are worn? In the crowd, he spots people of all the species that make up the 9-Star Congress, except the Mantodeans, who slipstream travel in their own vessels and by their own network of tubes.

There are even Asuna here – he has only seen them in person a couple of times, when his father received delegations as part of his duties as a commerce leader. He admires their pale green skin, the hints of yellow and white. Most of all, he admires their halos. The crystals sprout around the crown of their skulls and, like their eyes, appear in a multitude of colors.

An inner knowingness tells Jes he made the right call. He remembers childhood conversations with his grandmother when she explained the importance of that sensation. "Our intuition is the force of our life moving towards what will fulfill it, like a plant moves towards the sun. Follow its pull and you'll find what you need."

He hadn't been aware of it before but now, as he looks down at his all-travel pass, he gets it. He's grateful that even what he endured and witnessed at the Institute didn't overwrite this essential lesson his grandmother had imparted. He heeded it without thinking. It is a part of him still.

"*Last call for Port Ruby Station, Persephone-9,*" the smooth robotic voice of the attendant intones. He flashes his pass for the scanner and is waved on board.

He grabs an empty seat among some humans and straps in. Behind his eyes, his grandmother's face smiles – she is still teaching him about intuition. In his pocket, he carries his only memento from the life he is fleeing, a crystal shard on a delicate yet strong chain of tiny titanium links, threaded with colored spheres of other coded minerals. His grandmother had given it to him on his tenth birthday. It is the only tether he has to his past.

"I can't wait to hit the clubs," a young human behind him says to her Rijala companion. "We'll have a couple of nights before the forest gathering."

"I've heard the forest is beautiful," her friend responds. "This is my third trip to Persephone-9 and I still haven't been to that side of the moon."

"That's because you're a party whore," the original speaker teases.

"You flatter me!"

The two friends laugh as the shuttle vibrates, preparing to depart. With the vibration comes relief – he is *really* escaping now. He can see Matheson's face in his mind – the pale skin that obviously did not get enough sun, the pale, watery blue eyes, the limp ashy blond hair and the fake smile that didn't hide the man's impatience nearly as much as he thought it did. The man who thinks of Jes as his prize lab animal. He hopes to never see that face again. But a deep buzzing in his intuitive sense tells him that he will, someday. But right now he has to focus on getting away. He can only hope that "someday" is far, far away.

The chatter about party plans, and which casinos are best, and which clubs have the best vibes, all settles down as the engines increase their pitch. Jes leans back as the shuttle glides gently to the guiding strip. It hovers a moment before the press of speed pushes him into his seat and they launch out of the bay, away from the city, the ground, the planet of Rijal, the Institute and all its horrors.

In seconds they've pierced the atmosphere and zoom out into open space. From where he's sitting there's no porthole, but a viewscreen option is available. Once they're in space he shuts it off, knowing there will be a viewing deck when the lounge opens. Instead, he looks around at the rabble surrounding him. The range of species comforts him. Definitely the right call.

There are Rijala and Bezans. There are humans of various shades of brown and a bewildering array of hair textures and colors. A couple of Hydraxians occupy a wide bench on the side of the shuttle. They're orange-skinned and four-armed, and against his empathic sense are much softer than one would guess from the sour expressions they wear. As a hybrid himself, Jes feels more comfortable in this multi-species array than he ever did among homogenous Rijala society.

The ones who fully captures Jes's attention, however, are the Asuna sitting a row ahead on the other side of the craft. With their hoods down, the characteristic iridescence of their skin is visible from this distance. He can also see that the crystals that sprout from their heads are a deep emerald green. If he remembers his Asuna sociology correctly, emerald green is the Council Class of civic and cultural leaders. One of them looks younger than the others, and she doesn't have the shimmer yet – a characteristic only the fully mature members of the species manifest. He remembers being told that they often looked younger than they were and that their lifespans were much longer than that of the other known humanoid species. He guesses they are a family unit, as their halos are all the same color. But he is confused. If they are as upper caste as he thinks, why would they be taking a common transport?

The two females wear their long hair in ornate braids; the younger one's hair is the color of rose gold and her braids sit loosely around her face, while the older one's braids are knotted atop her head and are a deep auburn in color. The brilliant green of their crystal halos reminds Jes disconcertingly of the serum they shot him up with in the lab, the one that kept him sedated and unable to use his ability while they performed the more invasive procedures. He remembers the heavy, sleepy feeling falling on him. How everything moved real slow, how the places in his body where his ability usually buzzed went numb and dark and cold. But he is not numb now.

Jes wakes from a dreamless sleep to find the shuttle well into its time in the slipstream. The lounge is open, so he gets up to stretch his legs. Standing at the viewport that takes up almost a whole bulkhead, he stares out at the lightshow before him. The slipstream, gift of Zo, the sentient star who called to order the 9-Star Congress of Conscious Worlds, displays colors of violet and indigo and white as they writhe and intertwine and shift between shades. The stream cuts the length of interstellar travel to a fraction of the time that such trips take in regular space at sub-light speed. Jes doesn't fully understand how it all works. He suspects most folks don't.

"It's so beautiful," a voice says from beside him. "I've never seen it in person before. Have you?" It's the Asuna girl, and she's speaking Ninespeak without first asking if he knows it. But, he supposes, it's probably a safe assumption that anyone going to Persephone-9 would know the common language used in the unaffiliated sectors.

"Yes," Jes answers in Ninespeak also. "A few times. But it's been a while."

"Esmée." She bows slightly as she says this, then looks at him expectantly.

He struggles to remember what he learned in his Interspecies Etiquette class and dredges up a vague lesson on greetings. The Asuna simply state their names and bow, by way of introducing themselves.

He's about to give the name of his discarded alias, but then remembers that Asuna are empathic, in their own way. He reasons that in this moment, the truth makes the most sense to give. His intuition pings back to him that this is the right call.

"Jes," he says, bowing back.

She says something that sounds like "orkut". The r sound rolls like a purr.

"I'm sorry – I don't speak Mudra-nul."

She laughs. "It means 'well met.' I think humans would say 'nice to meet you.' Though it could also mean 'nice to see you.' You are human and Rijala? I hope it's not rude of me to ask." She seems about to say something more but holds back.

"Yes, I am. Human mother, Rijala father."

"I'm sorry if I'm prying. Hybrids aren't common where I'm from."

Jes is aware of the Asuna's reputation for xenophobia – their restrictions on other species visiting their homeworld is well known. "It's fine," he says.

"Is your human side Loran or Indran?"

He wonders if all Asuna are this direct or if it's just this Esmée person. "My mother's from Indra. But I was born and grew up on Rijal."

"So do you possess the Indran talents?"

"I can see auric fields when I concentrate. And I have the intuitive and empathic senses, but I'm not emerged so no telepathy or telekinesis or any of that stuff. But even if I were emerged, psi-abilities don't work away from the world of origin anyway. That's true of Emerged Ones from all species."

"Of course. I wasn't thinking." She pauses. "I haven't met many other species. This is my first trip off Opale."

This doesn't really surprise him, but he holds his tongue and looks back out at the lightshow. "Some people have questioned whether all Consciousness Holders could access their abilities if they were in orbit of Zo, since it connects all our worlds."

"That's an interesting question."

A few others join them on the observation deck. The Rijala keep their distance from the other passengers and look askance at everyone, especially the humans and Bezans from whom they turn away if one gets too close. It's as if they fear picking up some kind of parasite from them. Odd how the Asuna have the xenophobic reputation while it's Rijala who behave like this in public. A pair of Bezans, whose bright clothes give off the insistent smell of reef and incense, giggle together in a corner and point at the slipstream lights. He wonders if they experience the streaming colors differently than he does.

"Are they your parents?" he asks. "The two you're traveling with?"

She nods. The slipstream reflects in the golden glint of her eyes.

"I'm surprised to see Asuna of your status traveling by shuttle."

She smiles wryly. "Persephone-9 is a place of depravity. Any Asuna who wishes to sully themselves by going there may only do so by common means, regardless of status." She meets his eyes and adds, "Those are the rules. My mother isn't happy about it."

"So why are you going? Needing some depravity?"

She laughs. "You're funny. No. My mother must deliver some news to a relative who lives there."

"Do you not have comms where you're from?" Jes susses her curiosity, openness and a friendliness he hasn't encountered all that much in his life. He finds himself relaxing in her presence and is relieved he can still have a conversation with someone without having his guard up.

"This news must be delivered in person," she answers. "It is our custom. Most Asuna don't have to go off-world to do it though."

"I'm going to guess it's not happy news?"

"My aunt died. My mother's sister. We're on our way to inform my cousin."

"I'm sorry for your loss."

"Thank you." He senses sadness from her, but gets the feeling it isn't really connected to her aunt. She stands with her arms crossed, looking out the viewport; her halo's deep green crystals glitter in the reflection it holds. She has smaller crystals too, along her collarbone and at her wrists – these aren't as dark and shine a bit brighter.

"Are you training in an approved field for your caste?" It's an awkward change of subject, but he figures she probably won't mind not lingering on the death in her family.

"In my own way," she replies. "Emeralds are civic and cultural leaders, mostly in the realm of policy and administration. But I hope to be an artist. Artists are technically a type of cultural leader but it's rare for Emeralds to pursue the arts. It's not unheard of, of course, though Rubies are more typically artists. In my opinion, artists are the ultimate cultural leaders – I mean, they're the ones that actually give creative expression to a society, a culture. Somehow, bureaucrats took over that leadership."

He picks up a resentment that is familiar in its emotion, if not in circumstance. "What kind of artist are you?"

She brightens at the question. "I'm training in Mudraessa – do you know what that is?"

He susses from her that she expects his ignorance. He is happy to surprise her. "Asuna opera," he responds. "I've never had the honor of witnessing it first-hand. But I understand it is the most harmonically perfect music produced by any species in the 9-Star Congress. Are you sad to be missing the festival?"

Incongruently, she smiles at this. "You're familiar with the festival?"

He shrugs. "I know of it. I know it's a big deal for off-worlders to be selected in the lottery to attend." He can tell she's impressed. "So, you're a singer then?"

Now she is less impressed. "If you must boil my identity down to such simplistic terms." After a pause, "So why are *you* going to Persephone-9?"

Jes hopes his face doesn't betray the fact that he hasn't thought about this part of his story. He had been so focused just on getting away from Matheson and the Institute that he hadn't yet invented a cover story for himself. He panics a little, knowing that she is empathic too, but then remembers that the Asuna mode of empathy focuses almost exclusively on desire. Sexual desire. So his panic starts to ebb. But he wants to make a connection, so he makes what he hopes is a neutral-yet-cheerful expression. "Seeking my fortune, I guess."

"Surely finding your fortune relies on more than guessing?"

He smiles against the nervousness rising inside him as lies formulate on his tongue. "I have an uncle who runs one of the... casinos. I came to see him about a job. I didn't want to stay on Rijal anymore." At least that last statement is true. He brushes the knuckles of his left hand against the hem of his cape, taking comfort in the smooth coolness of the satin.

He stiffens reflexively as a green-haloed figure steps onto the deck, coming up behind Esmée. Her startling green eyes intimidate and judge, though she visibly relaxes as she gets closer to them, as if something she'd been worried about proved to be of no concern. Though he feels no desire, Jes's breath catches at the ripple of light and soft color across this older one's skin. The shimmer is truly hypnotic up close. Flashes of gemlike glamor glint across her face, up her temples, right up to the glittering crystal formation of her halo. She places a hand on Esmée's shoulder and the latter flinches at the touch.

"*Attention passengers,*" the smooth AI voice says over the intercom. "*We are about to re-enter simple space. Please return to your seats and strap down.*"